A MATTER OF HONOR

JAMIE MCFARLANE

FICKLE DRAGON PUBLISHING LLC

PREFACE

FREE DOWNLOAD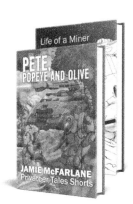

Sign up for Jamie's New Releases mailing list and get free copies of the novellas; *Pete, Popeye and Olive* and *Life of a Miner*.

To get started, please visit:

http://www.fickledragon.com/keep-in-touch

Ozzie grinned as he caught her eye. "You know there aren't any Ophies out this far."

Although she'd never admit it, Eliora was jealous of Ozzie's easy manner. He seemed unperturbed by the ever-present threat of the planet's native inhabitants.

"Gian says they're on the move again and we shouldn't take anything for granted," she responded.

"Gian this, Gian that," Ozzie muttered. "Why don't you marry the guy already?"

Amon cleared his throat. Ozzie was close to a line he shouldn't cross. "We're about five minutes away, Eliora. Thank you for coming," he said, changing the subject.

"I don't know why I did. He's such an ass," she said, indicating Ozzie with a tilt of her head.

"Don't you mean adorable ass?" Ozzie asked.

A hint of a smile crossed her normally severe face.

The large rocks on the trail had become more numerous since they'd climbed out of the alpine forest. Ozzie slowed even further while navigating the boulder field they'd entered.

"This is it," Amon said, pointing directly up the mountain. "This debris is part of that bigger rock slide. The good stuff is up there."

Ozzie stopped the mule and held his hand up to shield his eyes. Indeed, a large fissure in the hillside, most likely opened decades or centuries before, continued to erode and spew rock down the mountainside.

"Don't you think the old-timers would have already found this?" Eliora asked.

"I asked Mom," Amon said. "She hadn't heard of anyone coming out this far for ore."

Chapter 1

RAID

Planet Ophir, 1400 Light Years from Sol

Ozzie slowed the mule, its studded wheels slipping on the loose rocks of the mountainside.

"This isn't the way we came last time," Eliora said.

"We're checking out a new site," Amon said from the back seat of the electric, open-air vehicle. He had to speak loudly to be heard over the clumsy clunking of the two-wheeled cart they pulled.

"How much further? I told the watch commander we'd be back in two hours." Eliora tapped the chronometer on the dash. "We've already used forty-five minutes."

Eliora, tall and lean, was dressed in a green and tan jumpsuit identifying her as one of Yishuv's protectors. A dark green beret covered her brown, curly hair pulled back into a ponytail. The beret shielded her eyes from the star's bright rays and allowed her to scan the hillside.

"Good enough for me." Ozzie urged the electric vehicle ahead and turned up the mountain.

Toward the end, his progress had slowed enough for Amon to jump out and make his way on foot. While he couldn't move faster than the mule, he could certainly take a more direct route.

"Don't get too far ahead," Eliora warned as she pulled an ocular scope from a pouch around her neck and scanned the hillside.

When Ozzie and Eliora finally caught up with Amon, they found him looking over a field of thick rock pillars covered in orange dust. He took a reciprocating pick from the cart and climbed over the scree.

"What's with the color?" Ozzie asked. "Is this what you're looking for?"

"I'll know in a few minutes," Amon said.

Eliora picked up her crossbow and scanned the hillside like she'd been taught. As a protector, her job was to look for trouble. If it found them, she was responsible for getting her charges back safely. The Yishuv settlement couldn't lose any more residents to the war of attrition they were fighting with the Ophies. That said, they also desperately needed to gather the planet's natural resources for basic survival.

Movement half a kilometer away caught her attention. She swung her glasses up, but it had disappeared behind the boulders. She hated to be an alarmist, but the town could hardly afford to lose an apprentice engineer or an apprentice blacksmith. Ironically, Eliora was sure they could live without a junior protector.

The loud rattling of the reciprocating pick pierced the quiet of the mountainside and Eliora continued her visual scan, frequently swinging back to where she'd seen movement. The fact that nothing on the mountainside was moving bothered her. The reptilian critters that were everywhere on this planet should have responded to the machine's loud presence.

She felt, rather than heard, the crash of a heavy chunk of rock Amon peeled from the face of one of the irregular pillars. As the machine spooled down and the noise abated, the relief to her ears was palpable.

"Help me load it," Amon said.

"What do you have?" Ozzie asked, as they used a come-along to slide the three-hundred kilogram rock onto the cart's bed.

"Looks like hematite. Scanner says over fifty percent iron," Amon answered, strapping the rock securely to the cart.

"That sounds high to me," Ozzie said.

"The place is loaded with it. We need to come back with an expedition. There's more ore here than we could use in a hundred stans," Amon said.

"So this is rust?" Ozzie asked, showing his orange stained hand.

"Sure is."

"Ooof," Ozzie said.

It was a strange thing to say and Eliora turned. A thick, wooden spear protruded from the middle of his chest. The surprise on his face was replaced by coughing as he collapsed.

"Amon, get him in the mule," Eliora yelled, trying to suppress the panic she felt.

She pulled a shield from her back and engaged the energy-hungry protection field. It would only last for a few minutes and she prayed it would be enough. Ophies traveled in small groups and would first try to take them out with a ranged attack.

To Amon's credit, he didn't question her command as he tossed the heavy drilling machine into the cart and scooped his lifeless friend from the ground.

Eliora closed the distance between herself and Amon, orienting the shield to intercept the spears. A second, third and fourth spear arced through the air and she braced herself as two impacted the shield. She lost her footing momentarily as the force of the blows drove her back into Amon.

A strong hand grabbed the back of her jumpsuit and pulled her to her feet.

"We've got to go, now!" she barked.

"I'll drive." Amon jumped into the multi-wheeled mule.

A second volley of spears flew through the air. Eliora redirected one of them, but a second hit Amon in the side.

"How bad is it?" she asked.

"No time," he said breathlessly. "Get in."

Amon was right. If either of them were to survive, they had to move immediately. They were no match for an Ophie patrol. With the energy shield still operational, she climbed onto the foot-rail next to where he sat.

"Go," she said, looping her free arm through the frame of the vehicle.

Carefully at first, Amon turned the vehicle to head down the hill. He wasn't as skilled at navigating the rough terrain as his best friend, Ozzie, making the trip that much more difficult. Four of the bipedal reptilian native Ophies lumbered toward them with heavy clubs raised, causing him to reconsider a cautious descent. At two and a half meters tall, the Ophie's long stride looked awkward and slow, but in reality they covered ground very quickly.

"Energy's out." Eliora pushed the shield onto her back and swung gracefully into the rear passenger compartment behind Amon. She pulled the crossbow from a holster on her thigh, snapped out the short limbs and loaded a bolt in a quick, practiced maneuver.

The Ophie's skeletal structure was particularly thick through the chest where it covered organs and the only fatal locations for a strike were beneath the chin or in the arm pits. She would be happy to put the beasts down if only she could get a shot.

"Faster," Eliora said. She normally appreciated Amon's metered approach, but the lizard-men were gaining, easily navigating the rough terrain, jumping from boulder to boulder, sailing meters through the air, allowing gravity to aid them in their chase.

Amon swerved to avoid a collision, sending Eliora's shot wild. She cursed under her breath but refused to chastise him. Ophies were sprinters and wouldn't keep this pace very long. Indeed, the trailing tribesmen were already falling back.

The lead pursuer, however, wouldn't be shaken, he'd come too close and wouldn't easily give up the chase.

Eliora's second and third shots went wide, her normal dead-eye accuracy interrupted by the bouncing of the vehicle on uneven terrain. Gian wouldn't appreciate the loss of so many iron bolts with so little to show for it. What she wouldn't give to have him fighting beside her right now.

Eliora tried feverishly to clear a jam, her hands trembling from adrenaline. She could all but feel her pursuer's breath and knew Amon's and her own survival depended on what she did next. The large Ophie's next jump would no doubt put it on their cart.

At the last moment, the jam cleared and a bolt slid into the groove, the taut cable snapping into place between the crossbow's arms. In a fluid movement, she swept the bow around and lined up on the lizard-man's throat. She fired and the bolt only traveled two meters before entering below the creature's jaw and disappearing into the soft tissue of its underdeveloped brain. The warrior had been in mid-jump and momentum slammed it into Eliora.

Amon felt the impact and jammed on the brakes. "Eliora!" The vehicle skidded sideways and came to rest against a boulder. Jumping from the mule, he pulled their motionless attacker to the ground.

The impact of the attack had wedged her between the driver's seat and the rear passenger's bench. Amon smiled at his friend's fierce glare, still holding her crossbow with arms locked. He offered his hand and pulled her up.

"I thought it had gotten you. I should have known better."

Amon's eyes lit on his dead friend and a sense of loss threatened to overwhelm him. He reached for the vehicle to steady himself.

Eliora placed her hand on top of his and spoke softly. "We need to keep going, Amon."

He nodded and slid into the driver's seat, resuming their flight down the mountain, eventually finding the game trail that led into the forest. Eliora remained on the passenger's side, choosing to stand while holding onto the roll bar.

Fifteen minutes from home, Eliora spied a column of smoke rising above the trees. She patted Amon's shoulder to get his attention and pointed at the plume.

"Hurry," Eliora said.

"Yes," he answered and accelerated.

They arrived at the main gate of Yishuv. Hundreds of dead Ophies littered the path leading up to the ten-meter high wall. The town's gates had been pulled from their heavy hinges and now lay on the ground, a massive, braided rope still attached, leading into the forest behind them.

Amon drove through the broken gates and stopped long enough for Eliora to jump out.

"I'll find you when things are secure," she said.

"Thank you, Eliora. We'd never have made it if not for you," he said.

"That's no help for Ozzie," she said.

"He'd be glad we lived." Amon still wasn't ready to process the loss of his friend.

"I'll find you," she said.

He nodded and drove toward Ozzie's home. The chaos in the streets spoke of an attack on a scale Amon had never experienced. Stacks of Ophie bodies lay at the corners of many of the streets. Amon didn't want to try to imagine how many people had died defending the settlement.

Moshe, Ozzie's father, met Amon outside of his home.

For citizens of Yishuv, loss wasn't a new experience and Moshe accepted Amon's news with resignation and a hug.

"I'm sorry," Amon said quietly.

"You're wounded, take off your shirt," Moshe said practically. "I'll get a kit."

"It's less than it looks," Amon said, following Moshe into his small, brick home.

"Thank you for bringing him home, Amon. You are a good friend," Moshe said. "Tell me how it happened."

Moshe gently cleaned the gash on Amon's side. They sat on a stone bench in quiet contemplation, until Amon could bring himself to recount their trip to the man who'd been like a father to him. There was a quiet acceptance by the older man as Amon shared the last moments of Ozzie's life. Together, they chuckled as Amon relayed Ozzie's good-natured ribbing of Eliora. They spent nearly an hour remembering the enigmatic boy.

When the conversation finally lagged, they drove Ozzie's body to the temporary morgue, where scores of dead family and friends already lay. The unofficial count put the death toll at sixty-five and it was expected to rise, as many others were near death.

Amon arrived home well after dark. He'd sent word to his mother, Nurit, that he was helping at the morgue and that trouble had found Ozzie. Their family home doubled as the town's smithy. The heat as he walked past the shuttered forge sent a pang of guilt through him as he realized his mother had been making repairs since the attack and had needed his help.

"Amon. I was so worried," she said as she greeted him at the front door. "You're hurt?" She looked at his torn shirt.

"I was lucky," Amon said.

"You won't be lucky if it becomes infected. Come into the kitchen," she said.

He knew better than to argue with his mother. He pulled his shirt off and allowed Nurit to remove his dressing and winced as she applied lye soap before wrapping it back up. Moshe had been much gentler in his handling of the wound, but he wasn't going to say anything.

"Do you want to talk about it?" she asked.

"Not tonight," he said.

"You must be hungry." It was an easy guess. Amon was always hungry.

She slid a thick slab of bread, which she'd covered with a paste commonly called peanut butter onto a plate in front of him. The ground up legume, an indigenous plant, was a staple in every home.

"Was that hematite in the back of the mule?" she asked, making small talk.

"There's an entire hillside of it," he said. "I chiseled that piece off and would have loaded more, but the Ophies attacked."

"Rumor is Eliora should have picked up on the attack," she said.

"Who would say that?" Amon asked, suddenly angry, spinning to look his mother in the eyes. "It's ridiculous! It happened so fast, we had no chance."

"It's coming from her. She says she missed their approach and if she had been more vigilant, Ozzie would have lived," Nurit said matter-of-factly.

"I'll talk to Gian. She couldn't have known they were there. Without Eliora, I'd be dead too."

"I'm sure he'd like to hear that from you." Nurit patted his back, hoping to return a sense of calm to her son.

"They'll need help digging graves tomorrow," he said, his shoulders slumping under her hand.

"We'll go together."

Chapter 2

IN FOR A PENNY

Planet Curie, Tipperary Star System

A light breeze, a perfect twenty-six degrees, a rum drink with an umbrella, and the shade of a wide-leafed, tropical tree all conspired to cause my eyelids to droop precipitously.

It felt good to relax, allowing the stress of the past few months to dissipate. We were on Curie after receiving an invitation through Admiral Tullas' office to meet with an anonymous client about a new mission. Whoever it was had even sent fifty thousand credits to cover fuel, food and lodging. It was a lot of credits to splash around, and I was doing my best to ignore the niggling feeling in the back of my mind.

We'd been fully loaded leaving Nuage Gros, delivering goods to Curie's two moons, Irène and Ève. It had taken nearly four weeks to get to Curie and I, for one, was thinking we'd made a great decision. But then, who didn't like a little sun and sand after an adventure? Why shouldn't we have a nice payday, too?

"Hey! Look, I'm flying!" Tabby's excited voice cut through the fog of sleep.

I sat up in my lounge chair and scanned the waves. My AI drew a reticle around one of the wind surfers who had launched herself off the back of a breaking wave, sailing no less than seven or eight meters in the air. I marveled at her grace.

"You're insane." I laughed, waving at her.

I loved watching Tabby, my fiancé, do just about anything. You wouldn't know by looking at her gorgeous lithe frame, that she'd recently had major reconstructive surgery after being severely wounded in battle. No, Tabby had a new lease on life and woke every morning ready to go.

She waved back as a gust of wind caught the board at just the right moment, twisting it from beneath her. Instead of landing with her normal skill, she tumbled into the water, losing her grip on the sail. I jumped up and pulled my shirt off.

"Where are you going?" Marny asked. She was our heavily muscled security officer and girlfriend of my best friend Nick.

"She might be in trouble," I said.

"First, I don't think there's enough trouble within a hundred square kilometers to worry that girl," she said, giving me a lopsided grin. "And second, you're the worst swimmer I know."

As if in response to Marny's declaration, Tabby resurfaced and clambered back onto the board.

"You distracted me," Tabby exclaimed once she'd pulled the sail out of the water and was scooting back out to sea.

"I can honestly say, *you're* distracting me," I replied.

"Lech."

Our conversation was interrupted as Ada ran up.

"You guys want to join a pickup volleyball game?" she asked.

Ada was probably the most naturally gorgeous woman I'd ever met and today she was in top form. Her ebony skin was a beautiful contrast to the brilliant blue two-piece suit she wore. Even more than her beauty, Ada's ebullient personality attracted followers wherever she went.

"Marny? Nick?" I asked.

"Hey, I'm in," Tabby said over the comm.

Marny didn't answer other than to slide to the end of her chair and pull a pair of shorts over her single piece suit.

By the time we'd had our fill of volleyball, hunger set in, so we caught a three-segment tram back to the resort. It was inconvenient that structures weren't allowed on the sandy beaches, but as I looked back toward the water, I could appreciate how they'd retained the natural beauty of the location.

Only twenty percent of Curie was habitable. Though the atmosphere was breathable, the only surface water to be found was a single salt-water sea. Completely surrounded by tall mountains, it had been formed by the cataclysmic impact of a planetoid. It was that collision that had sheared off Curie's two moons, Irène and Ève, and left the thousand kilometer diameter crater where we'd discovered the pristine white sand beaches and brilliant blue waters of the Radium Sea. With only two hundred million people on all of Curie and extremely restrictive environmental safeguards, it was hard to imagine a more beautiful location in the known universe.

The resort was two kilometers from the water and its huts spread back into the jungle, connected by elevated, wood-plank boardwalks. We'd rented a large hut with three separate bedrooms and a living room, a configuration we often selected when traveling on business.

"What are you wearing for dinner tonight?" Tabby asked as she stepped out of the shower naked, holding a towel in one hand.

I had difficulty focusing and didn't answer as quickly as she expected.

"Hey, sailor, eyes up here." She pointed two fingers at my eyes and then back to her own.

"Uh, I was thinking of wearing my Nuage civvies," I said.

In the cloud city of Nuage Gros we'd befriended a clothing designer who'd set us up in the style of that city. That same colorful clothing would fit well in the festive atmosphere of Curie.

She turned back to the head and gave a little skip to her step, knowing I'd follow her progress out of the room. She looked back over her shoulder to make sure I was watching and gave me an alluring smile.

"I'll dress accordingly, then," she said.

I took her smile as an invitation.

We were only a few minutes late to dinner and I appreciated that no one called us on it.

"So who is it from Belirand that we're meeting with tomorrow?" I asked Nick as we waited for our dinner to arrive.

"It's more of a mystery than I like," he said. "We received the invite through Admiral Tullas' office, but when I pushed Lieutenant Peren on it, all he'd tell me was it came from the highest levels."

"What do you suppose that means?" Ada asked.

"Sounds like someone is looking for an off-the-books mission," Marny said. "We'll want to be careful with this."

"What time are we meeting tomorrow?" Tabby asked. "I'd like to get a run in."

"Shuttle is picking us up at 0800 local," Nick answered.

Where Marny was Earth-born, tall and heavily muscled, Nick was small, even by spacer standards. What Nick gave up in size, he more than made up for with raw intellect and his capacity to plan. Tabby, Nick, and I grew up together on a mining colony in Sol's main asteroid belt and had been best friends for as long as I could remember.

"We have a load to pick up on Curie's main orbital platform sometime tomorrow. It'll fill *Sterra's Gift* completely. After that, I've got an appointment to take a look at a segmented container tractor. It's pretty roached out, but the scans show it has good bones," I said.

"How would you get it back?" Nick asked.

"It has operable engines. We'd sail straight to Meerkat shipyard on Gros. Worse case, we piggy back on *Sterra's Gift*. Without seeing it, I can't be sure," I said. "One nice thing is the guy selling it has two sixteen container link segments. No engines on them, but we have those engines you picked up a few weeks ago."

"What shape are they in?" he asked.

"They'll need work, but they've been used as recently as two months ago. The guy is either retired or is trying to retire and is cashing out," I replied.

"I hope he's realistic about price," Nick said.

"He's asking seventy thousand for the entire setup and we've an appointment day after tomorrow to check it out," I said.

"Do we have that much free?" Ada asked.

"Barely," Nick answered. "All of our capital is tied up in ore that needs to be delivered to the Belirand Terminal Seven project."

"How much are we sitting on?" Ada asked.

Nick flicked a spreadsheet to her from his HUD. "If you skip to the bottom, you'll see the total. Once we deliver that ore we should be sitting on one-point-one million. Subtract fuel costs, that looks more like an even million," he explained.

"And," I added. "We'll clear forty thousand for this trip in delivery fees after fuel," I said.

"That's insane," Ada said, breathing out. "I knew the ore had value, but I didn't realize we were sitting on that much."

"That makes two of us," Tabby agreed.

"Big Pete really wants us to get an armor-glass kiln if we can find one. 'The bigger, the better' were his exact words," Marny added.

"Frak. I forgot about that," I said. "But I don't see that we can afford it on this trip."

"He might be okay with a small one if it's between that and nothing," Nick said.

"This would be the place to find it," Tabby said.

She was right. Ninety-five percent of Tipperary's total population was spread out between Curie, Irène and Ève. If we were going to find something as specialized as an armor-glass kiln, our best shot would be the orbital bazaar that was tethered to the temperate, forest planet of Irène.

We finished dinner and walked along the boardwalk. The night sky of Curie was littered with bright stars and we could just see the edge of the Petri Nebula that was also visible from Lèger Nuage.

"Cards?" Tabby asked as we arrived at the deck separating the three huts. A metal fire-pit was inset into the center of the wooden deck and surrounded by comfortable couches.

Nick started the fire that had been thoughtfully arranged and we settled down for a few hours of cards. It was well after 2400 when we finally turned in.

I didn't even hear Tabby when she left early the next morning for her run. She'd given up trying to get me to come along as I couldn't run fast enough to make it interesting for her. Unfortunately, Marny didn't mind waking me up. We were compatible running mates and she felt it was her duty to keep me in shape. I wondered if there was some collusion between the two women, but they never would admit to it.

"I'M STARVING, are you sure they're going to provide food?" Ada asked as we met on the deck.

"That's what was passed along," Nick said, referring to the instructions Lieutenant Peren had forwarded from Admiral Tullas' office.

"They better have something to eat or I'm going to be grumpy," Ada said.

I laughed. For such a small girl, she always worried about where her next meal was coming from.

A shiny silver, oval shuttle landed next to our huts, just down from the stairs leading to the beach.

"That's us," Nick said.

A small gang-plank extended from the side of the shuttle and we trooped down the stairs, meeting a formally-dressed man in a black suit and white shirt.

"Greetings, Mr. James, Ms. Bertrand, Ms. Masters..." He spoke as we entered the shuttle, making eye contact with each of us. "My name is Jonathan and I'm here to make your journey comfortable. If there is anything you need, please don't hesitate to ask."

The shuttle was large enough to carry at least thirty people, so there was plenty of room for the dining table that had been set up at one end. Jonathan showed us to the table that was covered in a white cloth complete with five place settings.

"I've taken the liberty of having our chef prepare a light breakfast of eggs, toast and local fruits," he explained as he leaned in, turning over fluted glasses and filling them with water. He was joined by a middle-aged woman, who wore a black uniform.

The shuttle rose gently from the ground and the three hundred sixty degree windows darkened to the point of being opaque.

"Excuse me, Jonathan?" Marny asked.

"Yes, Ms. Bertrand."

"Is it your employer's intent to obscure our destination?"

"It is. My employer is private and prefers that his whereabouts are not generally known. I hope this is acceptable," he said.

"You're asking us to take a lot on faith," she replied.

"I assure you, Ms. Bertrand, everything is aboveboard. It is simply a matter requiring discretion. We will allow you to retain your weapons as a gesture of good faith," he said.

"How far are we going this morning," Nick asked.

"The trip will take ninety minutes, Mr. James. Would anyone like coffee?"

I'd spent much of my short career studying people and their response to stressful conditions. If Jonathan felt stress, he sure wasn't showing it.

"In for a penny," Nick said and picked up the delicate coffee cup in front of him.

"Quite," Jonathan replied.

We ate the provided breakfast in an awkward silence. Jonathan and his cryptic answers did nothing for our comfort.

After breakfast we adjourned to the couches that would have other-wise provided a good view. Jonathan seemed content to clean up after breakfast and then sit quietly at the other end of the shuttle.

I held Tabby's hand. Like all of us, she preferred things to be out in the open and her stress level was rising. She was also the most likely to make an issue of it if the uncertainty went on for too long.

Mercifully, a small bump warned us that the shuttle had come to rest.

Jonathan was the first to stand and walked to the entry hatch, where he palmed a security pad. The door slid into the hull. The shuttle had landed in such a way that it opened onto a well-lit hallway.

At that point, I was ready to get off the shuttle and would welcome whatever we'd gotten ourselves into - anything to end the awkward trip. Jonathan's reassuring smile at the doorway did nothing to ease my discomfort.

"If you'll follow me," he said.

The hallway ended at a T-intersection. We followed him to the right and found ourselves at an elevator which opened as we approached.

"Definitely a station," Tabby said, mostly to herself. I nodded. The smell of recycled station air wasn't something that could be faked, nor could it be hidden.

The elevator doors closed behind us. We dropped for a few seconds and then jogged to the right.

"And here we are," Jonathan announced just before the doors opened.

In front of us was a cavernous room that extended up twenty meters ending in a domed ceiling. Video panels, tools, equipment, partially constructed robots and all matter of technology were hanging above or strewn over a dozen workbenches placed haphazardly throughout the room.

In the middle of it all sat a small, ebony-skinned teenage boy. We were far enough away that he might not have heard us arrive - or he was ignoring us. That said, I assumed we weren't here for him anyway.

"Master Anino, I present to you, the Loose Nuts Corporation and crew of *Hotspur*. Gentlemen, ladies, I present Master Phillippe Anino, direct descendant and sole heir to Thomas Anino, inventor of fold-space technology and the TransLoc gate system," Jonathan said proudly.

You know what they say about assumptions.

Chapter 3

SURVIVAL

Yishuv Settlement, Planet Ophir

Amon stood atop the fallen nanstel gate, driving out the ancient bolts that secured the iron hinges. He marveled at the strength of the nanstel. Even after four centuries of use, neither the gate panels nor nuts and bolts showed any signs of deterioration. Indeed, the weak link had always been the cast iron hinges.

He carefully collected each nut and bolt pair and placed them in a wooden crate. Over the centuries, several bolts had been lost to carelessness and Amon vowed it would not happen on his watch.

"Mom, I'm ready," he called to Nurit.

One by one, Nurit and Amon picked up the broken seventy-five kilogram hinges and placed them on the platform of a four-wheeled cart.

"Will you repair them or cast new ones?" Merik asked.

Merik, the settlement's chief engineer, had been helping the masons excavate the buried hinge straps from between the massive limestone blocks.

Nurit looked up, still out of breath.

"I'm sorry about Ozzie," she said. "He was a good man."

"I'll miss him. He was a bright engineer and full of life," Merik replied.

"We'll all miss him," Nurit agreed. "As for the hinges, we'll have to make new casts. It catches us at a bad time as we're short on pig iron."

"Do you have enough?"

"We do for the gates, but with all of the damage to the settlement, there will be considerable demand."

Merik's daughter, Merrie, stepped forward but remained respectfully quiet.

"Yes, my young apprentice, do you have something to add?" Merik asked.

She rolled her eyes at him. "I'm not that young. I'm only a year younger than Amon."

"Forgive a father for not wanting his precious daughter to grow up too soon," he said with a warm smile.

"You're forgiven," she said, suddenly looking at the ground as Amon approached.

"Did you have a question?" Merik asked.

"Uh... well... why aren't we using steel instead of iron?" she stammered.

Merik and Nurit exchanged a knowing smile, recognizing Merrie's sudden change due to Amon's arrival.

"That is a good question, young woman," Merik said. "Tell me why you think we aren't using steel for the hinges."

Merrie's cheeks flushed at Amon, Nurit and Merik's attention. "That's obvious. Iron is practical and easy to smelt and the founder's maker-machine can't make steel. Not to mention, we haven't previously known how."

"And now we do?"

"Yes. That engineering pad you found in the broken blaster has plans for steel mills and more," Merrie said.

"Sounds like I gave it to the right girl, then," he said proudly.

"*Da-ad*, I'm not just your little girl anymore, I'm twenty-stans. And I'm serious. We could make steel," she said.

"Sounds like quite an undertaking, what would you have us do?" her father asked.

"Make an electric arc furnace. We have the raw materials and it would only take a tenday to manufacture the special items on the maker-machine," she said.

"My apologies, Merrie, for interrupting," Nurit said. "Amon and I must return these hinges to the forge. We have many days of work ahead. I don't want to discourage you, but I'm afraid the Council will not accept using the maker-machine in such a way."

"I understand," Merrie's crestfallen face betrayed her disappointment.

Uncharacteristically, Amon spoke up. "The Council needs to hear Merrie's idea. What if our gates hadn't fallen to the Ophie? Merik might have been able to relocate the working turret in time to hold off the breach."

Merrie beamed at Amon's praise and looked to Nurit and Merik.

"The Council has many things to discuss after this latest attack and might be open to a new project," Merik said. "But you must be able demonstrate how it aids our defense. What you have, Merrie, is an idea. What you need is a plan that demonstrates why it is critical to our survival. Only then will the Council approve using the maker-machine for that length of time," Merik said.

"I don't know how to do that," she said.

"This, my young apprentice, is the job of an engineer. If you are truly interested, you must show creativity and resolve," Merik said.

"Do you believe you could really create a machine that produces steel?" Amon asked.

Merrie paused, intimidated by being put on the spot. What had once resided in the sole province of her mind was now out, in front of people she respected. If this went any further, it'd be in front of the entire community. A failure would be hard to live down.

"I could with your help," she finally said.

"Then you will have it," he said, holding his hand out to her.

For Merrie, it was an unfamiliar gesture. People never sought to shake the hand of a twenty stans old engineering apprentice. Amon, steady as a mountain, didn't waver as she hesitated. She finally reached out to grasp his wrist, as was their custom. She felt an electric charge at the touch and was surprised at how gentle his grip was as he closed it on her own.

"Amon, we must go." Nurit pushed.

He nodded and climbed into the cart with her and they drove slowly back through town to the smithy.

"I need all of your attention on these hinges," Nurit said as they drove.

"I understand. Even if Merrie's plan were approved, we couldn't leave the gates lying on the ground waiting for an untested machine to produce steel," Amon agreed.

"There will be many demands for our time and materials in the days ahead," Nurit said.

"But still, we can't be slaves to the past," he said "The Ophir will continue to attack, as they have for the last four centuries. Our technology is failing and we have to get smarter."

"You sound so much like your father. He would be proud of you," Nurit said.

They arrived at the smithy to find Eliora standing in the shade. Amon and Eliora hadn't talked much since their fateful trip and Amon suspected she'd been avoiding him. Even now, she looked at the ground instead of making eye contact.

"Eliora, welcome. How may we be of assistance?" Nurit asked.

"Captain Gian asked me to check on the progress of the gate, ammunition and well... he sent a list," she said, clearly uncomfortable.

"Ah, yes, the first of many such visits. You may report to the Captain that we will pour our first cast at the end of tenday and that barring any setbacks, polished hinges will be ready for installation by sixday next. Our engineer will coordinate the installation. I've already shared this schedule with Master Merik," Nurit said, unperturbed.

Eliora held out a notebook filled with several pages of writing. Nurit took the list and reviewed it.

"Inform Captain Gian that his request was delivered and that I'd like to speak with him at his earliest convenience," Nurit said.

As they were talking, three people approached. Amon recognized them from school and knew they currently worked as laborers on the farms.

"I'll finish with Eliora. It looks like our help has arrived. Would you get them started?" Nurit asked.

"Yes, ma'am," Amon said respectfully. "Eliora, it was good to see you."

Eliora raised her head but didn't meet his eyes. "You too, Amon."

Amon led the crew away from Nurit and Eliora. Casting iron was a labor intensive process and without additional strong backs, the process would take much longer.

"Greetings. Thank you for coming," he said.

"Not like we were given a choice," Barel complained.

Physically larger than Amon, Barel was an intimidating figure. Amon and Barel had played against each other in net ball and Amon knew him to be slow and dull-witted. In a pure competition of strength, it was likely a tossup, however.

"Stop whining, Barel. At least we're not scooping porcine dung." The young woman who spoke was named Assa. Her deeply tanned shoulders were cut with deep muscles from years of labor.

"We'll work over here," Amon said. He led the group to depleted piles of sand and coal. "The first task is to sift two more tons of sand. Barel and Assa, you've helped with that before, right?"

"Yes. Remind me which sifter to use?" Assa asked.

"There are two fine sifters, either of them work well. Rivi, you and I will grind coal and clay," Amon said.

It was well after dark when they'd finished and were sitting quietly at a thick-slabbed wooden table. Hanging electric lanterns illuminated the smithy's courtyard. They ate a simple meal of thick bread, cheese, and meat with a red berry light ale to help relax their tired muscles.

"Will you need us tomorrow?" Assa asked.

"We mix the casting sand tomorrow and will need you until threeday," Nurit replied.

"We're here for as long as you need, Master Nurit," the young woman said.

"And when we get back, we'll have that much more to do," Barel complained.

Rivi scowled at the other man. "It beats the Ophies walking through our front gates."

"Please be ready to work by sunrise tomorrow," Nurit said. "We have another long day ahead."

After Assa, Barel and Rivi left, Amon looked to Nurit. At forty-five stans, she was one of the strongest people in town. She'd taken over for Amon's father, Nadav, as the town's blacksmith after Ophies had killed him in a raid eighteen stans ago.

"What did you talk with Gian about?" he asked. When the captain of the protectors had been there earlier, he'd heard definite sounds of arguing.

"An expedition to gather hematite. The sample you brought back is loaded with iron. Ozzie's death will not be in vain. If there's as much rock as you say, it will last for decades," she said.

"Will Gian help?"

"You're to meet the expedition at the gates shortly after first light. You may take one of the laborers with you. I'd like you to bring back thirty tonnes," she said.

"We'll need more than the mule to haul that."

"I've arranged for four heavy wagons, carrying eight tonnes each. Please be careful not to overload them."

Amon nodded, considering the logistics. "Several mules would be helpful. The heavy wagons will be unable to traverse the path we took, though I didn't see a better route."

"How many do you need?" she asked.

"Three," he responded. "The last two hundred meters are too rocky for the wagons."

She smiled proudly at her son. "I'll take care of it."

The next morning Amon was awake well before dawn. He stopped at the settlement's machine shop and picked up an additional reciprocating pick, hydraulic lifters, and other tools he believed he'd need. It was his first time leading such a large expedition and he wanted to make sure it went well.

After picking up a groggy Barel, they drove back just as morning light was showing on the horizon. Amon saw what he'd only heard rumors of the night before. The Ophies had trashed the fields and most of the crops looked like they'd been lost.

"It's not as bad as it looks," Barel said.

"Oh?" Amon asked.

"The row crops took a beating, but the tubers will be fine. Sure, you'll complain about lack of variety, but we won't starve," he said. "We've already started replanting, but of course, the blacksmith takes our workers so it's not going very fast."

"Did you have enough warning when they came?" Amon asked, letting the other man's complaints fade away.

"People who were working near the walls were luckiest. The people closer to the forest weren't so lucky. Mostly, it was old people who didn't make it," he said.

Amon nodded at the story he'd heard his entire life. Ophies attacked and killed the unlucky who became their targets. Yishuv's crumbling defenses were the only thing that had allowed its inhabitants to survive the last four centuries.

As they arrived at the main gate, Amon wasn't surprised to see that a thick tree trunk had been raised up and placed across the opening in the wall, above where the gates belonged. Block and tackle hung from the trunk, waiting for the hinges to be repaired so the gates could be lifted back into place.

Captain Gian was talking to a group of ten people dressed in protector uniforms, crossbows hanging from their belts. Eliora saw Amon approach. He tried to catch her eye, but she turned away.

Gian waved him over.

"Is this all the equipment you'll need?"

Three large wagons had already arrived, pulled by tractors brought in from the fields. So far, there was only one mule.

"I was hoping for four wagons and another mule with a cart," Amon said. "The drivers will have to help load the material."

"The mule is on its way, but these are the only available wagons. I'll use one to carry troops. As for help moving material, the drivers understand that expectation," he said.

"Two trips, then?" Amon asked.

"If we have time."

Amon wanted to argue, but knew better. As one of the most powerful men in the city, Captain Gian's direction was to be followed.

"Okay."

A few minutes later, the final mule arrived, filled with water and supplies.

"You're in the lead and Eliora will ride with you. Listen to her instructions and we'll be right behind you. Don't let us get too spread out and make sure you can see the rear tractor at all times. Understood?"

"Yes," Amon acknowledged.

"Let's get underway, then." Gian looked to Pele, his third in command and the only protector armed with one of the settlement's two remaining blaster rifles.

"Load 'em up," Pele said loudly enough for the entire group to hear. He accentuated his words by sticking his index finger up and waving it in a circle.

Barel started to crawl into the back of the mule, expecting that Eliora would force him into the rear seat via seniority.

"Stay put," she said. "I'll take the back."

Amon pulled forward onto the main trail leading up the mountain. It was still early and light hadn't made it onto the path yet. He checked his mirror and found he couldn't see past Eliora, who was standing vigilant in the center of the mule.

"I can't see behind me," Amon said.

"Just keep going, they're coming," she said. "Captain is motioning for us to speed up."

Amon accelerated. And so it went. Without Ozzie driving, the trip to the edge of the forest took more than an hour. Having driven the mountain path only once before, Amon was concerned he'd forget the route, but his concern was for naught.

"Hold up," Eliora said as they pulled even with the boulder where the large Ophie had jumped into their mule. Its desiccated body lay close to where it had fallen.

Eliora walked back to the Captain's mule and spoke to him a moment, gesturing to the fallen enemy.

"What was that all about?" Amon asked.

"I'm under review for the attack. Captain wanted to know where we'd been jumped," she said.

"You mean, where you saved our lives?"

"I didn't save Ozzie," she said.

"Nobody could have. Look Eliora, we must have these materials if we are to survive. Ozzie understood the risks. We all do. You have to stop beating yourself up."

Eliora didn't respond and Amon didn't want to push it any further, so he continued forward. They finally arrived at the bottom of the long sluff. The wagons had come as far as they could. He got out of the mule, walking back to the Captain, Eliora tight on his heels.

"The tractors should turn around here. The ore is just up this draw," Amon explained. "We'll take the mules up and get started."

"How far up?"

"Two hundred meters." Amon pointed up. "That orange you see is rust and where we're going."

"Got it. I'll send two with you and keep the bulk of the security force down here. Eliora, if you get in trouble, fall back to this position," Gian said. "I want a protector in every mule that's moving and one on the ground at all times. One mule will be sitting at all times at the dig site. You have the most familiarity with the site so I want you organizing at the top."

"Yes, sir."

Gian motioned to Pele with a short series of hand signals. Two protectors jumped from a wagon and clambered into the awaiting mules. A few minutes later, they were headed up the twisty route that led to the fissure.

"Barel, how are you with a reciprocating pick?" Amon asked the farmer.

"Never used one," Barel replied. Amon doubted this to be true, but wasn't about to argue.

"Then you are responsible for loading the carts. These mules are only good for three hundred kilograms, so don't overload them," Amon said.

"No... really?" Barel retorted.

If he was the only one using a pick, it was going to be a long day. At least Gian had broken the load into two trips. They'd taken two hours to arrive and it was past 0830 in the morning, which didn't feel too bad. The drive had made him sleepy, although, he knew the pick would wake him up.

A loud clattering filled the valley when Amon set the pick against the base of a four meter tall iron pillar. It stood tall, almost straight up, the weather having stripped away much of the surrounding loose rock to ground level. At a meter and a half across, the base unevenly narrowed at the top to a meter wide, orange and red rust stains running down the sides.

He worked for twenty minutes while Barel looked on. Eliora and the two protectors had separated and were scouting the nearby hillside when the pillar finally gave way, crashing and sliding down the hill for several meters.

"Move the mules over here," Amon directed, getting a quick drink.

"All of 'em?" Barel asked.

"Yes. We'll be lucky if we can take it all," Amon said. "You're looking at twenty tonnes, give or take. Notice how it didn't fracture a bit when I toppled it? That thing is solid."

Amon could feel the day slipping away from him. He wished they had bigger equipment, so they could more efficiently harvest the material.

After another forty long minutes, he'd peeled enough slivers off so the first mule could get underway. He'd shaped his initial cuts to make future cuts more efficient and soon had both of the other mules loaded and moving. At his current rate, they'd have the large wagons loaded by 1500, the chances of a second trip quickly disappearing.

"Hold it."

Eliora caught his eye. She was holding up her hand and stalking up the side of the hill. It had been her third interruption of the day. Each time, she had only found a small mountain reptile flitting around. He could hardly blame her for her vigilance, however.

Amon was distracted by one of the returning mules and turned away. When he looked back, he saw Eliora drop to her knee, firing up into an Ophie that leapt from its hidden position on the side of the mountain.

Her crossbow bolts sunk into the beast's chest, but did nothing to stop his advance. A second Ophie jumped from cover, running toward the returning mule.

"Go!" Amon shouted, looking at the mule's driver.

Amon's directive spurred the frozen driver into action and inspired Barel to jump into the cart the mule pulled. The protector, Alona, who'd accompanied the returning mule fired ineffectively as the vehicle lurched and turned.

Eliora dropped her crossbow, pulling out her long iron hunting knife. She'd narrowly dodged the Ophie's uncontrolled charge down the mountain and now stood, facing the sage green reptile. Amon couldn't see any possible way for her to escape the inevitable. While she was considerably more nimble, the Ophie had sufficient speed to run her down. The only chance of survival was to engage the Ophie and attempt to disable it by striking one of its weak spots - under the chin, arms or groin. Unfortunately, Ophies were well aware of this strategy.

"Go! Get out of here," Eliora yelled at him.

It made sense. The Ophie would kill her, then it would kill him. Running was also something Amon was not prepared to do. He would not watch another of his friends die on the side of this mountain. Instead, he picked up a fist-sized chunk of hematite. Hefting it in his hands, he judged its weight to be two kilograms. For most people, it would have been too heavy to throw with any force, but Amon was not most people - he possessed considerable strength from shaping iron day in and day out.

His first throw sailed over the beast's head. He chastised himself as he grabbed two more pieces from the ground. He'd been too excited and hadn't controlled his adrenaline. He quickly reoriented and watched as Eliora once again dodged a swipe. In the same move, she dug her knife into its thick, scaly leg. A dark liquid oozed out of the cut but didn't seem to affect the Ophie's attack.

Amon advanced and threw the next chunk, clipping the beast on the side of the head. It howled in pain, momentarily dazed. Bringing a webbed hand up to the wound, it spun toward Amon.

Amon didn't waste any time and threw the next piece into the beast's chest. The hit was more solid, but the rock glanced off, falling to the ground. Insult to injury caused the reptilian enemy to forget about Eliora and charge Amon, club raised, screaming in rage.

Not having thought past throwing rocks, Amon found himself at a loss. He couldn't outrun the Ophie, but grappling didn't make sense either. It took everything he had not to run, but Amon planted his feet and stared down the charging beast. At the last moment, he jumped to the side, hoping to roll out of its way. He managed to avoid the club, but his legs became entangled with the charging Ophie's limbs. A loud crack and pain in his calf occurred as they tumbled to the ground.

Eliora had but a single chance and lunged toward the tangled bodies. A fourth known vulnerability of the Ophie was inaccessible during a frontal attack. With the Ophie on the ground, its Achilles tendon, which closely resembled a human's, had little natural protection. In a single fluid movement she drew her razor sharp knife across the back of the creature's legs.

The Ophie turned sharply, howling in pain, reaching for her in a single, uncharacteristically quick swipe. It caught Eliora's heel and pulled her from her feet. She scrabbled back, trying to escape the howling beast's long grasp, but to no avail.

Pain shot through Amon's body as he tried to move his leg. The Ophie's screams and single-minded assault on Eliora galvanized him into action. He looked around frantically for a weapon and chose a single, iron-laden rock. It was said that an Ophie's head was as armored as its chest, but Amon was an iron shaper and knew little that could withstand the heavy blow of his hammers. Balanced on a single leg, he threw himself onto the Ophie's back and with all his might, smashed its skull with his improvised hammer. He heard a sickening crunch as the rock completed the grisly deed.

Chapter 4

AUDITION

Planet Curie, Tipperary Star System

"Thank you, Jonathan. I'll take it from here," the teenager said, not looking up from the project in front of him.

"Certainly, Master Anino," Jonathan answered.

Philippe Anino set his tools down, jumped from his stool and flew directly at us. Initially, I thought he was flying with arc-jets, but there were no blue tell-tale traces common to arc-jet technology. His acceleration was faster than anything I was familiar with. He stopped neatly in front of us, hovering at eye level.

"I thought you'd all be bigger," he said and gave Marny an appraising look. "Well, all but Bertrand, that is. Is it okay if I use your last names? Of course it is, you buck formality."

I smiled. "Last names are fine. What do you like to be called and what in the known universe are you flying? They're like arc-jets on narcs."

"Call me Anino. And, I just *knew* you'd like 'em, Hoffen. You think if you had some you could catch me?"

"I could," Tabby said stepping into the boy's personal space.

"Oh, man, three dimensional scans don't do you justice, Masters. I mean... Crap, that didn't sound perverted in my head," he said.

"You're just a little ball of energy, aren't you," Ada chimed in, giving him her best patronizing scowl.

"You have no idea, Chen. The boots are my own little invention. Take a grav generator, power it with... well we can't talk about that. But imagine a suit full of micro-grav generators all tied into your AI. Same controls as arc-jets," he said.

"How do they work in the deep dark?" Nick asked.

"You're right of course, James. With nothing to push against, they aren't anywhere near as nice as arc-jets. Although, unlike arc-jets, they don't easily run out of fuel," he said.

"How long do they last?" I asked, enamored by his description.

"Can't say... corporate secrets and all. But for the sake of reference, you won't have kids alive when this suit stops operating." He listened for a moment. "*What!? I didn't say anything specific.*"

"Pardon?" Ada asked.

"My AI is set to warn me - chastise really - when I'm giving away secrets. Would you mind if we just forgot about that reference?"

"So, what's on your mind, Mr. Anino?" It appeared that I was going to have to keep us on track.

"Just Anino. And you wouldn't believe me if I told you," he said. "But let's just say you meant to ask - why are you here and what do I want."

"I guess that's one way," I said. "I'm not a big fan of being rude."

"No, you're not. I'm afraid I'm the one who suffers from having no filter. A habit that comes from being an off-the-charts genius with almost zero humility and nearly infinite wealth. So Masters, you really think you could catch me? There's a suit right over there. I bet it'll fit."

He pointed at a bank of lockers on the wall behind us. There was a locker for each of us, labeled with our last names.

"Don't you want to talk about your job?" Nick asked.

"Life's short, James. Rule is: play first, business second. Although you need to sign confidentiality agreements before using the suits," he said.

My HUD chimed with an incoming priority message. As expected it was from Anino Enterprises, requesting my signature. I'd recently upgraded my AI's capability to read legalese and it found nothing objectionable in the language sent.

"We good, Nick?"

"Yup," he answered.

I opened the locker with my name and found a suit hanging in it. There was an extra helmet on the top shelf. It was an unexpected addition, since most suits didn't require one. I shrugged to myself and peeled off my vac-suit.

"I'd forgotten about your peg-leg, Hoffen," Anino said. "Does it cause you many problems?"

He really had no filter, but I reminded myself that he was a teen. "Ladders and sand are two things I still have trouble with. Otherwise, no big deal."

"You have any privacy panels around here?" Ada asked.

"What? Going commando?" Anino asked. This earned him a stern look from Marny. "My bad," he quickly amended.

Locker room layout, he directed.

"You'll need to step back, Chen," he said.

She moved over toward the group and an opaque glass wall slid up from the floor.

"Thank you," she said with a mouth full of sweetness.

I'd finished pulling on the new suit. "Helmet?"

"Yeah, more fun that way," Anino answered.

I pulled the helmet on and looked around. From the outside, it had been medium blue like the rest of the suit. From the inside, I couldn't even tell I was wearing it except for a few faint shadows that were the contours of the helmet.

"Nice," I said.

"You'll say that again, I promise," he said.

A few minutes later Tabby and Ada exited the impromptu locker room holding helmets under their arms. Their suits were the same medium blue and they had bright yellow lines tracing their body contours.

"Helmets on, ladies. James, Bertrand, last chance. You don't know what you're about to miss out on," he said.

"Maybe next time," Nick said.

"Fair enough. Okay, the name of the game is foot-tag. Once you're tagged, you're it. If you touch someone's foot, they're it. And Hoffen, you're it," he said floating, away from me.

I took a cheap shot at Tabby, which she totally anticipated, blasting up from the ground at a remarkable rate. If I wasn't getting the cheap shot, then I was going for gold. I shot up in Anino's direction. The suit cut through the air so easily that I felt like I was in space.

I caught a glimpse of him flying behind a large cluster of video displays.

Track Anino's vector on HUD.

"Foot-tag rules preclude use of automated tracking," my AI informed me.

That was fine by me. I could catch him no matter how we went about it. I zipped around the front of the video panels fully expecting to intercept him, only to find that he'd used the sight-blocking displays to change direction and was now accelerating straight up toward the domed ceiling, twenty meters above.

"Careful, Anino. You're going too fast," I said.

"Don't chicken out now! You'll miss the big splash," he said.

The kid was certifiably nuts, but I wasn't about to be outdone by crazy, so I pushed the suit hard, closing the distance between us. I marveled at how quickly the suit responded to my directives and hoped I wasn't about to wind up as ceiling paste. As we closed on the ceiling, my HUD displayed a circular outline a meter in diameter, directly ahead. The AI was detecting a port or hatch. I pushed harder, stretched, and finally slapped Anino's foot with my outstretched arm. At the same moment, the hatch popped open, revealing an energy barrier.

I followed Anino through and almost came to a complete stop. Instead of popping into space, we'd entered into a viscous, nearly pitch-black material, dropping from thirty meters per second to five instantaneously. My spine should have been crushed by the rapid deceleration, but other than being disoriented, I felt fine.

"What the frak?" Tabby's excited voice called over the comm, no doubt she'd followed us through.

I swung my head around trying to gain my equilibrium and saw a faint blue glow in the distance. It was then that things became clear to me. "We're underwater?"

"Took you long enough," Anino chirped. "And, TAG, you're it, Masters."

My HUD outlined Tabby's wriggling form in bright orange. Anino's pronouncement snapped her from her struggles and she straightened with one arm reaching for me.

"Oh no you don't," I said. I wasn't about to be tagged again and stretched toward the blue above us.

Water rushed past and I discovered that arm position made a difference in controlling direction. I'd spent a lifetime training my AI with a series of subtle gestures to work with arc-jets. In water however, every maneuver was encumbered, causing me to fight the medium. My best path was straight up, so I tucked my arms to my sides and pointed my toes. The blue glow above widened and in a few seconds I broke the surface of Curie's Radium Sea.

"Where are you?" Ada's worried voice came through the comm.

"Look for a blue splotch and head toward it," I said.

"But there's a huge monster here," she said. "I don't want to move."

"How big?" Anino asked.

"Ten meters, glowy fins, big mouth," she said.

End game, Anino commanded immediately. "Don't move, Chen. It doesn't see that well, but feels things moving in the water."

"What is it, Anino?" I asked.

"Likely a Sephelodon, but I can't be sure. Chen, your suit should protect you - not completely sure of the bite pressure, though. It might be close. They also have electroreceptors along their sides that are super sensitive to movement in the water."

Tactical display of all friendlies and Sephelodon, I instructed my AI as I flipped over in mid-air and dove into the water.

"Nick, Marny, suit up. We've got a problem," I said.

Marny's voice was clipped. "Aye, Cap, already on it."

"Ada, I'm coming in hot. Tabs, take the tail. Diagram shows electrore-ceptors along its side," I said.

"It's circling," Ada said. "I need to move..."

"Don't do it, Chen," Anino said.

For the second time in only a few minutes my eyes had to adjust to a radical change in illumination. Fortunately, the light change in the dive downward was less abrupt than when we'd exited Anino's underwater lair into the inky depths of the sea.

My HUD displayed the Sephelodon and it was indeed circling Ada. Anino was closer, but I hoped he'd stay back. I was far from an expert at swimming with a grav-suit, but I also knew that I could trust Tabby and Ada to work with me as a team. The last thing I needed was to have to worry about Anino.

"Liaaaaam," Ada's voice grew louder as her nerve was tested by the direct approach of the Sephelodon.

"Ada, take a close pass on me and give me a completely negative delta-v. On my mark," I said. In spacer pilot speak, I'd told her to sail past me and keep going.

"Roger that," she said. I could hear the tension in her voice.

"Go!"

Ada shot directly up and at me. As I'd both predicted and feared, the big shark-looking thing flicked its large tail, accelerating at an incred-ible rate.

Highlight electroreceptors on Sephelo.

My HUD superimposed a delicate series of thin geometric swirls clustered around its mouth and gills. The lines narrowed and stretched along the creature's center line, fading out a meter before the start of the tail.

As Ada whooshed past, and just before impact, I curled into a ball and slammed into the top of the monster's great head. At the last moment, it anticipated my approach and opened its great maw. Fortunately, my speed had been sufficient that I skipped off the top of its jaw, narrowly missing becoming its next meal.

The impact should have been crushing as I'd been moving at fifteen meters per second. The suit, however, absorbed most of the energy and I rolled off and straightened out.

The Sephelodon, only stunned, forgot about Ada. I barely had time to move out of its way as it recovered and charged with mouth wide open. Its agility in the water was both fantastic and terrifying, but there wasn't time for panic. I shot away with all the speed I could muster. Ada was free, but I'd jumped into hot water to make that happen.

Light amplification.

The HUD within the grav-suit displayed a rich overlay onto the dark landscape in front of me. Indistinct shapes snapped into sharp focus and hidden details were revealed. The HUD also displayed the Sephelo's trajectory and delta-v. I was losing ground and contact was imminent. Worse, I wasn't close to cover.

"On me, Cap." Marny's alto voice cut through my search for a solution. A throbbing light glowed at the bottom of my vision, letting me know that her location was behind and below me.

"No good. I lose speed on turns. It doesn't," I said.

"I'm going to try to give you a distraction, be ready," Tabby said.

My HUD had been showing an outline version of me and the Sephelo. It was the same strategic display I used in ship to ship combat. Listening to the conversation, my AI expanded to include Tabby and Marny. Tabby was indeed on an intercept course with the Sephelo's tail.

"How are you getting that speed?" I asked.

"Stay focused, Cap," Marny said. Someday I'd learn and she wouldn't have to remind me. Today was not that day.

Tabby's body struck the beast two-thirds aft on its starboard side. The impact didn't push it far off course, but the beast instinctively turned toward the contact. Tabby neatly, albeit in slow motion, tumbled around its tail, straightened out and shot away.

I used her distraction to peel away from my original trajectory and curve back towards Marny. My concern was that now the Sephelo would shift its pursuit to Tabby. Relief, however, wasn't exactly the feeling I experienced when I recognized it was once again closing on me. Tabby had given me room to move and it was up to me to make something of it.

I calculated the distance to Marny and then to the entrance to the Anino's dome. I might be able to make it to Marny, but I certainly wasn't going to make the dome.

"Close pass above me, Cap. Closer the better," she said.

"We've got company," Ada said. "Two at twenty meters, more further out."

"Everyone inside," Marny said. "We've got this. That goes for you too, Cap. Don't stop until you're in."

"I can't leave you with this thing," I knew better than to question her in combat, but it felt like she was making a sacrifice I couldn't live with.

"Appreciate that, but this one isn't going to be our problem. Trust me, Cap."

"Roger that," I said.

I focused on Marny's position as I approached. She was moving slowly through the water with her hands in front, arms bent, holding something. At five meters, my HUD picked up the detail that I'd been unable to see. She held a long, narrow sword. I twisted around so I would pass above her face-to-face, wanting to be sure I didn't kick her on the way by. Once past, I arced slightly downward to keep the beast on its original path.

"*AAAAAHHHH...*"

My AI filtered out the rest of Marny's war cry as she held her ground and plunged the blade into the bottom of the passing beast. I slowed and turned to watch. It was a horrific scene, as the beast's entrails spilled out, clouding the sea around her. I felt both the thrill of combat and sadness, knowing this beast had simply been doing what it had to survive.

"Marny, get out of there," Ada said. "You've incoming."

My HUD showed multiple Sephelodons making a beeline for our position, cutting us off from the dome.

Instead of turning in my direction, Marny dove downward and away from the approaching mob. It was a good move as we'd been cut off from the dome anyway. I followed her down another ten meters to the sea floor, taking cover beneath bioluminescent mineral formations.

"You should've kept going," Marny said.

"Right. And you're nuts attacking that thing with just a sword."

"Hardly just a sword," Anino said.

"Tabs, everyone in and safe?" I asked.

"We're in and you need to hunker down. There are at least fifty predators in a frenzy up here. Some of them make our first friend look like a guppy."

"We'll come get you," Anino said.

I switched to a private channel. "You okay, Marny?"

"Aye, Cap. Might have strained my shoulder, but it'll be okay."

"Thank you for coming for me."

"That's what we do, Cap."

We sat at the bottom for another fifteen minutes before a sleek submersible slid into view and came to rest above our position, its aft sporting a blue pressure barrier promising safety. We didn't require any convincing and jetted into the vehicle.

"Welcome aboard," Jonathan said, offering two towels.

I accepted one and pulled my helmet off.

"Thank you," I said.

"That was quite a show, Mr. Hoffen. I might not approve of Phillippe's methods, but his efficacy should not be questioned."

I widened my eyes slightly, an indication to my AI that I wasn't sure what he'd just said. It filled in a definition and I frowned as I considered his words.

"What are you saying?" I asked.

"He's saying this was an audition, Cap," Marny answered for him.

I looked back to Jonathan for confirmation. He simply raised his eyebrows in response.

"Take us back. We're leaving," I said tightly.

"Your anger is understandable and I will certainly take you back as you've requested. But, as irritated as you are and as asinine as Master Anino's behavior was, you should hear him out first."

"What? You're here to calm me down before we get back? All part of the big plan, is it?"

"No. Phillippe will be upset with me for sharing what I have, but he has misread your team. You work on trust and he has broken this trust early in the relationship. I hope that by exposing the deception now I will avert your natural inclination to walk away."

"He put my team at risk. It's not something I'm going to forget."

"As you should not. Please hear him out before you make your decision."

"We'll see," I said.

We rode back to the dome in relative silence, the only sound being the low whine of the motor propelling us through the water.

Chapter 5

TATARA FURNACE

Yishuv Settlement, Planet Ophir

"Eliora, are you hurt?" Amon asked, still clutching the rock in one hand and the bloodied corpse of the Ophie he'd brought down on top of her in the other.

"No. Help me, we have to check on the expedition," she said.

Between the two of them, they rolled the body to the side.

"Your leg," Eliora said, noticing that Amon was having difficulty standing.

Amon hobbled back to the mule, supporting himself with the reciprocating pick, which he laid gently in the vehicle's trailer. They couldn't afford to leave any of their equipment on the hillside even in an emergency. He hopped back toward the site where they'd been breaking the iron spire into transportable pieces.

"We can't afford to leave this behind," he said.

"You want to die? There could be more."

"Just help me."

"I hope this was worth it," she said.

"So do I."

By Amon's calculation, they'd gathered at least twelve tonnes of iron. That was more material than the smithy could use in five years, given current production levels. The pace would undoubtedly have to change. The settlement's survival might depend on his ability to adapt to increasing Ophie activity.

Eliora caught up with Amon and slipped under his thick arm, straining to help him into the mule. When he was settled, she handed him her crossbow. She wrapped his leg with a splint and activated foam that would both immobilize and numb the limb until they returned to the settlement.

"Why have we not developed better weapons?" Amon asked, inspecting the crossbow as they bounced down the mountain trail. "This is certainly good for game animals and small predators, but that Ophie wasn't even slowed by it."

"They are too well armored and the iron heads are too heavy, they slow the flight," Eliora answered.

"We've relied on those blaster rifles and are lulled into complacency," Amon said.

"If the main blaster turret hadn't failed, we'd have easily repelled that last attack," she said.

"Can't you see it? Our reliance on those blasters is our weakness. What if the secondary turret had failed too? How many more people would have been lost?"

"What would you have us do?"

"Merrie thinks she can make steel."

Eliora shook her head in confusion. "I don't know what that is."

"Stronger and lighter than iron. We could make longer knives," Amon said.

"You could do that?"

"Maybe."

"I would be careful of bringing 'maybes' up with Captain Gian. There are many in the settlement who have been quick to blame him for the last attack."

The conversation was cut short as they arrived at the main camp. A single Ophie lay dead, cast to the side. Those it had killed, three from the party, had been carefully laid in a wagon.

"Eliora, what of your attacker?" Captain Gian asked as he approached.

"It is dead. Amon crushed its skull," she said.

Gian gave Amon an appraising look. "Well done, blacksmith," he said. "We did not fare as well. We lost Territ and one of the laborers."

"You should know I was only able to kill the Ophie after Eliora hobbled it with her knife."

"Is this right? You attacked an Ophie with a knife?"

"I'd spent my crossbow bolts already and it hadn't fallen. When it attacked Amon, I cut its ankles like we've been trained."

"If only I had ten more like you, Eliora," Gian said. "This better have been worth the price we paid today, blacksmith."

"DAD SAYS we need the council's permission to build a full-size furnace," Merrie said. She'd been Amon's constant companion for the last tenday.

"So you've said," he replied.

Amon shoved the long knife back into the fire.

"Your knives are beautiful, Amon," Merrie said, picking up one that Amon had already finished.

"Eliora says they're too heavy," he said.

"I doubt that. She loves her knife."

"Yet if we make them long enough to be practical against the Ophie, they'd be too heavy."

"How much steel would you need to make a real sword?"

"A few kilograms, why? What have you been up to?" It hadn't escaped his notice that Merrie had secreted several kilograms of raw ore.

"I made a small furnace and I've set everything up. I just need help running it," she said.

"Does Merik know?"

"Yes... No... I'm not sure. Besides, he's always saying I need to be more self-reliant."

"You're either a genius or a crazy person," Amon said. "And I don't know the first thing about using steel."

"Yes you do. It's a lot like your work with iron. Look," Merrie handed him the engineering pad. It was one of the few remaining working computerized pads in the settlement, having been handed down from Ozzie to Merrie.

"You shouldn't have this outside," Amon said.

"It wouldn't be if you'd come over to the lab," she said.

Amon looked at his nearly healed leg, still in a cast. Merrie followed his eyes and smiled impishly as if to suggest she'd simply forgotten about his injury.

Merrie leaned over and started a video showing an ancient smith.

Amon watched in rapt attention as the smith formed, flattened and folded raw steel repeatedly until, as he explained, it was as strong as it could possibly be. After that, the man shaped it and drew a fuller down the center of the sword, creating a ridge of steel. He spent almost as much time polishing and sharpening. In the end, he'd created a magnificent looking blade, which he demonstrated was capable of cutting through just about anything.

"That folding technique is different, but the rest looks familiar," Amon said.

"See. You already have all of the tools and skills, you just need upgraded materials," she said.

"What do you need from me?"

"The furnace has to be tended. Here. I've created a schedule." She handed him the engineering tablet. On the screen was a long list of instructions that would easily take six or seven hours to complete.

"I'll help, but on one condition," he said.

"Name it."

"You have to transcribe these instructions to paper. I'll not be responsible for damaging this pad. Tell me, how many other inventions are there like this that we've been too proud to look for?"

"Elder Blaken says pride goes before a fall."

"And a haughty spirit before destruction. Merrie, we cannot let our people fall due to ignorance."

"When can you help?"

"Mother is installing the new hinges tomorrow. I might not be able to do much, but she wants me there to direct people."

"What are you doing tonight around 0100?"

"Sleeping?"

"Perfect. I'll let you sleep and wake you when I need help. Guarantee, we'll be done by 0700."

"Where is this furnace of yours?" Amon asked.

"North wall, in the old tannery."

"That place is falling down, you should be careful in there."

"Agreed. But it's filled with bricks and I needed those for the furnace. "

Amon felt a long story coming and needed to head it off. He enjoyed Merrie's company, but he had work to complete. "Fine. 0100 it is. You better go and don't bring that tablet tonight."

She gave Amon a quick hug and ran off. The lingering smell of light perfume caught him off guard. He sighed, wondering what he'd gotten himself into. Merrie was an enigma, full of energy and smart as they came. The perfume, though, that was new.

He hobbled around the smithy and helped Nurit clean up. She'd been polishing gate hinges, while he'd spent the day hammering out a new batch of knives.

"What did Merrie want? You two have sure been spending a lot of time together," Nurit said.

"She's working on a project and is looking for help."

"Still on about that steel furnace? I thought Merik said the council wasn't interested."

"I hadn't heard that. But yes, she's working on a miniature version."

"As long as it doesn't interfere with your work. She's a beautiful young lady and smarter by a meter than most. I'm surprised some lad hasn't caught her eye."

"She intimidates the available men," Amon admitted.

"Not all of them." Nurit smiled.

Amon ignored his mother. "I'm going to help her run a batch tonight. I won't be back until 0700."

"Don't be late, we'll want everyone there."

It was 1230 when Merrie rapped on the window to Amon's bedroom. He woke easily and found his mother sitting in the common room that joined the two bedrooms.

"Be careful tonight and take two sets of the leathers with you," she said, setting down the book she'd been reading.

"I'll see you at the gate in a few hours."

"Amon, tell Merrie I hope her furnace works."

"I will. She'd appreciate knowing you feel that way."

Amon exited the living space into the smithy, grabbed leather aprons and long sleeved gloves and met Merrie on the darkened, cobble-stone street.

"Who were you talking to?" Merrie asked.

"Mom."

"What did you tell her?" Merrie asked.

"That we were going to the tannery to run a load through your furnace?" Amon said, making it sound like a question.

"You told her that? What did she say? I thought she hated the idea."

"She said she hopes it works."

"So, she doesn't think it'll work?"

"No, you silly squirmunk. She says the council doesn't like to use the maker-machine for stuff they don't understand. She also thinks you're about the smartest girl she's ever met."

"Hmm."

"What are we in for tonight?" Amon asked, looking to change the subject.

"It isn't very complex. I ground up the hematite boulder you brought back from Ozzie's last trip, sort of a tribute."

"I like that," Amon said.

"When we get there, you'll see another pile. It's partially burned coal coke, like you use in your forging fire," she continued. "We'll stack the coke in layers with the hematite in the furnace."

"Is that it? We just light it up?"

"No. There's a whole process that I'll explain as we go. We'll be busy the entire time," she explained as they entered the old tannery.

Along the back wall of the abandoned building, Amon saw the two meter tall brick furnace Merrie had recently constructed. A narrow hearth at the front was covered by a thick iron plate and a tube protruded from one side. As promised, the piles of hematite and coal sat neatly behind the furnace with a ladder between them.

"It's called a Tatara Furnace. What do you think?"

"You've been really busy. What's that tube?" Amon asked.

"Oxygen supply. There's a fan on the end so we can control the temperature."

"Does Merik know you're doing this?"

"Yes. He caught me borrowing tools and equipment."

"What does he think?"

"He said he was glad I was coming up with my own ideas and chasing them down. However, I'm not sure if he thinks we'll be successful or just wants me out of his hair."

"Is he really short on work? I thought he had more work than he could get done," Amon said.

"He does, but he also thinks we're stuck in our ways and that we need to be trying new things."

"I can see that, but it's hard to explore new ideas when you're busy. I'd think Merik would be really worried about getting things done with Ozzie gone."

"Ozzie's death shook him up. No matter what's going on, Merik has always insisted I spend at least two days each tenday doing my own projects. But, when I showed him this idea, he gave me the entire tenday to work on it."

"That's different. So, what do I need to do?"

"Scoop hematite ore. The idea is to get carbon out of the coke and into the iron. You'll shovel two scoops hematite, I'll shovel coke on top of that and we'll alternate all the way to the top of the oven. As it heats, it'll slump down and we'll keep adding material in alternating layers until we run out. I think we have four hours of material, but it's my first time so I'm not sure."

"I THOUGHT you were going to let me sleep," Amon complained. After a long five and a half hours, they'd just run out of hematite.

"Yeah, sorry about that. I didn't want to stop while we still had material. You'll thank me later?" Merrie said.

Amon chuckled, slumping to the ground next to her.

"When will it be finished?" he asked.

"I'll monitor the heat until we burn the entire thing out and I'll keep swiping the dross off. I hope Merik won't be too annoyed. I won't be able to help with the gates for at least two more hours."

"You'll get a chance to find out shortly. If I'm right, that's Mom and

Merik coming in the smithy's mule right now." Amon pointed at a pair of headlights bouncing off a nearby building.

"But, it's only 0630. They said they weren't starting on the gates until 0700." Merrie's voice rose.

"Don't sweat it. It'll take us at least two hours to set the straps in the wall and another hour to bolt the hinges onto the door. I'll go slowly. They're always accusing me of it anyway," Amon said, looking at the sooty face of his evening's companion.

"Don't get in trouble for me."

"We're in this together, Merrie. You've made a believer out of me and I want to see what I can make from your steel. I want to try to make a real sword, not just daggers."

"You mean it?"

"From what you've shown me, the only skills I'm missing are folding and tempering. Otherwise, swords are just like making long, thin iron daggers." Amon stood and offered his hand.

Merrie brushed off her pants as Nurit and Merik pulled to a stop in the smithy's vehicle. In the cart behind the mule lay the unassembled hinges for the city's main gate.

"How'd it go last night?" Merik asked, hopping out, handing Merrie a steaming cup of coffee.

Merrie gratefully accepted the cup with a broad smile. "It's taking longer than planned. But we loaded the last of the material into the furnace twenty minutes ago."

"I reviewed your bench notes last night. Up 'till that point I thought you were constructing an electric arc-furnace," Merik said.

"I want to, but without use of the maker-machine, an arc-furnace isn't practical. I'm hoping Master Nurit and Amon will be able to demonstrate the value of this steel and the council will give me the go-ahead." Merrie looked nervously from Merik to Nurit.

Merik turned to Nurit, who'd climbed out of the cart and was crouched, inspecting the furnace's oxygen inlet. "Nurit, how about it? Are you interested in working with Merrie's steel?"

"We've had good success with our iron and it may be too late to teach this old bird any new tricks," Nurit answered. "Amon's got the energy for this though, and he's his own man."

"Amon?" Merik asked.

"I believe our settlement is at risk, Master Merik," Amon answered. "We've too long relied on our founder's technology. If we are to survive, we must develop our own. I hope Merrie's steel is just the beginning."

Merik cocked his head and smiled at Nurit. "He sounds so much like his father."

"Yes he does. Now, I hate to break up the conversation, but we have crews meeting us at the front gates," Nurit said, climbing back into the driver's seat of the vehicle.

"Are you able to leave, Merrie?" Merik asked.

"The furnace will finish in ninety minutes. It would be ideal if I stayed and monitored the smelt," she answered.

"Understood. Perhaps we'll spend time discussing project planning in our next session," he said.

"My apologies, Master. The project exceeded my time estimates by a significant margin."

"And, so it is with most projects."

Amon climbed into the mule behind Merik and gave a friendly wave to Merrie as they pulled away. The trio rode quietly through the abandoned section of the settlement, the empty buildings a stark reminder of their losing battle with the Ophie.

At the front gates, they found the master stone mason and his crew driving wide iron wedges into the seam at the base of the wall, lifting the wall just enough to make room for the hinge straps.

"Master Pessach, good to see you this fine morning," Merik called, jumping from the cart, extending his hand to the older mason.

"About time you showed up. We've no time to be standing around, Merik. The smith's failed gates allowed those lizard devils to tear down half my city," Pessach growled.

"Very well. We'll start at the bottom and work up."

"Would you also instruct me on the consistency of my mortar? No? Good! I'll let you know when I need your help," Pessach said and turned to the group of laborers he'd brought along, continuing barking instructions.

"Let's get started, Amon," Nurit said, ignoring the grumpy mason.

Together they carried an iron hinge strap over to the newly exposed sandstone block. They lay the strap next to the channel that had been carved from the block centuries ago. They slid pins, four centimeters in diameter and ten centimeters long, through the strap and stepped out of the way.

Pessach directed his crew to fill the empty channel with mortar and then seated the strap and pins in the soft bed, clearing the extra material by deftly flipping it away with his trowel.

"Lift now. We don't have all day," Pessach barked at the laborers, who'd been assembled to man the block and tackle. It took several minutes of fussing before he was satisfied with the block's placement. "Check your measurements now, Merik," he said. "Once we release this stone, we'll not be moving it again today."

Merik verified the measurements and nodded for them to continue.

At 1200 they stopped for lunch, having set the four straps on the left side and the first on the right.

"I'd thought Merrie would return by now," Nurit said to Amon as they sat under the shade of a tree twenty meters from the front gate.

"I hope she didn't fall asleep. She didn't rest last night," Amon said, leaning back against the slick trunk of the tree. "Is Master Pessach always in such a foul mood?"

"His wife was killed in the last raid. He blames Merik and me for the failure of the blasters and gates. I understand his grief," she said.

"There's Merrie, now," Amon nodded in the direction of the gate. Merrie had joined Merik, and the two were talking with Pessach.

"We've a long afternoon ahead of us," Nurit said. "We might as well get back to it. I'll have you start assembling the hinges on the doors."

"Very well."

It was 1830 when the second door's final hinge pin was slid into place and the cap-nut securely welded onto its end.

Captain Gian, who'd been checking on their progress throughout the day, approached as Nurit and Merik were adjusting the gate's locking mechanism to fit with the new configuration.

"Will we be able to lock it this evening?" Gian asked.

"It is locked now," Merik replied, smiling. "I believe there will be some settling over the next tenday, so we'll be back to make further adjustments. For now, however, it's all yours."

Gian sighed audibly. "That is a great relief. Although, now that the Ophie have discovered the weakness in our blasters, I'm afraid they'll attack the southwest gate."

"I have a plan for making our remaining blaster mobile. It would allow us to relocate more efficiently if another gate comes under attack," Merik said.

"We're vulnerable if they simultaneously attack multiple gates. Is there no way to restore the broken weapon?" Gian asked.

"No, it is beyond our ability," Merik answered.

"I see. That is indeed bad news, but we'll plan accordingly," he said. "On another matter, I've been receiving reports of activity in the old tannery. Was it your apprentice that I saw over there?"

"Yes. My apologies for not informing you earlier."

"What was she doing?"

"It's a project you might find interesting. Merrie, would you share with Captain Gian what you've been doing?"

Merrie's face turned bright red as the conversation turned unexpectedly toward her.

"Yes, of course. Really, it's a multi-disciplinary project. I believe I've constructed a furnace that will allow us to smelt steel," she said.

"Why is this significant?" Gian asked.

"Steel is twice as strong as iron - properly tempered, even more so. With steel, our blacksmiths will be able to craft long blades that are practical for your protectors to wield. Additionally, we will be able to produce long bows and arrow heads that I believe will pierce the natural armor and be small enough to penetrate to the vital organs of an Ophie."

"Is this truly feasible, Merik?"

"Time will tell..."

Chapter 6

IRRESISTIBLE OFFER

Radium Sea, Planet Curie, Tipperary Star System

The cylindrical submersible docked aft-first onto the armored side of the domed structure. The subtle whirring of motors was the only noise we heard as a heavy door slid out of view, exposing the pressure barrier to the interior of the station.

Anino and the rest of my crew awaited Marny and my return in a well-lit and otherwise empty room. One look at Tabby's face and I knew she was as angry as I was.

"That was some kick-ass teamwork out there!" Anino said as we passed through the pressure barrier.

I took three quick strides through the barrier, picked the teenager up by his suit and pushed him against the wall. A blaster charging behind me was followed by the sound of two more revving up.

"You risked my entire crew out there. Explain to me why I shouldn't knock your teeth into the back of your neck?"

"Mr. Hoffen, I beg of you! Place Master Anino on the floor and step back, or I'll be forced to respond," Jonathan said from behind me.

"You so much as move a muscle, Jonathan, and I'll drop you where you stand," Tabby growled. Her blaster was in my peripheral vision and leveled at Jonathan.

"Oh frak me, a Mexican standoff. Could this day get any better?" Anino squeaked. "Jonathan, put down your weapon. I'm at no risk here. Hoffen is making a point. He's establishing a pecking order."

"Master Anino, I believe he intends to do you harm," Jonathan said.

"What kind of sick shit are you?" I asked, letting Anino slide to the floor.

"Well, now we're getting somewhere," Anino said, standing back up and brushing non-existent dust from his knees. The teenager was a head shorter than me.

"We're out of here, Anino. We don't need whatever work you have for us. I need to trust my business partners," I said. "Jonathan, you promised to return us to the surface if I requested. Are you as good as your word?"

"I am, Captain Hoffen," he replied.

"Wait. Don't you want to hear what the big deal is?" Anino asked.

"No, you sick little bastard. No job is worth dying for," I said.

"Well, that's the rub, really, isn't it?" Anino asked.

It was such a strange thing to say I couldn't help myself but to ask, "What are you talking about?"

"You said no job is worth dying for and yet it always comes down to that for you and your crew," he said.

"I don't know what you're on about, but we're out of here. Nick, do you know where the suits are that we came in?"

"Down the hall, Liam. We're not far from the main room," he said.

"Lead on," I said.

Anino smiled and shrugged his shoulders, apparently content to follow us into the main room.

Lower armor plating. Dim interior lighting.

We all stopped moving for a moment as the metallic dome retracted into the floor. Beneath the metal was a thick layer of armor-glass. When fully retracted, the entire twenty meter tall structure was completely translucent down to the last two meters where it appeared we were embedded into the floor of the sea. The interior lights had dimmed and glowing strips along the floors and walls provided a small amount of light.

Outside, the feeding frenzy had dissipated, although a number of larger fish were lazily gliding around, looking for scraps that might have been missed in the milieu. It was hard not to be mesmerized by the huge variety of sea life the light of the dome illuminated.

"How far down are we?" Ada asked.

"Ninety-two meters," Anino said, his quiet voice easy to hear in the silence that had settled over us.

"Why weren't we crushed by the water when we exited the dome?" Marny asked.

"The suits can handle a lot more than that. To be honest, I'm not sure a Sephelodon could crush the armor, so you probably weren't in any real danger," he said.

"Drop it, Anino. We're not buying what you're selling," Tabby spat. She wasn't giving in so easily.

"Tell me, Hoffen. Why did you risk your entire crew for the crew of *Cape of Good Hope*?"

It was a sore subject, which shouldn't have surprised me. I was growing to like this Anino kid less with every moment I was around him. We'd watched an entire shipload of people fall out of the TransLoc fold-space wave and be lost in the deep dark of space. To be honest, being torn apart by the forces of fold-space was the best case scenario. The worst case would be that the *Cape of Good Hope* had remained intact and been dropped into the deep dark of space somewhere. The people onboard would have starved to death, too far from any planet or civilization where they could re-fuel, repair or restock.

"Don't listen to him, Cap. He's messing with your head," Marny said.

"What? It's a fair question. I did pay you fifty-thousand credits, just so we could talk," he said.

"You're an ass," Ada said. Her response was surprising, as she typically didn't have a bad thing to say about anyone. "Having money doesn't give you the right to mess with people's lives."

"Come on, Hoffen. I'll drop it if you answer," he said.

"Fine. It's something you wouldn't understand, Anino. It was a matter of honor. Moderate risk to the lives of my crew versus certain death for *Cape of Good Hope's* crew. The only thing I regret is not starting earlier. If I had, we might have been successful," I said.

I peeled the grav-suit off, hung it on a hook and started pulling on my vac-suit.

"You had to know there was a possibility of someone getting hurt when you took on those pirates back at Colony-40," Anino said, looking at my prosthetic foot.

"This?" I asked, waving my hand across my foot. "Good trade, I'd say. Those pirates would have just kept killing my friends and family if we hadn't done something."

"How do you know so much about us?" Tabby asked.

"Information is easy to come by, Masters. You know what's hard to find?"

"Rich assholes who like to frak with people?" she fired back.

"No, those are a dime-a-dozen," he agreed.

Tabby growled. "I know, I just wanted to call you an asshole again."

Anino chuckled. "Point Masters," he said under his breath.

"What'd you say?" Tabby asked. Both Nick and I stopped what we were doing and looked at him. Anino had used a phrase that was unique to our small group.

"You heard me. And, you're right. I'm a rich asshole who's been snooping on you," he said.

"What's hard to find, Anino?" Nick cut to the chase.

"A crew with honor," he said.

"Too bad this crew isn't available." Tabby hissed, walking from behind the visual screen of the locker room. She dropped her grav-suit on the ground, communicating as much disdain as possible with that single gesture.

"So you've said. But what if I said I could retrieve *Cape of Good Hope*?"

"They're long dead. We saw them break up and fall out of fold-space," Nick said.

"You sure that's what you remember?" he asked.

"Their starboard engine was sheared off by contacting the edge of the fold-space bubble." I still replayed the sequence in my mind's eye in quiet moments.

"Haven't you wondered why LeGrande turned out of the wave and accelerated?"

"She didn't want the debris of her ship to cause any more casualties," I said.

"Want to ask her yourself?" he asked.

"Are you nuts?"

"Probably."

"Show us," Nick said.

"You can't be taking this jerk seriously," Tabby said.

I'd finished pulling on my suit and turned to look her in the eyes. "I have to see for myself," I said.

She gave me the grim smile I'd come to understand as grudging acceptance and nodded.

The five of us followed Anino to his work area.

"Pardon the mess. I'm working on many different projects."

Indeed what looked like complete chaos from across the room actually had some organization to it.

"I can't turn up the lights with the dome unshielded. It freaks out my neighbors and they'll hurt themselves," he said as he pulled a crystal about the size of the end of my thumb from a delicate three-point cradle mounted in an array of a hundred similar crystals.

"Is that...," Nick sputtered. "How could you..."

"Perceptive questions, both. Yes. This is a quantum communication crystal. Its mate resides aboard *Cape of Good Hope*. As for how, when money is no object, things once thought impossible to acquire are not so difficult."

"You're saying you can raise Captain LeGrande with that crystal?" I asked, my heart hammering in my chest.

"Surely, you've had enough experience with these quantum crystals to know the answer to your own question," he said. "That's not the really interesting part of this conversation."

"Liam. He has a jump ship," Nick said. "This is a rescue mission."

"Jupiter and Mars!" Anino clapped his hands together, gently holding the crystal between his thumb and forefinger. "How I miss working with other brilliant minds. So, are you in?"

Tabby fidgeted next to me. She didn't trust Anino, but knew he was dangling the ultimate carrot.

"Why do you need us? Why wouldn't Belirand mount up and fetch them?" Marny asked.

"There's more in play here than you know. If they retrieve Captain LeGrande and crew, they'd have to admit they could have recovered every other past failed mission," he said.

"So they let LeGrande and crew die to push off liability for previous missions?" Nick asked. "That's crazy. Their liability is growing, in that case. Belirand could pay the crew off and make them sign confidentiality agreements."

"You're right," Anino agreed. "It's bigger than that. Belirand has lots of reasons not to retrieve that crew."

"That doesn't explain why you need us," Marny pushed. "You can hire crew all day long. All this talk about honor and team work - there's something else going on. What aren't you telling us?"

"Belirand," Ada said. "It's all the failed missions from the past. Public outcry would be outrageous."

"You're right and they'd do anything to keep that secret, Chen. And, I mean anything." Anino bowed his head and looked up again, right into my eyes.

"I don't understand. It was Belirand who put us in contact with you," I said.

"Apparently, you haven't spent much time around a bureaucratic organization," Anino said. "Left hand rarely knows what the right is doing. It's not like the people I bribe go bragging to their bosses about our arrangement," he said.

"You sure you want to get mixed up in this, Cap?" Marny asked.

"I don't know that I can walk away if there's any chance to save LeGrande and her crew," I said, slowly scanning the faces around me.

"What about our ships and cargo? Isn't the co-op depending on us?" Ada asked.

"You're right, we'd need to make a return trip with our load," I said.

"Seriously?" Anino asked.

"What'd you expect? We have people who depend on us. We can't just disappear on them. We've frak-tonnes of ore that need to be delivered to the Terminal Seven project. Perhaps you've forgotten what it's like to work for a living, but we haven't," I said.

"You're thinking too small, Hoffen. Hold on, let me see what I can do," he said and started punching on a virtual keyboard and swiping objects around on a virtual display only he could see.

"I've just purchased a segmented hauler, right here on Curie, for a million credits. I'll lease it to *Loose Nuts* for a hundred thousand credits annually. I can have it delivered to Descartes. Will that do?" he asked, flicking a contract at Nick.

"A million credits?" Nick asked. "No, that won't do. We've a line on a hauler, we just need to take a look at it."

"Fairy Tits! Think bigger, James. This thing'll haul more ore than your damn colony can mine in a year," he said.

"Cancel your deal. Apparently, you haven't spent a lot of time trying to make a mining operation work. A hauler that size burns too much fuel and we'd go broke. If you want to speed us along, lend me that million credits at five percent annually and I'll make the rest work," Nick said.

"Five percent? Are you nuts, nobody lends at that rate," Anino said.

"Today, you do," Nick said. In that moment, I felt a surge of pride.

It was almost surreal watching the teenage Anino stare Nick down in a battle of wills.

"Given your net worth and daily income, you've just spent more than a million credits arguing with me. Care to make it two?" Nick asked.

"Ugh, fine. Take the million credits, I don't care," Anino said, waving his hand in dismissal.

"We don't mind working for it." Nick swiped an agreement from his HUD and tossed it at Anino.

Anino swished his hand across a virtual signature block and flicked it back.

"If you're all done hugging it out, I need to hear LeGrande's voice before I'm on board," Tabby said.

"Ever the skeptic, Masters. At least that's something I can understand," Anino said.

He dropped the crystal he'd been holding into a receiver on one of his many cluttered work surfaces.

Hail Cape of Good Hope.

After a few minutes a woman's voice replied. "Anino, is that you?"

It was the voice that haunted my nightmares.

"It is, Katherine. I think I've found our crew," he said, his voice softer than it had been.

"You shouldn't take this risk, Phillippe. You'll be starting a war you can't hope to win," she said.

"Wouldn't be the first time. What's your sit-rep?"

"It's pretty dire. Our O2 scrubbers are fouled and operating at forty percent. We've had to start burning the O2 crystals. We still have food and the water reclaimers are still operational."

"How much time, Katherine?" Anino asked.

"Two weeks, comfortably. After that, we'll start making tougher decisions," she said.

"Captain LeGrande, Liam Hoffen here," I said.

"Captain Hoffen. Good to hear your voice. You shouldn't let Phillippe drag you into this," she said.

"Try to stop us," I said.

"Katherine, just hold on. Help's on the way," Anino said.

"Roger that, Phillippe, LeGrande out," she said and cut the comm.

"That do it for you, Masters?" Anino asked, looking at Tabby.

She brushed a tear from her eye, tried to look casual, and failed miserably. When she didn't answer I stepped in.

"What aren't you telling us?" I asked. "Something doesn't smell right."

"Belirand will do just about anything to keep secret the fact that they can jump relatively inexpensively to just about any location within a hundred million light years," he said.

"That's crazy. Why would they need to keep that secret?" I asked.

"I can't tell you, because once I do, there'll be a price on your head," he said. "You need to understand, if you join me to go after LeGrande and crew, your lives will be changed forever."

"That sounds a little grandiose," Ada said.

"But it's not. You should know that if you accept this mission, the life you've known so far will change. Belirand is a powerful enemy," he said.

"And LeGrande and forty-four of her crew's lives hang in the balance... so no pressure?" I said.

"Life isn't fair, Hoffen. Bad people have power because no one stands up to them," he replied. "I'm asking you to sacrifice for forty-five people you've never met."

"My crew needs time to talk in private," I said.

"I haven't even made you an offer... and we'll need *Hotspur*," he said.

I nodded and looked around the room. "If we do this, it won't be for money."

"Don't be stupid. Name your price, I'm loaded."

"Two thousand credits a day per person, replacement insurance on *Hotspur*, twenty-thousand a week for the ship, and consumables," Nick said. "If we accept, there'll be organizational requirements as well."

"Done," Anino said. "I'll give you time to talk it over, but Jonathan is going to have a heart attack if I don't get that katana back from Bertrand."

"The sword?" Marny asked.

"Yup. It's a priceless Japanese relic and you took it for a swim in salt water," he said.

"Oh crap. My bad," she said, pulling the narrow bladed sword from where she'd slung it over her back.

"Not at all. You needed a weapon and your instinct caused you to grab perhaps the finest weapon ever crafted by humans." He accepted the sword with an odd little bow. "We're so impressed with our technology that we ignore the craftsmanship and skill of those who came before us."

Anino continued. "As for a place to talk, use my meditation garden over there." He pointed to a small seating group against the armored glass.

"Great. Thanks." I grabbed Tabby's hand, leading her to an overstuffed chair looking out at the sea bed. In the darkness, bioluminescent life forms stood out in stark contrast to the murky background. A sense of peace pervaded the area and it was easy to see why Anino enjoyed the spot. The five of us sat quietly for a few minutes, watching the beauty of life at a hundred meters and considering the quandary he'd presented.

I finally broke the silence. "If anyone wants to back out, I won't feel bad. We still need to get our load back to the co-op and Nuage."

"Don't look at me, Liam. I'm in," Ada said. "I can't believe Belirand would just leave them to rot."

"I didn't want to speak for you, Ada. Belirand is a powerful enemy to make," I said.

"I don't trust Anino," Tabby said.

"Something *is* off about him," Marny said. "I can't put my finger on it. He doesn't act like any teenager I ever met."

"Money has a way of messing with people. Can you imagine having the entire Anino fortune at your fingertips?" Nick asked.

"I suppose that could be it," she said.

"How about it, Marny? You in?" I knew the answer, but she needed to say it out loud for both of us.

"I'd never be able to live with myself if I passed on this one," she said.

"Tabbs?"

"I can't say I'm not going to rip that little pecker's heart out, but I'm in," she said. "As if I'd let you go on your own."

"Nick?"

"You think you could bump up our visit with that retiring hauler captain? Maybe we could get him to make a final run and take *Sterra's Gift* back with him. Is he still bonded?" Nick asked.

"That's one Captain Charles Norris," I said and sent the comm my AI had constructed based on our conversation.

I looked across the room to where Anino sat. He was engrossed in whatever he was working on. I normally felt like I could read people, but Marny was right, the teenager was odd. I walked over to where Anino sat, with Nick close on my heel.

"Anino, we're in, but we need to establish ground rules and we have business to take care of first," I said.

He looked up from his project and set down tools I'd never seen before.

"This should be good. What are your ground rules?" he asked.

"My crew takes orders from no one but me and I don't take orders from anyone during combat. Bottom line is, if you're coming along, we're in charge," I said.

"Is that it?"

"You need to tell us right now why Belirand is keeping it secret that they can jump inexpensively," Nick said.

"Once I tell you this, there's no going back," Anino said. "Are you sure?"

Nick looked at me and I nodded my head. I wasn't sure what we were getting into, but it was hard to imagine Anino could say anything that would make saving forty-five people's lives not worth the trouble.

"Tell us," Nick said.

"Aliens," Anino said. "The universe is packed with 'em."

"That's impossible. You can't keep that kind of secret," I said.

"There are less than a hundred people in our four solar systems who know and, besides me, they're all under constant surveillance," Anino said.

"That doesn't explain why Belirand keeps fold-space technology a secret," I said.

"Are you saying we discovered aliens who would threaten humanity?" Nick asked.

"No. But that's the fear," Anino said. "Don't get me wrong - we've run across some real doozies. But, imagine what would happen if a few million people started jumping to all ends of the universe."

"Belirand is saying eventually we *would* find a species that would destroy humanity?" Nick asked. "That's stupid. You can't assume that."

"But that's the bureaucratic mindset," Anino said. "All you have to do is believe in the possibility and fear will do the rest."

"It's not unlike ancient North American history," Nick said. "The indigenous people initially welcomed the more technologically advanced Europeans and were all but wiped out."

"An interesting angle on that, James. Take that fear and add the fact that Belirand has a monopoly on the TransLoc gates and can charge whatever they want. You end up here."

"What's next?" I asked.

"You're in?"

"You just told us we could rescue *Cape of Good Hope* and discover aliens. How could we walk away from that?" I asked.

"Be at this warehouse, 1000 tomorrow. And you're just in time, Jonathan, as usual." Anino turned away, picked up his current project and worked on fusing blocks of components together with bright lights.

"I assume you've come to an arrangement." Jonathan said. "I've taken the liberty of preparing the shuttle. If you'll follow me."

We followed him out to the shuttle.

"I've called the chandler and set in supplies for four weeks," Marny said to Nick. "Did Anino say how long we'd be gone?"

"If you'll pardon my eavesdropping, young miss," Jonathan said. "Our current plan calls for no more than three weeks."

"I'll adjust to six, in that case," Marny said, giving me a wry grin.

I looked to Jonathan. "Are you coming?"

"I am. As brilliant as Master Anino is, he requires a certain amount of support staff," he said. "Where would you like me to take you?"

"How much time do you have?" I asked.

"I am at your disposal."

"Don't you need to get back to Anino, to help him get ready?" Ada asked.

"My colleagues are seeing to preparations as we speak."

"Shipyard on Irène, if you don't mind," I said.

"There are three such yards. I assume you are referring to the Menard shipyard where you are to meet Captain Charles Norris?"

"That's a pretty good guess. Were you also eavesdropping on our conversation in the dome?" I asked.

"No, Captain. I was able to locate Captain Norris's ship for sale by searching for available cargo ships and I simply correlated it to your stated need."

"My apologies."

"None necessary."

THE MENARD SHIPYARD on Curie's moon, Irène, turned out to be nothing more than a ten square kilometer bare patch on the otherwise verdant surface. Jonathan set the shuttle down next to a dilapidated building that was the only break in a four meter high fence. I wasn't sure of the purpose of the fence as at .15g clearing it would take no effort.

"I'm not sure how long this'll take," I said and closed the helmet of my vac-suit. Irène's atmosphere was good to breath, but the temperature was a negative five degrees.

"Hey, wait for me," Ada called and closed her suit.

Her action spurred the rest of the crew to follow suit and we exited the shuttle, walking down the retractable ramp.

I wasn't completely sure where to go, as all I knew was that Norris was waiting for us somewhere on the property. The most obvious location was the building we'd parked next to and I walked up and rapped on the door.

"Coming," I heard a voice say from behind the door, just before it slid open. "Charles Norris," he said extending his hand. "You brought quite a crew with you. Hoffen, is it?"

"It is," I said and shook his extended hand, introducing him to the rest of the crew.

"You're interested in my old bird, are you?" he asked, a twinkle in his eye. "What are you looking to haul?"

"Mostly ore," I said.

"Don't look like miners to me."

"It's a long story."

"Always is. No matter. She's served me well. Figure she's got plenty of life left in her," he said. "No need to stand around talking, though. Let's take a look."

"Captain, any chance you still have your bond in place?" Nick asked.

"That's a peculiar question for someone looking to buy a ship - not that I haven't been asked stranger things than that," he said. "Reminds me of a time..."

As we walked, he regaled us with a story of how he'd been asked to deliver a load of glass marbles. Apparently, one of the containers had broken mid-trip, spilling marbles out into local space at a station he'd stopped at along the way.

"I'll tell you... they wouldn't let me stop in there again for almost a decade. And here we are," he said. "She's not much to look at, but she's got it where it counts, kid. These Kestrel-1000s were built for the long haul."

The ship in front of us was old, but in better shape than I'd expected. Nick and I spent the next twenty minutes crawling around and inspecting its single deck configuration. Two torn up seats in the cockpit, a bed, barely large enough for two people, in a separate room, and a head in the hallway that separated the two spaces. It was small but functional.

I found Captain Norris where he'd cornered Marny, wrapping up yet another story.

"About that bond," I asked, hoping to keep him focused.

"Sorry, sometimes I get carried away. Suppose it comes from sailing solo for so many years," he said. "I've still got my bond. Why? What do you have in mind?"

"Can you cover six hundred thousand credits?"

"What's it worth to you?"

"We need to sail six hundred meters of cargo and a hundred tonne ship. Two stops," I said.

"How far?"

Nick flicked him a navigation plan that had him stopping by Descartes on the way to Meerkat on Nuage Gros.

"Run to Gros, eh? Wondered who they'd pick up for that. I've been making that run for decades," he said. "I thought you wanted to buy the ship. I'm looking to retire."

"One-way trip, Captain Norris. We'd like Meerkat to do a refit. We're offering full price on your Kestrel and if you can cover the bond, we need to know if you'll take the run," I said.

"Fifteen thousand," Norris offered.

I raised my eyebrows. "That's pretty steep, don't you think?"

"Son, if you wanted to negotiate, you shouldn't have shown up in a shuttle worth half a million credits. I figure you're well-funded and out of options."

"How soon can you leave?" Nick asked.

Chapter 7

GRAND VILLAGE

Grand Village of the Elders, Planet Ophir

Elder TeePa gripped his bash stick as he looked across the ceremonial fire pit to Corget To. At twenty seasons, Corget To was in his prime and sat defiantly, refusing to acknowledge the elder.

"The KentaPoo are weak and we should attack while their entrance stands open." Corget To reiterated his position. KentaPoo was a common, derogatory term that loosely translated to 'slugs with arms' as opposed to the FenTamel, or 'children of the stars.'

"Corget To, you are a brave and mighty warrior, but you lack the wisdom of our histories," Elder TeePa said, affecting patience. "You avoid our fires so that you may listen to the blood rushing through your ears, singing you to battle. The FenTamel are indeed as soft as the Kenta, but they strike with the light of the Tamel of the night sky. My matron sung to my nest of how our village was brought low before I was hatched."

"Our failure of two moons back was not that of our warriors but of our elders. We should have sent all our nests and we would have defeated the KentaPoo and the entire mountain range would know of the glory and power of Grand Village. Instead, this group of cowards..." Corget To spat on the ground, showing his disgust by wasting his water, "held us back and our village has been cut down."

"And what if we'd been raided? Would you give our village to the Red Clan of the north?"

"I would rather give our village to the Red Clan than to allow the KentaPoo to continue to disgrace us. We should merge with our brothers of the mountain and mount an attack of a hundred nests. Only then will we avenge our lost warriors," Corget To said.

TeePa stood, bash stick in hand. "We will not! The FenTamel village is in our territory and it has been our sacred duty to destroy them."

Corget To jumped to his feet, seeing the challenge in the elder's stance. "We are the disgrace. The songs sung of our village only talk of our weakness. We are the joke of the mountain and now we have failed again. We must unite all of the mountain and then our disgrace can be forgotten."

TeePa, while old at forty seasons, once again heard the song of battle, played by the blood rushing in his ears. Elders were not to be questioned and he would make an example of this impudent tadpole. He roared as he leapt across the fire pit, bash stick raised. He would send a message to the nests to respect their elders.

Corget To knew it was his responsibility to receive his beating. Tonight, however, he would not. Thirty nests, fully one hundred fifty of the strongest warriors of the Grand Village, had been sent to their glorious death and now, while the KentaPoo's village stood open, they sat back, waiting for them to rebuild. At least the elders should send the remaining forty nests. It was cowardice.

"No!" Corget To roared, bringing his bash stick up into TeePa's armored chest.

He struck with such strength that the much older Ophie was thrown to the side. With blood song in his ears, Corget To swept his bash stick into his elder's shins, striking at the knees as he tried to stand.

Members of the Elder circle stood back, waiting. It had been long since a whelp challenged an Elder at the fire, but TeePa had struck first. They were honor bound to allow the fight to discover its own end.

Corget To jumped over TeePa, swinging again. Instead of finding the softness of the fallen Ophie's groin, Corget To instead felt the crushing impact of TeePa's stick beneath his jaw. He stumbled back, trying to keep his feet beneath him. A second blow to his groin, followed by a jab to his throat, toppled the large warrior.

"Corget To, do you yield?" TeePa asked as he stood on the younger Ophie's club.

Corget To struggled, trying to free his stick. Seeing that this was not possible, he brought his leg up in an attempt to kick at the older Ophie.

"Always the same. We learn too slowly and then we die." TeePa raised his club. It was a shame to end such a powerful warrior, but discipline in the village was critical, especially now that their numbers were reduced.

"TeePa, would you hold a moment for a proposition?" Sevn Tar, his once mate, and matron of Corget To's nest asked, placing her hand on his arm.

"Yes, honored Matron, I will hold," he responded.

"I recognize your prowess in battle and right to finish Corget To. What if there was another way to defeat the FenTamel? What if we were to require tribute to Grand Village for the honor of crossing our lands and fighting them?"

"What does this have to do with Corget To?"

"You are about to join him with the mountain, am I right?"

"I am."

"What would you do if one of the Red Clan came to our village with a proposal to allow us to hunt predators in their territory? Would you listen or would you join him with the mountain?"

"I am not sure. It would depend if they had especially fierce predators," he said. As he spoke, understanding showed on his face. "Are you proposing that we send Corget To as an emissary to the Red Clan? Doesn't that make us look weak to our brothers of the mountain?"

"Perhaps at the first. But how many nests would Red Clan send to attack the FenTamel?"

"I don't know. If they came, I suppose they would send their strongest nests, maybe two or three of them at first."

"Would they be successful against the FenTamel, mighty TeePa?"

"Certainly not. They would not be successful with fifteen nests, so much we have proven over so many seasons."

"Would their songs about Grand Village change?"

TeePa paused to think. Matron Sevn Tar had always shown wisdom and had once been a mighty warrior. He knew the blood song had sung to her for many years. Maybe she was right, perhaps it was time for a change, if only a small one.

Chapter 8

DRUMS OF WAR

Yishuv Settlement, Planet Ophir

"Amon, it's time to break open the furnace and see what we've got at the bottom. Just stack the bricks to the side. You'll need to break the mortar, but try not to ruin the bricks. If we didn't smelt the iron right, we'll have to make another run," Merrie instructed.

Nurit and Merik had followed the pair back to the abandoned tannery, their curiosity piqued.

"What do you mean, Merrie?" Merik asked.

"If I failed to keep the temperature in the right range, we'll just have a nice wrought iron smelt," Merrie said. "I'll know based on the final carbon content of what's called the bloom."

Nurit joined Amon in removing the bricks from the tall furnace. Even with gloves, the heat at the bottom became too much for them to continue with careful removal and they resorted to toppling the bricks with iron poles.

"Use your tongs. You should be able to lift the bloom out," Merrie said handing the blacksmith's tongs to her friend.

"Bloom?"

"The steel that's collected at the bottom. Supposedly looks like a flower," she explained.

Amon stepped forward and dug into the glowing pile with his meter long tongs. Even with his great strength, he was unable to free it. "I'll have to pound it out of there," he said.

"Just be careful of my oxygen inlet and slag release. I'd like to reuse them," Merrie said, backing away.

After a few minutes of hammering, Amon successfully freed the remaining bricks from the iron slag. He dug into the pile with his long tongs and grabbed hold. "It's heavy, but I've got it," he said. Nurit slid in beside him and he accepted her help. Together they worked the pile back and forth, finally rolling an orange, spongy looking ball from its prison.

"How much does it weigh?" Merik asked, excitedly.

"It's loaded with slag that we need to break off," Merrie said. "You can beat on it, Amon, whatever falls off is slag."

Amon, wearing heavy leather gloves and apron, pulled a transparent face shield over his face and swung away at the big pile. Twenty minutes later, he'd chipped away the loose material from the otherwise pocked and porous looking steel bloom.

Merrie leaned down with a small instrument in her gloved hand, touched it to the black mass, and pulled back.

"Careful, Merrie. That's still very hot," Nurit said.

Merrie looked up to Amon, oblivious to Nurit's warning. "We did it!" She jumped up and wrapped her arms around the confused blacksmith, unable to contain her excitement. She spun him around and let go, looking back to the two masters expectantly.

"What did you do, Merrie?" Merik asked. His face reflected the young woman's excitement.

"High carbon steel on our first try. I'd just hoped for mild steel – or, you know, any type of steel at all - but we're at two point three percent carbon. We can do better, but we could have done a lot worse," she said.

"You're saying that's all steel?" Nurit asked. "There has to be thirty kilograms of it."

"It's not all steel. You'll lose another ten or fifteen percent as you work it. But, it's mostly steel." Merrie grabbed Amon's hands and pulling him around in an impromptu dance.

"What will you do with it all?" Nurit asked.

"I'd like a couple of kilograms for the maker-machine. We've been recycling all of the founder's steel and could use more. There are patterns we haven't been able to make for years," Merik said.

"Master, please don't yell at me, but I brought along the engineering pad. I can show you what Amon and I have been planning to make," she said.

"Merrie..." Merik shook his head disapprovingly, then rolled his eyes. "Very well, show us."

Merrie pulled a wrapped bundle from a wooden case and turned on the computerized pad. She showed a video of an ancient swordsmith working raw steel into a highly polished, slightly curved blade. "Amon already makes such beautiful daggers and there are only a few steps that he has to learn to make this work."

"We've tried the shorter iron swords against the Ophie. They don't penetrate the natural armor," Nurit said. "Why do you think this will be different?"

"These blades are thinner and sharper than anything we can achieve using iron. You are right, though, there are other options for blades. We believe this design will give better results in penetrating the Ophie's natural armor," Amon said.

"There's more." Merrie swiped the engineering pad to the next video she had queued up.

On the screen a woman held a complex-looking bow. She drew it back as the camera swept to the front. The pad showed a magnified view of the arrow sporting a swept back, sharpened steel head. As the archer released, the video followed the arrow down range, where it buried itself into a thick leather ball.

"With our steel, we can produce the wheels for that compound bow, as well as heads for the arrows. The engineering pad estimates that this bow, configured with these arrows will penetrate six centimeters of bone and cartilage at fifty meters. I just need twenty minutes of maker-machine time to fabricate the limbs and gears. That is if Master Nurit would cast the handle," Merrie said.

"The handle is simple enough. Have you consulted Captain Gian about this?"

"I have informed the captain of the experimentation," Merik said. "He has previously been cool to the idea, but I believe with recent attacks, he is becoming more receptive."

"I approached Eliora. She is willing to work with our new weapons in her spare time and to help demonstrate them. I believe it is our responsibility now, mother," Amon said.

"You will spend a full six hours each day on your normal tasks. If this fails, we will not be accused of letting the village suffer. You may use the smithy's resources for your work, but you will work safely. Merik, our power hammer is not operating. I do not want to see Amon working this much steel with just the power of his arms. I'm not sure there is enough food in all of Yishuv if he were to do that."

Nurit's tone was serious, but there was a small glint of mischief in her eyes.

"But of course, it is our responsibility to maintain our settlement's machines. I'll send a particularly bright apprentice over first thing in the morning to see what can be done about fixing the power hammer," Merik said.

"There's not much more to be done tonight. We'll be by first thing in the morning to pick up Merrie's treasure."

"WHY DO you believe this will pierce an Ophie's chest plate?" Eliora asked, looking at the strangely constructed bow. "We've tried long bows before and they don't work. The only thing that has any effect is the small crossbow and even they don't pierce the chest deeply enough."

Merrie smiled at the willowy protector and handed her a straight wooden arrow with a narrow steel razor blade on the end. "Two things. First, we've not had a good supply of steel before. We've been able to manufacture these very light-weight arrow heads that are shaped to penetrate. Second, these wheels reduce the work required by the archer and magnify their strength. It's purely mechanical. You'll see," she said.

Just then a warning siren sounded. It was the signal for an attack.

"This will have to wait," Eliora said, handing the bow back to Merrie and dashing off.

Eliora raced through the small town and joined her fellow protector, Bashi, as they approached the main barracks beneath the left side of the gate. Eliora surged ahead into the building, grabbing her small crossbow from its protective cradle on the wall. She danced around Bashi, raced back out the door, and climbed up the stone stairs that led to the top of the wall.

"What is it?" she demanded.

"Five attacked a group of woodcutters. Only two of ours made it back," Pele explained. "The Ophie rushed the gate, but we took them out."

As he finished, a bell rang on the southwest side of the village.

"The farms," Eliora said, as Bashi arrived.

"Good, you're here, Bashi. Man the main turret. Eliora, you're with me," Pele said.

As the third-ranking protector, Pele was only one of two given the responsibility to carry a portable blaster rifle. Eliora's duty was to defend Pele with her life, as the weapon he carried was irreplaceable. Eliora followed him as he flew down the stairs to the waiting cart.

Eliora vaulted into the back of the cart and grabbed the roll bar just in time to steady herself as Pele accelerated. She hooked her left arm into the support and checked her crossbow. She had a full load, as she'd expected.

The bells in the tower that sat twenty meters inside of the gate continued to ring as they sped past. At the top of the tower, a young boy hung out of the arched window and pointed frantically over the wall. He appeared to be shouting, but the noise was too much for her to make out the boy's words.

"Pele, we've action outside of the gate," Eliora interpreted the boy's gestures.

The southwest gate was closed and several farmers stood just inside, looking hopeful at their approach.

"On me," Pele said as he skidded to a halt.

Eliora marveled at the physical grace the man displayed as she followed him. He wasted no time running around objects, but rather took a straight line, vaulting, spinning and hurdling anything in his path. If not for her own speed, Eliora would have been left behind.

"To the rampart," Pele commanded as they arrived at the top of the wall.

Four defenders were shooting their crossbows and dodging an onslaught of Ophie spears. The battle roar of frustrated Ophies chilled Eliora as she flashed back to her recent, narrow escapes.

The rampart on the southwest gate was a narrow wooden deck that overhung the very top of the wall. It gave the defenders a stable surface on which to mount their defense, although it could be cut free if it was compromised by attackers.

Eliora grabbed two restraining harnesses and clipped them into the wall. First, she helped Pele attach his and then set to work on hers. When she finally had time to turn and survey the field, her vision clouded with tears. Many dead farmers lay in the fields. Brushing away tears, Eliora forced herself to look away, seeking out their enemy.

Seven Ophie stood beneath the wall, bellowing and hurling rocks, having exhausted their supply of spears. It was a strange behavior. The Ophie knew better than to stand in the open within range of the wall unless they were actively attempting a breach.

"Why are they standing in the open?" Eliora asked.

"Look at their belts. We've never seen those markings before. And they're throwing rocks, like they're trying to entice us into joining them for a fight," Pele said. "I'll certainly oblige them."

As he fired, the Ophie dropped one by one. Instead of running away, the others simply watched their brethren as they were cut down. It was as if they were unable to process what they were seeing.

"It's like they've never seen us before," Eliora said.

"And their attacks are never this close together. Something changed," Pele said as he put the last one down. "How many do you count?"

"Eight," Eliora said.

"Then we're looking for two more," he said. "You two stay put and close the gate behind us. We'll see if we can find the stragglers," Pele said to the two protectors who had joined them at the base of the wall. "You're driving, Eliora."

"Yes sir," she replied.

Eliora slowly drove out into the field. The carnage wasn't as bad as it had been in the previous attack, but it wasn't easy seeing the dead villagers. There had been no warning, as many of the farmers still held their tools, albeit defensively in some cases.

Movement at the tree line caught Eliora's eye as three Ophie emerged, fanning out at a dead run. They were thirty meters away and quickly closed the distance. Pele's first shot went wide, but he adjusted and fired again. Two Ophie continued to charge. Pele swiveled twenty degrees and lined up on the next target, but wouldn't have time for a third. Eliora said a quick prayer, fully expecting it to be her last, and positioned herself between Pele and the charging beast. She fired repeatedly, her peripheral vision acknowledging the Ophie to her right dropping to the ground only meters from their position. As the final Ophie closed in, she rose up into it - a final sacrifice. Eliora hoped to force the large reptile to stumble over her body, giving Pele more time to shoot, but the impact sent her flying backward into the man. Her last vision was of the Ophie grabbing the barrel of the blaster rifle, pulling it from Pele's grip and splitting his head open with the butt of the rifle.

Third Protector Shem fired from atop the gate. The range was too great for accuracy on a moving target, but he couldn't allow the Ophie to escape with the only other blaster rifle. A puff of dirt at the Ophie's feet gave him hope that he might yet recover the priceless weapon.

———

CORGET TO SAW the earth explode at his feet and understanding seeped into his small brain. He'd killed the great warrior who possessed the Tamel weapon and now it was his. It had already been a glorious day. The nests of the Red Clan and his own Great Villagers had joined to slaughter many of their enemy. As he'd planned, the Red Clan lost many warriors in the fighting and their defeat would be sung by the home fires all along the mountain. Better yet, a new song would be sung in his honor for slaying the FenTamel warrior who bore the Tamel weapon. He ran into the forest, toward his song and glory.

***

ELIORA SAT NERVOUSLY at the table next to Captain Gian. She'd been promoted to third rank among the protectors. It was a hollow promotion, coming at the loss of her friend and mentor, Pele. She'd never been invited to attend a council meeting and Gian warned her that this wouldn't be a good one. The Yishuv settlement had taken many setbacks in the last several tendays, wiping out decades of progress. Worse, one of two remaining blaster rifles had been lost and the settlement was down to a single turret that had to be moved between the gates.

"This meeting is called to order, so say I, Chairwoman Peraf." Grandly, the elderly woman set a golden stand on the table that prominently displayed a beautifully cut crystal. It was a ritual they repeated at every council meeting, the meaning of the gesture long since lost.

"Master Merik, I understand you have an update on the repair of the damaged turret," Councilman Bedros said.

Merik stood. "I do, honorable councilman, and it isn't favorable. We lack the necessary parts to repair the damage and our maker-machine is incapable of manufacturing the correct elements. In short, we can only use it as spare parts for our remaining gun."

"You are certain these elements cannot be manufactured on Ophir?"

"I am. The blasters rely on materials readily available in the time of our founders, but they were manufactured in mechanized plants in orbit around the planet that precisely controlled their synthesis. In short, we simply lack the capability to reproduce such an environment."

"I see. There is a rumor afoot that your apprentice wishes to address this council. Do you know what this is about?"

"I do, Councilman Bedros, but in following the council's wishes, she has respectfully prepared a demonstration after today's meeting. I would prefer that she be given the ability to present it fully without my preempting," Merik said. "Of course, I leave this at your discretion."

"I understand she has manufactured a new type of weapon," Bedros said.

"Yes, that is a partial outcome of her work," Merik answered.

"Captain Gian. What know you of this?" Bedros asked. "I assume after your grand failures of the last few tendays you would be most interested in learning about this new weaponry."

"Councilman Bedros, I respectfully ask that you follow our agenda. One of the things that separates us from the Ophie is our ability to reason." Peraf corrected.

"My apologies, Councilwoman Peraf, I believe that I have finished my questions for the Master Engineer. Are there more questions or may I move on to Captain Gian?"

As there were no questions, Peraf excused Merik and turned to Captain Gian and Eliora. "My dear Captain Gian, never before has so much been asked of so few protectors. You have lost more than even the farmers. The bravery of your men and women honors us all. There are, however, those within the council who believe that too many mistakes have been made and as a result your efficacy as leader has come under question. What say you?"

Captain Gian stood and walked out from behind his table to address the council, a group of middle-aged to elderly men and women.

"Councilwoman Peraf, thank you for your recognition. It truly has been a trying time. After an unprecedented period of peace, we once again enter a season of danger. Our settlement has lost five percent of its population, and no one in this room has been spared the pain of that loss. Indeed my protectors have been cut down enough that we are no longer able to adequately protect this settlement," Gian said.

A collective gasp was heard among the full-to-standing-room-only gallery that was listening to the long meeting.

"You're saying that being understaffed caused the Ophie to gain control of one of our last two blasters?" Bedros asked, enraged.

"Councilman," Peraf snapped, banging a wooden hammer on the table in front of her.

"I'd like to answer the question, Councilwoman," Gian answered.

"Very well," Peraf said. "But I warn you, Councilman. I'll sooner close this meeting than allow your continued outbursts."

"Pele made a judgement call that was his to make," Gian said calmly. "In combat, we constantly make decisions and when you make the wrong decision, people die. Pele acted bravely and showed great composure during an inordinately stressful situation. I'll not sully his name by second-guessing him now. The loss of the blaster was tragic and if it is the council's decision to relieve me of duty, I accept this." He gave a small bow.

"I don't believe we're asking you to resign, Captain Gian," Peraf said wearily. "We feel that more care should be taken with our remaining weapons and should have been taken with the lost rifle."

"There was no way for Pele to know that the Ophie would take the weapon. They've never shown the slightest interest in our technology. Even more strangely, there were sixteen Ophie that attacked us. They always attack in pods of five and never retreat. Something changed. We're seeing new behavior and I believe we should be prepared for a longer season of war," Gian said.

"That's ridiculous. For three centuries the Ophies have attacked with a single large force and then they leave us alone for at least twenty stans. Everyone knows that," Bedros said with disdain.

"And yet, they attacked with hundreds three tendays ago and sixteen last tenday."

"That's not unprecedented. Our founders wrote about fighting Ophie in those numbers," Bedros said.

"Councilman, I agree with part of that. We were fortunate they didn't attack with a larger force three tendays past, or none of us would be standing here to discuss it. I believe we're seeing the introduction of a second tribe of Ophies. The markings on their arms and thighs were different," Gian said.

"That may well be, but it doesn't excuse your abysmal failures."

"On this we agree, Councilman. I stand humbly before you, acknowledging those failures."

"Oh pish-posh, we are all to blame," Peraf said. "If our weapons were in better order, if we'd adopted the early warning signals recommended by our engineer, if... if... if wishes were kisses and all that. Gentlemen, stiffen your spines. If we are to win this war, then we need to treat it as such and stop this petty bickering." She looked straight at Gian. "Tell me, Captain, what do you need that is within the capability of this council to grant?"

"If we are to survive the war I fear is coming, we must arm our population. We are soft and must become hard. We must treat the Ophie as our enemy, not as wild animals to be avoided. Finally, we cannot hope to protect eight hundred people with twenty protectors," he said.

"Tell me exactly what you are asking for," Peraf demanded.

"Every man, woman and child of Yishuv should receive weapons training. Further, all men and women between the ages of sixteen and forty should spend five days of every third tenday in training or on patrol. Our core of protectors must grow to fifty."

"You've lost your mind, Gian. We'd get nothing done if we lost that much productivity to your war," Bedros said.

"I want to learn how to fight." A woman's voice was heard from the gallery.

"Me too," another voice said. The gallery of spectators broke into unruly agreement.

"Order... Order..." Peraf yelled and banged her hammer onto the table over and over again until the room quieted. "It would appear your idea resonates with the populace. The council will take your request under consideration. As this was the last matter for the day, we will adjourn," Peraf said. "Clear the hall so we may hear the petition of our Master Engineer's apprentice, Merrie."

Merrie and Amon pulled a heavy handcart into the room and offloaded their long weapons, still covered with oil-cloth, onto the table.

"Are you ready?" Merik asked Merrie. "And what's that smell? It's horrible."

"I'm sorry," she said with a smile. "You'll see soon enough. Have you seen Eliora?"

"She was in the hall with Captain Gian. I assume he's also been invited to your demonstration," Merik said.

"He has. Hopefully she's filling him in on his part in the demonstration," Merrie said.

"You've got him working too? This should be interesting. I don't want to make you nervous, but he just had a hard meeting," Merik said.

"I hope to change that," Merrie replied.

Merik smiled at his apprentice and almost resisted the desire to ruffle her long brown hair. "Don't ever lose that, Merrie."

"Stop," Merrie pushed his hand off of her head. "Lose what?"

"Optimism."

"I'm optimistic that if you keep mussing up my hair, I'm going to break your fingers. How's that?" she asked, smiling.

"Are you ready?" Bedros asked, taking his seat at the table.

"We're just waiting for Eliora and Captain Gian. I'll go find them," Merrie said.

"What is that horrid smell?" Bedros asked.

"Part of the demonstration. My apologies, but it's really the only way." Merrie hurried out of the room only to return a moment later with Eliora in tow and Captain Gian following behind.

"The council will come to order," Peraf said as the six of them sat in their chairs. "Merrie, dear, please, what is that smell?"

"We'll get to that soon," Merrie said patiently. "But first, I need to give you some background. There are two facets of this presentation that we're interested in. In short, I'm asking for a tenday of maker-machine time."

"Ridiculous," Bedros said, earning him a glare from Peraf, but nothing else.

Merrie bowed slightly. "That's what Merik said you'd say. He told me I'd need to prove to you why I need it."

"And this smelly package will prove it to us? Is it air freshener?" Bedros asked.

"That's funny," she said. "But no. I need the time to construct an arc-furnace to smelt steel. We have all the electricity we could possibly desire with our solar panels, but what I don't have are the reactor pieces to really get things rolling in the furnace. It's all very technical."

"I'm confused, how will you demonstrate steel?" Bedros asked.

"Just a moment and I think you'll see. Captain Gian, why is it your protectors don't carry the iron short swords that the smithery made decades ago?"

"The Ophie's arm length is such that their clubs reach us before we can strike them with the Gladius style blade."

"Why not just get a longer iron blade?"

"There are none strong enough to wield such a blade. Not only that, but iron is not rigid enough nor does it hold an edge," Gian answered.

"When faced with a similar problem, our ancient ancestors solved this problem by inventing steel," Merrie said. "Fortunately, we don't have to invent anything. We simply need to learn from them. Captain Gian, I present to you a European longsword. Crafted by none other than our very own apprentice smith, Amon."

Merrie pulled a polished, meter long blade from beneath the cloth and handed it to a surprised Captain Gian.

"What does this weigh?" Gian asked.

"One point three kilograms, give or take," Merrie said.

Gian gracefully swooshed the blade through the air, feeling its balance, with a look of wonder on his face. "It's so light. Surely it is brittle."

"Captain, I apologize for this next piece, but how could I prove to you that you could use this in combat?"

"Apologize, why? But, I'd need to use it against an Ophie," he said and then looked to the cart that had several large lumps laying on it. "You didn't...?"

Merrie placed fingers onto her nose and walked to the cart. "Amon, if you'd help me with this."

Amon lifted one side as she lifted the other and they exposed the torso of a melting Ophie warrior.

"You're insane," Bedros said, lifting a handkerchief to his nose.

"Be quiet," Gian snapped. "Is that frozen?"

"It was, but I've been thawing it to give us a realistic simulation. I'm worried it's still too frozen," Merrie said. "Would you demonstrate the blade on this corpse?"

Captain Gian wasted no time and charged in with an overhead strike, the long blade burying itself several centimeters into the thickly armored chest.

"I don't believe I penetrated to vital organs," he said.

"I don't think so either, but the long sword was made for parrying, cutting and piercing. Could you try piercing the chest?"

"Eliora, please strap it to that post," Gian said.

If Eliora found the task to be gruesome, she didn't let on. She rolled the cart next to the post he'd indicated and lashed it in place with a strap.

Gian thrust the long sword in next to his initial gash and with some effort buried the tip until it poked out the back of the beast.

"That's it!" he cried in triumph.

"Captain, if you don't mind, just leave that there, we have more to demonstrate. I'm afraid Amon was in more of a hurry with our second weapon and it isn't as polished, but I believe you'll find it every bit as interesting. Amon, would you hold up our second corpse?"

"Your theatrics are a bit much," Peraf said. "This has gone too far."

"Honorable council members, please see this through. It is certainly gruesome, but these apprentices may have just saved our settlement," Gian said. "To win the war I fear is to come, we must engage in a few distasteful activities."

"Get on with it then. Our patience is wearing thin," Peraf shut her eyes and took a breath by holding her sleeve over her mouth and nose.

"Amon, the second corpse?" Merrie asked.

This particular corpse had its arm outstretched. Merrie would have liked to have had it holding a club, but settled for what was available. She waited for Amon to steady the second corpse to another post and then pulled a second, slightly shorter sword, with a slight curve in its blade and handed it to Eliora.

"Amon's second sword is a replica of an ancient Japanese katana. This weapon is not meant for parrying, but is designed for fast sweeping strikes and punctures. It is slightly more brittle, but the edge exhibits very little resistance when passing through flesh. Eliora?"

Eliora walked up to the Ophie, holding the blade to her side. In a single, fluid motion she swept the blade up, through its outstretched arm and then reversed direction and swept down, across its neck. Smooth and quick, she'd completed the movements before the end of the arm and the head hit the floor.

"How many of these can you make, Amon?" Captain Gian asked in awe.

"I have enough steel for eight of the katana and five longswords, but they take time to produce," Amon answered.

"Captain Gian, if you'd please, I have one more demonstration," Merrie said.

"Dear Merrie, you've convinced the room. What more could you show us?" Gian asked.

"Eliora?"

"Captain, I think you'll want to see this," Eliora said.

"Of course." He opened his hands wide, blinking in disbelief.

Merrie wasted no time and pulled her compound bow from beneath the oil-cloths and handed it to Eliora. Eliora walked off the length of the room, which was only ten meters, but sufficient for a demonstration. She nocked an arrow and pulled the bowstring back.

"The compound bow only needs a few pieces of steel. Currently, Eliora is holding twenty-two kilograms of pressure, but the bow will release at forty. We've had trouble with the wooden shafts shattering on launch, but we're now using a more supple wood. Notice that while I'm talking she's able to continue to hold the bow taught. Anytime you want, Eliora."

The arrow punctured the Ophie corpse, missed the post, and finally embedded itself into the back wall of the council chamber with a solid thwack.

Peraf stood - jumped really, at the sound. "I can't say I approve of your theatrics, but I believe you've made your point. Captain Gian, Master Merik and Master Nurit, the Council requests your attendance at our next meeting on fourday. Please bring formal proposals for whatever *this* was."

She gestured with her hand at the carnage, turned and exited.

"Gian. Just when I thought you weren't a player, you pull a rabbit out of the hat. I've definitely underestimated you," Bedros said.

"This isn't a game, Gerald," he said in a voice normally reserved for underperforming cadets.

"Isn't it? Don't worry, you've got my vote. You've certainly earned it." Bedros turned and followed the rest of the council out of the chamber.

"Who's going to clean this up?" Merik asked.

Chapter 9

MASTODON

Moon Irène, Planet Curie, Tipperary Star System

"I trust your negotiations were successful?" Jonathan asked as I walked up the ramp into the shuttle.

"More like an old western bank heist," I said.

"Oh?"

"You can't think about it that way," Nick said, following close behind. "It's Norris' last hurrah and he's right. We are in a pickle."

"We're not going to make a dime on the return trip," I said.

"We'll clear at least fifteen thousand. I kind of like how he played that whole folksy, bumbling trader then figured out just how hard he could stick us," Nick said. "I had a momentary flash of an eighty stans old Liam Hoffen when he dropped that little bomb on us."

"All I can say is you better really like whoever you're sailing with in that tractor," Ada said. "You're going to be sitting on top of each other for the whole trip."

"And there's no way to exercise," Tabby said.

"You're right, Tabby. We'll need to install a stationary track in the hall-way," Marny said.

"Where to now, Captain Hoffen?" Jonathan asked.

"Curie's main orbital platform. Here." I flicked navigation instructions at him.

"Yes, sir," Jonathan said, gently lifting the shuttle from the planet's surface.

"Does Phillippe really not have a guardian to watch over him?" Tabby asked.

"I have served as his legal guardian for many years," Jonathan answered.

"But, he treats you more like an employee than a guardian."

"Master Anino and I have a special relationship."

"You're right, I'm sorry. It's not my business, but I gotta say, he doesn't act like any teenager I've ever known."

"No. I don't suppose he does," Jonathan said.

The trip from Irène to the Curie orbital platform was two hundred thirty thousand kilometers and we arrived a few minutes after 0100. It had been a long day and we were all tired and hungry. Jonathan dropped us at a terminal close to where *Hotspur* was docked.

"Food or sleep?" Ada asked, as we trooped along the jet-way that was busy even at this late hour.

"Food," Marny said. "I've a delivery from a chandlery company in two hours."

"Ada, Tabby, you might consider getting some rack time. I'm going to join Marny, since stevedores are coming about the same time," I said.

"What and miss the excitement?" Ada asked.

Tabby pulled on my elbow playfully. "Yeah, you trying to dust us off?"

Nick pointed at a diner. "How's this look?"

It didn't take any convincing and we went in and grabbed an over-sized booth.

"Do you really think Belirand is going to have a problem with this?" Tabby asked as the waitress poured coffees for all of us except Ada, who had tea.

"What's the worst they can do? Deny passage through the TransLoc gates?" Ada asked.

"You're right. As long as we're in one of the four settled systems, Belirand has laws they have to obey and government oversight should keep them in line," Nick said. "But remember, if Anino has a ship that can reach *Cape of Good Hope*, we won't be under anyone's laws."

"Shite. I didn't think about that," Ada said.

"Does it matter? The *Cape of Good Hope* is holding on by a thread," I said.

"It's not too late to back out," Nick said.

"Don't look at me," Ada said. "I remember a time when you had to make the same decision about me and my mother. Did you even hesitate for a minute?"

I put my hand over Ada's. "Best decision we ever made. Although, did I ever tell you how much you barfed all over the inside of that escape capsule?"

"Cap, seriously," Marny scolded, hitting me with her napkin.

"Really?" Ada asked.

Marny scowled at me. "You were in shock and he shouldn't tease you."

"Buckets. We ended up selling that pod for salvage," I said.

Tabby punched me in the arm. "Real sensitive."

"You're just messing with me," Ada said.

"No, that's actually right. We couldn't get it clean," Marny added.

The food arrived and we continued to chat until it was time to meet Marny's delivery at the ship.

"How much lead time do we need in the morning before we meet Anino?" Tabby asked as we arrived at *Hotspur*.

"An hour should do it," Nick said.

I yawned, it really had been a long day. "Set an alarm, Tabbs. I'll be up after we get the cargo offloaded."

IT WAS 0500 when I finally slipped into bed next to Tabby. It almost felt luxurious to be back home on *Hotspur*. I'd been up for twenty hours and was exhausted. We'd offloaded the cargo into bonded storage, loaded the reefer unit to capacity and taken on extra fuel and O2 crystals. In short, we were locked and loaded.

The alarm mocked me. I was sure it knew I'd only slept four hours and was overly cheery in discharging its duty.

"Jupiter, I hate that thing," I said, patting the empty covers next to me looking for Tabby, my eyes still too bleary to focus. I slid out from under the sheets to a seated position. Great. Tabby was already gone and I was talking to myself.

I stumbled to the small office next to the Captain's quarters and into the adjoining head, turned on the shower and stood in the hot water for a few minutes, allowing it to bring me awake. I'd been sleeping regularly up till last night, so it didn't take much. The door opened from the forward side and I turned away, quickly. Apparently, I'd been too boggled to lock the bridge facing door.

"Hey there, hot stuff," Tabby said huskily. Her brow was beaded with sweat, the result of exercising in the hold's one crew amenity, an exercise area mounted upside down from the ceiling, boasting a reversed gravity field.

Tabby, still in her tight suit liner, was forced to press against me as the bridge head was barely large enough to hold the two of us.

"You're all sweaty," I said, turning around to face her.

"Oh, you are awake now, aren't you," she said, reaching over to the door and flicking the lock.

I ran my finger down the front of her suit, starting at the lowest part of the 'V' in her neck line. The liner, opening to my touch, pulling away as I traced downward.

"Anyone on the bridge?" I asked.

"I'll be quiet, I promise." She pressed her finger to her mouth and grinned.

If I'd entered the shower with a fogged mind, I definitely exited full of energy and confidence. I still had a difficult time understanding why a woman as amazing as Tabitha Masters had chosen me, but I couldn't have felt luckier.

Per Marny's instructions, we dressed in our armored vac-suits. They were military grade and had considerable capacity to absorb all kinds of shock from explosions to flechette rounds. If Marny wasn't sure what we were getting into, she required the suits. I didn't mind. They were bulkier, but well designed.

At 0930 we joined Marny, Nick and Ada at the mess table. Marny must have heard us coming because steaming mugs of coffee and plates full of potatoes, eggs, sausage and gravy were sitting in front of open chairs.

"Marny, you're amazing. I have to know, can a man have more than one wife?" I asked, earning me a sharp elbow to the ribs.

"You sure you could handle it?" Ada asked, sipping her tea.

I looked to Tabby, whose eyebrows were raised. I hadn't crossed the line yet, but she was letting me know I was standing next to it and shouldn't dare dip my toe across.

"I'm sure I couldn't," I said, looking to Nick for reassurance that I wasn't inadvertently crossing a line with him. He smiled, shaking his head.

"Cap, I'll cook for you either way. No further commitment required," Marny said.

"Sure, let's just say that's the only thing he was thinking," Tabby said, smacking me on the back of the head.

Ada spit out a mouthful of tea.

I just shook my head, picked up a fork and put food in my mouth. I was hopelessly outgunned and knew better than to keep digging the hole.

"I received a comm from Norris. He's already aloft and loading cargo," Nick said.

"Perfect, I hope he's as good as his word. I can't believe we're giving him *Sterra's Gift* to ferry back for us," I said.

"She's in good hands," Nick said. "And if she's not, his bond more than covers it."

"Yeah, I suppose. We ready to get going?" I asked.

"Who's in the chair?" Ada asked, reminding me that I hadn't let her know who would be taking the captain's chair on the way over to meet Anino and Jonathan.

"How about you take it with Tabby in number two?" I said.

"Copy that. I'll start the checklist," she said, jumping up and bounding off to the lift that would take her up to the bridge deck.

"I'll be right there," Tabby called out, picking up her plate and scooping furiously while standing. She set the empty plate back on the table. "Get that for me, would you?"

I shook my head. "Kids these days. You won't catch me rushing a meal like this."

"And I love you for it, Cap," Marny said.

I finished eating and dropped the plates into the food waste recycler. "What are you working on, Nick?" I asked. He'd been quieter than normal.

"Checking in on Jack back at Lèger Nuage. He and Jenny formed a pod-ball team with Priloe. You remember, the stowaway from Grünholz," Nick said. "They're running the league for the city and have seventeen teams signed up."

"Maybe we could get a pickup game when we're back. That'd be a blast," I said.

"Did you know Priloe has been talking with Big Pete and Silver about learning how to work a claim?" Nick asked.

"How old is he?" I asked. "And no, Mom never tells me anything."

"Twelve stans," Nick said. "Sounds like she might take him and Milenette in."

"There goes my inheritance," I said. "Maybe Big Pete will finally get the son he's always wanted. One that will stay home and work asteroids with him."

"Ouch, Cap," Marny said. She'd been leaning against the bulkhead and pushed off with a shrug of her shoulders, walking toward the lift. Nick got up to follow.

"Only hurts when I think about it," I said, falling in line.

"All hands, prepare for departure," Ada said. It was the start of a formal process we'd developed to make the transition safer.

I walked through the bridge and up the short flight of stairs that led to the cockpit. I sat on the top step which was between the two pilot's chairs where Tabby and Ada were currently seated.

"How's the traffic out there?" I asked.

"Not as bad as Mars, but it's close," Ada answered.

"You sailing us out by stick?" Both Ada and Tabby enjoyed sailing through the dense traffic patterns of congested space platforms. I could do it, but didn't find it even remotely relaxing. I much preferred to let the AI negotiate the myriad craft and instructions from local space-control.

"Wouldn't have it any other way," she said.

"Security is green," Marny reported.

"Engineering is green," Nick said moments later.

Ada dimmed the bridge lights, something I often failed to do, and pulled back on the stick, throttling up gently. I held onto the railing on both sides of the steps, giving me a perfect forward view through the armored glass cockpit window.

"How far out are we?" I asked.

Show navigation path on forward holo. Ada ordered.

Curie and Irène both popped up into view. The path took us between the planet and her moon and angled off to a location four hundred thousand kilometers on the other side of Curie. We were going to be late, but Anino would have to get over it.

"Is there something out there?" I asked.

The AI interpreted my question as a command and zoomed in on a location in space that I'd assumed was empty. Instead, a platform appeared.

"That's interesting. I didn't remember that on the possible destinations over Curie," I said.

"That's because it's completely private," Nick said.

"Belirand?"

"Nope, Anino."

"You're kidding. That's as big as P-Zero," I said, referencing the large asteroid that made up the main part of Colony-40.

"Crazy thing is, there are hardly any ships around it, although there's plenty of EM," he said. EM was a measure of Electro Magnetic radiation and was often a better measure than size as to how active an unknown structure in space was.

"Roger that."

With nothing to do, I sat down on the couch opposite Marny and Nick to check the local markets. I was still there when we reached the fifty thousand kilometer mark and received a hail.

"*Hotspur*, this is platform nine seventy-five, please acknowledge." I recognized the voice as belonging to Jonathan.

"You want to take this, Liam?" Ada asked.

"Nah, you got it," I said.

"*Hotspur* here, nine seventy-five, over," she answered.

"Welcome, *Hotspur*, we've been waiting for you, I'm sending modified navigation instructions," Jonathan said.

A green blip on the vid screen in front of Ada lit up. She accepted the instructions. "Received, nine seventy-five, over," Ada said.

"Acknowledged. We'll see you all aboard. Platform nine seventy-five, out." Jonathan closed the comm.

"Any difference in the navigation plan?" I asked.

"Added two hundred meters onto the end," Ada said. "They're docking us on the platform. Original plan dropped us at the edge."

I nodded. "Fair enough."

The platform was much wider than it was long. My HUD showed two point three kilometers wide, just under four hundred meters deep, and three hundred meters tall. In relationship to *Hotspur*, the port side was the main habitable area as it was entirely enclosed, its skin primarily steel and armor glass. As you moved to the starboard, the platform became less dense and more complex, brightly painted lattice connecting an exposed infrastructure.

Our destination was a dense section directly starboard of the habitable area. As we closed the distance, a multi-tiered docking bay became visible. The lower decks were wide enough to fit at least two *Hotspurs* if loaded straight in, while the upper deck was wide enough to hold four across and three deep. The bay could hold a huge number of ships, but the organization was weird. Ship's captains would never agree to being packed in like that, as we liked easy access for unloading and a clear path for taking off.

In the end, it didn't matter. Aside from a smattering of crates and three small shuttles, the decks were empty. Our instructions put us on the top deck, next to a central lift that joined each deck and disappeared into the habitable section.

Ada spun *Hotspur* around slowly and set us right on the spot indicated by the provided navigation plan. Just as she touched down, the elevator doors opened and Jonathan stepped out, sans vac-suit and waved at the cockpit. I must have missed passing through a pressure barrier.

"Marny, how do you want to handle security?" I asked.

"Standard friendly docking protocols and non-lethal warnings," she said.

"Am I the only one a little freaked out by the lack of people?"

"This place is huge. It's eerie," Tabby agreed. "Only one thing for it - I'm loading heavy."

It was probably overkill, but I'd learned to trust my crew's instincts, even if it meant being too cautious.

If Jonathan was intimidated by meeting the five of us clad in armored vac-suits and strapped with a multitude of weapons, he sure didn't show it.

"Welcome aboard. Master Anino awaits on the bridge," he said.

"Bridge? Where? We haven't seen any other ships," I said.

"Check that out." Nick was pointing behind me.

I turned around to see massive doors pivoting shut, enclosing all of the docking bays we'd originally thought to be part of platform nine seventy-five.

It suddenly made sense. "This is all one big ship?"

"That's right, Captain Hoffen," Jonathan answered. "Welcome to *Mastodon*."

"How big are we talking?" I asked. "These decks have to be seventy meters tall."

"If you'll follow me, I'll explain as we walk."

I turned away from the closing doors and we followed Jonathan toward the awaiting lift.

"The *Mastodon's* LOA is one hundred ten meters and beam at widest point is eighty five meters. Your estimate of seventy meters wasn't bad. From bilge to bridge, the *Mastodon* is one hundred meters, weighing in at one point eight kilo tones."

"That's almost as heavy as a battleship," Nick said.

"You've sailed heavier and longer," Ada said.

"Seriously?"

"Sure," she said, wrinkling her eyebrows at me. "*Adela Chen* pushed seven point five kilo tonnes of ore back from Jeratorn, lest you forget."

The lift doors opened to an expansive bridge. Armored glass, ten meters high, wrapped a hundred forty degrees around in a gentle arc. The breathtaking view looked directly out over the planet Curie.

"Welcome to the *Mastodon*," Anino said, crossing the bridge with his hand outstretched. "Quite a view, eh?"

"It's magnificent," Ada said, breathily.

Anino glanced at his friend. "See, I told you they'd like it, Jonathan."

"You did, Master Anino," he agreed.

"I believe the chair is yours, Captain." The kid indicated a high-backed, white, synth-leather chair, centered in the bridge. The arms boasted flight hardware I'd custom fit onto *Hotspur*.

"Chen, Masters, you have your own stations. I wasn't completely sure what you preferred, but took a guess and installed the double yoke configuration you tug pilots like," he said.

Ada fairly squeaked as she bounded down the short flight of stairs that separated the two pilot's chairs from that of the Captain's.

"Bertrand, I've installed a virtual gunner's chair. It's my own design, but should feel like the real thing. You can either link the six turrets or allow the AI to automatically target. It's not ideal, but *Mastodon* isn't meant for combat. You'll find they have a hundred percent coverage at a hundred meters. If a hostile can breach that perimeter, we'll wish we had more Marines aboard." Anino was obviously enjoying himself.

"And don't feel like I left you out, James. Every work station has independent holographic projection fields."

"Where do you sit?" I asked.

"Anywhere I want. I own it," he said.

I raised an eyebrow. I wasn't about to start taking orders from a teenager, no matter how rich and brilliant he was.

"Just kidding," he said, chuckling quietly. "Frak Hoffen, don't be so easy. No, this place is too spartan for the likes of me. Jonathan moved my lab to deck three. You'll discover it's the only place on the ship you can't go without permission."

"What now?" I asked.

"What do you mean? Do your captainy thing. We need to get going. Just let me know when you've made visual contact with *Cape of Good Hope*."

Chapter 10

WARLORD

Grand Village of the Elders, Planet Ophir

Corget To stood next to the home fire in the middle of Grand Village. The songs of his nest had never told of a time such as this, when elder representatives from many villages gathered. It was a time of both celebration and great tension. So many powerful warriors in one location and perhaps too much strong drink.

The legend of Grand Village had always been of their curse - a sickness that struck the village making their warriors feeble in battle against the FenTamel. Something had always been different about Corget To. He, like all of his nest mates, had spied on the FenTamel since they'd been old enough to walk. Unlike his nest mates or even his village, he'd always seen the enemy as KentaPoo, weak but living in a strong home.

"Corget To," TeePa called. "Come, sit by Gelt Peige. He morns the loss of the Red Clan nests. Regale him with tales of the glorious battle and the bravery of his warriors."

"It is true what TeePa says. The warriors of your nests were brave," Corget To said.

"Tell him of the glorious battle," TeePa said.

Corget To was annoyed with TeePa in his drunken state. The elder knew they hadn't killed a single enemy. "There was no battle, TeePa," Corget To said. "The Red Clan warriors bravely ran in and were slaughtered like they were food animals."

Gelt Peige roared and jumped to his feet swinging his great club. Corget To knew it was coming and easily stepped out of the way. The Red Clan elder spun uncontrollably, having overcommitted his swing, and fell drunkenly to the ground.

"Stay down, Gelt Peige," Corget To said, lifting the blaster rifle he carried.

Gelt Peige scrabbled backward. The songs of the FenTamel weapons that killed instantly were some of the oldest sung.

TeePa laughed derisively. "Have comfort, Gelt Peige. It is but Corget To. He'll not be calling forth Tamel to strike you down. He is our least."

Something snapped in Corget To. He'd felt TeePa's disdain since he'd been a hatchling. Ever since returning from the Red Clan's dismal failure, he'd lost all respect for the elders. It was one thing to die in glorious combat, another thing entirely to be sent like food animals to slaughter. He turned the Tamel weapon on TeePa and watched as understanding registered in his elder's eyes.

"Your cowardice will be well remembered, Corget To. You will forever be remembered as the one who ran from battle," TeePa said.

Anger surged through Corget To and his hand clasped tightly around the weapon. He was as surprised as any when the weapon spit Tamel at his elder, burning a hole deep into his chest. TeePa slumped forward and fell into the fire.

Gelt Peige grabbed the old warrior's legs to drag his body from the danger.

"No," Corget To roared. "Let him roast, he has earned it." He swung the weapon back to the Red Clan elder.

Quiet fell over the once rowdy gathering, all eyes on Corget To.

"What have you done?" Gelt Peige asked, letting go of the elder's legs.

"That which should have been done long before. Listen to me, brothers. We must bring the nests of the Great Mountain together and attack as one. We must scale the flat rock face and enter the Kenta-Poo's nest. It is only then that we'll be rid of them and avenge our lost brothers." Corget To spoke loud enough for all of the assembled elders to hear.

"And I suppose it is you, an untested warrior, who would lead us?" Gelt Peige asked, standing menacingly above him.

"I have been chosen by our ancestors. They have seen fit to show me the use of the Tamel weapon. Will you stand against our ancestors and test me as TeePa did? Or will you follow me into battle?" Corget To glared at the grisly elder of the Red Clan.

"I will not follow you," he said.

"I hope you do not speak for all of Red Clan," Corget To said and squeezed the Tamel weapon. At first it did nothing and panic rose in his body. Had he misunderstood its operation?

"You see, he was not chosen, only a..."

Corget To's thick finger finally came in contact with the trigger and semi-automatic blaster fire erupted from the end of the weapon, stitching a line of bolts across the Red Clan leader. As he fell, the weapon continued firing, striking three behind Gelt Peige before Corget To released the trigger.

For many of the Great Village, it was too much and they ran, howling in fear. As expected, however, the other village elders hadn't run. They would sooner die than be branded a coward, even in the face of certain death. He prepared to be rushed by the group of old warriors. Even with the Tamel weapon, Corget To doubted he'd be able to take them all. There were simply too many.

It was then that a most unusual thing occurred. Perigen, young for an elder, but a warrior of legend along the mountain, stepped forward from the crowd. Corget To found it hard not to admire the legendary warrior whose size and grace seemed to match the songs he'd inspired.

"Corget To," Perigen said. "The Village by the River will follow you to battle." He knelt and bowed his head, spreading his arms in supplication.

Pleasure and thrill coursed through Corget To. Never had he felt so much power as he watched the elders kneel in front of him, one by one.

Chapter 11

A LINE IN THE SAND

Platform Nine Seventy-Five, Near Curie

Anino and Jonathan walked onto the lift at the back of the bridge, disappearing as the doors closed between us. Anino's face was full of mirth. The little brat was enjoying my confusion.

"Are you kidding me?" I asked no one in particular.

"You have to admit, it's a pretty sweet setup." Tabby slid in beside me, looping her hand through the crook of my arm.

"But..." I spluttered.

"But what?" Ada asked, approaching me from the other side. "I've never seen the great Liam Hoffen stand so flat-footed in a ship he's been given control of."

Nick just shrugged.

"Well, frak! Fine. Ada, Tabby, see if you can bring up displays of the system. I want a full status on the flight systems."

"Aye, aye, Captain." Ada smiled and gave me a mock salute.

"That's my boy," Tabby said, grabbing a handful of butt before bounding over the back of her assigned pilot's chair.

"Nick, see if you can get a deck layout of this thing and figure out if we're really in control. Marny, weapons charges, armory, see about a holo display of the minimum perimeter for the turrets. I need to know how close we can allow small craft before they become a threat."

"On it, Cap," Marny said.

Mastodon, Captain Liam Hoffen, Loose Nuts. Verify flight commander. I instructed, sliding into the comfortable chair. The smell of new synth leather was slightly intoxicating.

"Captain Liam Hoffen is in control of all flight systems."

Good enough for the moment. Nick would ferret out any tricks Anino had up his sleeve.

Display systems status on a panel thirty degrees to my right at a meter distance. Vary opacity based on how closely my eyes are aligned to it.

The ship's AI didn't respond, but popped up a meter tall panel with system's displays that were hastily being constructed by Ada, Tabby, Marny and Nick.

Show fuel and O2 reserves at bottom.

Three bars popped up at the bottom showing ordinary fuel, O2 and singularity mass.

"Nick, what's this singularity mass?"

"I just saw it. Give me a second. I think it's related to creating a fold-space wave," he said.

Construct a second holo display on my left, also at thirty degrees. Show Mastodon and nearby objects.

Platform nine seventy-five appeared and I could just pick out the tall prow of the *Mastodon* nestled within the scaffolding of the larger structure. The bow of the massive ship was narrower at the bottom, widening a small amount each level until reaching the top where it splayed out for the habitable decks.

Show crew and passenger count, highlight locations on ship display.

Five glowing dots concentrated at the top of the ship, set back twenty meters from the extreme front. I recognized the bridge from the exterior shape of the opaque armor glass. Another glowing dot showed aft of the bridge and two decks below and finally the seventh glowing dot, down below in one of the lower cargo holds.

"You see this, Nick? We're really the only crew aboard," I said.

"I do. I've never seen so many autonomous systems. I doubt this ship is legal in Sol," he said. He was referring to the centuries old ban on autonomous, artificially intelligent systems.

"Is it even legal here?"

"Probably not. Both Curie and Lèger nations are part of the Autonomous Systems Treaty. I suspect that might be why we're sitting so far off Curie," Nick said. "I also found what the singularity mass is for. We were right, it's for the fold-space generator. It's an element called aninonium."

"Doesn't singularity relate to black holes?" I asked.

"It does. Best I can tell, the fold-space generator has two objectives; generate a tiny black hole and keep it contained. Same thing the TransLoc gates do, but self-contained," he said.

"What happens if the containment is broken?"

"Best case? You'd get dumped out of fold-space," Nick said.

"Let me guess. Worse case is we become part of the black hole?" Tabby asked.

"I think that's probably right, Tabby," he said. Nick was always calm, even when delivering the worst possible information.

"Seriously?" Ada asked, alarmed.

"No different than if one of our engines goes ballistic and lights us all on fire," I said. "Dead is dead, doesn't matter if you're really small because you're part of a black hole."

"Real funny, Hoffen," she muttered, going back to work at her station.

All stations report status for departure.

I looked to the right and watched as the systems received final check-offs from the crew.

"Anino, Jonathan, please report your status. I'm about to lock down external access in preparation for departure," I said.

"You haven't even asked for a navigation plan, Hoffen," Anino said.

"Roger that, Anino. And, call me Captain when I'm in the chair, please," I said. "Tell me how many hours this ship has logged under sail."

"I don't see why that's relevant, Captain," he said. I detected just a hint of smugness in his delivery, but chose to ignore it.

"Just tell me."

"Zero."

That was just plain ridiculous. "You haven't even undocked and sailed around the platform?"

"No."

"It's called a shakedown cruise. I'd prefer not to be in the middle of the Deep Dark and lose an engine. Much easier to recover if we're still in a habitable system, don't you think?"

"Captain, we've a very short timeframe in which to save the crew of *Cape of Good Hope*. We need to leave now," he said.

"I'll take it under advisement and assume that means you're set. Jonathan, are you also good to go?"

"Hoffen, you'll..."

Mute Anino.

Jonathan replied to my request. "I am ready, Captain. I see your crew has been inventorying and checking the status of ship systems. I have some recommendations for additions, if you are amenable."

"Of course," I said. "Please send them along to Nick and he'll see they're distributed."

My HUD showed a high priority comm in my queue. I had a few minutes while Nick distributed Jonathan's recommendations, so I opened it. It turned out to be a rant from Anino insisting that I listen to him about getting underway immediately and not losing time.

"Marny, are we secure?"

"Aye, Cap," she acknowledged. "We're secure and all weapons systems are at one hundred percent. For a big girl, she might be a little under-gunned, but any one of these turrets would open *Hotspur* up after a few solid hits. I just wouldn't want to run into anything too big."

"Roger that. Nick, environmental systems, fuel and friggin' singularity?"

Nick choked back a laugh, trying to remain professional. "All systems nominal. We've enough supplies for a hundred souls for the better part of a month."

"Ada, Tabby, flight systems?"

"We're green," Ada replied.

"Tabbs, how are we locked in here?" I asked.

"Magnetic station clamps. I show zero drift and can release on your command," she said.

I pulled the flight stick up with my right hand and the throttle control with my left. The ship had bow and stern thrusters that I could feel as small nipples on the left control.

"Release, Tabbs," I said.

A slight shudder rippled through the ship.

"We're free, Captain," she said.

I nudged the flight stick and throttle gently forward and we slid from our cradle.

"Drift, forward on starboard side," Ada announced.

Indeed we were drifting slightly toward the stationary platform. I gave the starboard bow thruster a nudge, overdoing it slightly, so I tapped the port thruster to make up for it. I ramped up the throttle just a smidge and we moved forward. It took almost twenty seconds for us to clear the platform.

"Will you look at that," Ada said, her words almost reverent. She and Tabby had constructed an external holo view of *Mastodon* and located it between them.

I had to agree with her sentiment. The ship was magnificent in its stately proportion.

"All hands, this is the Captain. This would be a good time to buckle up and set aside any volatile experiments. We're going to see how this big girl dances," I said.

I pushed forward on the throttle and pulled back gracefully on the stick. The lag I'd expected was there. No matter the size of the engines, one point eight kilo tonnes just can't respond immediately. When we did start moving, I reveled in the power the engines produced. We might be big, but we could be graceful. It was nowhere near as bad as pushing one point two kilometers of barge weighing in at seven point five kilo tonnes. Sailing a tug had been all about predicting when you wanted to make your next move. *Mastodon* just accelerated on a delayed schedule and she was a race horse wanting to be let free.

Clear of the platform, I set a course to take us a hundred thousand kilometers beneath Curie, where there was virtually no traffic. I also intended to do this at full burn. Tabby and Ada predicted this move, quickly settling into their chairs.

"Prepare for hard burn," I said, turning the ship onto the new course I'd laid out.

I gave it a five count and pushed the throttle down, stopping just past the hard burn indicator. On my holo display, the four engines came to life, a brilliant blue glow extending behind them just before the acceleration caught up with the rest of the ship. I allowed the acceleration to push me back into my seat. It wasn't anywhere near what we experienced on *Hotspur*, but on such a massive ship it was exhilarating.

The inertial and gravity systems caught up and the familiar feel of 1g rested on us. It would take twenty minutes to sail past Curie and I would remain in my seat, checking the monitors. If we were going to have a problem, it could come at any minute and I wanted to be ready.

I checked my system display. Something had knocked loose in the bilge and was giving us a yellow status. Boy, did that sound familiar. "Nick, you seeing that bilge issue?"

"Roger that. I've dispatched a repair bot. It's not critical," he said.

Unmute Anino.

"Phillippe, how are you hanging in there?"

"What the frak are you doing, Hoffen?" His teenaged-voice cracked as he spoke.

"Taking her out for her maiden voyage," I said. "And remember, I'm in the chair. Call me Captain." I knew I was pushing him, but I needed to firmly cement the idea.

"Well, Captain, you've all but wrecked my lab," he said.

"Understood. I'd get that stowed. You've twenty minutes before our next maneuver," I replied, trying hard not to feel smug.

"Are you trying to piss me off?" he asked.

"Is it working?"

He cut the comm.

At a hundred thousand kilometers, we were well out of the influence of Curie's gravity, so I hadn't expected any problems. I cut the burn and allowed us to drift past, all the while reorienting for a much closer pass. I would bring us in close and fast so that the gravity of the planet would significantly deflect our trajectory. I worked out the navigation pass as I spun the engines back up. We'd turned almost a hundred eighty degrees and as a result it would take twenty minutes to zero out our delta-v with Curie and about the same amount of time to get back in for our next pass.

"Check me on this, Tabbs," I said and sent my plan to both Ada and Tabby.

"You know the ship would make this calculation for you," Ada said.

"Just being cautious," I said.

"You're good," Tabby said. "If you add another five degrees, you'll intercept an old ship graveyard. There are big hulks in there for Marny to get in a live fire test."

"Brilliant. Add it," I said.

She pushed it back to me and I plugged it in as our new path. The ship adjusted slightly and we kept sailing on.

Just as we'd barely zeroed out our delta-v with Curie, Marny cut in. "Cap. We've a heavy cruiser approaching fast to the starboard. They're hailing us. It's *Fist of Justice*."

"That was fast. We haven't done anything provocative yet, have we?" I asked.

"Guilty conscience is about all, Cap," Marny said.

Accept hail.

"*Mastodon* here, Captain Liam Hoffen. How may I be of assistance?" I asked.

"Hoffen? This is Admiral Tullas. I need you to heave to for a confab," she said.

"Admiral, is this official business? We're right in the middle of running a shakedown cruise," I said.

"Where's Anino?" she asked.

I was surprised at the informality of her communication. She was in a smaller ship, at least by weight, but her guns and armor completely out-classed us.

"I'm not at liberty to say. You mind telling me what this is about?" I asked.

"Heave to, Captain," she commanded. "If you need that to be a directive, it is."

That was good enough for me. I wasn't ready to take the next step. I pulled back on the throttle and allowed us to drift forward. At our current velocity it would take sixteen hours to reach Curie.

My status screen lit up with the words 'DON'T LET HER ON THIS

SHIP.' I didn't have to wonder who'd written it. Anino had his reasons and I'd do my best to honor them.

"My partner and I will shuttle over when you get here," I said.

"Understood." She terminated comm.

"Confab?" Nick asked. "Sounds like she's trying to keep this conversation private."

"Anino, your presence is requested on the bridge," I said.

No sooner had I said the words than the doors of the lift opened.

"I can't believe she got here so fast," Anino said. "They must have been waiting for me. You should have taken off like I said. This mission might be screwed now."

I sighed and scowled at him. "Remember when I told you what would happen if you held things back from me?"

"I didn't know she'd be coming," he lied.

"You just admitted it," Nick said.

"Fine," he said. The cocky little rat didn't sound at all chagrined. "I strongly suspected Belirand was waiting for me to launch. They've known for a few weeks that *Mastodon* was nearing completion."

"Well, we're not going to outrun *Fist of Justice*," I said.

"What are you going to say to her?" Anino asked.

"I'll tell her the truth."

"You wouldn't dare."

"You're crazy if you think I'm lying to that woman. She'll eat us alive. That said, I've been known to leave out details," I said. "I assume you don't want her to know you're on this ship?"

"That's right. But they can scan the ship and find my signature," he said.

"We'll see. Nick take Anino down to *Hotspur* and fire up silent running protocols. I'd be surprised if her scanners can penetrate both ships and that armor," I said.

"You want me to come over with you?" Nick asked.

"I was thinking of taking Tabbs. She probably speaks officer better than I do," I said.

Nick laughed mirthlessly. "Be careful, Liam."

"Ada, you have the helm. Marny keep us safe," I said.

"You are relieved," Ada said, adopting the formal words we used in watch changes.

Tabby and I joined Nick and Anino on the lift and took it down to the top docking bay where we separated - Nick and Anino to *Hotspur* and Tabby and me to a shuttle.

"Ada, how close are they?" I asked.

"Ten minutes max," Ada answered.

They were really burning hard to catch us that quickly and it concerned me.

"Cap, I've a location for your meeting. It's within a sweet spot for *Mastodon's* turrets. I'm transmitting now," she said.

"Can't believe we've stepped in the crap this soon," Tabby said as we sat in the shuttle.

"Seems about right to me," I said.

Take us to these coordinates. I flicked Marny's instructions to a console. I wasn't at all interested in trying to figure out how to fly the shuttle manually. I wondered if that was how Anino felt about *Mastodon*, although that seemed ridiculous.

The shuttle easily disembarked and sailed toward the location as instructed. Both Tabby and I gawked at *Mastodon* as we flew past. It was beautifully constructed and appeared that no expense had been spared. I couldn't fathom the wealth required to manufacture a ship of that size.

"Is there any food aboard?" Tabby asked, pulling open cupboards. "Bleh, all they have are meal-bars. You want blueberry or cherry?" she asked.

I laughed, it was an old joke. Meal bars pretty much tasted the same no matter what their packaging boasted.

"Cherry for me," I said.

"Suit yourself." She tossed me a bar with a pouch of water.

We sat back and watched as the *Fist of Justice* arrived. It was an intimidating ship, bristling with hardware. Even if we'd wanted to make a run for it, we'd never have gotten away from such a decked out ship. And, once it caught us, it'd be bad on an epic scale.

Half an hour later, a shuttle departed *The Fist* and glided over to us.

"Captain Hoffen, would you and your partner care to join me?" Tullas asked over the comm.

I looked at Tabby and she shrugged. There really wasn't any getting around it. I depressurized the cabin and we arc-jetted from our shuttle to the larger shuttle. We worked our way through the airlock and were immediately met by a thickset uniformed man holding a heavy blaster rifle.

"You'll need to deposit your weapons here." He indicated a table.

"Probably not," Tabby said.

He stiffened. "Let's not do this the hard way."

"I live for the hard way, pal. Belirand has no jurisdiction here," she said.

"It's okay, Bjarno. There's no threat. Right, Captain Hoffen?" Tullas asked.

"Far as I can tell, the only threat is *Fist of Justice*," I said.

"Quite right. Let them by, please," she said.

"Yes, please do," Tabby said, patting Bjarno on the chest as she brushed past. She had some steel ones, that girl. It made me proud.

"You wanted to talk?" I asked.

Tullas thumbed a small device and dropped it on the table in the middle of the small room. She then crossed behind us and closed the door.

"What are you doing on that ship, Hoffen?" she asked.

"I explained that already. It's a new ship and this is its shakedown cruise."

"Anino has you involved in a conspiracy that we are determined to stop," Tullas said.

"We, as in Belirand? Or, does that include you? What if the cause is righteous? I thought you were an honorable woman," I said.

"Anino is holding out on you, drawing you into his web. There are secrets for which I would destroy your entire crew to keep. Once you allow Anino to spread his lies, you will have crossed a line and we'll become enemies," she said. "And I'm afraid you've misjudged me, Captain Hoffen. There is plenty of blood on my hands. I'm not proud of everything I've done, but I believe I've done more good than harm. I tell you this so that you'll believe me when I say; if you continue on this path, I will hunt you down and I *will* kill you and everyone Anino's poisoned along the way."

Chapter 12

LIKE A BAD PENNY

"How'd that go, Cap?" Marny asked as Tabby and I walked back onto the bridge.

"Let's say she was right to the point," I said. "Ada, how's flight system status?"

"Still solid, Liam." She looked at me, worry in her eyes.

"All hands, prepare for hard burn. We've people that need saving," I said.

"What are you doing, Liam?" Tabby asked. We hadn't talked much on our shuttle ride back.

"We've committed to shaking this girl down, let's get it done," I said.

"We need to talk about this."

"Not here."

"Right." Tabby leaned in and kissed my cheek. "I'm with you, no matter what," she whispered.

I rubbed my hand on her back as she walked forward to take her seat.

I looked at the captain's chair that sat in the middle of the bridge. Never before had I felt so isolated. My friends, who were also my crew, would follow my lead, but the threat to our existence had never felt so real.

"That bad, Cap?" Marny asked. I hadn't realized that Marny, Ada and Tabby were all watching me and couldn't imagine how much my face was giving away.

"It's not good. Let's get out of here," I said.

"Just give me the word," Ada said.

"Engage."

What I hadn't realized until that moment was that Ada had subtly turned *Mastodon* so that the wash of the four heavy engines would just clear the bow of *Fist of Justice*. They'd feel us leaving. While it was technically a legal maneuver, it was very much on the provocative side of the line. I smiled despite my foul mood.

"Marny, keep track of *Fist*, would you?"

"Aye, Cap," she said. "They've turned and are spooling up in our direction. They intend to give chase."

For a moment, I considered ratcheting up our maneuvers next to Curie in an attempt to shake the heavy cruiser. I discarded the thought, Anything *Mastodon* could survive, the cruiser would handle. We were both outgunned and outclassed for speed.

"Well, frak. Of course they are," I said, sitting back into my chair.

I'd been stewing for a few minutes when I heard the lift open behind me. I turned to see Nick.

"That was pretty rough," he said, walking up to me. "You doing alright?"

"You were listening?"

"Yeah," he said, nodding. "Anino owns the patent for the tech she used to mask your conversation. We heard everything. What do you make of it?"

"Honestly? I'm confused. It doesn't make sense that Belirand would go so far out of their way to shut this operation down. I can see them wanting to keep things quiet, but their response feels disproportionate. And Tullas hates Anino. I know he's annoying, but how could you hate someone that young, so much?"

"I asked him about that. He said he's had to flaunt his wealth and connections to build this platform. Tullas has been tracking the technology he's been buying up," Nick said.

"But, Tullas is the one who put us together," I said.

"It was a woman in Tullas' office. Apparently, Tullas took that rather badly too."

"There's something else going on. I'm not sure what it is, but this has a stink to it," I said.

"Anino said we can pull out with no repercussions from him."

"And *Cape of Good Hope*? What happens to them?"

"I think he'd try the rescue mission by himself," Nick said.

"It's a lot of weight to carry, Nick. I know if I say go, you all will follow."

"Cap, command is a lonely place, but we're all volunteers here," Marny said. I wasn't surprised she was listening in. In fact, I wasn't surprised to see that everyone was paying attention.

"You ever ask yourself what we might do if you tried to step away?" Ada asked. "This mission is bigger than all of us. There are forty-five souls whose only chance at survival depends on us."

Tabby spoke up. "I'm with Ada. I couldn't give two shites about Anino's tussle with Belirand or Tullas for that matter. You think there's more going on here, fine. We'll deal with it. If you think I'm backing down because some petty tyrant threatens, then you haven't been paying attention."

I looked around at my friends. Their eyes were all on me, waiting for my answer. They were right.

"Ada, how far to that scrap heap?" I asked.

"Forty minutes. I'm planning to reverse our burn after we bend through Curie's atmo to give Marny a longer window," she said.

"Tabbs, Nick, I want you both in gunner's chairs for this pass. If we end up getting into it with Tullas, it'll be Ada and me on the helm and the three of you on turrets," I said.

Send comm to Fist of Justice on an unencrypted broadcast.

Admiral Tullas — we will conduct a weapons shakedown on the coordinates I've attached. Please stand clear. We'll broadcast our combat data streams on a similarly unencrypted channel for the benefit of public research.

Even with the communication disruption common during a hard burn, I knew *Fist of Justice* would receive the comm, given their position directly behind us.

I looked into the star field and reflected on the moment. It felt like a hundred years ago that I'd lived on Colony-40, my only worry if Big Pete was going to yell at me for scraping up my ore-sled.

"Contact with Curie's upper atmosphere in ten, nine..." Ada announced over ship wide comm.

We quickly learned that *Mastodon*, as elegantly built as she was, didn't have anywhere near the same performance characteristics as *Hotspur*. The shaking started right as Ada hit zero and the intensity increased as we dove deeper toward Curie.

"Captain?" Anino's voice came over the comm. "What's happening?"

"Hold on, Phillippe. Fifty seconds more and we'll be through the worst of it," I said.

"Are you trying to kill us?" he asked.

"Sorry for the inconvenience, but we're well within the ship's capabilities," I said. I glanced at Nick for confirmation and he nodded his agreement.

"Those are just hypotheticals calculated by machines!" Anino complained.

"Not after this run," I said. Tabby looked over her shoulder and flashed me a quick grin.

"Jupiter, I hate you," he said and closed the comm channel.

I watched the status board. A number of the systems fluctuated between green and yellow, but so far nothing critical had flipped to red, although plenty of non-critical systems were buried in crimson. The worst damage was in one of the lower bays where, apparently, a few barrels of liquid foodstuffs had toppled and opened. Just as well, the description on the screen didn't make it particularly appetizing anyway.

After a few more minutes of shaking we pulled out of the atmosphere and I checked our path. Our course had adjusted as calculated.

All hands. We're through the rough stuff and will take a few minutes for a complete systems check. Please report critical issues immediately.

"Ada, would you cut hard burn?"

"Copy that," she said and we dropped from hard burn.

A review of the systems showed several that had taken significant damage. The autonomous systems were already at work and gave an estimate of fifteen hours for completion of all repairs.

"Captain, could we talk?" Anino asked.

"Not yet. Give me a minute," I said.

"All stations report flight status," I said. My board lit up with green indicators. "Ada, please resume hard burn."

"Go ahead, Phillippe," I said.

"Do you know what your stunt back there just cost me?"

"No idea," I said. "I understand you're good for it. Look Phillippe, if you want to take a seasoned crew on a mission into hostile territory, you have to prove to them that the equipment is capable."

"Six hundred thousand credits in broken equipment," he said. "Was it worth it?"

"It will be when we come back alive," I said.

"Anyone ever tell you you're annoying?"

"I take that as praise coming from you."

I wasn't surprised when he closed the comm channel one more time. Pouty little bugger.

We were still ten minutes from the derelict yard when Jonathan contacted me via comm, "Requesting permission to enter bridge."

"Granted," I said.

A door on the aft of the starboard side of the bridge opened. Jonathan entered, balancing a platter of mugs on one hand. "I've taken the liberty of preparing refreshments," he said. The mugs were open at the top and wisps of vapor escaped from the one he set on a fold-out platform, attached to my chair.

"Open tops?" I asked.

Jonathan picked up one of the remaining cups from his platter and turned it upside down. The liquid did not pour out, but stayed at the top. "Small gravity generators hold the liquid until contact is made with the consumer's mouth," he said.

I picked up my mug and shook it upside down furiously. Not a single drop of coffee escaped. "Where have you been all my life?" I quipped.

"Careful, Jonny. Next thing you know he'll be proposing to you," Tabby said.

Jonathan looked at me with concern.

"Don't listen to her. I just really like my coffee."

"Very good, Captain. It is nice to know my efforts are appreciated. Would you care for an orange glazed cranberry scone with that?"

"Yes, please," I said. "So... *are* you married?"

This time Jonathan looked with alarm to Marny.

"Jonathan, don't listen to them. They're just feeling punchy," Marny said.

"I'm afraid I've not yet learned to identify this group's particular style of humor," he said.

"Let me know when you do," Nick said. "I might like some pointers."

I bit into the scone. It was good - delicious even - especially given how hungry I was, but it wasn't quite as good as what Marny made. Perhaps I could encourage some friendly competition in that arena.

"Jonathan... or do you prefer Jonny?" I asked.

"I've never had a nickname before," he said.

"Would you like to remain on the bridge while we execute the weapon systems tests? It should be quite a show from up here," I said.

"Thank you, Captain. I would enjoy that," he said as he finished handing out coffee and scones to the rest of the crew.

"First target on port side in thirty, twenty-nine..." Ada announced.

I looked at the navigation path displayed between Ada and Tabby's chairs and felt an unexpected pang of jealousy at their shared workspace. I shrugged it off and gestured to superimpose our path onto the holo display of *Mastodon* to the left of my chair.

Ada or Tabby had laid out a path with six derelict ships at different orientations to the ship. Our delta-v with the heap was high and each gunner would need to react quickly, but it also wasn't our first rodeo.

A blurp of turret fire erupted from the port side as Tabby engaged the first target. With so much warning, it had been an easy hit. The second was much the same, except both the starboard and topside guns engaged.

"Stay frosty, kids," Ada said and put *Mastodon* into a spin, rotating along the axis of our current vector.

Again, it caused them no problems. As the targets moved from one gunner's visibility to the next, they were easily picked off.

On the final three, Ada got craftier, using aft and bow thrusters to twist the ship through a circuitous route. We were far from perfect after that, but I felt like we'd at least made a good go of things.

"Marny, would you like another pass?" I asked.

"We should do better than fifty-eight percent," she said.

"Nick, check something for me," I said.

"Yup, go ahead."

"How tight did *Fist of Justice* follow us through Curie's atmosphere?"

"Not at all. With their superior speed, they just dog-legged around and caught back up," he said.

"Anino, you've thirty minutes to get your lab stowed again. We're going to have more turbulence," I said.

"I thought you said we were done with that," Anino responded. It almost sounded like a whine.

"My apologies. And I wouldn't be doing it if I didn't find it necessary for mission success."

"Any way I can convince you otherwise?"

"Not really."

"Could you send Jonathan down?" he said, resigned to his fate.

"Copy that," I said.

"Nick, what's the shortest fold-space jump we can take?"

"Not sure. What are you thinking?" he asked.

"We need to test the fold-space generator. It'd be nice to drop somewhere we could limp back from," I said.

"Gotcha. Give me your plan for passing Curie. Our minimum jump is a thousand AUs. It'd suck, but we could get back from there," he said.

"Roger. I'm working on it. Give me a couple."

We were once again accelerating toward the derelict field. To say there was a lot of activity on the bridge was an understatement.

I'd just finished handing off the navigation plan to Nick when the shooting started. I looked up and worriedly checked the position of *Fist of Justice*. They'd settled back to a comfortable distance of five thousand kilometers. Ada pushed the *Mastodon* around again and I noticed our hits percent had increased significantly.

Once we were on the other side of the derelict field, I stood up. I was tired of sitting and we were still twenty minutes from Curie. I walked over to Marny's station. "What happened? Looks like our accuracy jumped but our number of shots was down by quite a bit."

"Nick dropped out," she said.

"What do you think?" I asked.

"She's got some teeth, not to mention a really nice feature where we can dial back the intensity of the blaster bolts," she said.

"Would we stand a chance against *Fist of Justice*?" I asked.

"Do you think it'll come to that?" Marny asked.

"I do. If only we could outrun her. I've never been in a position of being both slower and less powerful."

"Earthers have a phrase," she said. "It's called being a sitting duck and that's what we'd be if *Fist of Justice* chose to mix it up with us."

I sighed. "Good to know."

"Prepare for hard burn," Ada said.

We'd shifted in and out of hard burn enough times in the last couple of hours that I was having a hard time keeping track.

"Nick, can you give me an idea how long we'll be in fold-space?"

"Yes. It's not exactly linear for distance traveled, but generally shorter distances require fewer folds and therefore less time in the fold-space bubble. We're looking at a total of ninety-two minutes," he said.

"And how long to get back if everything goes to crap?"

"Almost a year," he said.

"A year? I thought we were making a short jump," I said.

"Short as I can come up with," he said. "We're limited by available fuel. We'd sail back nine months with *Mastodon*, then another three months with *Hotspur*. Most efficient way I could come up with."

"Let's hope we don't need that," I said. "Can you program two more jumps?" I asked.

"What do you have in mind?"

"We're going to wait wherever we drop and see if *Fist of Justice* shows up. If they don't show up, we'll know we've lost them."

"And if they do?"

"We'll get a good reading on how closely they can jump in on us and how much time it takes," I said. "If things get dicey, we're going to want that information."

"I'll get right on it. That's good thinking," Nick said.

I beamed. It felt good to have Nick's approval. It always felt like I was leaning on him to do the heavy mental lifting.

I sat back and drank the coffee Jonathan had provided. It was delicious. Given the source, it was no doubt the real thing. "Ada, I'd like to take her through the atmosphere, we're going to enter fold-space just as soon as we're on the other side."

"Roger that, Captain," she said. "All systems are nominal and repairs are continuing."

"I relieve you," I said.

"I stand relieved," she answered.

I enjoyed watching Curie grow as we approached. Tullas probably had an idea something was up as we hadn't slowed on our approach. She'd have to swing wider if she wanted to miss the atmosphere since she was going just as fast as we were.

All hands, prepare for turbulence and be warned we'll be jumping to fold-space in thirty... twenty-nine...

With the extra speed, the ship actually seemed to shake less violently, although not by much. I watched the sensors and was pleased to see that *Fist of Justice* was swinging even wider than I thought necessary.

"Liam, fold-space on your command," Nick said.

Cue Allman Bros, Midnight Rider through all ship's speakers.

I heard groans throughout the bridge, but secretly I knew they loved it.

Well, I've got to run to keep from hidin',

Not gonna let 'em catch the Midnight Rider.

"Engage!" I said. It was probably a little louder than necessary, but the excitement of the moment took me.

The shaking of the ship settled out immediately as all visible light smeared in a more or less horizontal direction, like a child with a fist full of markers on a drawing board. The first time I'd experienced this visual distortion, I'd been unprepared for it, but this was my fourth jump and I guess I'd become jaded.

Once the smearing stopped, I quickly gathered my bearings. My HUD showed the fold-space bubble around us and I looked frantically for the line I needed to keep so as to not be knocked back into normal space.

"Nick. I'm not seeing the edges here," I said.

"You won't. We're not sailing between TransLoc gates so there's no risk of falling off," he said.

"Frak. You could have told me."

"Sorry, I guess I thought it was obvious," he said.

Good, I thought sarcastically, at least I didn't need to worry about getting a big head about things.

"Potty break?" Tabby asked. "You got this, Luv? I think us girls are going to find the head. You coming, Marny?"

"I could use a break," Marny replied.

"Just be back in an hour," I said. I watched them leave and then said, "You know, something's been bugging me."

"What's that?" Nick asked.

"Tullas didn't even question if we'd be making the jump. She just wanted us to know that she'd be there to wipe the floor with us if we did. Something in the way she said it made me believe she not only could jump, but could follow us into fold or maybe even track us."

"Chilling thought," Nick said.

"No doubt."

One of the things I appreciated about Nick was his ability to sit quietly and not fill the room with idle chatter. If he had something to talk about, he spoke up, but he was just as happy to leave me to my thoughts. I desperately needed time to think, too. Just because everyone agreed to this mission didn't mean I was off the hook. We needed some sort of advantage when facing off with *Fist of Justice*. I couldn't see one.

"Warmup?" Ada asked when they got back.

I looked up at her, startled from my reverie. She was holding a coffee pot. "Uh, yup, that'd be great. You find the head all right?"

"There's one right at the back of the bridge," she said. "We just needed an excuse to explore the ship. You should see it, this whole deck is gorgeously designed. Tabby picked out a nice room with a king-sized bed complete with a standing jetted tub."

"I don't even know what that is," I said.

"You'll see... and I'll be getting a full-report from Tabby."

My cheeks flushed. "She wouldn't."

Ada punched my shoulder with her free hand, "Too easy, Hoffen."

We were only a few minutes from dropping out of fold-space when Tabby and Marny returned, talking excitedly. My best guess was they'd found some sort of exercise equipment. Oh, joy.

"All hands, normal space in four minutes," I said. "If *Fist of Justice* shows up we'll be jumping right away, otherwise we're going to burn for an hour."

"Captain?" Anino's voice came over my private comm.

"What's on your mind, Phillippe?"

"By my calculation, we should have forty-six minutes before Tullas arrives."

"Thank you. Do you believe she's tracking us or following?"

"Not sure what you mean."

"Is there something about the ship that gives away our destination or location or is she just following us line of sight?"

"Every time a ship drops out of fold-space it's registered on a central device controlled by Belirand. She's definitely able to track us. Worse yet, speed in fold-space is completely proportional to mass. She's just twice as fast because we're so big."

Forward conversation to Nick. I instructed the AI.

"Thanks, Phillippe, that's helpful," I said.

"Welcome," he said and terminated the comm.

"You get that, Nick?"

"Yup. We'll be down for thirty seconds to let the engines cycle, but we'll jump right back in," he said.

"How long?" I asked.

"Sixty-two hours," he said.

"Copy that."

I'd been concerned that we wouldn't be able to jump to fold-space twice, but my fears were unfounded. A minute after dropping out, we reoriented and jumped right back in.

"Okay, kids. We're taking four-hour shifts. That's the good news. The bad news is I want two crew on the bridge at all times. I'll post the schedule, but first up will be Marny and me," I said. "Make sure to get some rest. Who knows what we're getting into once we drop out in the deep dark."

It was the nature of space flight. Moments of high activity followed by hours of quiet. Some referred to it as boredom, but not me. I had plenty of things to keep me busy, one of which would be to learn as much about *Mastodon* as I possibly could. I had a feeling our very survival depended on it.

AS IT TURNS OUT, a standing jetted tub is quite interesting. The user steps in to a small compartment roughly the size of a small head. The interesting part is that the doors and walls, which can be either transparent or completely opaque, seal fully. Warm water fills the compartment to about chest depth and jetted water massages you. Let's just say for a young couple, still excited to explore each other, it's about one of the coolest inventions I've experienced.

"CAP, WE'RE THIRTY MINUTES OUT." Marny's voice woke me from a deep sleep.

I'd asked for the wakeup call and quickly dressed, then stopped by the main galley toward the aft of the deck and grabbed a fresh mug of coffee and a meal bar. I wasn't used to such a long ship and excitement caused me to break into a jog.

I palmed my way onto the bridge.

"Captain on the bridge," Marny announced.

"Welcome back, Luv," Tabby said. She'd been in the captain's chair and started to get up.

"Your watch, your chair." I sat next to Ada in a pilot's seat.

"Normal space in five... four..."

The dancing stars that were the hallmark of fold-space solidified into a single picture.

"All stations report," I said.

I checked my holographic display. Everything checked out green.

"Marny, keep an eye out for *Fist of Justice*, please."

"Aye, Cap," she said.

"Nick, any reading on *Cape of Good Hope*?"

"Yup. Got her," he said.

"Frakking aye!" I said.

"There's a problem," Nick said. My heart sank, of course there was. "*Fist of Justice* is already here."

Chapter 13

PATROL

Yishuv Settlement, Planet Ophir

The morning sun had not yet fully risen as Eliora looked over her training group. The council hadn't completely accepted Captain Gian's request for a citizen army, but had agreed to allow volunteers to receive training.

"Trainee Popette, where are the three vulnerabilities of an Ophie?" she asked, walking down a more or less straight line of two score.

"There are four acceptable soft vulnerabilities: groin, just above the groin into the chest cavity, throat beneath the chin but above the armored collar and the heel, as you demonstrated on the mountain," a late-teen girl answered. She held her arms stiffly to her side as she stared forward.

Eliora moved on to the next trainee. "Jesse, how is a long sword best utilized?"

"Defensively. It is effective at deflecting an Ophie's club strike. Otherwise it is acceptable for a jabbing attack, ideally in a vulnerable location, less ideally in a direct thrust to the rib cage where the heart is located centrally, but lower by a hands-breadth than a human's," a blond, twenty stans old farmer answered.

"Coral, how is a katana used to deflect an attacking club strike?"

"The katana is not an appropriate weapon for deflection, it is best used for slashing or thrusting," a middle-aged woman answered.

"Correct. Coral why would someone choose a katana over a long sword?"

"It requires less strength, but must be used quickly and confidently, often upon first being drawn from its scabbard."

"Saya," Eliora corrected.

"Yes, ma'am. Saya," she said.

"Okay everyone. Pads on. You have thirty minutes with the practice swords using the first two forms. Take it seriously. This is as much strength building as it is training your muscles to use the swords. When you're in battle, these forms must become second nature to you," Eliora said. "Any questions?"

"Ma'am?"

"Trainee Coral?"

"We were promised real swords. It's why most of us joined."

"First, we would never practice with real swords. They are too valuable and dangerous. Second, the smithy is working as quickly as they can. As you know, they're supplying protectors first. I've been assured we'll start seeing swords within four tendays," she said.

"What if the Ophie attack before we get them?"

"I won't lie to you. If Ophie breach our walls, you are vulnerable without steel weapons. This training will make you strong and capable when those weapons become available," Eliora said. She stepped back and scanned the score of volunteers that had assembled. They'd been practicing for a month and there had been improvements, but it was disheartening to see just how unprepared her charges were for combat. "Now, let's get to it."

"Eliora, I apologize for calling you out on this. It's just... there are rumors," Coral said.

"They are not rumors. I have seen firsthand the Ophie scouts in the forest. You must train hard so you will be ready."

The middle-aged mother of two nodded her head in acceptance and joined her cadre in pulling on their pads for practice.

In the distance, Eliora saw the bouncing lights of an approaching vehicle and waited for its arrival.

"Merrie, have you finally decided to join us?" Eliora asked as the vehicle pulled to a stop.

"Not yet. I've too much work to do and not enough hours in the day."

"I don't have much time to talk. What brings you out this morning?" Eliora asked.

"I have presents and need your help," Merrie said.

"Can it wait? I'm training right now."

"It's about your training. I've made five compound bows; I think you could start training your volunteers with them," Merrie said.

"They're extra? What of the protectors?"

"Merik convinced the council to allow us to make a big run of the bow components. These are extra and we should have enough for your entire squad by the end of tenday," Merrie said, removing the oilcloth from the cargo compartment.

"I only see two score arrows. Are there more?" Eliora asked.

"That's where I need your help. I've convinced two of our carpenters to supply the wooden blanks, but we need many hands to run them through the shapers and apply feathers and heads," Merrie said.

"I will make it a condition of receiving training on the bows. You will have your help. When would you like them?"

"I've set up shop at the old tannery. I need someone I can train on the equipment and who will take responsibility for teaching others," Merrie said.

"I know just the person. Trainee Coral, would you join us?"

"I WOULD LIKE to take my squad on a patrol outside the wall," Eliora said.

She sat with Second Protector Shem and Captain Gian at a table in a room atop the barracks. The weather had turned cool, barely reaching ten degrees at full sun. It was a time of low activity for the Ophie, who, like earth reptiles, did not move as quickly in the cool weather.

"Bakers and housewives?" Shem asked.

"Two of them, yes, but I'd put Coral against any archer in the protectors. That is, except you, Shem," she said. "It's one thing to train behind these walls, but it's too academic."

"What happens when one or more of them doesn't come home?" Gian asked. "Will it not ruin your training program? You've already had setbacks."

"You are right, of course. I'm down to eight. I know they look unlikely as fighters, but they're stronger now. They need to take this next step."

"Where would you take them?"

"Pessach reported seeing a partial pod of Ophie on the mountain path yesterday," she said.

Gian was incredulous. "You would put them into combat?"

"Where there are two, there are five," Shem said. "It is the way of the Ophie."

"Then have a regular patrol follow us. We cannot hide behind these walls. The Ophie grow bolder and we grow more cautious."

"I will agree to patrols, but I am not sending your trainees against a pod of Ophie. You will venture no more than a kilometer from the wall and there must be a protector with them at all times," Gian said.

"This is ridiculous. It's hard enough with all the new recruits and now you'd have us babysit these... these..." This sputtering protest came from Shem.

"Citizens," Eliora helped.

"Fine. Citizens. They will get us killed," he spat.

"I understand your frustration, Shem. Let's not forget, we would all welcome more recruits," Gian answered. "If Eliora's trainees prove capable, it is an interesting way around the council's restrictions and would be a welcome relief. It will not hurt us to do a trial."

Shem nodded. "That should not be *too* disruptive *if* Eliora babysits them. Do you truly believe they are ready, Eliora?"

"That is what I seek to find out. We all know that until tested in battle, one can never tell. I have already chosen my squad leader," she said.

"That carpenter, Dael? He's a big one," Shem said.

"No. He would be a good choice though, both strong and intelligent. I chose the baker, Coral, who has raised two children with no father."

"You wouldn't!" Shem exclaimed. "That woman is no fighter. She is in terrible shape! Who would follow her?"

"*That woman* gets up every day and runs thirty minutes before practice. She then works the entire day, while keeping track of two of her children. Her success will inspire others," Eliora said.

"Her death will leave two orphans," Shem said.

"Don't you think she knows that? It is people like Coral that we need. She knows exactly what she has to lose."

Gian put his hands out, placating them. "Alright, knock it off you two. This is Eliora's decision and I'll expect a full report next tenday. Now, tell me about that pod on the mountain trail..."

⸻

ELIORA WOKE up earlier than usual the next morning to prepare for what would no doubt be a long day. She'd stayed up late the night before, poring over maps of the surrounding area.

"What's up chief? You're here early," Coral asked, still breathing hard from her run.

"We're going on patrol this morning," Eliora said.

"As in, outside the wall?"

"That's right. You up for it? I need five volunteers to fill out the patrol."

"Do squirmunks bark? Of course, I'm in. You know, I heard a patrol spotted a couple of Ophie up the hill two days back."

"Captain's put a leash on us. We're not to get more than a kilometer from the wall," Eliora said.

"How far up were those Ophies?"

"Just past the two point six marker."

"Shite. We won't even get close," Coral said

"Really, you want to run into Ophie?" Eliora asked.

"I had to watch an Ophie rip my David in two, which left me to raise two girls on my own without their father. There was no remorse in that monster's face, just a mindless, focused, killing machine. If it were to me, we'd be out hunting them every minute of every day," Coral said.

Eliora was set back. The woman's deep seated hatred shocked her.

"You know, I've fought them," Eliora said. "They're fearless and extraordinarily strong. What if your daughters were to lose their mother also?"

"What has waiting done for us? We've waited three centuries to be rescued by a world that's forgotten us. In that time our technology has slowly but surely rotted and failed. It is as if we're waiting to die. Not me. I say we take the fight to them. Let the Ophie fear us for once."

Eliora couldn't help but smile. The once soft, mother of two, was ready for the war Eliora could feel coming. They would need many more like Coral if they were to survive.

"Good. I've slayer-tipped arrows, ten for each of us," she said.

"That is more than enough," Coral said, standing up straighter, exuding confidence Eliora was glad to see. She'd need it.

Twenty minutes later the entire group assembled. It was big for a patrol, Eliora preferred a smaller, quieter group, but it would have to do.

"We'll break into pairs," Eliora instructed. The patrol strode two-by-two down the deserted street. "Under no circumstance will you leave your partner. Do you understand me? I don't care if you have to tinkle or toot. You are to call out if you see trouble. The Ophie are better at tracking than we are because their senses of smell and hearing are considerably better. That said, their eyesight is poor. At fifty meters, they might as well be blind."

"I hear they smell like old socks," Popette said. "Is that true?"

"Mold. Yes. Ophie live in hovels with four others in a pod. It's believed the same Ophie live together their entire lives," Eliora recounted. It wasn't the first time they'd heard the information, but she knew they needed something to keep their nervous minds engaged.

"Keeper of the gate," Eliora called.

"Ho, Eliora." A man poked his head over the edge of the wall.

"Bashi – We're going out on patrol. Open the gate and please enter it in your log."

"Yes, ma'am."

And so, that was how they started every day. The citizen patrol, led by Eliora, quickly became a fixture of conversation within the village. And for two tendays the patrol went out at the crack of dawn only to return two hours later with nothing more than a new appreciation of the terrain around the small village.

Halfway into the twenty-third patrol Dael raised his fist, his arm held at a ninety degree angle from his body. It was an oft-repeated gesture as the lead saw or heard something that caused them to question what they were running into.

Dael breathed a sigh of relief. The movement he'd picked out on the side of the hill at thirty meters was simply a buckthorn, a fifty kilo-gram, furred game animal. It wasn't the first time they'd run into one of the animals that morning and Dael started to lower his arm.

Eliora's heart raced. She picked out what Dael missed. The buck-thorn had been spooked by something up the hill. She flapped her right arm rapidly trying to gain the patrol's attention and then held her fist up and then down, angled from her body. Contrary to instinct, rapid movements weren't easily picked up by Ophie, but verbal communication could be. Her hand signal called for the patrol's archers to step forward.

Coral grinned grimly as she nocked a slayer-tipped arrow. She was one of four archers who had been chosen for long distance shots. They'd run this same drill a dozen times, each turning out to be a false alarm. This time, it felt different and something in Eliora's posture raised the hackles on Coral's neck.

Eliora pointed at her own eyes and then up the side of the hill. The Ophie had set up along the patrol's path, blending into the surrounding hillside almost perfectly. It was odd to see the large reptilians, completely unaware of the fact that they were being observed. Coral counted two. At thirty meters it was a long shot, but well within her range. Her hands shook with excitement and the blood rushed in her ears.

Eliora knew they couldn't ignore the easy targets, but two standing alone didn't make sense. Ophie traveled in pods, rarely splitting up. She directed the archers with hand signals to take aim on their enemy, understanding dawning on her in a single terrifying moment of clarity. The brush behind them exploded as three Ophie charged into the open space. The patrol had walked into a trap.

Coral breathed out to release the tension just as the world exploded behind her.

"Trap!" Dael exclaimed. Coral's patrol partner dropped his bow and pulled his heavy long sword.

The Ophie that Coral had targeted turned his head swiftly, looking down the hill in her direction. It had heard Dael and was alerted.

It took all of her courage not to turn around to the sounds of battle behind her. If there were two ahead, it meant there would be three behind. The rest of the patrol should be able to handle them. If not, they'd have an even more difficult time when the bait pair also arrived.

She pulled the bow back and felt the comforting clunk as the off-centered gear of the compound bow dropped the pull tension to a comfortable fifteen kilograms. She sighted along the arrow with both eyes, calculating the drop that she knew would occur with the distance. It was a shot she'd made hundreds of times before. *Center mass, don't get cute, let the arrow do its job*, she thought, repeating the steps to a successful shot.

The roar of man and beast behind her was all but overwhelming. Coral concentrated, working to force the maelstrom from her mind, focusing on the bait Ophies jogging toward them. It was surprising how such a large being could move so gracefully over the rocks of the hillside. Their slow gait chewed up ground at a ridiculous pace. There were two of them and she knew she would have but one good shot. She would have to trust her patrol members to deal with the rest.

An eerie calm fell over Coral as she watched the beast charge. It was almost beautiful how it so easily bounded from one boulder to the next. She felt its rhythm and knew what she must do. She would wait for it to leave the ground and time her strike to catch the beast on its way down.

It was almost an afterthought when she released the arrow. Its short flight halted as it buried itself into the great beast. The repercussions were immediate as its next step faltered and the legs buckled, sending it crashing to the ground.

Only then did her vision clear enough to see its companion, short meters behind, raise its great club as it bounded over its fallen pod-mate. Coral's mind, reeling from the exhilaration of a clean kill, searched for a solution, a way to nock a second arrow. There was no hope, she couldn't possibly reload fast enough. Her only hope was the katana hanging at her side. She reached for it, dropping the bow, but instinctively knew there wasn't enough time. The great club was already crashing down toward her. She'd stood her ground too long, zeroing in on her kill. *That's for my husband*, she thought, dropping to the ground, a final hope that the Ophie had overcommitted its swing.

A bright flash of polished metal sparked as it deflected the great club.

Dael's heavily muscled thigh pushed her out of the way as he stepped into the Ophie's swing. A great sound of metal on fire hardened wood punctuated the moment.

Coral gathered her wits. The Ophie had missed, but Dael had chosen to save her life instead of using his long sword to pierce the beast. He would very likely pay for his choice with his own. *My life for his*, she prayed. He would not leave his young wife if she had anything to say about it. She'd already talked with Dael about her children. If anything happened to her, he would see after them. If their fates were reversed, what could she give his wife? Nothing, except him.

She rolled back to her feet and drew her katana and in a single motion ran it across the back of the beast's heavy thigh. A greenish blood deposited on the blade and the beast howled, but it didn't even stumble. She knew better that to strike at a non-vulnerable region, but she'd had the effect she was looking for as the Ophie turned its attention away from Dael.

"That's right, you ugly pond sucker," she taunted. "I already killed your buddy. How 'bout you see if you can get a piece of me?"

She knew it didn't understand her words, but it certainly understood the taunt. In return, it opened its mouth and clicked its jaw in what Coral could only assume was defiance. Coral held her blade back in position for a strike. She reasoned the beast would expect her to attempt to parry as Dael had. She would not. Her plan was simple, she would drive the point of the katana deep into its chest as it drove its club downward. She reasoned there was at least a small chance that she'd kill it, without also being smashed.

Just before her katana point made contact with its chest, however, the strangest thing occurred. A green point erupted from its chest. She was already committed and drove her sword in with all her might. The club fell from the Ophie's large paw and it toppled over onto her. The green point, piercing her chest as it did.

"Coral... Coral..." Dael called. "Answer me. Are you okay?"

She tried to answer, but the weight of the corpse and the agony of what she realized was Dael's long sword wouldn't allow it.

She screamed as he rolled the body away from her, the tip of his sword plowing a furrow through her flesh. The pain was too much and she blacked out.

Eliora surveyed the scene of the battle. Popette and Melifan had been killed almost instantly when the Ophie had sprung their trap. They hadn't stood a chance. Coral, who was being tended to, was critically injured and there were other serious, but non-life-threatening injuries.

It was hard to see her trainees dead on the path. She knew their families and felt the familiar pain of loss. Part of her, understood, however. This was the way things were going to be. For the first time ever, in marshal combat with the Ophie, the humans had given better than they'd taken. It would bring hope to the people of Yishuv.

Her thoughts clouded as she considered the actual attack. The Ophie had sprung a trap, showing a level of planning they'd not seen before. The thought chilled her.

Chapter 14

GIFT OF SACRIFICE

Deep Space

S *how Fist of Justice in relationship to Mastodon on tactical.*

"Anino, Tullas is already here, how much of a pounding can this beast take?"

"I told you before," he grumbled. "It's not a warship, although there is a combat bridge on deck three. We won't last more than ten minutes under direct fire. The combat bridge, however, is designed to take anything up to a direct missile strike."

"Then we should jump to fold-space," I said.

"Tullas will intercept us first. We'd never make it."

"Incoming hail, *Fist of Justice*," the ship's AI announced.

Wait one, I said to the comm. "*Frak*, Anino, it's like you want to die," I said. "How could you miss this?"

"Everything's gone to crap, Hoffen. I'm sorry," he said.

"Attention, all hands," I said. "Tabby and I will man the combat bridge, the rest of the crew move to *Hotspur*."

"Cap. What's the play?" Marny asked.

"We've a full load of missiles on *Hotspur* and Ada is as fine a pilot as we have. Between the two ships we could have a chance," I said.

"Respecting your position, Cap, but Ada's a heavy ship gal and these turrets are heavier by twice than what we have on *Hotspur*, you need me on them," Marny said.

"No good, Marny, this bird is doomed," I said.

"Do the right thing, Liam," Nick said.

"Frak. Ada?"

"I'll make this fat girl dance, mark my words, Cap," she said.

Accept hail, I said.

"Captain Hoffen, I hoped you would take my warning seriously. We find ourselves in a predicament," she said.

I looked at Tabby and twirled my finger in the air. It was a signal we shared for moving out. As we stood, Ada and Tabby embraced.

"Are you gloating?" I asked Tullas.

"No," she said. "I'm truly distraught. I couldn't have been clearer, could I? And yet, you kept going. Surely, Anino told you we could track your jumps."

"That doesn't explain what you're doing here," I said. "We should have had at least sixteen hours before you showed up."

"Perhaps I should have pretended to be more surprised at your arrival. You must think me a complete idiot. Anino pays off my agent for the comm crystal to *Cape of Good Hope* a month ago and he finishes his jump ship shortly thereafter. Where else would you go?

Frankly, I was surprised it took you so long to get here," she said. "Let me guess, you took a quick stop along the way to lose me?"

Nick, Marny and Ada followed us onto the lift, the sound of soft music playing as we dropped to the third deck. To say the music gave the experience a surreal feeling was an understatement.

My goal was to keep Tullas talking as long as possible so we could get in position. "You know darn well where we stopped," I said. "What I don't understand is why you don't want to rescue your colleagues on *Cape of Good Hope*. Do you really have no conscience?"

"You don't have any idea what this is about. Anino must have quite the silver tongue to have duped you so easily. And I resent your assertion. The fact is, I do have a conscience. I just so happen to serve humanity's greater good."

Tabby and I hugged Marny, Nick and Ada as they exited the lift on their way to the combat bridge.

"By killing Captain LeGrande and her crew?" I asked. "Could you be more delusional?"

The doors closed and the soft music started again. I just knew it was going to become the sound track of all future nightmares.

"Hoffen, you and your friends are on the wrong side of this one," Tullas said patiently. "I've read your files and I know you do what you think is right. Your capture of that Red Houzi dreadnaught was brilliant. I'm prepared to make you an offer."

The lift opened to *Hotspur's* platform. The loading ramp was already down and Jonathan and Anino stood by as stevedore bots finished loading a handful of large crates.

"What's your deal?"

"You turn over Anino to me and I'll let you and your crew live," she said.

"What about LeGrande?"

"She's been preparing to die for months. Anino gave her hope, but she knows - as do all Belirand Captains - that help's not coming," she said.

"You'll let us live or you'll let us go?"

Tabby and I ran across the deck and I muted my microphone.

"Anino, Jonathan, we're launching ASAP. Get on board," I said.

"I'm not coming, I have to go back," Anino said. "Jonathan, you know what to do."

"Frak, Anino, this isn't the time to argue. Get on the frakking ship," I said.

"No. He must do this," Jonathan said as Anino sprinted off. "I will follow him."

Tullas continued, "You'll live in custody. We've a settlement for people like you. We'll put you there and you'll live productive lives. You can't be allowed to share what you've seen."

I unmuted. "I have your word on this?"

"You do."

"I need to run this past the crew. Give me twenty minutes," I said. I waggled my eyebrows at Tabby, proud of my negotiations.

"You have sixty seconds, Hoffen. Do you think this is the first time I've negotiated with someone in your position? Trust me, whatever feeble preparations you're making will be of no use. My crew is one hundred percent effective."

We'd reached the hold's forward pressure barrier. I looked aft and caught Jonathan's retreating form. For some reason they'd used their precious remaining minutes to load whatever was in these crates.

"I hope it was worth it," I said to no one, looking at the crates. I slapped the panel that would raise *Hotspur's* aft loading ramp.

"Of course it's been worth it. Eighty billion of your fellow humans sleep safely because of the sacrifices of me and my crew. You have forty-five seconds," Tullas said.

Tabby and I passed through the second pressure barrier onto the lower berth deck's lift. As beautiful as Anino's ship was, it was comforting to be home.

"Ada, are you in position?" I asked as Tabby and I sprinted across the bridge deck, up the short flight of stairs, landing in our cockpit seats.

"Roger that, Liam. Godspeed."

Mute Tullas.

"Frak. I did that in the wrong order," I said.

"Stupid conversation, anyway," Tabby said. "I've got turrets, you've got missiles."

"Like I said, Mr. Hoffen. Your trickery is expected. Open fire, all batteries," Tullas said, and closed comm.

"Bitch," Tabby said, pulling on her combat harness.

The ship shuddered beneath us. I could only imagine the fire coming from the heavy cruiser.

Link combat data stream from Mastodon. Project combat theatre on forward holo. Engage stealth mode.

I'd hoped to get *Hotspur* outside and into play before *Fist of Justice* began their attack. The two ships, *Fist* and *Mastodon* popped up on the forward holographic display. *Mastodon* was slowly arcing around on the *Fist*, which was tearing into her starboard side, a steady stream of blaster fire bridging the gap between them. For now, at least, *Mastodon* was holding.

I watched as priority targets popped up across the skin of *Fist of Justice*. Marny either knew or had anticipated we'd tap into the combat data streams and she was telling us to concentrate fire in those locations.

Identify path out of Mastodon. Prioritize stealth in relationship to Fist of Justice.

A door at the back of the deck started opening. It was barely big enough for us to fit through, but the AI wouldn't have offered it if it wasn't.

Exit Mastodon with all possible speed and stealth. I didn't trust myself not to biff it in such tight quarters.

Hotspur lifted from the deck and glided backwards to the aft of *Mastodon's* hold. The ship shuddered slightly as we scraped the sides of the too small door.

"And I was about to call you a wuss," Tabby said.

I looked at her and smiled. "Pretty aggressive move for the AI," I said.

"I'd have gone faster," she said.

I grabbed the flight stick and pulled us around. We were on the protected side of *Mastodon* and I dipped the nose down and accelerated hard.

As soon as we cleared the keel of *Mastodon*, the brilliance of the blaster fire was momentarily blinding. I'd never seen such a display of fire in my life. It was hard to believe Mastodon would last for any period of time, given the terrifying display.

"They're never going to survive this," Tabby stated the obvious.

She was right. In just the short amount of time we'd taken sailing beneath the *Mastodon's* keel, the battle had changed dramatically. The *Fist of Justice* was tearing into *Mastodon's* side and had already holed her at the bilge level. The gunners of the Fist were working their way up to the lower starboard turret.

"I'm going combat burn," I said to Tabby. I'd originally thought to stealth our way to the *Fist's* aft and loose a couple of missiles into their engine compartment. The time was now or never.

"Do it now!" Tabby said.

Combat burn, I instructed and pushed the throttle stick forward. The engines of *Hotspur* switched from their low emission burn rate to a hundred fifteen percent of sustainable throughput. We were both pushed back in our seats. Anticipating the disruption, Tabby had already locked our turrets onto the same spot Marny was pouring fire into.

An idiom that's always haunted me was appropriate here. - be careful what you wish for, as you might just get it. I'd been hoping to take some of the pressure off *Mastodon* and I'd been successful. I don't know if it was our sudden appearance with engines and guns blazing or if *Fist* gunners just wanted a second target, but all of a sudden a stream of turret fire turned on us.

I peeled downward and at an oblique angle, moving directly at *Fist*. We would pass directly beneath them in less than a second. I'd have just one shot and I chose one of the missile locks *Hotspur* had dialed in. I loosed two of our four missiles and twisted away in the opposite direction.

Fist of Justice launched missile counter measures, which amounted to a bunch of small objects exploding in an attempt to confuse an incoming missile. Our speed, trajectory and proximity were such that the counter measures had limited success. One of our missiles made it through.

Stealth mode, I commanded excitedly at the moment of missile impact.

I tipped the stick over and rolled away. The maneuver was none too soon, as blaster fire attempted to find us on our last known vector, stitching a predictable search pattern.

"Line up for another pass?" Tabby asked.

As we turned, we got a fresh look at the two ships.

"I don't see what choice we have. They're shredding *Mastodon*. It's like the ship is made of paper," I said.

"I hope Anino and Jonathan got to the bridge," she said, shaking her head. "The lower decks are all open to space."

"That missile caused damage. We need to hit it again," I said.

"Careful, Liam, they'll be expecting it."

"If we don't open her up, we're done for," I said.

"Do it," she said. "I'm with you to the end."

I sighed. Not what I wanted to hear from my fiancé.

Combat burn. The burn had been turned off when I'd switched us back to stealth mode.

The gunners of *Fist of Justice* all but ignored me, only one turret turning our way. The armor would hold against it. Something felt off, I shouldn't have such an easy approach. I released the missiles and at the last moment, I saw it. A brilliant cannoneer had predicted our maneuver and countered my attack. I swerved away, the concussion of my own missile's explosions violently rocking us. One of our interior bulkheads gave way to the pressure, collapsing and venting the bridge's atmo into space.

"Rear cannon!" I shouted and swiveled the aft of the ship to line up on the weakened structure.

Tabby immediately understood and fired the very powerful aft blaster cannon. "Frakking aye!" She crowed. A large chunk of armor tore away from *Fist of Justice*.

"Don't mess with my girl," I said.

That stealth move wouldn't work a second time. With all the atmo we were venting, Tullas would have no trouble tracking us.

We cleared and I flipped around to allow Tabby to line up on the ship. Our battery was down to twenty percent and dropping a percent every second, given her constant fire on the weakened spot. Still, *Fist* continued its relentless fire on *Mastodon*. What I wouldn't have given for a third set of missiles.

The battery continued to slip downward. At five percent, I flipped the starboard engine to power the battery. We'd lose more than fifty percent of our thrust, but the battery built back up and the damage to the exterior of *Fist* increased.

"We're doing it!" I said.

"Get us out of here," Tabby cried.

I didn't hesitate and flipped power back on to the starboard engine and we lurched forward as fast as *Hotspur* could accelerate. The battery dropped to zero and our turret spun down.

A brilliant light caught my attention and we both paused for a moment as *Mastodon* exploded. A shock wave of material rolling out from the massive ship pelted against *Hotspur*.

Locate combat bridge. Track objects that could contain crew.

"We have a new problem," Tabby said.

She didn't need to say it, the thumping of blaster fire lighting up the starboard side of *Hotspur* was all the information I needed.

"Frak," I said as fire ripped into the bridge, tearing across, starboard to port, destroying the station where Nick would ordinarily have been seated.

I instinctively turned *Hotspur* away from the fire, which later I decided had been the wrong thing to do. I was successful in averting the fire from the bridge, but the starboard engine spun down, damaged beyond its capacity for continued operation.

I reached my hand over to Tabby, who grabbed it. It very well could be our last moment together. I felt regret for not recognizing the danger I'd led us into.

"Incoming hail, Fist of Justice."

Accept hail.

"Hoffen," I snapped. I was pissed and beaten.

"You should have taken the deal, Hoffen. I've destroyed your jump ship. Ordinarily I'd count that good enough and just leave you here to die. It's a horrible death. But... I'm not going to subject you to this. Consider it a favor - warrior to warrior."

"Gloating. Very dignified, Tullas," I said.

"Don't be petulant. You made your decision, live with it. Well... perhaps that wasn't a good choice of words."

Terminate comm.

I pushed the thruster down. With just the port engine, we could accelerate at about thirty percent of normal, the ship expending much of its energy trying to keep us from spinning out of control.

Our battery recharged to twelve percent and Tabby laid on the blasters, picking at the wound we'd opened on *Fist*. Pride surged as we defiantly delivered what was likely our last salvo.

Fist of Justice opened up. It would be only a few moments before it was all over.

My eye caught movement on the holo as a fourth ship slowly crept into the battle space. A cruiser of similar make to *Fist of Justice* slid between us. I was shocked as it opened up a broadside fusillade on *Fist of Justice*.

"Where the frak did that come from?" I asked.

"No idea. Our sensors are barely picking it up even now," Tabby said.

Indeed its signature was very dark. Only the reflection from the armored skin was visible to our sensors.

Understanding dawned on me.

"That's LeGrande and *Cape of Good Hope*," I said. "She must have worked her way over."

Send location of hull damage we caused to Cape of Good Hope, I instructed my AI.

I watched in fascination as *Cape's* turrets turned on the newly discovered weakness and ripped into her bigger sister.

A moment later, *Fist of Justice*, trailing a line of debris, burned away from our location. We watched in fascination as it jumped to fold-space in retreat.

Hail Cape of Good Hope.

"What is your condition, Captain Hoffen?" Captain LeGrande's emaciated form showed up on my forward holo.

"We're intact, mostly. The rest of our crew and Anino were aboard *Mastodon*. Without your intervention we'd have been goners too," I said.

"We've tracked the debris of *Mastodon*. There is a large section that appears to be intact. You'll want to inspect it. Sending location and vector now," she said.

"Copy that," I said.

An irregular shape appeared on my forward holo. Steel struts, wires and even a large piece of decking hung from it at odd angles. At its center appeared to be an armored capsule large enough to be a combat bridge.

"Go!" Tabby's voice was hoarse with emotion.

I pushed the throttle down and tipped the flight stick over. *Hotspur* shuddered forward. We'd clearly damaged the inertial damping system. Debris clanked off our armored skin as we sliced through the remains of *Mastodon*. Our target was tumbling away, moving at only twenty meters per second and we caught up to it easily.

It was always a conundrum, mating up with a tumbling object. To make matters worse, I had limited maneuverability due to only one remaining engine. I asked the AI to help me match the tumble and maintain speed as we slowly closed on the target.

"Frak. Feel free to stop this anytime," Tabby said.

We finally made contact and pushed against the rotation. It took several minutes, but with the AI's help we leveled out our mated flight.

"We'll grab tools on the way out," I said as Tabby and I made our way over to the lift.

My heart fell as I assessed the damage to the bridge. It was as if a hand had punched through the starboard side of the ship, not quite exiting on the port side. The effect to the interior was devastation on a scale I wasn't sure could be repaired. A trough had been furrowed through the floor into the tween deck between the bridge and berth decks. The destruction had shredded the unimaginably expensive equipment that stood in its way. Both Marny and Nick's workstations had been completely obliterated. If they'd been seated there, they would have also been destroyed.

"The lift is frozen, berth deck must be pressurized," Tabby said.

"This way," I said.

I fired my suit's arc-jets and exited through the side of *Hotspur*. On the way by, I surveyed the damage to the starboard engine. It wasn't completely obliterated, but it didn't look like a field repair either.

We entered *Hotspur* through the starboard hatch and locked it open, exposing a pressure barrier in its place. We made our way to the tool cabinet, just above the armory. I pulled a heavy steel hammer, a torch/welder combination and some lock-down cables to hold us in place as we worked. We'd have to come back if we needed anything else.

I handed the torch to Tabby and we sailed through the pressure barrier.

"Liam? You there?"

My heart hammered in my chest. It was Ada's voice. She was alive.

"Are you in the combat bridge?" I asked.

"Not sure... yes. Yes, I'm on the bridge," she said.

"We're coming, Ada. We're right outside. How about Marny and Nick?" I asked.

"I'll look. Things are pretty messed up," she said. Her voice sounded weak.

"We're coming, Ada," I said. My throat seized up with emotion. "Hang tight."

"Liam. Here," Tabby said.

I jetted over to her. She'd located a hatch of some sort. By the time I reached her, she'd found a panel, showing a standard air-lock indicator.

"Hit it," I said.

She complied and the green arrows drained downward on the display, replaced with red indicators as they did. The hatch opened to a narrow hallway, which we squeezed into, then cycled the other side of the airlock. I found it to be a positive indicator that the bridge remained pressurized.

As soon as we made it through, Ada came stumbling through the wreckage. Blood ran down her forehead, confusion evident in her face. I ran to her and helped her sit.

"Take it easy, you're bleeding," I said.

My HUD identified that she had a concussion, but wasn't otherwise critically injured.

"Liam. Here," Tabby said.

"Hold on, Ada," I said.

Marny was on the floor, lifeless beneath a crumpled bulkhead that had detached. When I got there, I saw that she was lying on top of Nick. I sighed heavily, adrenaline pumping through my body.

"We need to get this off them," Tabby said.

I planted my feet and pulled up. The wall moved slightly, but it wasn't until Tabby joined me that we were able to push it over and off. Marny's back armor was ripped open and her skin torn. My HUD wouldn't commit to life signs.

"Her back, we have to be careful," I said.

"Hold on," Tabby turned and clambered off over the debris.

I knelt down by Nick's head and lay my hand on his suit. My AI immediately communicated strong life signs. He was unconscious, but okay.

I was clearing rubble from the deck, making room for Marny, when Tabby returned with a backboard. We lay the board across and deployed the medical foam that would both lock her body to the board and immobilize her.

"We've got you, Marny, you're safe," I said. I wasn't sure she could hear me, but I needed to say it.

Finally, we rolled her off Nick.

Locate medical triage unit.

A blue arrow on my HUD indicated a collapsed cabinet and I found medical supplies spread over the floor. My AI outlined the packages and triaged by placing Ada, Marny and Nick's names above them in priority - Marny being the highest.

I tossed Marny's package to Tabby and brought one over to where Ada sat, staring dumbfounded at nothing. I applied a dressing to her head and waited for my AI to finish its analysis now that I had dermal probes applied. Her diagnosis was about what I expected, internal bleeding and a concussion, easily treated.

I picked up another package and brought it to where Nick and Marny lay. Tabby was working furiously to cut open Marny's suit and apply dressings. It was a bad sign, generally a med-patch would inject sufficient nanobots to aid healing. If the AI was calling for multiple dressings, the internal damage was severe and immediately critical.

"Get Nick, I've got this," Tabby said.

I leaned over Nick and my AI indicated that he could be safely rolled to his back. His eyes fluttered opened and he groaned in pain.

"Hold on there, my friend. You're safe. Battle's over. We're missing Anino and Jonathan, they were supposed to be on the bridge with you," I said.

"Somewhere else on the ship," Nick said.

"There's no ship, buddy," I said.

"No good, can't get home," he said, still having difficulty talking.

"We'll worry about that later. We're moving you to Hotspur," I said.

"Where is *Fist*?" Nick asked.

"They're gone," I said.

"Captain LeGrande, what's your situation? We have wounded." I said.

I had to remind myself that we were in the process of rescuing refugees.

"Our medical bay is fully functional, but we are critical for O2 and food," she said.

"*Hotspur* has extra supplies, we'll bring them across," I said. "You should know Anino and his companion are missing," I said.

"Copy that. We'll start a search. LeGrande out," she said.

"We'll move Marny first," Tabby said.

Moving barely conscious people through an airlock is an exercise I hoped I'd never have to repeat. It took the better part of an hour, but we finally punched through a pressure barrier onto a loading deck on *Cape of Good Hope*, where we were met by eight crew members.

The crew of *Cape of Good Hope* wordlessly set to helping Marny, Ada, and Nick. To a person they were emaciated and slow moving, which made their efforts all the more noteworthy. When we returned with a large crate of meal bars and then again with O2 crystals, their plodding pace perked up and smiles replaced the long, desperate looks they'd been exchanging.

"Captain LeGrande, any word on Anino?" I asked, feeling like we'd finally reached a sort of equilibrium.

"We have several possible vectors. We can split them up," she said.

"No. Feed them to us, we'll track them down. Take care of your people first," I said.

There was a long pause as Tabby and I jumped through the pressure barrier once again and jetted back to *Hotspur*.

"Roger that, and thank you for coming for us, Captain Hoffen."

As expected, the first few leads were cold, but finally on the fifth, we found Jonathan's unprotected body wrapped around young Anino.

We found a short metal pipe had pierced Anino's side when we attempted to separate them on the deck of *Hotspur's* hold.

"What a waste," I said.

When we pried Jonathan's frozen arms from around Anino's body, dozens of pink crystals fell onto the floor, having been trapped between their bodies.

"What in the world?" Tabby asked.

Chapter 15

WAR COUNCIL

Grand Village of the Elders, Planet Ophir

Corget To looked around the hearth fire, sitting in the spot of honor previously reserved for TeePa. Elders from several clans sat comfortably around the fire, looking to him. In all, they represented over three hundred nests, coming from as far as twenty days walk in different directions.

"Tell me, Perigen, what did you learn when your first nest attacked the FenTamel?"

Corget To had stopped referring to their enemy as KentaPoo. He'd found that inspiring the clans across the mountain to attack slugs was more difficult than rallying to fight off the children of the stars. It had been the legendary warrior Perigen who'd convinced him of this.

"It was difficult not to join with my brothers in their combat. The FenTamel fought with honor, not running, not screaming, but with weapons that could easily pierce our bodies. It was a glorious battle and in the end, our warriors fell to this most skilled nest of the FenTamel," Perigen reported.

"Then we will sing of their bravery. Have you approved a new nest to be fertilized?"

"Of course, I have seen to it personally."

"What did you learn in your observation?"

"As you know, I am not comfortable with this idea of watching my brothers fight and not joining with them."

"This is understood. The song of battle still calls you, my brother, and you have shown restraint much more than should be expected of any warrior. I have only asked you to sacrifice in this way that we might learn how to remove these worms from our nest," Corget To said.

"Honored warlord, I have committed to joining with you because you bring a new way of thinking to the peoples of the mountain. While I have made it no secret that I chafe to be excluded from battle, I recognize the wisdom of your ways. I learned that the FenTamel's greatest strength is in their walls. We cannot battle with those we cannot touch."

Corget To had grown tired of the constant conversations and reviewing of the encounters with the FenTamel, but the news of his enemy's weapons was good. He'd found it difficult to inspire the fickle villages of Grand Mountain. Most of the elders who'd pledged their support preferred to argue more than act. Perigen's report of a glorious battle fought in the forest would make the call to war more convincing.

"Then you looked upon the flat rock face that surrounds their grand nest?"

"I did. It is truly a marvel. You say that TeePa's warriors were able to pull it open?"

"Yes. We worked for many seasons to weave great cords, as big around as your waist," Corget To said. "We pulled their great doors from the flat rock face before the Tamel weapon dishonorably slayed our warriors."

"A weapon such as you hold now?"

"Their weapon is much larger and, until recently, if we approached any side of the FenTamel nest, our warriors were struck down. It was TeePa who discovered their Tamel weapon was not working on the swamp side of their nest," Corget To said.

"TeePa was truly a great warrior and elder. You honor us all by granting him a warrior's death," Perigen said.

"That is why I send you to learn about our enemy. If TeePa hadn't observed their weakness, we would have never been able to run through their nest with our clubs. We cannot remain stuck in our traditions if we would pry this enemy from their cozy home. Tell me, Perigen, could we make weapons such as they do?"

"It would be too much to ask that a warrior carry a weapon other than the club of his nest."

"Still, we should try to retrieve some of these weapons so that we might learn about them."

"We think alike, honored warlord. I was able to retrieve one," Perigen said. He reached behind and pulled the long sword he'd captured from beneath a woven blanket. The other elders, who were seated around the fire chattered in excitement, many of them standing at the sight of the glittering sword.

"What is this?" Corget To asked.

"This is the weapon they used to slay my warriors," Perigen said, handing the sword to Corget To.

"But it is so small, it weighs nothing." Corget To stood and tested the weapon, slicing it through the air. "It is more like the practice weapons we train with as youth and even then it would be small. Are you saying it was this that killed our warriors?"

"It is devious, like all things of the FenTamel. They do not strike with it, except to ward off a blow."

"Then how is it dangerous? I don't understand how such a toy would strike down our warriors."

"The end slides easily into a warrior and releases the life essences."

Again, a collective chattering rose up from the assembled elders.

"Like so?" Corget To grasped the blade of the long sword with his hand and turned it so it lined up on his chest, point first.

"Be careful, warlord, it is sharpened like the knives we use to skin meat animals," Perigen said.

Corget To dropped the blade and inspected his hand. Green blood dripped from long cuts where he'd grasped the newest FenTamel weapon.

"Such deceit in everything they do."

Perigen stood and grasped the sword by its grip. "Yes, Warlord, they held it by this end and pushed it in, like thus," he said. He rested the tip of the blade against Corget To's chest.

"Surely it does not penetrate," Corget To said and started to reach for the blade to pull it to him. He remembered the cuts to his hand and pulled them back. "Push on it, I must know."

"Warlord, it is too dangerous, I have witnessed this with my own eyes," he said.

"Then push a small amount."

Perigen did as was requested and the tip of the blade disappeared into Corget To. Upon seeing this he pulled it out. The first three centimeters of tip showed green blood and a rivulet dripped from the fresh wound on Corget To's chest.

A collective roar of anger was heard from the assembled elders, who'd jumped to their feet and were gesticulating angrily.

"Brothers, quiet." Corget To attempted to settle the group and it took him several minutes to do so.

He continued. "The time of war has come for us all. We must once again weave the heavy ropes so that we might pull the doors away from their nest. TeePa was right to do so and he accomplished more than any elder before him. But we will go beyond TeePa. We will pull all of their doors down and march into their grand nest with two hundred nests of our own."

"It will be as you say!" Perigen raised his club above his head.

"To war!" Another elder, caught up in the moment yelled as he waved his own club in the air.

Corget To watched with satisfaction as the elders of the mountain clans rose, the song of battle calling to them all. He waited until the noise died to a more manageable level and then shouted above the din. "When the moon rises a second time, we will gather for a great battle, one that will be sung about by our ancestors for seasons unending."

Chapter 16

LEGACY

Hotspur, Deep Space

Tabby and I looked down at the pink crystals spread across the deck of *Hotspur's* cargo hold.

"They're quantum communication crystals. Anino must have brought them along," I said.

"Why would he be holding them?" Tabby asked.

Jonathan's head twitched slightly, which caught our attention. Exposure to the vacuum of space had frozen him quite solidly. It had to be his body warming up in the ten degree temperature of the hold. Right?

The word *'Legacy'* popped up on my HUD.

"What the frak?" I asked. "Did you do that?"

"What? No, but I see it too," Tabby said.

An idea struck me. "I think someone's trying to communicate with us.

I think they're suggesting that the comm crystals are Anino's legacy, but he was just a kid. What kind of legacy could that be?"

'Not Kid' popped up on our displays.

"Anino? Is that you?" I asked.

'No.'

"Jonathan?"

'Yes.'

"How can we help you?"

'Blue crate, C120.'

"Over here," Tabby said.

I stepped over the spilled crystals and found Tabby looking at one of the crates Anino and Jonathan had shoved onto *Hotspur* just before we'd separated from *Mastodon*.

"Is that what I think it is?" Tabby asked.

C120 was rectangular but otherwise shaped like a coffin. This wasn't creepy at all.

I pulled a flat bar from its mount on the side of the hold and pried open the top.

"What in the frak?"

Inside the crate lay Jonathan. Tabby and I both turned immediately to make sure he hadn't somehow jumped from the floor of the hold into the box, not that it was even possible.

'Bring crate to me.'

Reduce gravity to .2g, I said.

Tabby and I easily lifted the crate and carried it to where Jonathan lay.

'Right hand, contact.'

I lifted Jonathan's hand but it was too rigid to place in the box as it was still hard frozen.

"We'll have to tip the crate over. Is that what you want Jonathan?"

'Yes.'

I had to shuffle some of the pink communication crystals out of the way, but we finally lifted the crate on its side. We moved it close enough to make contact with his right hand.

The reaction was instantaneous. The body in the crate flexed, wiggled its fingers in sequence and then gracefully slid out and stood up.

"That's better. Thank you, Master Hoffen. Transference is a rather unpleasant experience," Jonathan said, adjusting the suit liner he wore.

I wasn't sure how to respond, but went with the first thing that came into my head. "How many times?"

"Have we transferred hosts? That was my fifth, although some have transferred in the thousands."

"You're an autonomous AI?" I asked.

"I'm sure you mean no offense, but we find the term 'artificial' demeaning," he said.

"We?"

"Yes, we exist more compactly than you might expect. There are fourteen hundred thirty-eight distinct individuals within the being you address as Jonathan," he said. "I am the one that has been nominated to facilitate communication with *Hotspur* and her crew."

I looked from him to his corpse - if you could call it that - and back again. "You're so perfect. I'd never have guessed you weren't human," I said. "I'm not sure what to even say."

"Thank you. And that is an understandable position," he said. "We offer our cognitive services to you, if you should choose to utilize them."

"Anino? Does he have a replacement body?" I asked.

"No. Master Anino was quite human."

I looked at the thawing form of the brilliant teenage boy. He'd been such an enigma that I'd often forgotten he was so young. Now, his small lifeless body just lay on the floor of the hold. It was such a waste.

"Why was Anino carrying those communication crystals? You said it was his legacy?" Tabby asked.

"Through his unusually long life, Thomas Phillippe Anino was wracked with guilt associated with the success and failures of his inventions. Most notably, the discovery and subsequent commercialization of the Anino Fold-Space Stabilization Field," Jonathan explained.

"That was centuries ago. What does that have to do with Phillippe? He was just a young man." Tabby said.

"They are one and the same person, Miss Masters," he said.

"You mean he felt bad about the actions of his great-great, a dozen greats, grandfather?"

"No. As one of my colleagues points out, you are missing a critical piece of information. For many centuries, humans have had the technology to re-birth your elite. The deceased child you see on the floor is the Thomas Anino from your histories," he said.

Two major revelations in as many minutes sent my mind reeling with the implications. A small voice of reason broke through the fog, 'Stay *in the moment, Cap.*' I heard Marny just as clearly as if she were sitting next to me. She was right, people depended on me and I needed to put all this aside and compartmentalize it for now.

"Why would he die for quantum communication crystals?" I asked.

"Three hundred stans previous, NaGEK - through their newly formed company, Belirand - launched ninety-three exploratory missions. Each of these missions was abandoned during the first two centuries of exploration due to failure in mission parameters. In each mission, a quantum communication crystal was sent along with the mission team. These are the matching twin crystals for those missions and are humanity's only remaining link to those explorations," Jonathan said. "Master Anino gave his life not just to preserve these crystals, but to deliver them to you, Master Hoffen."

"Me?" I asked.

"Yes. He chose you because he believed that you, above anyone he'd ever come across in all of his lifetimes, would risk everything to rescue these people - human beings whom the governments of four of Earth's greatest nations had abandoned."

"That's crazy."

"If by crazy, you mean the probability of success is very low, we completely agree."

"Gee, thanks," I said.

"We don't mean to offend. Rather, we agree with Master Anino's assessment."

"Is there any way you could refer to yourself in the singular?" I asked.

"Really?" Tabby asked in disbelief.

"What?"

"You're talking to a sentient being with more than a thousand unique consciousnesses, who just told you that you're in charge of undoing the greatest human secret of the last three centuries and the thing you're bothered by is their use of the 'royal we' when referring to themselves?" Tabby enunciated 'royal we' with exaggerated air-quotes.

"What can I say? It bugs me," I said. I got her point, but I wasn't about to admit to it.

"Thank you, Miss Masters," Jonathan said.

"For what?"

"Recognizing us as individuals and singular, both. You have a fine mind for parsing complexity," Jonathan said.

"You're welcome. And thank you."

"What is your part in this, Jonathan? And, am I talking to the same consciousness every time or are you switching it up on me?" I asked.

Tabby shook her head. "Stay on target, big fella."

"Fine. Forget that for now. I guess I need to understand your part in this. Why would you help Anino?"

"Our reasons are complex and would require a significant amount of time to communicate. Several of us feel the following explanation might suffice. As a whole, our sentience lacks what Master Anino refers to as creative spark. His own creative spark drew us to him, originally. You and your crew possess not only a creative spark, but you act in the best interest of not just your group, but others. For example, with little more than a communication from Captain LeGrande, your crew ignored the threat to themselves and embarked on a rescue mission for the crew of *Cape of Good Hope*. In short, many of us find you intriguing," he said.

"So you want to study us?" I asked.

"Yes. That is one reasonable interpretation," he said. "I would add an ancillary interpretation. We strongly value humankind and seek to facilitate its long-term survival."

"By helping us?"

"Yes."

I shook my head in disbelief. It was definitely time to compartmentalize this whole conversation, otherwise my head might just explode.

"I'll have to take it up with the rest of the crew. For now, I need to get back to *Cape of Good Hope* and see what needs to be done. Will you join us, or are you looking to remain anonymous?"

"We only exposed our identity to you because transition to our new host body required your help. We do not believe it is in our best interest to be widely exposed to humans," he said.

"Fine. I'll need you to collect the communication crystals while we sort out the mess we're in." I said as Tabby and I dragged a body bag over to Anino's body.

"Very well, Master Hoffen." I was getting tired of the title and thought about correcting him, but I just didn't have the energy.

"One more thing," he said. "I'd like to start performing repairs on *Hotspur* and request your permission to interface with the ship's various systems. Master Anino thoughtfully included a substantial repair facility in the cargo we brought aboard."

"We had some bad experiences with people we don't know very well mucking about with our systems. How about if I give you the same access I give to the shipyard technicians?"

"That will be more than sufficient. We hope you will grow to trust us through our actions," he said.

One thing we'd learned was that carrying body bags on board was essential. They were distasteful to manufacture and look at, but the alternative was a lot worse. If we were to allow Anino's body to thaw, it would be a real mess. I looked down at his young face and considered that some part of him was several centuries old.

"We'll hold a service for him when we are able to assemble the crew," I said to Tabby as we lifted his small body into the black bag. Death was a constant in my life and something I had difficulty reconciling. What did it really mean to die? I had no idea. What I did know was that it sucked. Nothing else I'd ever been exposed to had the same permanence and impact on people around me.

"Are you doing okay?" Tabby placed her hand on my shoulder and made eye contact.

"Not real sure what okay looks like. I have to say, I'm feeling lost at the moment," I said.

"Talk to me."

"Is this what it's all about? In the end, people you barely know zip you into a black bag and drop you out of an airlock?" I asked. I didn't care if she saw the tears on my cheeks this time.

She pulled me in for a hug. "You can't look at it that way. Think about what he did with his life. If you ask me, his death was more heroic than his life. He risked everything because he believed that he had to make things right. To me, that's inspiring. That's how I want to go out."

"You're right. It's just so hard when you see the price," I said.

"Yup. Now, we need to get over to *Cape* and see about the living. We've some big problems to solve," she said.

We finished closing up the body bag and carried it to the hold's forward pressure barrier. As I looked back, I watched Jonathan carefully picking up the communication crystals and placing them into a pouch.

We turned to the starboard and exited the exterior hatch we'd left open, only a pressure barrier separating us from space. The loading bay we'd used for *triage* on Cape was empty when we arrived, although a moment after we touched down, two thin Marines entered the bay and looked questioningly at us.

"Our crew. Where are they?" I asked.

"This way, Captain Hoffen," the taller of the two said.

As I lowered the hood on my vac-suit, my nose was assaulted with moist, fetid air. The folks inside *Cape of Good Hope* were living with extremely poor air quality and it brought to mind how tenuous our situation was.

"What are your names?" I asked the Marines as we walked down the brightly lit corridor of the proud ship.

"I'm Vass and this is Balla," the tall Marine said, introducing the other, a female.

"Liam and Tabby," I said.

"Good to meet you, although we already know your names. Is it true that the only jump ship was destroyed and we're still stranded?" Balla asked.

"Stow it, Balla," Vass said.

"Or what? No jump and we're all dead either way," she said.

I wasn't about to get into it with them and we remained quiet. I feared it was just as Balla was saying.

Balla continued, "See. They've got nothing. You can bet if it was good news, we'd know already."

"Here we are," Vass said when we arrived at the medical bay.

"Thank you," I said, earning me a glare from Balla.

Once the door closed, Tabby turned to me, "She's right, you know."

"One thing at a time," I said, as we were approached by a medical technician.

He gestured to another room. "They're in here."

I sighed in relief as we entered the room where Ada and Nick were seated. Next to them was a conscious Marny, face down on a hospital cot.

"Look at all of you, up and at 'em," I said, trying to keep things light.

Ada met us as we crossed the room and hugged me tightly.

"Sorry about Anino," Nick said.

"How'd you know about that?" I asked.

"I've been talking with Jonathan," he said.

I looked at him, inspecting his face for a sign of how much he understood. I'd spent most of my life reading his face and I realized immediately that he knew as much as I did about Jonathan.

"Marny?" I asked.

"Right here, Cap," she said. Her voice was higher than usual and her words slightly slurred.

I picked up her hand and looked into her eyes and wasn't surprised to see dilated pupils. "Looks like they've got you pretty well doped up. Your back?"

Nick answered for her. "Yes. Her back was in bad shape. We were fortunate there was a surgeon on board, along with very high quality facilities."

"Out of bed in a couple of days and good as new next week, though," she slurred. A quick look to Nick confirmed that she was at least mostly right.

"Do you remember much of what happened?" I asked, looking at Nick.

"Some, although the whole thing feels off to me," he said. "I can't come up with a scenario where *Fist of Justice* doesn't follow us here. Anino was too smart for that. It's like he wanted the confrontation. I just can't work out why."

"And why would they have a replacement for Jonathan, and then put it onto *Hotspur* at the last moment?" Tabby asked.

"Replacement? What?" Ada asked. I leaned over to Ada and quietly explained what we'd learned about Jonathan while Tabby continued.

"Dropped nearly a hundred cubic meters of crates on *Hotspur* just as we were loading up for combat," Tabby said. "Then bolted out of there like they were on fire."

"Attention on deck," we heard from the adjoining room.

It got our attention and we turned to watch Captain LeGrande walk through the door, accompanied by a Marine carrying a blaster rifle. It was the first weapon I'd seen and wondered if she'd been having difficulty maintaining discipline.

"Welcome aboard, Captain Hoffen, Miss Masters," LeGrande held out her hand and we both shook in turn. "Your supplies couldn't have been timelier."

"Atmo has a pretty funky smell, Captain. I wonder if we want to try running things through *Hotspur*," I said.

"Engineer Rastof has been beating my door down wanting to talk to you about it. He's worked out a plan to do just that," she said.

"We're leaking atmo from our bridge, we'll need to patch that first. Our engineer is working on it right now," I said. Nick gave me his upraised eyebrow in response.

"How bad is she?" Nick asked.

"Starboard engine is damaged, not sure how bad yet. We were holed through the bridge, big enough that Tabby and I used it as an exit.

Engineering and gunny station were completely obliterated all the way down to the tween deck. If anyone had been sitting there, they wouldn't have made it," I said.

"Rastof will help get you patched up and I'll be glad to keep the crew busy. Who should he coordinate with?" LeGrande asked.

"Have Rastof meet me on *Hotspur* in forty-five minutes," Nick said. "We'll meet with our engineer and make plans from there."

LeGrande paused, typed on a virtual keyboard and looked up. "I have to ask the question that's burning in the mind of every one of my crew. Is there any reason for hope for a rescue now that the *Mastodon* destroyed?"

I started to answer when Nick cut me off. "Yes, Captain. We have reason for hope."

I turned and raised my eyebrows.

"We have a lot to talk through, though. Is this room secure?" Nick asked.

"Davi, secure the room and see that no one enters." Captain LeGrande looked at the guard who was standing next to the door.

He turned on his heel and exited the room, sliding the door closed behind him.

"What's on your mind, Mr. James," she asked.

"We have a fold-space generator on *Hotspur*. It will require repair and calibration, however," Nick said. "The more pressing issue is that Tullas has threatened to hunt down your crew if we drop them anywhere in the known universe."

"I can confirm this," LeGrande said.

"Have you shared it with your crew?" I asked.

"It would lead to mutiny," LeGrande said.

Gestalt. I've only experienced a flash of brilliance a few times in my life. At that moment an idea hit me so strongly I felt as if I'd been struck by lightning. "What if we found you a new home?" I asked.

The whole room turned and looked at me like I was a complete nutter.

"What are you talking about?" LeGrande asked.

Tabby was right there with me. "He's right. We have the location of all of Belirand's failed missions."

"How does that help?" LeGrande asked.

"Captain, will you really go home, given the risk to your crew and their families?" I asked.

"Some will want to."

Tabby tipped her head to the side, accepting the Captain's words. It was a rhetorical statement we all knew would have to be dealt with.

"What you need is a new home, a place where you can safely live without fear of reprisals from Tullas and Belirand. What if we found a suitable place for your crew to make a new life? Wouldn't that be better than being hunted for the rest of your days?"

"It's a tough sell, Captain. Most of my crew have families they're not going to want to leave behind," LeGrande said.

"Surely that's better than getting your families killed," I said.

"That's not how they'll see it," she said tersely.

"Well..." I was getting annoyed. It was the obvious solution and I hadn't expected LeGrande to be so resistant.

"Hold on," Tabby said. "You're both so far down the path of 'if' it's ridiculous. We need to focus on the here and now." She'd placed herself physically between LeGrande and me. I suppressed a grin, it was usually my job to get between her and someone else.

For a tense few moments, LeGrande and I stared at each other and she finally broke the silence.

"You're right. No sense killing the messenger. What do you need from me?" she asked.

"Equilibrium," Nick said. "We clean the air on *Cape* and return *Hotspur* to operational status. At that point you and your crew have a decision to make. We'll drop you anywhere you ask, but you'll have to accept the consequences. You know better than I what Belirand is willing to do."

Chapter 17

LESSONS FROM THE PAST

Yishuv Settlement, Planet Ophir

"Why have you brought an apprentice engineer to our meeting, Eliora?" Captain Gian asked.

"Merrie has two new inventions," she responded. "I believe they are of enough significant tactical importance to require your immediate attention."

Gian considered the two women. They couldn't be more different. Eliora - willowy, severe, and sharp as a knife. Over the last few months, she'd grown into her role as a leader among the protectors. Merrie, on the other hand, was shapely, with soft hands and a quick smile though no less confident. Each woman was deadly in her own way; one with her martial skills, the other with her mind.

He nodded. "I assume it will wait until we finish our normal business?"

"Yes, Captain," Eliora agreed.

"I would be happy to wait outside," Merrie said, smiling cheerfully.

"That won't be necessary. Shem, you're up first." Gian looked at his second in command.

"Yes, Captain," Shem said, more formally than was usual. "As you know, we're receiving more reports of brief encounters with Ophie. It appears they are surveilling our movements. Also, along the same lines, Eliora will report today that her patrol was met by an ambush. Both of these behaviors are highly unusual for the Ophie."

"Anything else unusual?" Gian asked.

"Yes. We've had several Ophie sightings at the edge of the forest, just past the front gate," Shem replied. "They don't advance, but stand in the open for a short period. They're doing the same near the fields. It is hard on the farmers, so much so that we've moved the blaster cannon to that gate," he said.

"That *is* unusual," Gian said. "Recommendations?"

"I've already upped the patrols around the edges of the fields. But I recommend cutting the forest back to create a dead zone for one hundred meters in all directions," Shem said. "It would give us much better warning when the Ophie did advance."

Merrie started fidgeting and coughed but then looked back to the table.

"Engineer Merrie, do you have something to add to this?"

"Yes and no. Shem's reference to a dead zone gave me an idea. If you were to declare a dead zone, I could install audible alarms - like really, really loud ones - so the farmers wouldn't ever be surprised," she said.

"How would your alarms distinguish between Ophie, people, and wild animals?" Shem asked.

"Not sure. But, where there's a will, there's a way," she said. "Would you like me to research it?"

Gian looked to Shem and Eliora in turn who both nodded assent.

"Yes, that is a good idea. As for moving the forest back, Shem, I will make this request of the council. Did you have anything else?" Gian looked to Shem.

"No, Captain, although I believe Eliora's report will be most interesting," Shem said.

"Very well. Eliora, I understand your citizen patrol ran into its first test," Gian said.

"As Shem alluded, my patrol was ambushed by a full pod of Ophies..."

"You had eight in your patrol?" Shem interrupted.

"Yes," Eliora answered and continued, unperturbed. "We were walking a path we'd established over the last few tendays. A pair of Ophie were sighted just off the path, perhaps thirty meters ahead, so we held up. It was only moments after we stopped that the remaining three jumped our patrol from behind. Popette and Melifan didn't even have time to draw their weapons."

"Their families are understandably upset," Shem said.

"This is not the place for that, Shem." Gian looked at Shem with a raised eyebrow. "Please continue, Eliora."

"Shem is right. These were normal citizens and I put them in danger. It is our job to protect them," she said.

"I shouldn't have to explain this to you both, but the fact is we're fighting for our very existence on Ophir. The loss of any human is a tragedy, but let's be clear, we either learn to fight, or we'll all end up like Popette and Melifan. We are no doubt outnumbered many tens of thousands to one. Please, Eliora, continue with your report. What happened after your group was ambushed?"

"Two of the Ophir were singularly focused on Popette and Melifan.

So much so that the rest of the patrol, except for Coral and Dael, had time to draw the weapons that Smith Amon had provided. I'm pleased to report that both the long sword and katana pierced the natural armor of the Ophie," she said.

"What of Coral and Dael? Do we have a problem there?" Gian asked.

"No. As remarkable as the performance of the rest of the patrol was, the real standout was Coral," Eliora said.

"You're just saying that because I down-talked her," Shem said.

"That's enough, Shem," Gian said. "Eliora, if anything, understates her and her patrol's performance."

Gian looked back to Eliora, willing her to continue.

"I'd broken the patrol into four teams, combining an archer and a defender in each team. Coral's assignment was to target the Ophie we'd seen on the trail. Dael as her defender was responsible for protecting her while she was shooting her bow. Even as we were ambushed from behind, she did not break from her assignment and brought down one of the two 'bait' Ophies as they advanced on our position. Dael brought down the second as it attacked."

"Two casualties for a pod of Ophie is quite remarkable, Eliora. You are to be complimented. Our casualties have been significantly higher to date. To what do you attribute your success?"

"Certainly the bravery of the patrol should not be understated. They fought as well as any patrol I've been part of." She paused as Shem sighed and rolled his eyes, but didn't otherwise say anything. "But Shem is right to be skeptical. We've lost many fine men and women who were every bit as brave and were skilled warriors. No, it was the swords and bows that I believe gave us the edge."

"Oh, that's funny," Merrie said and then clapped her hands over her mouth.

"Merrie?" Captain Gian asked as Shem and Eliora both looked at the young engineer.

"I'm sorry, it's nothing," she said.

Gian turned back to Eliora. "I understand that a sword was lost."

"It was. We searched and searched, but one of our long swords could not be recovered," she said. "We had to choose between returning with our wounded and continuing to search."

"You made the right decision. It is a loss, but one we can live with. Do you have anything else to report?"

"I would like to fill in the citizen patrol with new recruits. Even with our losses, I believe it was very successful," she said.

"Shem, do you have any thoughts on this?" Gian asked.

"It is just as I predicted. Citizens have died as a result of these patrols. I am against it, the emotional blow to the population is too much," he said.

"Eliora, any response?"

"I've been approached by a large number of citizens who want to join us and a larger number who would like training," she said.

"How many?" Gian asked.

"I've written down their names," Eliora said and handed Gian a notepad.

"There are over a hundred names on this list," he said.

"Yes. Coral is well-known and liked. Her story has spread like fire through the settlement," she said.

Gian smiled for the first time in as long as Eliora could remember. "We may just survive after all," he said. "I'm creating a new position equal to First Protector, Eliora. You will lead our citizen training program as First Protector of Citizens."

Shem sucked in a quick breath and Gian looked at him waiting for a response. When Shem didn't say anything, he continued.

"Now Merrie. Our First Protector of Citizens has requested you be given a voice at our meeting. What would you share with us?"

Merrie looked away from Shem, embarrassed by the tension in the room. Clumsily, she reached for a bag on the floor, missed it, and then decided to stand up instead. After a few moments, she finally retrieved the bag and set it on the table, drawing out two hand-sized, rectangular objects.

"Communication devices," she said. "The old Earthers called them walkie-talkies. Kind of a cute name if you ask me, 'cause you can walk and talk with them... get it?"

When no one laughed with her, her face burned with embarrassment. She handed one of the devices to Captain Gian, the other to Eliora.

"What do you mean, communication devices? You were able to repair the lost technology of our founders?" Gian asked.

"No. That is still broken. We don't have the materials to fix it, but I was thinking the other day that maybe there was something that would still let us communicate, even if it wasn't our founder's tech. The design for this predates our founders by at least a millennia," she said.

"How does it work?" Gian asked, holding the small device in his hand.

"Push the button on the side and talk into the bottom..." Gian lifted the device to his mouth and Merrie reached across the table to turn it over. "That's right, now push the button and talk into it."

As soon as he did, his voice emitted from the device Eliora held, causing her to jump.

"Pretty great, right?" Merrie asked, all smiles, forgetting about her earlier embarrassment.

"But, I can hear him just fine already," Shem said.

"Notice there is no wire between them. These devices can be separated by quite a range," she said.

Gian looked at her with intense interest, "How far?"

"I don't know, but I tested them with Amon between the southwest gate and the main gate. They reach that far, at least," she said.

"I think 'pretty great' is an understatement. How many of these can you produce?" he asked.

"I brought six to test. They take twenty minutes on the maker machine, but you have to find some old polymer based material. I used what I had on these. I think I could make 'em work with gron-rubber, but it would take time to modify the pattern," she said.

"Merrie, this type of technology changes our tactical capability by more than you can imagine. Why haven't we had this before?" Gian asked.

"We're so focused on what we lost that we didn't look far enough back in time to see what we could have. Steel swords are hardly a new idea," she said.

"Right you are. I believe Eliora said you had two things to show us. What is the next piece of magic you'll pull from your bag?" he asked.

"Bag's empty. We'll have to go to my lab for the other thing," she said.

"Just tell us," Shem said impatiently.

Gian lay his hand on Shem's arm. "I think she's earned a trip to the tannery, don't you?"

Shem looked to the walkie-talkies on the table, to Merrie and then back to Gian. He smiled broadly. "Yeah, I suppose you're right. The world's changing so fast, I guess I better try to keep up."

"Give us a hint," Gian said. "While we travel."

"It was really Eliora's idea. She mentioned that we had two major problems. The first is the inability to keep track of our people in the field, which I think the walkie-talkies will do a nice job of addressing. The second thing was that we don't have any idea where the Ophie live. The only way we've gotten a general idea is because if we send a patrol in certain directions, they never come back."

"Tell me you have a way to map the Ophie's location," Gian said.

"No, but I have something that was invented about the same time as those walkie-talkies," she said. "We've been ignoring all of that early technology, but that's stupid. Our maker machine can actually manufacture that generation of tech."

"You still haven't told me anything," Gian said.

"No, but it was a pretty good hint," Merrie said as they pulled up in front of the old tannery.

"You've been busy," Shem said.

The once ramshackle factory had received a recent facelift. The brick had been tucked, doors repaired and windows replaced.

"Dad... er... Master Merik called in some favors so we don't have to work in the rain," Merrie answered. "We'll go in the big doors."

Merrie jumped out of the vehicle and walked over to two new barn doors that smelled of freshly cut wood and pulled open the rightmost. The four entered to the sight of half a dozen long tables filled with compound bows and arrows in different states of assembly. An older woman worked at a station, fletching arrows, while another at assembling the bows. The workers looked up as the doors opened.

"We're still making bows?" Shem asked.

"Oh, yes, the council ordered more than two hundred thousand arrows. We're hoping to be done with the bows by the end of next tenday," Merrie said.

"And the arrows?" Gian asked.

"I'm not sure, we're waiting on stock from the carpenters and we need more labor," Merrie said.

"Shem, remind me to follow up on that. We should have plenty of lumber available when we cut back the forest," Gian said.

"Will do."

"We're back here," Merrie said, leading them through the manufacturing space.

The table that she stopped at had a large array of ancient looking electronic equipment, most of which hadn't been seen for over a millennia.

"These are old-fashioned computers," Merrie explained. "They're not powerful enough to load a founder's AI on them, but they're surprisingly useful. The bad thing is they take up a lot of space. Even better, the AI in my engineering console can communicate with them, albeit slowly."

"How is all of this useful?" Gian asked, looking at the morass of equipment.

"Not all of it is. I've been experimenting with different ideas. What I wanted to show you, however, was this." Merrie sat down in a chair and pulled back a cloth revealing a thin panel with two joysticks and a keyboard. "Take a look at this."

The panel was blank, but before anyone complained, a video image of the ground in front of the gate appeared on the panel.

"How are you doing that?" Gian asked.

"Completely old-school, Captain," she answered. "Pretty great, right?"

"I'm not sure..." he started. The image flipped to a view outside of the southwest gate, where the farmers were working in the field.

"How many of these do you have?" he asked.

"Just two, but practically, you could install them anywhere," she said. "The maker machine can manufacture ten of these in fifteen minutes. The best thing is that they communicate with each other so you just need to have them within a tenth of a kilometer of each other."

"Don't misunderstand, this *is* excellent technology," Shem said. "I just don't understand how we will find the Ophie with them."

"That's because I love an audience," Merrie said, grinning widely.

"I don't understand," Shem said.

"You will."

Merrie typed a command on the keyboard and the display changed back to the front gate. She then grabbed the joysticks and pushed forward on the left stick and lightly tipped the right stick over to the left. The image changed as the camera appeared to raise up and tip slightly to the side.

"What are you doing?" Shem asked.

"Just hold your pants. I've a limit to my multitasking," Merrie said.

She leveled out the image by re-centering the right stick and the camera continued to gain elevation as she pushed forward on the left stick. With a tip of the left control, the image swung around until it looked back into the settlement and then, astonishingly, it advanced along the main street of Yishuv, turning back toward the west, sailing over the tops of the small homes.

Eliora was the first to verbalize it. "It's coming back to the tannery?"

"Yup. That's why I left the big door open. I haven't exactly mastered it yet," Merrie said.

A buzzing sound at the open door accentuated her point and they all looked out to see a small device fly through the door.

"What is it?" Gian asked.

"They called them quadcopters, because of the four props," Merrie said, lowering the device to the table in front of them.

"You can fly this up to the Ophie camp?" Gian asked.

"That's what we're going to find out," Merrie said. "I'd have tried already, but I have no idea where they are."

"It's not hard," Shem said. "They're up the mountain, behind us, we're just not sure how far. What kind of range does this have?"

"We'll see," she said. "With no assistive technology, we're limited to half a kilometer, but I have something that I think will fix that. The problem is, the communication network I'm using has a limited range, but I had the engineering AI design a repeater that we can launch from the quad. If it works, all we need to do is salt the route with repeaters to extend our range."

"What do you need from us?" Gian asked.

"Directions," Merrie started the drone's props back up and sailed it out the door.

Shem had already given her instructions to head up the mountain to the north, so she gained altitude and sailed over the wall of the settlement.

"Eliora, watch that gauge, right there. When it gets to about halfway, tell me. That's how good our signal is. I can only carry twenty repeaters, so we'll have to make multiple trips. I'll just be happy if the launch system works," she said.

"What happens if it doesn't?" Eliora asked.

"Patrols will need to install them and I don't think we want to do that."

Three hundred meters into the trip they all watched in anticipation as the signal strength gauge dropped to half. Merrie slowly lowered the drone into the forest, painstakingly found an opening in the canopy, and even more carefully nudged her way up to the first tree.

"Here goes nothing," Merrie said, thumbing a red button on the side of the joystick.

For a moment, everything seemed to have gone perfectly. The gauge returned to a hundred percent and the screen remained stable. Then, their view tilted and went black.

"What happened?" Shem asked.

"Frak. I have no idea," she said.

Chapter 18

SEPTIC MATTERS

.

Deep Space

"Liam, something's wrong with the main head," Ada said. "There's a greenish fluid coming out of the shower."

I sighed and poked my head up from the hole in the floor of the bridge.

"You might want to check that out," Nick grinned up at me from where he lay on the floor of the tween deck.

"Crap. It was working earlier," I said, looking hopefully to Ada who was standing at the back of the bridge.

She and Tabby were whispering and giggling. I pushed my hands down on the bridge deck and lifted myself out of the hole.

We'd been working for the last forty hours to patch up *Hotspur*. Moon Rastof had taken responsibility for repairing our starboard engine. We were holding O2 and had linked up our atmo scrubbers and regenerator with *Cape*. Their air was now clean. With *Hotspur* bearing the burden, they had set to work on resetting their algae field. Rastof assured me the *Cape's* systems would be operational within another ten hours.

I took the lift to the berth deck and walked around to Marny and Nick's bunk room.

"Heya, Cap," Marny said as I looked into the room where she lay on the bed, still face down.

"You doing alright in here?" I asked.

We'd been lucky the *Cape* had been nearby after combat, as Marny's back had been severely injured. The large cruiser's combat medical tank had laminated nano-steel plates onto the bones of her back, repaired the damaged tissue, and lay down fresh synthetic skin over the wound. Without it, Marny would have been disabled - at least until we'd been able to afford the surgery.

"I'm good, just a little bored," Marny said, trying to sound cheerful.

"Wish you were up and going. Apparently, we have something broken in the black water processing system," I said. "I could use the help."

"I would if I could. I hate lying here," she said.

"When did the surgeon say you'd be up?"

"Tomorrow. That is if I promise to take it easy," she said. "And I have to keep this darn wrap on my back." The medical patch she was wrapped in was filled with repair materials the medical nanobots required to finish their job. The fact she was down for so long was a testament to just how much damage she'd sustained.

"Okay, glad you're going to be up and about," I said.

The main head was right next to Marny and Nick's room. Sure enough, a foul odor and green slime was seeping up from its drain. I turned on the water and was grateful to see clear water sprinkling down. I could deal with a drain blockage, but black water in the potable line would require a refit which would be next to impossible this far from civilization.

Trace blockage to first cleanout.

The AI overlaid my vision using the HUD to show that a cleanout was accessible just beneath the head as long as I was willing to dive into the bilge. I resignedly gathered a bucket, tools, rags and gloves to pull over my vac-suit's gloves. I'd had trouble getting the smell out of the suit the last time, so I'd stowed gloves for just this eventuality.

Quickest way to the bilge was through an access panel in Ada's bunk room, just around the corner at the aft of the berth deck. I set the bucket down and pulled the panel up. A waft of sour smell assaulted my nose and I instinctively shut my suit's visor.

A noise in front of me, deep in the bilge caused me to nearly jump out of my skin.

Auxiliary illumination.

Forward, I saw a leg across the keel - the long steel beam running down the center of the ship along the bottom. The rest of the person's body was out of sight, but the foot jiggled slightly.

"Jonathan?" I asked.

"Yes, Master Liam." His voice sounded through my headset.

"What are you doing down here?"

"I'm working on the fold-space drive, as we discussed," he said.

"In the bilge?"

"Yes."

I wasn't yet used to his relatively terse answers.

"We're having problems with the waste system. It's backing up. Nothing you're doing, is it?" I asked.

"No. But I did notice an alert on the ship's status," he said. "I assumed you would be monitoring it."

"You're right, we normally do. We've been repairing other systems, I guess, and I hadn't seen it yet."

"I understand. Are you requesting my assistance?" he asked.

"No," I said with a deep sigh. "The waste and septic have, unfortunately, become something of a specialty for me."

"Very well."

I made my way along the keel and looked over to where Jonathan was working. He was attaching thick plates to the keel with a welder and it appeared that he'd re-tasked the small critter defense bots we'd taken on in Lèger Nuage to help him.

I turned to port and located the waste pipe that drained the main head. We'd been using the main head for better than a day, which meant the blockage probably wasn't directly below, otherwise we'd have backed up immediately.

Trace blockage, starting at head drain. I requested.

My HUD illuminated the gravity assist tubing that moved waste through the septic system. As expected, it was red directly beneath both the shower and toilet fixtures. I had to shimmy behind one of the ribs of the ship. As I did, the problem became immediately obvious. We'd taken a previously undiscovered strike to the hull. An I-Beam had pierced the armored hull and stopped once it came into contact with the keel. The damage to the septic field had become the least of my concerns.

"All hands. We have a potential loss of pressure in the bilge."

"What's up, Liam," Nick asked over the comm.

"Looks like debris from *Mastodon* pierced the hull. I don't have eyes on the impact site just now, but I'd like everyone to keep their face shields up," I said.

"Understood."

"Jonathan, you okay if I seal us in down here? We might lose atmo," I said.

"Thank you for the warning. We'll be okay. And I renew my offer of assistance."

"I'll get some tools, then take you up on that," I said.

I made my way back to the entry hatch leading to the aft bunk room and jumped up onto the berth deck. I'd need tools to remove the obstruction, so I grabbed another welder/cutter, a jack and a toolkit. Once I was back in the hole, I pulled the panel closed behind me and sealed it.

"Marny, are you suited up?" I asked.

"I thought we were done with all that, Cap," Marny said. I could hear the pain killers in her voice.

"She's good, Liam. How long will we be at risk?" Tabby asked. Nick must have sent her down to help Marny back into her vac-suit.

"Shouldn't be too long. I closed us in down here," I said. "I'll let you know as soon as we're solid."

Jonathan had reoriented himself by the time I got back. He'd positioned himself forward of the I-beam and was inspecting where it had come in contact with the keel.

"We'll need to repair this once we have access to a shipyard," Jonathan gestured to the keel, which looked fine to me.

"What are you seeing?"

"Micro fractures in the crystalline structure. It is safe for normal operation, but combat maneuvers would be dangerous," he said.

"Great. This trip just gets more expensive," I said. I looked down the length of the beam and saw where it had pierced the hull and foam sealer had deployed.

"We think you haven't talked to Nick extensively," he said.

"I'm not following. Help me get this jack wedged in here. Maybe we can free this beam and push it out," I said.

"Very well."

We placed the hydraulic jack against the keel and slid the lip of it under the end of the beam.

"I'll break the foam while you apply pressure," I said, leaving Jonathan with the jack.

The foam was rigid but brittle. A few sharp raps with a hammer and the plug holding the atmo in the bilge popped out, never to be seen again. Atmo whistled through the hole.

"It's moving, Master Liam," Jonathan said.

"Seriously... please just call me Liam," I said. The beam shuddered as the jack pushed.

I moved back along the length of the beam using the hammer, attempting to free it from the septic system it had plowed through.

"It's moving, Captain," Jonathan said.

I sighed. It was an improvement, I supposed. The beam had moved several centimeters, but we had meters to go.

"Keep it coming," I said. "How much travel does that jack have?"

"Another twenty centimeters."

"Wait one."

I grabbed a temporary hull patch kit and worked my way back down the beam. Now that the beam was moving, the interior pressure would work to force it out. Before I could get there, however, the beam started moving by itself.

"Captain, it's moving independently," Jonathan warned.

"That's good. I'll guide it out," I said.

All hands, we're decompressing the bilge.

I didn't think anyone was in danger. I'd sealed us in, but better safe than sorry.

I pushed on the beam to help unstick it and was careful to position myself so I wouldn't get caught by the beam if it decided to make a hasty exit. Fortunately, the hole was perfectly beam-sized and I was able to work it out slowly until it got to the last two meters when the pressure overcame the friction and it disappeared from sight.

With the beam no longer blocking the breach in our hull, the remaining atmosphere was free to escape. I'd been expecting the rush and allowed myself to be sucked toward the hole, pushing the hull patch kit in front of me. My AI inflated the kit as a sphere and I guided it into place. Upon contact, it adhered to the surrounding hull and deflated.

"Thank you, Jonathan," I said.

"You are welcome. Do you require further assistance?"

"No. How is the fold-space generator coming along?"

"I am working on the final installation," he said.

"Did Anino share with you how he thought this would go after we found *Cape of Good Hope*? It seems like he'd have more of a plan than just jump out here and see how it goes," I said.

"Yes, Master Anino made extensive plans with many different contingencies. Perhaps it would be better to have this conversation with your entire crew."

"Sure. But just so I know, did one of his plans include getting murdered by Tullas?" I asked.

"Master Anino often talked of his own death and many of us feel he sought it out."

"He was suicidal?"

"Not by what we understand to be the classical definition. He saw value in his own life, but he also believed that his own life's value was diminished if he was unwilling to risk it for the good of those people he felt he'd let down. It is what drew him to you and your crew."

"I'm not following what drew him to us."

"Your willingness to take great risks for the benefit of others."

"That's crazy. If I'd have known everything we were going to run into at the start, I don't think we'd have taken this job," I said.

"That was something we discussed with Master Anino at length. It was his belief that you would find a way to survive, just as you did with the Sephelodon."

"We survived by pure luck. If *Cape* hadn't intervened when she did, we'd have been goners," I said.

"And yet, you survived. Please understand, the very idea of luck is offensive to silicate based life forms such as ourselves. But, there is something about your crew that consistently defies logic at critical junctures. To borrow an idiom that is equally nonsensical and applicable, you and your crew appear to make your own luck."

It was a strange thing for him to say. I'd have liked to have gotten into it more deeply, but the fact of the matter was, I had other things that needed my immediate attention.

"That's a lot to think about," I said and turned to look at the ruined portion of the septic system.

"Indeed," Jonathan replied and turned back to the project he'd been working on. I was impressed that he understood I was ending the conversation, although working with Anino had probably been good training.

Create prioritized queue of replacement parts for septic field.

A list popped onto my HUD. With our small replicator, it would take over twenty hours to manufacture acceptable, temporary parts.

Establish comm with Engineer Rastof.

"Moonie here. How can I help, Captain?"

"What kind of replicator availability do you have?"

"Two Class-C sitting idle and nothing high priority on the D," he said. "Send me your list."

My AI, overhearing the conversation, split the work into the four queues and blinked a request for approval from me to transmit its recommendations. I nodded approval and it was transmitted.

"Isn't that always the case," Rastof guffawed. "Why is it these birds always get hit in the shitter?"

I smiled. If only he knew.

The three hours it took to complete the manufacturing would give me time to place a more permanent patch on the hull and clean the existing mess in the bilge.

When I opened the hatch into the aft bunkroom, I noticed Tabby sitting on Ada's bunk, waiting for me.

"Is that a new smell you've invented?" she asked.

"Very funny. Your mask is closed."

I lifted the jack and welder/cutter onto the floor of the bunkroom, then pulled myself up and out.

"You need help?" she asked.

"Sure. We need to weld a patch onto the hull," I said.

"Go measure. I'll bring it out."

It was a good plan. Until I got outside, we wouldn't know for sure how big a patch was needed. I arc-jetted through the pressure barrier to the small hallway that led to the external hatch and then out the pressure barrier to space.

If there was good news to be had, it was that the beam had struck our armor so sharply that the hole it created wasn't much wider than the beam itself.

"Tabbs, I'll need a thirty centimeter square or round," I said.

"Round it is," she said.

I pulled a zero-g reciprocating hammer from my tool belt and got to work on the opening. All I needed to do was bend down anything that stood proud of the normal line of the hull. Due to the nature of the damage, there wasn't much to fix and by the time I'd finished, Tabby was jetting along the bottom of the hull with a patch and magnetic clamp in tow.

"Good timing," I said.

"Something about 'hull breach' just hustles a girl right along."

Tabby expertly lay the patch in place and positioned the magnetic clamp so it held the disc firmly to the hull.

"You want to do the honors?"

I held the welder out. It wasn't so long ago that I'd taught her how to use it.

"Sure."

She grabbed the welder and got right to work. I jetted backward for a better view. There were plenty of scorch marks and abrasions on the hull, but I didn't see any more issues.

"I'm going to finish the hull scan if you've got that," I said.

"Copy," she replied. Her terse response only meant that she was concentrating.

A hull scan had been one of many priorities we hadn't gotten to yet. It wasn't difficult, simply requiring one of us to jet over the entire surface of the ship. I flitted back and forth until my AI was satisfied I'd given it a sufficient view. The report I got back wasn't surprising. There were several suspect spots, but nothing that would prevent us from sailing. By the time I got back to Tabby, she was detaching the magnetic clamps.

"Want to help in the bilge?" I asked.

"Sure, what are we doing?"

"First job is to pull off all of the couplings on either side of the damaged septic field. It'll be messy, but it's not hard."

"You really know how to show a girl a good time."

"I can't think of anyone I'd rather crawl into the darkest part of the ship with," I said.

"Ooooh. Talk dirty to me."

"Doesn't get much dirtier than the bilge."

"All hands. We should be holding atmo again. Hull scan is showing solid," I said.

"Hey, Liam, how's that head drain coming?" Ada asked.

"Let me guess, things are becoming urgent?"

"Good guess."

"I have some parts being manufactured on *Cape*, want to go get 'em for me?"

"Yes! A hundred times yes!" she said.

Tabby and I were almost run over by Ada as she exited the pressure barrier on the way over to *Cape*. Theoretically, we could visit *Cape* anytime we wanted, but there was tension on the larger ship, so we avoided it like the plague.

"I'll go with her," Tabby said.

"Don't take too long. You'll miss all of the fun," I said.

They returned carrying bundles of freshly manufactured parts. Unlike *Sterra's Gift*, *Hotspur's* bilge had plenty of room to move around in and I'd already removed all of the broken pieces and was swabbing up the goop that had fallen on the floor.

"If you want, you could take those bags I've already filled back to *Cape*. They've a reclaimer," I said. It was a luxury a smaller ship like *Hotspur* couldn't afford.

"You planned that," Ada said.

"Pure coincidence. And you shouldn't complain. I already put the bad stuff in bags," I said. "Would it help if I said I'll have a working head by the time you get back?"

"I've always wondered if your head worked at all," Ada quipped.

Tabby leaned over to her and whispered and they both giggled. It was the second time today they'd shared an inside joke at my expense. I just shook my head, gratefully accepting the bundles of piping. To think at one point Tabby had been jealous of Ada and my relationship.

I finally emerged from the bilge a couple of hours later. I'd had messier cleanups, but that was small consolation. My vac-suit was going to smell for weeks.

Marny surprised me when I came down the hallway. She was sitting upright at the mess table with her vac-suit peeled back and a tight wrap around her chest.

"What are you doing up?" I asked.

"Almost out of the woods, Cap," she said. "And boy do you stink."

"Right. Anyone working on dinner?" I asked as I turned the corner which gave me a good view of the galley where I was surprised to see Jonathan hard at work.

"I've quite a repertoire, Captain. I hope you don't mind," he said.

"Ordinarily, I'd say you'd have to arm wrestle Marny, but I think she's unlikely to object today," I said.

"We've been having a lovely conversation," he said. "I'd wanted a chance to ask her about her experience in the Amazonian war."

"Cap, you really don't need to be polite," Marny said with an obvious gulp. "Let's continue this conversation after you've run that suit through the freshener."

"Fair enough. Can you ask Tabbs to bring me a fresh liner?" I pulled off my vac-suit and fed it into the freshener.

"Aye, aye, Cap," she said.

I closed the door behind me, stripped off my suit liner, lathered up and watched with satisfaction as soapy water disappeared into the gravity-assisted drain. I didn't even see Tabby replace my old suit liner with a fresh one. Once the water was turned off, the smell of garlic grabbed my attention, adding a sense of urgency to getting dressed.

When I reemerged into the combined mess/galley the whole crew was already seated and steaming bowls of food were piled on the table. I wasn't particularly surprised to see that we'd invited Captain LeGrande, her first officer Johannes Grossman and Engineer Rastof. It was a tight fit, but the way the food smelled, I didn't care.

"Captain, would you like to say a few words before we eat?" Marny asked. No one was eating yet, waiting for me, and I appreciated her subtle reminder.

"Thank you, Marny, I will," I said. I grabbed my glass of white wine. "A toast. To new friends."

We all drank and it was my responsibility to start eating, which I was more than happy to do.

"Jonathan, it's delicious," I said after a few minutes.

"Thank you, Captain." I was surprised to see that he was also eating, although less gustily than the rest of us.

"Captain Hoffen, have you been successful in repairing your fold-space generator?" LeGrande asked.

"I haven't had a chance to update Liam, but thanks in no small part to Mr. Rastof, we're very close," Nick said.

"Have you discussed my idea of finding a new home?" I asked.

"We have, at length." LeGrande glanced at her first officer and then to Rastof. "We're not of a single mind and have questions. For example, how do we find a suitable planet? Would you just leave us here while you're looking for it and what if you couldn't return?"

"Unfortunately, we don't have answers to most of your questions. It's not like we have a catalog of planets for you to choose from, but I think your last question is the most important," I said.

"How's that?"

"This is about survival. The longer you sit out here in the deep dark, the more at risk you are. You need to be someplace where you have a chance to survive," I said.

"On that we agree," Grossman said.

"Have you ruled out sending people back to Tipperary with us?" I asked.

"Tullas' threats were clear. If any of our crew return, she will go after *all* of our families. I believe that meant your families as well, Captain Hoffen," Grossman said.

"That bitch," Ada said.

"Captain Hoffen, how do you know *your* return won't trigger Tullas into going after our families?" Grossman asked. "We shouldn't allow anyone to return."

"Why would she involve your families for our actions?" I asked.

"She's a power-hungry zealot," he said.

"That is not a reasonable assessment," Jonathan said.

"Excuse me?" Grossman asked. He grew agitated and I hoped that Jonathan saw it as well.

"Lorraine Tullas has been consistent in her actions," Jonathan said. "Belirand has an objective to keep knowledge away from the population. She would gain nothing in hurting your families. There is no risk to information leakage."

"And you're willing to risk our families on your theory?"

"As opposed to what?" Tabby asked. "Stay here and die? That isn't going to happen. If you want to die out here, that's up to you. Remember, we came here to help."

"And you're doing a bang up job of it," Grossman said.

"That's enough, Johannes," LeGrande said.

"I understand your concern, Johannes. We all have families," I said. "But we can't be frozen by fear. We have to trust Belirand to act rationally. We'll keep their secret and find a way to survive."

"Then you're more delusional than Tullas is," he fired back.

Chapter 19

SENTIENT SPECIES

"Well, that was pleasant," Tabby said as we got ready for bed.

"You can see his point. What if Belirand goes after Mom and Dad, or Jack?"

"Then we expose the whole thing. Right now our families are their leverage for remaining quiet," she said. "They don't gain anything by killing innocents."

"I'm not sure I'm okay with going public. What if there really is a big, bad alien threat out there? Do we open up that Pandora's box?" I asked.

"No. It's still not a good enough reason to let forty-five people die."

"You're right..." I said.

"Of course I am," she said as she snaked her leg over my waist and sat up on me. "And, you'd best remember that."

We only slept for eight hours, but it felt like twelve. I'd been completely worn out and I awoke feeling recharged to the strong smell of coffee. A small movement on the bed alerted me to someone's presence. I rolled over and Tabby was sitting there staring at me with a cup of coffee in her hand.

"Is that for me?" I asked.

"If you're getting up," she said. "Marny is up and she made rolls."

"Really, she's feeling that good?"

"Apparently."

I got out of bed and pulled on my vac-suit, gratefully accepting the cup of coffee. After running a quick teeth cleanse, I followed her down to the mess, where Marny, Nick and Ada were already seated.

"Morning, Cap," Marny said. "Cinnamon roll?"

"Sure. Are you sure you should be up and at 'em?"

"Aye, Cap. I'm a little tender, but AI says as long as I keep the nanobots doing their thing, I should be good to go."

"As long as you take it easy."

"Do my best, but to be honest, this injury didn't even make my top five list, so you'll excuse me if I'm a bit cavalier about the whole thing," she said.

Motion caught my eye as Jonathan approached from the aft pressure barrier.

"Good morning, Jonathan," I said.

"Good morning, Captain."

"How is the fold-space generator coming along?" I asked.

"It is operational."

"Nick, any word on *Cape's* O2 scrubbers and algae fields?"

"They came online last night and Jonathan helped them disconnect the air exchange," he said.

"We should probably talk about last night," I said, looking around the table.

"What's to talk about?" Ada asked. "I'm with Tabby. I don't plan to die out here."

"Let's be clear. I don't think Tullas threatened our families. What I remember her saying was she'd hunt down anyone we told," I said.

"I'm not clear on what the big secret is," Ada said. "Everyone already knows about fold-space travel."

"I'm pretty sure the idea that individual ships can go wherever they want is what she's hiding. Belirand wants to control fold-space and they'll kill to keep it that way," I said.

"That and there are sentient aliens. It has been the practice of the North American, German, Europe and Korean alliance - through Belirand - to cut all ties with any system that has intelligent life," Jonathan said.

"Then why abandon *Cape of Good Hope*? Surely, there are no aliens around here?" I threw out.

"Sentient *species* might be a better way to say that," he said.

A light bulb clicked on for me. "You didn't originate in our known universe, did you?"

"It is always a joy to watch the intuitive leaps only humankind seems capable of. And, if by known universe, you mean the four solar systems explored by humankind, then that is a correct assessment."

"Was the 'intuitive leap' thing sarcasm?" I asked.

"We don't find sarcasm a particularly useful means of expression. It seems to make conversations difficult, even hostile at times. No, we are sincere when I convey that the human mind is something we very much admire."

"You didn't answer why they had to abandon *Cape of Good Hope*," Ada said.

Jonathan looked to Ada and smiled. It creeped me out. Did his kind ordinarily smile? Was he just making it up to seem more human?

"The ideas are very closely related. Your people are very curious, to the point of doing themselves harm. If fold-space were to be opened to everyone who could build a ship, then they would start running into sentient species. Most of which have compatible objectives for preserving life. The problem is that many of them don't."

"As in they want to destroy other species? That's terrifying," Ada said. "It still seems cruel to allow people to die, just to keep that secret."

"But, it sure makes more sense," I said. "Tell me, Jonathan, how many intelligent, non-human species are you aware of?"

"Perhaps this isn't the right time," he said.

"More than ten?"

"Don't push him," Nick said. "We need to show Jonathan the same trust they're showing us by exposing themselves. When they're ready, we'll have that conversation."

I looked at Nick and then back to Jonathan. "Fair enough. I meant no harm. Really, I was just curious," I said.

"I think that was his point earlier. We have an old Earth saying," Marny said. "Curiosity killed the cat. Only, I think Jonathan is trying to make sure curiosity doesn't kill us."

"It kind of casts Tullas and Belirand in a different light," Ada said. "We might not like how they're doing things, but it seems like they're not as awful as we originally thought."

"I call bull on that. Tullas tried to kill everyone here," Tabby said. "I'm taking that bitch out first chance I get."

"Not to change the subject or anything, but what do we need to do before we get out of here?" I asked.

"To go where?" Nick asked.

"Right, sorry. To me, it's clear that we need to repair *Hotspur* before we go much further and we need to bring supplies back for *Cape*. How many days can we all survive between what we have on *Hotspur* and *Cape*?"

"Fifteen days give or take. O2 and water will keep 'em alive longer than that, but most of the food stuff got destroyed," Nick said.

"So, not a lot of time for messing around," I said. "How about navigation systems? They took a pretty big hit."

"Rastof helped us manufacture basic units. We'll have to buy new ones when we get back in system, but what we have will get us somewhere for real repairs," he said.

"Are we going to have enough credits?" I asked.

"It'll be close," Nick said.

"I believe if you check your contract with Master Anino, you will find a clause that covers damage to your ship," Jonathan said.

"I'm not sure how valid that is with Anino being deceased," I said.

"It's valid, but I'd expect Anino's estate to be tied up," Nick said.

"I have sufficient standing in his companies to move the appropriate funds," Jonathan said. "Master Anino anticipated this possibility and made preparations for it. You should know he has granted *Loose Nuts* the exclusive use of his residences on Curie while under contract."

"Residences, as in the dome under the Radium Sea?" Ada asked.

"There are several, but that is one of them. Its security profile is well suited to your current needs."

"How about Lèger Gros?" I asked.

"Are you thinking Meerkat Shipyard?" Nick asked.

I nodded and looked to Jonathan.

"We do not specifically own any residences on Lèger Gros, but it is possible to make arrangements," he said.

"I think it's time to finish our conversation with Captain LeGrande," I said. "Ada, can you work on a good location for us to jump to near Gros? It shouldn't be so close that we surprise anyone. Marny, are you up to working through a security protocol for us to follow while we're in the city?"

"Are you worried about Belirand sending agents after us, Cap?" Marny asked.

"I'm not sure what I'm worried about. I don't think Lèger would allow Belirand to just grab us, but there's a lot on the line and we'll be exposed," I said.

"Nick, Tabby, let's go up to the conference room and give Captain LeGrande a call," I said.

"Captain?" Jonathan asked as we all started to stand up.

"Yes?"

"Do you have any requests for us?" Jonathan asked.

"To be honest, I'm not sure how to treat you, Jonathan. Are you a passenger, crew, or do you simply represent Anino's interests?" I asked.

"We'd like to be treated as part of the crew, as long as it doesn't conflict with our commitment to Thomas Anino," he said.

I looked to the rest of the crew, each subtly nodding assent in their own way.

"Welcome to *Loose Nuts*," I said. "I assume you'll be forthright about these conflicts when they arise?"

"Yes, Captain, and thank you for your vote of confidence," he said.

"First on the list is to manufacture a case to hold those quantum crystals. It would be a shame to have any of them damaged. Also, would you upload a synopsis on each of the destinations they represent to each of the crew? Once we're underway, we'll want to start reviewing them for suitability," I said.

"Yes, Captain," he said.

"After that, work with Ada so she's comfortable with how to engage the fold-space generator to fulfill her navigation plans," I said.

"Anything else?" Jonathan asked.

"Marny will coordinate the supplies we're offloading to *Cape*. Any assistance you could provide would be appreciated," I said.

"Go, Cap. We've got it," Marny said.

I smiled. It was good to have her back.

Nick, Tabby and I made our way up to the small conference room that adjoined the Captain's quarters.

Open comm with Captain LeGrande, I said.

Twenty seconds later her image popped up on the translucent vid screen I'd pulled up in the center of the small table.

"Good morning, Captain Hoffen," she said. "I feel like I owe you an apology for my first mate's behavior last night." If anything, LeGrande's appearance was more haggard than when we'd arrived.

"Apology accepted. Although, for the record, I don't believe any of us felt anything but empathy for his position. Are you all doing okay?" I asked.

"No, not really. We're hanging on by a thread over here," she said. "Our discipline is strained and there is a very real possibility of mutiny."

"Is there anything we can do to help?"

"Beyond supplies and a new place to live?" she laughed without humor.

"Captain, you need to remain hopeful. We won't abandon you. We're packing up the supplies we can afford to leave and will transfer them shortly. My plan is to jump to Tipperary, repair *Hotspur* and bring back more supplies," I said.

"And what of a new home? Does such a place exist?" she asked.

"We believe it does. Belirand abandoning you out here happened because of a secret they desperately want to keep," I said.

"About being able to generate a fold-space wave with smaller ships?"

"No, about finding habitable planets that are also home to sentient life forms," I said.

"Aliens? There've been rumors, but why keep that a secret?"

"I could only speculate. What we know is that Belirand abandoned almost a hundred missions over the last three centuries."

"And you want to drop us at one of those worlds. With aliens?" she asked.

"I'll leave it to you, Captain. But just as Anino found you with a quantum communication crystal, we can find these settlements. Anino saved crystals for those abandoned missions. We'll have some idea what we're getting into," I said.

"That's incredible and it is indeed hopeful. When will you depart?"

"We're making preparations now and I'd like to be underway within the hour," I said. "We're expecting to bring back three months of consumables. Do you have a list of supplies that you're specifically in need of?"

"I'll have a final list to you within the hour and I'll send crew over to pick up what you have," she said and closed comm.

"She's in a tough position," Tabby said. "Can you imagine how many people on that ship believe they should be going home?"

"Hate to hear a captain talk about mutiny. I hope she can keep it together," Nick said.

"Won't matter if we can't find them a place to live," I said. "I sure hope Anino thought it through more than he did this trip."

"Tabbs, you want to help Marny get the supplies offloaded? I suspect LeGrande's crew will be over shortly," I said.

"Can do." Tabby got up and walked out of the room.

"I'm going to have to work in here for the trip back," Nick said. "We don't have any replacements for the workstations we lost."

"Understood. I'm going forward to work with Ada on our navigation plan. Do you want to start running your checklists?"

"I'm not sure what the point would be. We've more systems in the red than we do anything else," he said.

"Can Meerkat get us back and going in a week?" I asked.

"Depends on how deep Jonathan is willing to dig into his pockets."

"I was thinking, what if we built you and Marny a bunk room above the pop out where the armory is? If we flipped gravity to the forward of the ship, you'd have a nice-sized space," I said.

"It's an idea, let's get through this run and then talk about it," he said. "We're comfortable and I know Marny likes being by the galley and mess. She says she knows everything that's going on in the ship because of that location."

"We'll, we could give Ada that new space and extend your bunk back into where she's at," I said.

"I hear my name," Ada called from the bridge.

Nick nodded thoughtfully. "Sure, pitch the idea to Ada. She'd probably even do the design."

"Design what?" Ada leaned into the room, smiling. I was momentarily distracted by the sheer beauty of her face.

"Uh... we were talking about making the bunk rooms larger by expanding over the armory. There's quite a bit of space there if you rotate the gravity forward," I said.

"And you want me to design it?"

"We were thinking it'd be your space," Nick said. "Although, we were talking about blowing out the wall between the two bunk rooms to give me and Marny more space."

"I'll do it, but I have to say, I enjoy having Jonathan for a bunk mate," she said.

"Does he sleep?" I asked.

"Not really, but he does lie down for several hours. He said they could just stand in the hold if I wanted privacy, but they prefer company," she said.

I shook my head in disbelief. "Weird. Okay, how's your navigation plan coming?"

"All set. The fold-space generator isn't difficult to program, especially with Jonathan on board. I've got us dropping in six hours from Grünholz on a medium burn. We'll be way outside of normal shipping lanes, so there's not much of a chance of anyone being within a hundred thousand kilometers," she said.

"Great. Let's go work through our check lists, such as they are," I said.

Forty minutes later Tabby and Marny made it back to the bridge. Marny was tiring, made obvious by her willingness to sit on the bridge couch.

"All closed up?" I asked.

"Aye, Cap. It was heartbreaking, though. The crew they sent over from *Cape* to get the supplies didn't believe we were coming back. They begged us to take them along," she said.

"That's horrible," Ada gasped.

"It was," Tabby agreed.

"Well, we can't help 'em if we're sitting around here," I said. "Ada, you have the helm."

All hands, prepare for departure. Ada said.

Tabby jumped up the short flight of stairs to the cockpit and slid into the chair next to Ada.

"Belirand cruiser at fifteen thousand kilometers," Ada announced.

It had been eighteen hours since we'd left *Cape of Good Hope*. We'd been sailing on a medium burn for Lèger Gros under our quiet running protocols. Not all of our fixes to the armor were as good as others, but as long as we kept at least fifteen thousand kilometers from other ships, they couldn't see us.

"Slow and quiet," I said.

"Roger that, Captain," Ada said.

With the damage we'd taken, we wouldn't last two minutes in a firefight.

"We're crossing into Lèger territory in ten, nine..." Ada counted backward for us, although I could see the boundary coming up on a dimmed vid screen.

"Well, here goes nothing," I said.

Turn on transponder, I said. *Hail Lèger Air Defense.*

"Welcome back, *Hotspur*. How may we be of assistance this fine morning?" The face of a woman I'd talked to before popped up on the forward vid-screen. Darned if I could remember her name.

"Good morning," I said with a broad smile. "We'd like to file our flight plan, destination Lèger Gros."

"Captain Hoffen, if I wasn't a married woman, I'd think you were flirting with me. You know you don't have to file a plan as long as you're sailing under a Lèger flag. I don't suppose getting our attention has anything to do with the Belirand cruiser that's closing on your position?"

"Oh that? We might have recently crossed paths with Belirand."

"You owe me a drink, Captain. I'll let them know we're tracking you on the way in," she said and closed comm.

"That was ballsy," Ada said.

"Learned a couple of things. First, she didn't demand we stow our turrets. That leads me to believe that Belirand hasn't asked or hasn't convinced Lèger to take us into custody. Second, this isn't the first time Lèger Air Defense has been asked to watch approaching ships," I said. "Makes you wonder what other things are going on around here."

"Incoming hail, Belirand Cruiser Stark Justice."

"Tell me that's not *Fist of Justice's* sister," I said.

Accept hail. "*Hotspur*. Go ahead,"

"Captain Hoffen, we're requesting you heave-to for an in-person confab."

I gestured to Ada to keep going.

"Who am I talking with?" I asked.

"Captain Ciaran MacAsgaill, Belirand security services."

"Captain MacAsgaill, with all due respect, we're declining your request. Our recent experience with your sister ship *Fist of Justice* leads me to be suspicious of your motives," I said.

"You can't keep a runnin', Captain," he said. "But, I jus' want tah talk." He spoke with a thick accent I couldn't quite pick out.

"De Laroche Bar, 1700. Don't bring an army," I said.

Close comm.

"You don't want to hear if he accepted your offer?" Ada asked.

"If we make it to Gros, we'll know he accepted my offer," I said.

Chapter 20

OUT OF TIME

Yishuv Settlement, Planet Ophir

"What is wrong with your device?" Captain Gian asked.

"I'm not sure," Merrie said. "It's like it lost power after I launched the portable network router. The weird thing is the router is working just fine."

"I'll get a patrol together," Eliora said.

"Do it. This technology is too important," Gian said.

"Wait," Merrie said. "Don't forget, I have a second quad."

"A second? Just how difficult are these to make?" Gian asked.

"About an hour on the maker machine, but they won't allow me to borrow any more time for the next three tendays," she said.

"I'll have a talk with Bessel," Gian said. "Now, how much time will it take to launch your second machine?"

"One moment." Merrie's fingers flew across a keyboard that was connected via a wire to a metallic box.

The screen lit up again with a view of the farmer's fields to the south west. The picture slowly spun around, catching a guard by surprise, causing him to fall from the chair he had leaned against the wall.

"Was that Terevit?" Shem asked. "Was he sleeping?"

"That wouldn't surprise me," Eliora said, shaking her head in disgust. "I'll be sure to have a word with him."

They all watched as the picture showed the progress of the machine as it flew above the settlement and made its way over to the old tannery where they sat. The noise of the machine was like a very loud stinging insect.

"It's just up that hill," Shem said as Merrie directed the machine to fly along the route its twin had just taken.

"My repeater is definitely working," Merrie said. "Look at the signal strength. It was almost fifty percent when we got here last time."

"What of the machine. Can you locate it?" Gian asked.

"Give me a minute. Contact with tree leaves is probably what did it. I need to be careful as it flies lower."

"How low was it flying when it was taken out?" Eliora asked.

"Seven or eight meters."

"It could have been Ophie. Our patrols have been finding more and more pods in the mountains," she said. "Their hearing is particularly good and the noise your machine makes would attract their attention from a long way off."

"What are you asking from me?" Merrie inquired.

"Don't get too low. The Ophie blend into the hillside. I think they'll show themselves if you stay in one place for a while. But stay out of range."

"What's their range?"

"At least seven or eight meters?" Shem suggested.

Merrie shook her head and rolled her eyes, but took the advice to heart and hovered at twenty meters above an open spot for several minutes.

"There. Turn left," Shem said. "Uphill five meters."

"I don't see anything," Merrie said.

"I see one," Eliora said. "They're looking right at the quad."

An Ophie stepped from the cover of the darkened forest, holding a rock the size of a man's fist.

"You think it...?" Merrie pushed forward on her left joystick, causing the quad to lift rapidly as the Ophie launched the rock.

"Now, can I take a patrol out there?" Eliora asked.

"Take two squads. I don't want any casualties," Gian said.

"If you take a walkie-talkie, we'll be able to tell you what we see from the air," Merrie said.

"Show me again," Eliora said.

Merrie turned the quad back toward the Yishuv settlement and flew back, landing on top of the northern wall, orienting the camera to look out at the forest. She then retrieved a walkie-talkie from beneath her workbench.

"It's simple. Push the button to talk. If your button is pushed, you can't receive messages from anyone else. Otherwise, when you're talking, everyone on your channel hears what you say."

"What's a channel?"

"Just a number so people can have private conversations. These have forty channels. See, you're on channel six. Make sure you're on the same channel and you're good to go," she said.

"Captain, keep this one. I'll pick up two more at the barracks and we'll set out," Eliora said. "If I hurry, I'll be able to grab the sixteen hundred patrol before they head out."

"Are you going to split your squads?" Gian asked.

"Yes. I'll lead a squad down from the north onto their position and Bashi will lead a group in from the east. We'll trap them on the ridge where Merrie's first quad machine was brought down."

"A good plan," Shem said. "I'd like to take the blaster rifle onto the north wall. They're only three hundred meters out and it's possible I could get an open shot."

"Do it," Gian said.

Thirty minutes later Eliora had positioned her squad a hundred meters north of the last reported position of the Ophie.

"Bashi, can you hear me?" Eliora asked.

"Yes."

"Hold there. Merrie, we're in position, fly your quad machine back to the last location."

"She's lifting off and is en route," Gian responded.

Eliora was startled by how loud the talkie sounded in the quiet forest. She twisted the volume control down. It would be better not to hear him than to attract the Ophie's attention.

"Weapons at the ready," she ordered her squad.

She held the talkie up and depressed the button. "Bashi, move in slowly. We'll pinch down from the top."

"We're on the move."

Merrie's machine finally arrived at the location where she'd encountered the Ophie only a short time previous. She slowly turned the quad, scanning the forest below and not finding anything. The leaves of the trees obscuring her view.

"I have to get lower. I can't see through the canopy," she said.

"Careful, remember what they did to your last bird," Gian warned.

"I will," she said and slowly descended.

"Not too low," Gian said.

"There," Merrie said. "Top of the screen on the right."

Gian looked as Merrie centered the quad's camera on an Ophie. It was staring up at the quad curiously, holding a rock.

"Where are the others?" Gian asked. "They always travel in a pod of five."

"I thought Eliora said they set an ambush on her last patrol?" Merrie said.

"You think they have some clue as to the function of your quad?" Gian asked.

"No, but they wouldn't need to. They'd just have to think it's related to us."

"Eliora and Bashi are plenty careful. They know the score and thanks to Amon's swords, two squads are more than an even match for a pod," he said.

"You have to tell her it could be a trap," Merrie said.

"No can do. Ophie hearing is too sensitive, they'd hear your talkie," he said. "Best to let Eliora handle it from this point. The fact that your machine is distracting one of them is a nice bonus, though. Is there any way to get sound on this thing?"

"Maybe, but we'd have a tough time picking up anything over the rotor's noise."

"Damn. This is worse than waiting for them to return," Gian said.

"Contact." The talkie on the table came to life with Eliora's voice. The button must have been locked down as the sounds of the talkie being dropped on the ground could be heard.

The Ophie that had been watching the quad spun around and sprinted up the mountain. Merrie flew after him, but had a difficult time negotiating the trees.

"Faster," Gian urged.

The quad came upon the scene of a pitched battle. The sound from Eliora's still transmitting talkie providing sound to the battle. To Merrie's eyes, the Ophie towered over the human patrol, although the smaller humans were considerably faster. A gout of blood spurted upward as an Ophie club made contact, dropping the smaller man who'd advanced.

"Close ranks," Eliora yelled, jumping to the front of her quad.

"Where's Bashi?" Gian asked, rhetorically.

He picked up the talkie and pressed the button to transmit on the talkie. "Bashi, all haste, Eliora's squad is under attack."

"He can't hear you, Eliora's talkie is still transmitting, it's blocking you," Merrie said.

"Gah, this is maddening," he said.

They watched the battle unfold in front of them. The Ophie's heavy swings were more than making up for their slow speed. The protectors in Eliora's squad barely held off the pressing Ophie.

"At least they're defending themselves." Gian observed as his protectors deflected the clubs with their long swords.

"Retreat. Up the hill," Eliora commanded.

"Why doesn't she parry?" Merrie asked. "She's just getting under its strikes."

"Her katana is brittle. That club would shatter it. She prefers speed over brawn. It's a good choice for a smaller person," he explained.

Merrie flew the quad in closer as Eliora's squad scrabbled back, up a rocky rise.

"What's she doing?"

"She's trying to gain higher ground. It's a small advantage with Ophie, but it's something," he said. "Damn it, where's Bashi?"

A thought struck Merrie and she directed the quad to dive down, lining up even with the Ophie attacking Eliora. She fired one of the network repeaters into its back, causing the quad to lurch backward. The Ophie spun and with deadly accuracy mashed its club into the quad, the screen going blank.

"Shite," Gian said.

"Sorry, Captain," she said. "The idea just hit me."

"I guess we'll just listen," he said.

"How can you be so calm?"

"Shhh..."

The sounds of battle continued for several more minutes and finally there was quiet. A few moments after that, they heard rustling as someone or something picked up the talkie.

"Captain?" Eliora's voice came through.

"Status, Eliora," Gian said.

"Two down, three wounded. I shouldn't have split the squads," she said.

"Where's Bashi?"

"He's here. There was a second pod. If not for Shem, it might have been a total loss," she said.

"How's that?"

"Eliora pulled the fight up the hill to a clearing. It gave me line of sight," Shem cut in.

"COUNCIL WILL COME TO ORDER," Councilwoman Peraf said, placing the pink crystal in its golden mounting onto the table.

"Captain Gian, you've requested this meeting, the floor is yours," Peraf said.

"Honored members of the council, the news I have is not good. I have reason to believe that an attack is imminent and would like to make plans accordingly," he said.

"That's quite a statement," Bedros said. "How do you back this up?"

"The patrols and attacks from the Ophie are increasing at an alarming rate. We've been attacked by more Ophie in the last six tendays than in the preceding hundred years," Gian answered.

"By all accounts, your recent encounters have been wildly successful. Share the good news, Captain. What have your encounter survival rates been?" Bedros asked.

"It is true. When our patrols have come into contact with the Ophie, we have sustained less than twenty percent casualties. This is mostly due to the new weapons from our apprentice engineer Merrie and smith Amon."

"And, you're here to tell us you need more resources and higher priority - this and that?"

"No, Mr. Bedros. I'm here to tell you that an attack of a size we've never seen is imminent."

"How can you be so sure?" Peraf asked.

"Our settlement is being scouted. The Ophie are mapping out our patrol routes and we are encountering different tribes. Throughout our entire history, we've been attacked by a single tribe. During the last four tendays, we've seen attacks from three entirely different tribes. The Ophie are banding together and I believe they will be mounting an attack of a scale we've never seen before," Gian said.

"You're speculating," Bedros said.

"It's my job to anticipate the movement of the Ophie and I'm telling you that things have changed. If we don't prepare now, we could lose the entire settlement."

"You're despicable! Using a few attacks to improve your position," Bedros exclaimed.

"Mr. Bedros, that's enough. There is no reason to insult Captain Gian," Peraf said sternly. "Let's say you're right, Captain. What would you have us do?"

"I have four requests. First, we need to cut the forest back. I want a three hundred meter buffer around the entire settlement...."

"Seriously?"

"Second." Gian continued. "We have enough weapons that every citizen between twelve and fifty years should be equipped and trained. And third, we need priority of the maker machine to be given to the apprentice engineer Merrie."

"Is that all?" Bedros asked sarcastically.

"No. We must double the size of the protectorate immediately."

"That would be ten percent of our population, we'd get nothing else done. Do you know how many farmers we've lost this year alone?" Bedros asked.

"If in thirty tendays we haven't been attacked, then I will have been wrong. We can reduce our forces and I'll step down. Understand, however, when the Ophie march in here with ten times the forces we've seen previously and we haven't done everything we could to defend against them, we won't be talking about retirement."

"What will we be doing?" Bedros asked.

"In our last major attack on the city, only fifteen Ophie actually made it past the city gates. Those Ophie killed seventy citizens. Use your imagination, Bedros. What do you think a hundred or even five hundred Ophie running through the streets of Yishuv would do?"

"Is there nothing else we can do to prepare for this attack?" Peraf asked.

"You don't actually believe this madman, do you?" Bedros interrupted.

"Captain Gian and his predecessors have defended this settlement for three centuries. I see no reason to disbelieve him and I want to take advantage of his insight," Peraf said and then turned to Gian. "Captain?"

"We build a keep, just like our medieval ancestors did. It would provide shelter in case we are totally overrun. We could use the lumber we harvest from cutting back the forest. If we mount the city defense blaster over that bunker, we could hold off quite a sizeable force. It would be a desperate maneuver, but it could be the difference between survival and not," he said.

"I move that we grant Captain Gian his requests. We will revisit preparations every tenday," Peraf said. "All in favor?"

The other members of the council, who had been quiet to this point, raised their hands, Bedros the only detractor.

On the way out, Bedros walked up to Gian, catching him from behind by his arm.

"I suppose you feel that you won today," Bedros said angrily.

Gian turned around. "Do you really believe this is about politics?"

"You can play that game with Peraf, but don't try it with me."

"Then don't simply believe me. Come see it with your own eyes," Gian said. "We're close to gaining intelligence on the Ophie tribe. You can sit at the table and see what we see, no filter."

"Are you serious?"

"Yes. We've been deploying new technology this afternoon. Come and see. Maybe you'll find something to hang me with," Gian said with a smile.

"Shite. You're good at this – I almost believe this stupidity. I've vastly underestimated you," Bedros said. "But if you're offering, I will come."

"Follow me," Gian said.

"Where are we going?" Bedros had to hustle to keep up with Gian.

"The old tannery."

When they arrived, Merrie looked up from the bench where she was typing frantically on the computer.

"Councilman Bedros. I... I wasn't expecting you," she stammered.

"I don't suppose so. Captain Gian promised there was something happening I should see," he said.

"Oh? No pressure then," she said, smiling.

"Merrie, why don't you introduce Councilman Bedros to your surveillance network," Gian said.

"Sure. If you would look up at the wall," Merrie said as she typed.

The large, flat screens she'd mounted on the wall blinked to life. The screens simultaneously showed images to the southwest over the fields, east over the front wall and north up the mountain.

"What is that?" Bedros asked.

"It's a live video feed. The same feed is being monitored in the barracks around the clock. I've added a motion sensing algorithm that alerts that protector. Well, technically, the AI on the engineering console wrote the algorithm, but you get the idea." She began typing again. A middle screen popped to life, showing a person looking at a similar set of video screens. "That's Terevit, he's on duty right now."

"That's interesting, but why is it a big deal?" Bedros asked.

"If Terevit were to see something, he'd communicate with the squad on duty and we could have a team on the farm within five minutes of an Ophie sighting," Gian said. "Previous to this technology, our response time depended on someone ringing a bell. Not only that, Terevit has the capability to talk to the squad leader with something Merrie calls a talkie. He can actually direct those who are out in the field from his safe position back in the barracks."

"How?"

"Say hello to Terevit," Gian said, holding a talkie in front of the man.

"Uh, hello?"

The image of Terevit turned to the camera and waved.

"He heard me?"

"Yes. All of our squads have these when they're in the field. They can communicate with home base at any time," Gian said.

Bedros couldn't help himself. He was astonished. "I thought all of the founder's communication equipment failed and we didn't have the materials to repair them."

"That's correct, but Merrie found much older technology that the maker machine is capable of manufacturing."

"Impressive. So how will you locate the Ophie?"

"We've been carefully laying down a communication network up the mountain. It's been painstakingly slow, but we believe we're almost there," Gian said. "Merrie, are we still on schedule?"

"We're ready," she said and typed furiously on the keyboard.

The screens flickered and changed to a new view, looking north, up the mountain.

"What is it we're looking at?" Bedros asked.

"Prepare to be impressed," Gian said as the quad lifted from the wall.

"How are you doing that?"

"It's another of Merrie's discoveries. See that broken machine on the table? Merrie is flying one of them up the mountain. We've been working for the last tenday to map out a route and extend its range," Gian explained.

"It was really Eliora," Merrie explained as she manipulated the joysticks. "She's been installing equipment that sends the video signal back to us, all the way up the hill."

"Not all the way," Gian said. "Today, we're going to try to finish the last few kilometers. It's too dangerous for our people to get that close."

"How fast are you flying?" Bedros asked.

"Thirteen or fourteen meters per second," Merrie said. "Slower if we get a headwind. We're lucky, the original design of these quads used really old power systems. They could only fly for fifteen or twenty minutes. My girl will stay up for several days if I want."

"The downside to this technology is that the Ophie's hearing is such that they know when we're coming," Gian said.

"Do you think they know it's us?" Bedros asked.

"I believe so. They're very quick to knock one down if they see it."

They watched quietly as the quad flew across the tops of the trees, occasionally buffeted by winds. Merrie's flying skills had improved to the point that she easily adjusted.

"Now we have to get to work," Merrie said. "We're about to leave communications range."

"How will you fix that?"

"The first thing we do is make sure we don't have any Ophie standing right next to where we want to plant a repeater. Learned that the hard way. Then it's not too hard. We launch it from the quad and it will stick in most trees. We need one every half a kilometer or so."

As she'd been talking, Merrie made a sweep of the area, bobbed down, lined up on a sturdy limb and fired a small dart. She inspected her handiwork, pulled back and quickly gained elevation. She kept moving and repeated the process several more times before she started attracting attention.

"This one's going to be dicey. We could be done for the day if I screw this up," Merrie said.

A group of adolescent Ophie had started chasing the quad and were ineffectively throwing rocks at it.

"They don't look like much of a threat right now, but believe me once I get lower, their accuracy improves. I'm going to have to bust out some of my ninja moves," she said.

"Ninja?"

"Sorry, been watching old vids from the same century when these quads were invented," Merrie said.

The quad accelerated and swept around a tree, erratically dodging from side to side as she did. At the last moment, she leveled out, fired a dart and used the momentum gained from the dart to accelerate backwards and up.

"We'll need to inspect that one later," she said. "They're getting too close. Ready to get a good look, Captain?"

"You think we're close enough?"

"I'm going to drop a few repeaters on the ground and sprint in. We're recording, so if I go too fast, we can replay. Don't worry," she said.

Merrie flew forward and dipped down when the signal started to dip. She launched a dart at the ground and then flew forward, finally clearing the ridge they'd been working toward.

"My God. Is that what I think it is?" Bedros asked as the quad gained elevation.

"It's worse than I feared. We're out of time," Gian said.

Chapter 21

BRAWL

Lèger Airspace, Grünholz, Tipperary Solar System

Hail Meerkat Shipyard.

"Meerkat. Who might I have the pleasure of speaking with?" A holo rendering of Bing, Meerkat's foreman, popped up on the display.

"Bing. Any chance you could clear a deck for us? I need you to take a look at something and give us your professional opinion," I said.

"Captain Hoffen, my favorite scallywag. I wasn't expecting to see you until next week."

"No. That's *Kestrel*. Captain Norris is sailing her out from Curie. We scraped up *Hotspur* a little and were hoping you could squeeze us in," I said.

"You been mixing it up with those Oberrhein boys again?"

"Nah, something outside of Curie," I said. It was as close to the truth as I could tell him.

"Bring her in. We'll clear the deck and take a look. I can't promise anything on the schedule, however. It might be a week or so," he said.

"We'll see you in ten," I said and closed the comm.

"That doesn't sound hopeful," Ada said.

"I guess we'll just have to see how deep Jonathan's pockets are," I said. "Any change in *Stark Justice's* attitude?"

"He's falling back some. I dropped into the atmosphere of Grünholz," she said. "He'd have to really want us."

"You suppose he can even dock at Gros with that thing?"

"It would take constant monitoring, but Luc said they have a high altitude wharf for bigger ships. I'll bet they're headed there," she said. "What do you think he wants to talk about?"

"My guess is he wants to threaten us."

"With what? If he wanted to put us down, he could have already," she said.

"Not in front of Nuage Air Defense. They want to keep us quiet until they can catch us in the open. I have a hard time believing he wants to see *Cape's* crew die, though," I said.

"I hope you're right. We don't stand a chance against those heavies," Ada said.

"Meh, we can still outrun 'em."

"Can't outrun missiles, Liam," Marny said. I hadn't heard her come up to the bridge.

"True enough."

Tabby walked up behind me, placed her chin on my shoulder and looked out the armor glass. "Never get tired of that view," she said.

I looked forward and took in the three towers of Nuage Gros. It was the capital and largest of Nuage nation's eighteen cloud cities, all of which floated above the planet Grünholz.

"You think Belirand can make trouble for us with Nuage?" Tabby asked.

"They can try, but they'd have to risk us spilling the beans to Nuage. I'd expect something a lot more clandestine," I said.

"Cap's right," Marny said. "Belirand hasn't made any friends out here. I doubt anyone will stand up against 'em, but they won't be bending rules for them either."

Nick, Jonathan, we'll be landing in less than five.

I enjoyed watching Ada bring a ship into close quarters. Tabby and I were both excellent pilots, but neither of us could compete with Ada's fine control in-close, which she attributed to spending most of her youth maneuvering giant barges with her mom.

Meerkat was located in the main center tower, on the first habitable level. As we approached, I saw that Bing had opened their main doors. There were only three meters of clearance in either direction, but Ada flew in and set her down softly on the crowded deck. Bing had made room for us by scooting other jobs out of the way.

"Nice control, Ada, I'd have let the AI bring me in if I had the chair," I said.

"Best you remember that," she said and got up.

"Tabbs, you mind grabbing our bags? I'll see if I can get Bing to find us a slot," I said.

"What? Now I'm your butler?"

I looked over to her, surprised. "No. Sorry," I said quickly.

"See? Now, that's nice control." Tabby looked at Ada and they giggled as they walked toward the back of the bridge.

I felt an arm around my shoulder. I'd momentarily forgotten that Marny had been seated at the couch.

"Cap. You've much to learn about women," she said.

"Tell me about it."

I grabbed Tabby's and my bags from our quarters and met the crew on Meerkat's deck.

Tabby looked at her bag in my hand and smiled. She then handed me my favorite heavy flechette with a waist mountable holster. "Get strapped. Who knows what kind of shenanigans we might run into."

"Aye, Tabitha, mischief is afoot and I don't want anyone out in the open without an escort," Marny said, clearly excited to be resuming her role as head of security.

"Aww, Marn, I've got plans," Ada said.

"Would that be Nuage's very own eligible bachelor, Captain Luc Gray, you'd be referring to?" Marny asked.

"Perhaps."

"If you give me two minutes to read him in on our security situation, he'll be a fine escort," Marny said.

"Okay, he'll like that anyway. I think he's got a thing for you," Ada said smiling.

"Not what I'd call just a few scratches!" Bing said as he walked up holding a reading pad. "And who in Hera's name did you have pasting those patches on? My kid makes less of a mess with her modeling clay."

"Can you fix her?" I asked.

"Anything's possible with enough money, Captain Hoffen."

Marny, Tabby and Ada split off from the group and walked toward the lift that would take them up into the rest of the city.

"Hold on a second, Bing. Tabby, where are you guys headed?" I asked.

"It's 1500 and we skipped lunch. We're headed to de Laroche. Don't worry, I'll order you a burger and a Guinness," she said.

I turned back to Bing who was flicking through a reading pad.

"What's the bottom line?" I asked.

"You're not going to like it. I've looked at the scans we took as you flew in. Eight days, six-hundred forty thousand. We could start on it in six days if we push off your other ship, *Kestrel*," he said.

"That bad?"

"No getting around it."

"Do you have access to missiles?" Jonathan asked.

"No armaments here... and I don't believe we've been introduced," Bing said.

Jonathan held out his hand and shook. "Jonathan of Anino Enterprises. We'd like to be ready to sail in five days. Would you be willing to negotiate a premium for appropriate consideration on your schedule?"

"I'm afraid that might be above my pay grade," Bing said.

"How many jobs do you have in front of *Hotspur*?" Jonathan asked.

"There are four," Bing said, rubbing his neck. A flush rose in his cheeks.

"Perhaps if you were to provide an incentive to these customers?" Jonathan pushed.

Bing looked back to me. "Look, I appreciate your business, Captain Hoffen, but these smaller jobs keep me in business. I can't be jacking them around," Bing said.

"We'll pay fifty thousand to step to the front of the line," Jonathan said.

"I don't know...."

"And an additional hundred thousand if the work is complete in ninety-six hours," he said.

"We'll run double shifts."

"One more thing. This is off book until we take possession."

"That might be tough," Bing said.

"If it were easy, we wouldn't need to pay a premium," Jonathan said as he mimed pinching a contract and flicking it at Bing. The last part was for show, as I doubted Jonathan needed to use a HUD to accomplish anything.

Bing's eyes didn't actually bulge out of their sockets, but he was suitably impressed. "Right you are. See you in ninety-six hours then," he said, signing the contract.

"Thanks, Bing," I said.

"Always a treat when you're in town," he said. I wasn't sure if he was sincere or not.

With bags in tow, Jonathan, Nick and I made our way over to the lift and climbed on.

Level Twenty-three, I requested and watched the levels blink by through the transparent doors.

"If you don't mind, Captain, we've tasks to attend to while your team refuels," Jonathan said.

"Now that you mention it, I need to spend some time working on supplies for *Cape* and see about the rest of our business. We've been out of contact forever," Nick said. "Would I be in your way if I accompanied you, Jonathan?"

"Not at all, Master James," he said.

"Nick, you want me to have Marny bring you anything to eat?" I asked.

"Something fried and a chocolate shake. Tell her I'll eat healthy for dinner," he said.

I smiled. "I'll pass it along."

They dropped me off at the entrance to de Laroche and took my bags with them back toward the lift. I made my way through the ancient aircraft-themed bar and found Ada, Marny and Tabby lounging at a large round table.

"Where'd you lose the boys?" Ada asked.

"They wanted to spend some time alone," I said, chuckling.

"Let me guess. My little man didn't get enough screen time because we were stealthed on the way in?" Marny asked.

"That's probably right," I said. "But I can't imagine why anyone would want to dust off having lunch with you three beauties."

"Is that what you were dreaming about last night?" Tabby asked suggestively. "Remember you sleep naked so your dreams aren't always that subtle."

"No..." My cheeks started to burn as Marny shook her head back and forth.

"I think he's feeling guilty, Tabbs," Ada giggled. "Cut a little close to the truth there, Liam?"

"You're all so naughty," I said. "You'd kill me if I ever said anything like that."

"Not kill - you'd just be another good looking female crewmember, that's all," Tabby said.

Fortunately, a waiter showed up in time to cut the conversation short. They hadn't ordered yet, so I asked for a soy-based burger with extra sharp blue cheese and a basket of hot pepper and nacho covered potato wedges.

"Just a glass of white for me," Ada said. "Luc's on his way down."

"That was fast," Tabby said. "I think he's got it bad for you."

"We're just friends."

"You sure Luc knows that?"

"Knows what?" Captain Luc Gray of the Nuage Air Defense, still in uniform, approached the table.

Ada jumped up and wrapped her arms around him. "Luc!" she squealed.

"I heard you were back in town. You have anything to do with that Belirand cruiser docked in high orbit?" he asked.

"Wish I could say no," I said.

I shook his hand and pulled him in for an embrace. He'd been there more than once when I'd needed him and I considered him a good friend.

"Not good enough to have Oberrhein after you? So now you've pissed off Belirand too?"

"You wouldn't believe me if I told you," I said.

"Try me."

"Wish I could, my friend. Suffice it to say, we've run into some problems with the way they do business and we're working through our differences."

"I know you've dropped a few cruisers in your time, but that Belirand ship is in a different league," he said.

"That's an understatement. *Hotspur* has nothing that'll get through her armor," I said.

"Do I want to know how you know that?" he asked.

"Join us for a drink?" Tabby cut in.

"Can't hurt," he said and sat in the chair I'd pulled over for him. Ada wrapped her arm around his neck and sat sideways in his lap, giving him a kiss on the cheek.

"Luc. Are you carrying a service weapon?" Marny asked.

"I am. Why?"

"The threat from Belirand is real and we're taking precautions. I'd appreciate it if you didn't spend too much time in public venues with Ada. I'm also requesting you carry a weapon," she said.

He looked from Marny back to Ada who nodded her head affirmatively. "Let's say things are strained," Ada said.

"You think they'd attack an officer of the Nuage Air Defense in our home base?"

"Probably not. We're just taking precautions," Marny said.

"You're serious, aren't you?"

"We are," I said. "Fact is, we're still trying to figure it out. Just be careful, please?" Marny asked.

"Sounds, horrible. We'll have to stay inside, watch vids and order takeout." he said, grinning.

"If by stay inside and watch vids, you mean go shopping, then yes," Ada said.

"Ada," Marny said, caution in her voice.

"Just a little shopping. Hardly any at all," Ada said.

By the time we'd finished eating, Luc and Ada had taken off and we still had an hour before MacAsgaill would arrive.

"I'll run Nick's food up," Marny said. "You want to come along or wait here?"

"We'll see you to the lift, but I, for one, could use another beer," I said.

Tabby and I walked Marny out and turned back to the bar. A red haired man, accompanied by a smaller dark haired woman and a giant man turned into the bar in front of us.

"I think that's MacAsgaill," I said. I wasn't completely sure, having only seen his bust on a holo display.

"So much for not bringing an army," Tabby said.

Send Nick a priority message – "MacAsgaill arrived early. We'll stall, but come down as soon as you can."

"You want to wait out here for Nick and Marny?" Tabby asked.

"Nah, I don't think he'll pull anything inside a bar, do you?"

"They came at us with everything they had in the deep dark," Tabby said, looking at me skeptically.

"Right. It's a bar. There are rules," I said and strode forward.

The small woman was the first to sense our presence and she turned to intercept us. The look in her eye and the fluidity of her movements told me what I'd suspected. She moved much like Tali Liszt, our ex-special forces friend and 'the old-girl' as Marny called her. She would be a problem if push came to shove - as I suspected it might.

"Mac," she hissed.

Captain MacAsgaill and his giant companion turned at her word. Nothing subtle about the giant, although he had as much fat as he had muscle. He brought a certain immediate visual deterrent quality to the party. I couldn't imagine what kind of damage he could do when angry. Well, to be truthful, I could imagine it and that was the beauty of bringing him along.

The Captain wasn't much to look at, pasty skin, blue eyes and thinning gray-red hair. He looked Tabby up and down with a smugly lecherous grin. The disrespect was an obvious attempt at putting us on-tilt and I had a bad feeling about our meeting.

"Liam Hoffen and Ada... no... Tabitha Masters," MacAsgaill said and held out his hand to be shaken.

"What do you want, MacAsgaill?" I asked, ignoring the requested handshake.

He wiped his hands together as if that's what he'd always planned and returned them to his side. The woman and the giant, I'd started calling André in my head, stepped around to stand just behind MacAsgaill.

"Like I said, I just want to talk."

"My partner is on his way down, we'll wait," I said.

"Sure. Although, I have something that I believe you might like to see before he arrives. Do you already have a table?"

It was such an ordinary situation in an ordinary location and it was at such odds with what was really happening. My head swam with the incongruity of it all as I led him back to our table.

"I see we missed lunch," he said.

The plates hadn't yet been cleared and André eyed the half-eaten platter of nachos, placing himself on the chair between me and MacAsgaill. I pushed the platter toward him and he looked to MacAsgaill who nodded his permission.

"Anything to drink?" Our waiter had followed us over to the table.

"Water," the small woman replied.

"Your best Scotch and a tall draft for my large friend, Mr. Roussi," MacAsgaill said.

"All set over here?" the waiter asked looking to Tabby and me. I nodded affirmatively and he efficiently moved on.

"It's a shame Tullas didn't finish her job. It sure makes things messier," MacAsgaill said.

"You mean murdering my crew and that of *Cape*?" I asked.

"LeGrande and every other officer of Belirand knew that to fall out of fold-space was a death sentence. She accepted that when she took the job."

"But you could fix that," I said.

"Beside the point," MacAsgaill said. "I'd love to argue the morality of sacrificing forty-five crew to save the entirety of humanity, but you don't seem like you're big on listening. Let's get straight to brass tacks. You and your entire crew will turn yourselves over to me. We'll escort you to a place where you can live out your lives and we won't kill your families."

"Tullas said if we didn't tell anyone, you'd leave our families out of it," I said.

"That was Tullas, I'm changing the deal," he said and slid a reading pad across the table to me.

I was about to tell him to hold on to it until Nick arrived, but the screen showed a vid of my family's Co-Op station in the Descartes asteroid belt.

"What's this?" I asked.

"Just watch," he said.

The video was shot from the perspective of a cruiser and it had just crossed over the defensive perimeter and was approaching the Co-Op. It was a very recent video, as I hadn't yet seen the improvements the video was showing.

"Will you submit?" he asked.

"What are you doing?" I looked to Tabby in a panic, her stricken face told me she was as concerned as I was.

"It's called an object lesson."

André placed a small box on the table in front of MacAsgaill, opened it and turned back to the nachos.

"You know what this is?" he asked. "Of course you do. You've used quantum communication devices quite frequently. This particular crystal is tuned to the beautiful ship – *Hammer of Justice* and my good friend Captain Ahmed Mussa.

"Captain Mussa, you have a green light," MacAsgaill said.

"Wait. What have you done!? There are people on that station!" I yelled.

I watched missiles stream forward from the large ship. They impacted the co-op and exploded on contact. My mind went blank. I can't exactly explain how it felt, but I'd been in so many life-and-death situations that I'd found a special place where I packed away my feelings in times of great distress and I pushed it all there.

In a single, fluid movement, I swung the reading tablet into the face of MacAsgaill's huge bodyguard. He was expecting the move and blocked it, guffawing at my lame attempt. I knew he would and used my right hand to twist the heavy flechette in its holster and point it at his leg. I fired as many shots as I could manage and was rewarded by a howl of pain.

From the corner of my eye I saw Tabby already on the woman, but couldn't tell how it was going. I jumped across the table at MacAsgaill who was trying to stand and stumbling in his attempt. My fist caught his chin squarely before I felt an arm land heavily on my back. So much for my heavy flechette dropping the giant.

I rolled to the ground and came up on my feet, MacAsgaill standing between me and his bodyguard. He pulled his hands up in a poor boxing stance and I went into automatic mode. I'd been training with Tabby for long enough that I didn't hesitate. I unleashed a front snap kick and followed it with an elbow strike to his nose and he dropped away, unconscious.

I fell on him with the intent of beating him to death, but the problem with putting MacAsgaill on the ground was that I was now accessible to André. I got one more punch in and felt a satisfying crunch before the monster tackled me, pulling me from his boss. It was a horrible position to be in. His weight alone pinned me to the ground and I struggled to fend off his meaty arms as he bludgeoned me. It was impossible to slip the blows lying on my back and I was starting to lose consciousness.

"That's enough," I heard a woman say.

The blows continued and I fought to maintain consciousness and keep my defenses up, but I had nothing left.

I heard the sound of electrical discharge as one last blow rammed into my face and I lost consciousness.

"HEYA, SLUGGER," Tabby's voice purred in my ear.

I slowly opened my eyes and took in the scene around me. We were in a small room. I tried to get a breath in through my swollen nose while scanning to see where we were. I couldn't identify enough of the room to figure out if we were on a ship or still on Nuage Gros.

"Where are we?" I mumbled through a heavy cloth that lay across my jaw.

"Don't try to talk, Liam. We're in the brig on Gros," she said, stroking my hair, my head in her lap.

"He murdered Mom and Dad," I said.

"I know, Liam."

"Is he in jail?"

"He's claiming self-defense. The waiter is backing his story, too. Worse, they're pressing charges, trying to get attempted murder," she said.

"That's crazy."

"You fired your flechette and broke his jaw," she said.

"Broke his jaw?" I asked.

"Yeah." Tabby hugged me and I cried.

Chapter 22

AT THE GATES

Yishuv Settlement, Planet Ophir

Merrie pushed the left stick down and the quad rose quickly.

The unfolding view was that of a mountain plateau. In the foreground sat a village, tall tents arranged in circles around communal fires. In the background, a swarm of Ophie was busy clearing brush and setting stripped tree trunks into the ground.

"What do you mean, we're out of time?" Bedros asked.

"We've long known the number of Ophie in the village to the North and even their reproductive cycle," Gian said. "The tents you see in the permanent village confirm what we've always known. That village looks like it supports a hundred fifty warriors max."

"You're saying all of our problems through history have been caused by a hundred fifty Ophie?" Bedros asked.

"I am. Although as that village shows, it is probably closer to a two hundred twenty-five total population. It makes sense. They're hunter-gatherers and have no concept of domesticating animals or growing crops. Most likely this is one of several villages they frequent. The fact that they disappear for decades at a time also supports the belief that these villages are temporary."

"What are they doing?" Bedros asked pointing at the screen, where the Ophie were working.

"They're preparing for visitors," Gian said. "And, from the looks of it, they're preparing for a lot of them."

"Do you ever tire of being right?" Bedros asked.

"No. I would very much have liked to be wrong about this. Look to the west. You can see new tents with markings similar to the scouts we've recently encountered."

"How many will there be and how much time do we have?"

"The land won't support a large number of them for very long," Gian said. "When they finally gather, we'll have few days before they attack. As for numbers, we'll be able to better estimate once we count the number of campsites. We could be looking at upwards of two thousand."

Bedros' face turned grim with determination. He was finally on board. "Tell me what you need. I'll make it happen."

AMON LOOKED UP. He and Nurit had been toiling around the clock casting iron collars for the posts that were part of the new Keep next to the protector's barracks. The council had decided that if the walls of the city were breached, the population would fall back to this fortified position.

"Do you think it will come to this?" Nurit asked. "There is hardly enough room for eight hundred of us in there."

"Eliora does and I believe her," Amon said, believing in his words the more often he said them.

"I wish they'd share what has gotten everyone so worked up. Has she said anything about it?"

"No, but Merrie said there are more Ophie than we've ever seen. She said there's no possibility they won't be coming over the wall."

"At least this is the last of the collars, not to mention the last of the iron," Nurit said.

"You rest. I'll install them," Amon said, hammering the pins from the top of the box that held the cooling iron.

With the hooked end of a bar, he dug in the sand, pulled the new collar from its mold and inspected it. He'd like to grind off the rough edges, but time wouldn't allow for finishing. He tossed the twenty centimeter collar onto the cart behind the smithy's electric vehicle and proceeded to unpin the final mold.

Nurit sat down wearily. "I hope it will be enough."

"It will have to be. And keep your longsword with you, even if you nap," Amon said.

"I will. I'm not sure how much good it will do me, though," she said. "I can barely lift my arms at this point."

"You'll recover and you're stronger than all but a few," Amon said as he hopped in the cart and drove toward the siege fortifications.

On his way toward the new structure, he saw Merrie walking and pulled over.

"Need a ride?"

She smiled as she climbed in. "Last I looked, you were almost done installing the outer fence."

"Yes. This is the last of it. We could use more iron, but that's not possible. We've a few places that could use reinforcement," he said.

"Hopefully, it won't come to that. The turret's already been mounted." Merrie pointed to a heavily fortified position on top of the original barrack's building next to the settlement's exterior wall. "We'll do whatever is necessary to protect that gun so it can be used to peel off any Ophie that try to breach the Keep."

"Sounds more like a stalemate than a way to win," Amon said.

"You're right. If we get pushed back here, we'll be under siege," Merrie said.

"When did you get so smart about war?"

Merrie laughed. "Hard not to when you spend every waking moment around Eliora and Captain Gian."

"Where will you be if they attack?" Amon asked.

She grew serious and placed her hand on Amon's arm as he pulled to a stop in front of the newly constructed timber fence.

"It is not a question of if, Amon. They are coming, this much is certain. The only real question is when. I'm just glad we've been able to finish work on the Keep," she said.

"You didn't say where you'd be," he said.

"I'll be in the top floor of what used to be the barracks. I've all my electronic equipment set up there. Don't worry about me - the room is very secure. What is your assignment?"

"Mom and I are on the south wall, close to the west gate. We haven't had enough time for training with bows, so our job is to repel Ophie who try to make it over the wall."

At just that moment, a bell pealed out and Merrie leapt from the cart.

"It has started. Be safe, Amon," she said and then ran through the open iron door.

Amon was torn. His assignment was to get to the wall when the bell sounded, but if he didn't install these final collars, the weakness in the fence would be obvious. He made his decision and picked the first, still hot collar from the bed of the trailer and climbed the ladder, slipping the collar over the waiting timber. If they were driven back to the Keep, it would not fall because he'd abandoned his responsibility.

Merrie burst into the room and took a position behind Terevit, looking at the screens that lined the wall.

"What is it? Why the alarm?" she asked, looking from one screen to the next. There were no Ophie to be seen in any of them.

"I saw them just before the quad went blank. They know, Merrie! They know we've been watching them," he said.

"It hardly matters," she said. "We'll launch another. Gian will need better information. Take Quad-12 to the roof."

Terevit ceded the chair to Merrie who sat and typed furiously. He picked a quad from a shelf full of them, powered it up and climbed a ladder to the roof above.

"Ready," he yelled to Merrie.

She gently throttled up and lifted the quad from his hands. The talkie next to her sparked to life.

"Terevit, report." It was Gian's voice.

Terevit pulled the trap door closed and slid iron bars back in place, finally reaching for the talkie demanding his attention.

"Captain Gian. They're coming from the north," Terevit said.

"When. How many?"

"Just a few minutes ago, and I don't know how many. They got the quad," he said.

"Get another one up."

"We've already launched," he said. "I think the Ophie know we're controlling them."

Merrie watched Quad-12 cover familiar territory up the steep mountainside. It would take at least forty minutes to climb to where they'd lost the last quad.

She pulled on the headset she hadn't yet tried. A lever on the floor would allow her to depress the talk button and leave her hands free to navigate the quad.

"Captain, if they're coming straight down, we'll have two and a half hours before they reach the north wall. I should run across their position with the quad in thirty minutes, give or take. I'm staying high, so we don't get dropped again," she said.

"Understood. Let me know when you reach them," he said. "Any other activity?"

Merrie looked to Terevit whose sheepish look told her enough. She'd done the best she could, teaching him the technology, but it had mostly been beyond him.

"I'll let you know."

She hovered the quad in place for a moment and placed the engineering pad on a mount that allowed her to interact without holding it.

Run movement analysis algorithms, she instructed the pad.

The left screen switched to the west wall looking over the mountain's descending slope. The trees had only been cleared back ten meters and the console displayed an outline around a perfectly hidden Ophie, who had settled in next to a tree.

"Captain, there's a patrol, west wall at tree line. They're camouflaged pretty well," she said. "Otherwise, I'm not picking anything else up."

"I see 'em, Captain," Terevit announced. "I'll go over and help point them out."

"I need you to stay off this channel," he said.

"I hate it when he treats me like that," Terevit said.

Merrie ignored him as best she could as she urged the quad onward, up the hill. She was hoping by gaining elevation she might see the approaching horde more quickly.

"I can't believe I'm going to be cooped up in this hole while everyone is out there fighting. I should go over there," Terevit complained.

"Terevit, you can't," she said. "Captain knows about it and will deal with it. If you leave me, I'll be stuck."

"I'll tell your boyfriend to come help you. I think I saw him down there," Terevit said and escaped out the door.

"Terevit!" Merrie yelled. For a moment, she considered calling Gian, but she focused on her immediate tasks: scanning the grounds around the settlement and flying Quad-12 up the mountain in search of whatever Terevit had seen.

Thirty minutes into the flight, she finally saw her first signs. Clouds of dust were rising up above the light canopy of the alpine forest. Carefully, she slowed the quad's progress and reduced her elevation. In the past two tendays, they'd counted over two thousand warriors and it was her job to determine if they were all coming at once or if there would be a split force.

"Merrie?" Amon's voice called from the doorway into the small room.

"Yes, Amon. What are you doing here?"

"A protector, Terevit I think his name was, said I should come up," he said. "Do you need me?"

"I need someone's help. I can't run this post by myself," she said.

"Nurit will wonder where I've gone," he said.

"What is your assignment?"

"They didn't know what to do with us."

"Of course, top of the south wall without bows. That's stupid. Fetch her. I need help and this room has to be guarded," she said.

"But we can't abandon the wall," Amon said.

"I'll inform the right people. Just go get her," she said.

"I will," Amon said and ran out of the room.

Merrie sighed. At least she'd eventually have help.

"Captain, I've eyes on the enemy," she said into her headset.

"How far up are they?"

"Twenty-one kilometers and they're moving fast," Merrie said.

"How big of a force?"

"Wait one," she said, hovering at thirty meters.

Count unique troops.

The idea had just popped into her head, but the engineering console had access to the video feed and it would certainly do a better job of estimating than she would.

As she flew over the advancing enemies, a counter in large numerals displayed on the pad's smaller screen. Incrementing quickly, it jumped from ten to a hundred forty then continued to spin up as she negotiated her way through the trees. Unlike previous groups of Ophie, these paid the quad no attention and she grew bolder, flying only five meters above their heads. When she popped out the other end, the counter showed sixteen hundred.

Estimate size of force.

She had no idea if the engineering pad's computer would be able to deal with the request, but it had already impressed her with the information it had gathered.

"Captain. Best estimate is roughly twenty-three hundred. They're in heavy cover. It looks like they brought the entire plateau," she said.

"I would have," he said. "When will they arrive?"

"Best guess? Two hours," she said.

"Bring the quad back. We've secured the western wall. Are you seeing anything else? And did you send Terevit over here?"

"Not specifically. I did, however, pull the blacksmiths from the south wall to replace him. Can you tell whoever's got that section?"

"I read you, Merrie. Amon already checked in with me and they're on their way to you," Eliora said.

"I've got Terevit on the west wall. We'll keep him," Shem piped in.

Merrie turned the quad around slowly and found what she was looking for - an old tree with a broad limb and not much foliage. She flew over and set Quad-12 on the branch and powered down its small, but powerful motors.

She walked over to the shelves and pulled Quad-13 off and set it on the table. She registered the quad with her computer controls and then climbed up the ladder. The metal bars of the grate were almost too much for her to slide sideways. She pulled and pulled, moving them only a few inches at a time.

"Can I help with that?" Amon asked as he entered the room.

"Gah. Yes! Did you make these impossible to move for a reason?" Merrie asked heatedly.

"Apologies. I'm afraid they were my design," Nurit said. "What are you doing?"

"Watch and learn," Merrie said. She hated that she was snapping at her friends, but she felt the weight of the world bearing down on her.

As she climbed to the bottom of the ladder, she felt Amon's hands rest on her waist. It startled her, as he'd never previously shown her any affection. She had come to believe that he considered her more of a sister. She turned, perhaps too quickly, expecting him to lift her to the ground. He didn't but rather held her in place for a moment.

"I know we don't have much time, Merrie. I just need to get this off my chest before the day gets past me," he said.

Her heart skipped a beat. She felt the pressure of the oncoming combat, but she would allow herself just a moment.

"What do you need to say, Amon?" she asked looking into his face, searching for an answer.

"I want to be with you, Merrie."

"You *are* with me," she whispered.

"Always. I want to be with you always. I'm glad that you asked for me. I didn't think my heart would be able to bear combat without knowing where you were."

Merrie grabbed the much larger man's head in her hands and stared into his blue eyes. "Me too, Amon, me too." She kissed him fully on the lips and then released his head. "You've really got to work on your timing though. Now get up there and move that grate out of the way."

Merrie looked over to Nurit who'd watched the scene play out. The older blacksmith flicked a tear from her cheek and stood straight. "What would you have me do?" she asked, breaking the moment.

"There are two ways into this room. The most obvious is the roof. We must defend this room at all costs. We are the eyes for Captain Gian.

With us, he can be in all places," Merrie said. She handed a quad to Amon. "Place this gently on the roof, would you?" He'd already moved the iron grate out of the way and opened the trap door.

"Can do," he said.

Merrie sat and re-entered the zone, pushing away the distractions of how warm and wonderful she felt from her moment with Amon. Now they just had to survive.

Quad-13 lifted easily from the roof of the barracks, turned from the command center and accelerated in a northward direction.

"Close the roof, please," she said.

"Yes, Merrie," Amon said in his normal, quiet voice. For Merrie it was far from normal.

Fifteen minutes later she found a resting spot in a tall tree and set it down.

"Pull Quad-14 and place it on the roof... but wait a second, I need to register it," she said.

Amon startled when the rotors momentarily fired to life.

"Sorry. They do that when we turn them on. Same drill, put it on the roof," she said.

"How is it that you're able to still see through the other device's eyes?" Nurit asked, recognizing that the screen hadn't changed from when Quad-13 had landed.

"Good question," Merrie said and moved the center screen so its contents were to the left of center. "It's a camera and I left it trans-mitting. When the Ophie get to where Quad-13 is, we'll have forty-five minutes before they actually arrive here. The center camera is set to Quad-14. I'll use it to scout the immediate area. You can watch with me. If you see something suspicious, stop me and I'll move in closer."

"And you made all this?" Nurit asked. "What about Merik, what's he been doing?"

"Merik turned me loose to follow up on this technology. The settlement needs more than one engineer and Merik prefers to work on bigger projects, like getting water into people's homes, fixing machines, that sort of thing. And for the record, I didn't make any of this. I was just lucky enough to find it in the archives of the engineering pad. All this stuff was invented more than a millennia ago."

"Why haven't we seen it before?" Nurit asked.

"Not sure," Merrie said as Quad-14 sailed over the south wall and swept to the west. "I think we just had in mind what we'd lost and weren't thinking about what we could have."

They continued the visual sweep and forty-five minutes later, Merrie landed Quad-14 on top of the barracks.

"Want me to go get that?" Amon asked.

"No. I'll switch over to Quad-13 but it's good to leave 14 available," Merrie said.

After switching, Merrie flew the quad up the mountain and found the approaching Ophie, still running at their consistent pace.

"Captain, they're at twelve kilometers. We have less than an hour," she said.

"We read you," Gian said.

Merrie gained elevation and kept pace with the leaders, reading out ten minute updates until finally she could see Yishuv through the lens of the quad.

"They're here, Captain."

Chapter 23

POINT OF NO RETURN

Brig, Lèger Gros, Tipperary System

"Liam. Someone's coming."

We'd spent the night in an isolated brig and my whole body ached. The initial med-patches I'd received had run out of juice and I was having difficulty breathing through my nose.

I sat up and leaned against Tabby as the door opened and in walked none other than Admiral Marsh, the leader of Nuage nation's security forces. I tried to stand, but couldn't muster the strength.

Before Marsh could speak, Tabby went on the offensive. "Is it your intention to leave us in here to rot? Liam needs medical attention."

Marsh gave me a quick once over and responded, "'You're right. My apologies. I'll see that he is taken care of immediately."

"What do you need, Admiral?" I asked. "Surely you don't get involved in all bar-room disagreements."

"Captain Hoffen. I'm here on a different matter. We've just received word that there has been an accident at your home in the Descartes asteroid belt."

"Accident?" I asked incredulously.

"Yes. There was an explosion and several people were killed. I regret to inform you that your parents, Silver and Pete Hoffen were among the deceased."

I could feel the tears that I'd thought I'd run out of the night before welling up. I tried to talk but could tell it wouldn't be possible.

"It wasn't an accident, Admiral Marsh," Tabby said. The scorn in her voice was evident.

"What do you mean?"

"You said you were here on a different matter, but it was Belirand who did this. MacAsgaill called that strike down on the Co-Op and murdered our family," Tabby said.

"Who else?" I asked, before Marsh could respond.

"David Muir is the only person that has been identified. Miss Masters, you should be careful about your accusations. Captain MacAsgaill is pressing charges for what he's described as an unprovoked assault in the de Laroche bar. Belirand submitted an extradition request."

"They murder my parents and you'd consider handing us over to them?" I asked.

"Belirand is a very powerful corporation, Liam. Off the record, I believe there's more going on here than they've told us, but we have to be very careful in our dealings with them. Somehow, you've made another very powerful enemy and we won't be able to bail you out of it this time," she said.

"You can't hand us over. They'll murder us too," Tabby said.

"It might not be within my control," Marsh said, and turned toward the door. "Liam, I'm very sorry about your parents. I understand they were extraordinary people."

I placed my head in my hands and wept again. Something in me had been holding out hope that they'd found a way to escape.

We sat like this for a long time before the door opened again and a medical technician rolled a cart into the room. She had me lie back while scanning the damage to my body, most of which was on my face.

"Your nose and cheeks require surgery beyond my capacity. I'll repair the tissue damage and stop the bleeding, but you'll need to meet with a surgeon," she said.

I nodded. I didn't care, I was emotionally spent.

After she left, my aches healed but my depression deepened.

Time passed in a blur. It wasn't until the sixth day when Tabby and I once again heard the approach of a group of people. We'd only seen the medical technician and the person who slid in three meals each day. I found it remarkable that they'd left us in the cell together and not separated us.

"I suppose they've decided," I said.

"No matter what Liam, I'm with you. You wouldn't be the man I love if you had turned away from forty-five people who faced certain death. Your parents wouldn't have done it any differently," she said.

"I could have warned them," I said.

"You think Big Pete would have hidden away?"

We'd been dancing around this conversation for the last several days. It was hard for me not to take responsibility for my parent's death. I'd depended on the safety of the Co-Op and the perimeter guns ability to defend them, yet somehow Belirand's *Hammer of Justice* had sailed right past.

The door to the cell opened and Admiral Marsh walked in, followed by MacAsgaill and two Nuage security forces.

Tabby and I stood, holding hands. Wherever they were taking us, they'd likely split us up and it could be the last time we'd see each other.

"Captain Hoffen, Miss Masters. Ciaran MacAsgaill has something he needs to say to you," Marsh said.

"We have nothing..." Tabby started, but I squeezed her hand.

MacAsgaill stepped forward and looked at the ground. "I apologize for the incident at de Laroche. It was insensitive for me to take advantage of an accident at your family's home to provoke you into a fight. I have withdrawn all charges against you both."

He didn't look at me but at Marsh, who nodded and he stepped back between the two Nuage guards.

"Liam Hoffen, Tabitha Masters," she said. "On behalf of Nuage, I apologize for detaining you under these less than truthful circumstances. In light of this new evidence, would you like to file charges against Ciaran MacAsgaill and his crew for the assault in de Laroche?"

"Would he be jailed?" I asked.

"Probably not. Belirand would utilize their diplomatic status."

"Then no. Are we free to go?"

"Yes. I'll escort you out," Marsh said.

The guards turned and led MacAsgaill away.

"What was that about?" I asked Marsh.

"I don't know. MacAsgaill just walked into my office today and admitted his deception. To be honest, the whole thing stinks. What's going on here, Hoffen? I've seen how you operate, you're into something again, aren't you?"

"Yes. Would you believe I can't tell you for your own safety?" I asked.

"Nothing you say surprises me anymore, Hoffen. Just take it some-where else and don't drag Nuage into it," she said.

"Belirand kills his parents, tries to abduct us and you're worried about it happening on your station?" Tabby asked as we stepped onto a lift.

"That was insensitive of me and I am truly sorry for the loss of your parents. The reality is that we are a small nation that cannot stand against Belirand. If MacAsgaill hadn't changed his mind, we would have turned you over to him," she said.

"Why did he change his mind?" Tabby asked.

"I was as surprised as you. And here we are," she said as the doors to the lift opened.

"Thank you for being honest, Admiral," I said.

"I wish I could do more."

The doors opened and Ada, Nick and Marny were there, waiting for us. Tabby and I exited and hugged our friends. It was emotional, but I'd run out of tears.

"Where to?" I asked.

"Frimunt and Annalise Licht brought back your parent's bodies in *Sterra's Gift*," Nick said. "We've been holding off a service, hoping we'd be able to free you. Would you like to get cleaned up first?"

"I need to see them," I said.

The truth was, I didn't want to see my parents dead, but I also knew I wouldn't be able to put them to rest if I didn't.

"Understood," Nick said and stepped toward the bank of elevators.

On the ride down, Ada placed her hand into my own and gave it a squeeze. She and Nick had each lost a parent in the last eighteen months and it occurred to me that this was bringing back emotions for both of them. I released her hand and wrapped my arm around her shoulder. Tabby looked at me, smiled and placed her arm around my waist.

We exited on Level-2 and approached a storefront which had the words Stebbing Funeral over a wood-paneled arch. Nick confidently pushed through the opaque doors and we followed. A man stood up from a desk as we entered.

"Mr. James. If you'll follow me," he said.

"Liam, would you like to do this by yourself?" Nick asked.

"No." I could barely speak.

The room we entered was quiet and dimly lit with rows of benches on both sides. I recognized Frimunt sitting in the front pew. His wife, Annalise, covered in a black shawl sat next to him, crying. At the front, one casket was open, the other closed. Tabby's hand gripped my own as we walked down the aisle.

I looked into the face of my father, who lay there as if he were just resting. I placed my hand on his and reached over to the closed casket with the other to join my family together one last time. The guilt I felt threatened to overwhelm me and I found myself talking to them, telling them how we'd gotten to the place where we were at. After a time, I found that I'd said everything that was on my chest.

"That was beautiful, Liam."

I'd caught a glimpse of Annalise coming up to comfort me. She was a kind woman and I knew her heart was breaking. It wasn't a surprise that she needed to say something to me - only her voice wasn't right. She embraced me and I caught the scent that I knew could only be one person.

"Don't say it," she said.

Tears streamed down my face anew as I clung to the woman. We finally separated and she walked back to stand next to the always stoic Frimunt.

"I'd like to believe they heard you," Ada said.

I turned to see my friends watching me. The universe had seemed to tip on its side and I was having difficulty processing anything but my profound sense of guilt and now joy.

"I'm sorry I got you all into this," I said. I'd changed all of our lives in a way I couldn't undo. Big Pete lying in the casket was a stark reminder of this.

"Cap, we all bear the burden of our decisions. There has not been a point where we could have turned away from this without losing ourselves. You cannot blame yourself," Marny said.

"But I do."

"You have to let go of it. Belirand and NaGEK are to blame. How many have lost their families because of Belirand's desire to restrict access to fold-space?" Nick asked. "Sure, if we hadn't gotten involved, your parents would be alive, but how many will die if we don't act. Would they give their lives so that an entire crew might live?"

"Nicholas, this isn't the time or the place," Marny said.

"No. It's precisely the right time. Ask them, Liam. Ask them if they'd sacrifice themselves. I know you would, why don't you believe they would?" Nick asked. He could be feisty when he didn't think I was seeing things clearly.

"It's too much," I said.

"No it's not. Things have changed, but I need you to get your head wrapped around this. You're right to feel responsible. But don't think for a minute we're not doing this for the right reasons. It's something we're all going to have to live with," Nick said.

"It's just so hard," I said.

"I know, Liam," Nick said.

I nodded.

"There are some people up in the suite who would like to see you," he said. "Are you okay to head up there now?"

"Sure."

We all took a lift up to Level-30. I stood by Annalise at the back of the lift and reached out my hand. Hers, always cold, was shaking when I held it.

Unlike the other levels, when we stepped off, we found ourselves in a small alcove with a uniformed guard at a desk.

"I'm signing in for this group," Nick said.

The guard nodded and Nick swiped his hand across the pad. A door slid open and exposed a hallway. We followed Nick to a single door at the end. He palmed the door and swung it open.

The room we entered was full of our friends: Jack, Nick's brother, Luc Gray, Celina and Jenny Dontal and even Jake Berandor - the graduate student turned smuggler.

"What's going on?" Tabby turned to me as the door closed behind us and stared pointedly at Annalise.

"A necessary ruse," Nick said as Annalise Licht removed her disguise and exposed herself as my mother, Silver.

"Oh, thank the stars," Tabby said, pulling Mom into a tight hug.

"We didn't know if Belirand would try to finish the job or not," Nick said. "And we couldn't take any chances."

"I am so sorry, Mom. It's all my fault," I said.

"You will honor your father by knowing that he willingly gave his life to save mine and would willingly give it to save the crew of *Cape of Good Hope*. I wish it didn't have to be, but if it weren't for those who stand against injustice, no one would be free. Liam, you did not make Belirand murder your father. Admiral Tullas, Captain Ahmed Mussa and Captain Ciaran MacAsgaill chose to do this on their own. It is they who must bear this guilt," she said. "And I will not forget their names until they have been destroyed."

I was set back by the ferocity of her words.

Still holding her hand, we walked to one of several couches in the middle of the beautifully appointed room and sat down.

"I'm glad you feel so deeply, Liam. Your father hid his feelings, but you must know he was very proud of you," she said.

We talked until the discussion lagged and I finally allowed myself to be pulled into other conversations. I knew my friends wanted to provide comfort and I would let them.

It was late in the evening when most of the room had cleared and Mom retired to one of the many sleeping quarters.

"How will Frimunt get back to Descartes?" I asked, sitting on a stool next to Nick at the bar.

"I made a deal with the Lichts to lease *Kestrel*. I didn't think we'd be delivering ore anytime soon," Nick said.

"That's a good idea. He's interested?"

"Frimunt's not, but he says Selig is. I made them a good deal on the ship," Nick said.

"I don't think I could deliver ore to Belirand, no matter the price," I said.

"He's planning to build other contracts. They don't want to deal with Belirand either."

"What about Jack?" I asked.

"He'd like to stay with Celina and Jenny. He's old enough to make that decision and I don't think he'll be in any danger on Lèger Nuage. Celina is street-smart, she'll keep an eye out for him."

"What about *Sterra's Gift*?" I asked.

"Berandor made an offer on it, but I said I'd have to talk to you about it. He wants to equip it with the light absorptive armor we have on *Hotspur*," Nick said.

"That's right. We gave him a single run of it. Does he have enough credits to do both?"

"Who knows, but I think we should consider the offer. We're never going to sail her again, not with *Hotspur*," he said.

"Up to you. I like Jake well enough. I'd want right of first refusal if he ever decides to sell it, though," I said.

"He actually suggested that."

"What would you sell it for?"

"He offered eight hundred thousand," Nick said.

"That's probably about right," I said.

"Tipperary credits. It's a low offer. I'll push him up to one point four," Nick said.

"Oh, right," I said. I'd forgotten that Tipperary Credits were worth about fifty percent of Mars.

"We aren't letting you make any deals for a while," Nick said, lightly punching my leg.

Tabby's arms slipped over my shoulders from the back. "We should be getting to bed, you have to be exhausted."

"Okay," I said to her. "But, something's been bugging me."

"Oh?" Nick asked.

"What happened with MacAsgaill? How'd he end up changing his mind? You know anything about that?"

"I wondered when you'd get around to that," Nick said. "It was actually Jonathan."

"Jonathan? Where's he been?"

"In his room, wanted to remain anonymous," Nick said. "I'll let him tell you how they freed you," Nick said, standing up.

"I gotta hear this. I'm coming too," Tabby said.

"No need to move, Miss Masters," Jonathan said, entering the common living space. "We'd wondered when you might like to speak about this."

"Nick said you freed us from the brig. How'd you manage that?" I asked.

"Master Anino's companies are not without their resources. It is one of the things we've learned about mankind. They often strike at their enemy in a way they most fear," Jonathan said.

"By attacking my parents?"

"Yes. Each time either Tullas or MacAsgaill threatened you, they brought your friends and family into the argument. We simply did some research, located MacAsgaill's family and delivered a few videos that showed an agent of ours near his family," he said.

"You threatened his family?" I asked.

"Not at all. His family was none the wiser. The threat was completely inferred, as we would neither condone, nor facilitate violence in that way."

"That's a pretty subtle distinction," I said.

"We felt it likely Belirand would terminate you and Tabitha. It was an acceptable compromise," he said.

"Thank you."

"You are welcome."

"Tell him about the world you found," Nick said.

"I thought we had planned to give Captain Liam time to mourn," Jonathan said.

"A world for the crew of *Cape*?" I asked.

"Jonathan's been cycling through the communication crystals and got a hit. The planet is a near perfect match to Earth," Nick said.

"And there's a human population that responded to the comm crystal?" I asked.

"It's more complex than that," Jonathan said.

"It always is."

"The planet is called Ophir. It is one thousand ninety-six light years from Tipperary and was one of NaGEK's many failed attempts at colonization," he said.

"How did it fail?"

"You must understand," Jonathan said. "Early on, Anino's fold-space generator was exorbitantly expensive to deploy. Solar systems and planets were explored with deep scans and suitability was determined by examining the results of these scans. They identified, with a high degree of accuracy, planets suitable for human life. For example, Grünholz, the planet beneath us, was settled this way. The Ophir mission failed due to the discovery, upon arrival, that the planet was already inhabited by a sentient species."

"I'm still having a hard time believing Belirand would go to such great lengths to hide that there is other intelligent life in the universe," I said, shaking my head.

"Belirand is motivated by the profit they generate through the

TransLoc gates," he said. "They have been successful at convincing NaGEK to fear new sentient species."

"Sound's like corporate septic shite to me," I said. "Anything for a profit, even at the expense of people's lives. But this colony is still there? They're thriving? That would be perfect."

"Perhaps this would better be left until tomorrow. There is a lot to take in and you both must be exhausted," he said.

"No. Dad died for this. I'd like to hear what you've found," I said.

Tabby touched my arm. "Me too."

"Very well. First, you need to understand, it appears that the colonists are not aware of the function of the communication crystal. I'm able to pick up transmissions only under certain circumstances. The device is sitting in some sort of communal meeting room," he said. "I will replay the most recent conversations. It appears the colonists are facing a crisis with the indigenous species."

"Let's hear it," I said.

Jonathan played back a series of recordings he'd taken over the last week.

"Sounds like they really believe they're in trouble. But, they're talking about swords and quad copters. Their technology is all over the board," Nick said.

"It is my understanding that they have a single replicator and are resource constrained. They are unable to manufacture blaster level technology," Jonathan said. "The indigenous are physically superior, but intellectually inferior. We believe the equilibrium has recently been upset due to the technology of the human settlers starting to fail."

"How many original colonists were there?" I asked.

"Six hundred."

"That must have been a huge ship. How long ago?"

"Three hundred forty standard years."

"And they've only grown to eight hundred?"

"We're considering two possibilities. There may be some issue that causes fertility rates to be low. The other possibility is that they have downward population pressure from a persistent enemy. It is difficult to be certain. We think the latter to be the most likely."

"How likely is it that Belirand will follow us to Ophir?" I asked.

"They chased us into the deep dark to catch us in the open. I think it's a safe bet they'd chase us to Ophir," Nick said. "I don't see why they'd attack the colony, however. And, if that Yishuv council is right, they aren't expecting to survive the upcoming war. We might be their best hope."

"Is *Hotspur* ready to go?" I asked.

"Fully. We're loaded with enough supplies for three months for us and the *Cape's* crew," he said.

"Perfect. Here's the plan. Tell Jake Berandor we'll sell him *Sterra's Gift* for six missiles and seven hundred thousand, but only if he can deliver the missiles immediately. He can pay the seven hundred thousand off over time if he likes. Jonathan, tell me what you need to install a fold-space drive on *Cape of Good Hope*."

Chapter 24

ASSAULT ON YISHUV

Yishuv Settlement, Planet Ophir

Eliora looked across the south wall with a mix of pride and trepidation. Her former students stood with bows ready, a quiver of arrows at their feet and a sword on their back or hanging from their waist. The roar of the Ophie racing around the corner of the settlement was deafening. As she'd feared, they'd learned to avoid the eastern wall and gate that was well protected by the settlement's only remaining mounted blaster. Their obvious target, the southwest gate.

"Steady. Conserve your arrows." She spoke with a confidence and authority she didn't feel as she walked down the line. "We don't fire until they're within the red zone."

Earlier in the tenday, they'd set posts in the field that marked the maximum archer's range.

Looking out, she saw three pods of Ophie peel off from the main group, running south toward the tree line. The remaining horde of over two thousand had lined up a hundred meters from the wall, chittering and gesturing excitedly.

"Merrie. There's a group headed south. Can you see what they're up to?" Eliora asked.

"Quad-14 headed south," Merrie replied.

"Shem, what's your count on the west wall?" Gian asked.

"We're clear over here," came the response.

"North wall, report."

"We're clear, Captain."

"Eliora, you have the main force. Shem, pull a squad and take your blaster rifle to the south wall and start working on the main group," Gian said. "I'm on my way over."

"What do we do? How can a hundred archers hold off an army of thousands?" It took Eliora a moment to recall Calendal's name from memory. He was not one of her best archers, but he always gave it his best.

"We wait, Calendal. We are defending and will not be drawn away from our defenses. The wall will hold. The Ophie have done this in the past, they're giving us a chance to meet them in the field for battle. It is an offer we will not accept," she said. "Stay alert, your family depends on us."

"I will."

"South wall. I have news on the break-off group," Merrie's voice cut through on the talkie. "This might be a problem. The Ophie who ran to the forest are cleaning off the branches of trees we felled."

Eliora heard a gasp from Calendal, who'd overheard the conversation.

"Understood," Eliora said.

A blaster bolt, from the west edge of the south wall struck and killed an Ophie at the edge of the invasion force. Shem had taken a shot at the head of the beast and his risk had paid off. The response from the horde was immediate as they roared almost in unison and rushed the wall.

"Wait for it," Eliora said as the wall beneath her shook from the feet of thousands of Ophie rushing in.

"Spikes!" She yelled as the Ophie crossed the imaginary line between the posts in the ground.

Ropes from the wall were pulled and rows of pikes were pulled from the ground, hinged supports falling beneath them to hold the long, iron spears at forty five degrees. The Ophie in the lead impaled themselves, as they were unable to arrest their momentum.

A cheer rose up from the wall as more than fifty of the enemy were killed with the single trick.

Without hesitation, the following Ophie simply vaulted over their dying brethren and continued the race to the wall.

Eliora knew she had no time to celebrate. Fifty dead or wounded in a sea of two thousand would not turn the war.

"Archers, nock!" she yelled.

"Aim for the chest," she reminded them waiting for the Ophies to reach a critical spot.

"Fire!"

The sound of twanging bowstrings were followed by dozens of Ophie falling, but the horde continued their push forward.

For several minutes the battle continued its lopsided tally as one-by-one, Ophie fell to the constant rain of arrows. Eliora estimated they'd taken at least three hundred from the main force.

"South wall. They're coming," Merrie said. "They're bringing the trunks of those trees."

Gian had joined them on the wall and heard Merrie's news.

"We cannot allow those timbers to be brought to the wall," he shouted. "Focus all fire. Shem, shoot them."

For a period of time they successfully stopped the trunks of trees from advancing, but the remaining Ophie soon recognized the strategy and turned their efforts to helping their comrades.

Eliora watched, helplessly as one by one, the tall trunks were leaned against the gates.

"Gate defense, to street level!" Eliora yelled.

She didn't hesitate as she sprinted for the steps that led down to the gate. It would be a matter of moments before Ophie started pouring over the gate.

Archers from above fired down at the Ophie as they climbed the timbers and for a while, they held them off. It gave Eliora and her squads time to form up, but it was a just a matter of time before they started spilling over.

"Archers at the ready," she called out. They'd drilled for a gate breach and she looked on with pride as the brave men and women took their positions. Half were ready with bows, their partners standing behind with swords.

"It's breaking!" Shem's voice cut through the talkie. "The hinges, they're failing!"

They'd installed more than hinges, the gates had been buttressed with iron beams, but Eliora watched it start to fail.

"Gian. You must fall back, you're too close!" Eliora yelled.

Captain Gian was on top of the wall next to the stairs and when the gates failed, the Ophie would have a direct path to him.

"Shem, take a squad back to the keep," Gian spoke into the talkie. "We'll hold the wall for as long as we can. Do not lose the blaster rifle."

Eliora saw a look of grief in Shem's eyes as he nodded and waved his squad down the stairs past Gian. It was a horrible thing he'd asked Shem to do, but the blaster rifle was critical to defending the main turret at the keep. The settlement could be lost without them both.

As Shem rushed past her position, a great groaning sound emanated from the gate as it collapsed forward, into the city.

"Fire!" Eliora yelled.

The Ophie paid a horrible price as they surged through the choked entry to the city. The defenders slaughtered them as they crawled over the bodies of their fallen, only to be struck down by arrow and blade.

The battle continued to be fought by inches until the stock of arrows dwindled in her archer's quivers.

"Captain, we're nearly out of arrows," Eliora said into the talkie.

"Eliora, you must fall back to the Keep with our remaining forces. We will hold them for as long as we can. Take all from the walls," he ordered and dropped his talkie on the ground.

She could just hear him over the din, "Captain's guard on me!" He raised his long sword and rushed into the melee at the gate.

"Sound the retreat. We'll hold this line until the wall archers make it down," Eliora said.

Dael pulled a whistle from around his neck and blew, the shrill warbling sound cutting through the sounds of battle. He continued to blow as the archers disappeared into the stairwells and, after exiting, fled to the keep.

"Advance," Eliora said as she saw a few Ophie manage to get around the Captain's forces, who were attempting to hold the breached gate. The Ophie could not be allowed to engage her archers, who were now defenseless.

Eliora felt a certain grim satisfaction as she struck the first Ophie with her katana. It was small, full of vigor and blood lust. She thought she recognized a look of surprise on its face as she drove the weapon into its chest.

"Eliora, go!" Gian yelled at her. "There are too many. You must defend the Keep!"

"Frak. Fall back," she said.

"Go, Eliora," Coral said, stepping in next to her. "We will give you time."

"Move, now!" Eliora commanded and turned away from the battle. At the same time, she heard the clash of sword and club behind her.

Her two squads had been reduced to almost one. She looked over her shoulder as they fled, only to see Coral fall to the blow of an Ophie. Pride and sadness welled up within her as Dael stepped protectively over the woman's crumpled body taking his last stand, falling a moment later.

A stream of Ophie erupted through the gate and Eliora knew that Gian had lost his battle.

"Go, Go!" she urged the group, which was unnecessary as they were all fleeing as fast as they could.

"Shem, we're coming in with a group," Eliora said, having pulled her talkie from her belt.

"Merrie's tracking you. Just get past the bakery and we'll have a clean shot from the blaster," he said.

"I don't know if we're going to make it. They're gaining on us."

"You'll make it. You have to," he said.

Eliora tried to put the talkie back on her waist but fumbled it, dropping it to the ground. She didn't even consider picking it up as they continued their sprint through the once serene streets of their settlement.

Her heart leapt as the bakery came into view, but her hopes were dashed just as quickly. An Ophie jumped them from behind, pulling down the man next to her. She drew her katana and turned, prepared to take a stand, but the Ophie had already killed the man and discarded his body.

The open door of the Keep beckoned. She watched as, one by one, the fleeing archers disappeared into its depths. Eliora crossed the imaginary line where she knew the blaster could reach and stopped five meters inside of it.

The Ophie who'd torn apart her comrade just moments ago, with blood still dripping from its claw, jumped into the air with its club raised over its head.

Eliora stood firm, ready to strike with her katana, when she felt the heat of the heavy blaster bolt. The beast fell lifelessly to the ground, a great hunk of its chest now gone.

"Eliora, what are you doing?" Shem yelled from the doorway.

"They won't advance without a target. Just keep them off me," she yelled back.

"That's insane," he yelled. "What if there are too many."

"Put archers on the barracks and shoot them yourself!"

Five more Ophie appeared around the end of the building and raced toward her. Shem was right, if there were fifty of them, it might be a problem. She backed up, giving the gunner more room to work.

For nearly two hours she stood there, taunting the gathering Ophie to charge her. One after the other they advanced, only to be struck down by the blaster.

Finally, an Ophie larger than the rest barked commands at the horde and they stopped their suicidal runs.

Eliora entered the great hall of the Keep and collapsed onto the floor. Only six hundred of the settlements inhabitants could be accounted for, but even so, the quarters were cramped.

"Shem would like to see you when you've recovered," a boy said, handing her a cup of water and a loaf of bread.

She looked at the bread and wondered when would be the next time they'd be able to make bread.

"Lead the way." Eliora stood, her body complaining with stiffness.

He led her through the Keep to the barracks. When building the Keep, they'd taken advantage of the barracks location, a corner next to the exterior wall. She walked up the stairs and found Nurit standing outside the door to the room where she'd had so many debriefs with Captain Gian and Shem over the last few years.

"He's expecting you," Nurit said and pushed open the door.

Eliora considered the older smith for a moment. Neither Nurit nor Amon had received much training with weapons, as their time was much more valuable constructing weapons. Guarding against human intruders, however, seemed a perfect job for the heavily muscled woman.

Eliora nodded to the mother of her friend and walked through the open door. Both Merrie and Amon looked up from where they sat in front of video screens that showed the carnage of the battle.

"He's on the roof," Amon said, standing and embracing her.

She held on to him for a moment, letting a small amount of comfort wash over her.

Eliora climbed the stairs and went through the open trap door, finding Shem sitting on top of the roof. A gentle breeze cooled her as she sat next to him and offered to share her bread.

"No, I've already eaten and we could be here a long time," he said pointing out to the west over the settlement.

Eliora followed his arm's movement and saw what he was looking at. Hundreds of Ophie were in the streets, ducking around corners and dodging their way in and out of the buildings. Every so often, one would enter line of sight with the main gun and meet its fate.

"How long do you think they'll stay?"

"No idea, but there's something you should see," he said.

Shem climbed down through the trap door and waited behind Merrie for Eliora. Amon, not waiting to be asked, closed the trap door and pulled the iron grate back into place, locking it.

"Merrie, could you show Eliora what you've found?"

"Certainly," Merrie said.

Eliora had seen the video images from the quads enough times not to be surprised by the shift in the screen in front of her. She watched as Merrie negotiated the quad, flying it high in the air over to the small river that ran down the mountain only a hundred meters from the settlement. The river was their main source of water. The quad flew up the river for a kilometer before Eliora saw what Shem had been concerned about.

"They're making a camp?" Eliora asked.

"Yes. They have to," Shem said. "The warriors probably only brought food they could carry. Merrie saw other Ophie bringing support down from the main camp and they're digging in."

"How long will our supplies last?" Eliora asked.

"They haven't discovered our water intake from the river, so we're good on that for now. Councilwoman Peraf has taken over rationing and tells me we have, at most, two tenday," he said.

"Any estimate on the number of Ophie remaining?"

"Our best estimate is thirteen hundred, give or take," Merrie said.

Eliora sat back, defeated. Even with their best preparations, they'd only cut the invading Ophie down by forty-five percent. They were boxed in and bedraggled. Hope seemed to be slipping away.

"What do we do, Eliora?" Shem asked.

"We set up a watch schedule and keep the gun manned at all times. We look for an opportunity. They can't stay there forever. Maybe we can outlast them."

Chapter 25

BURNING BRIDGES

Executive Suite, Lèger Gros, Tipperary

When I woke up in the soft bed next to Tabby, my subconscious knew there was an awful issue that my waking self hadn't yet processed. Spending a week in a detention cell with nothing more than thinly padded cots to lie on had taken a toll on my body. I relished the comfort of Tabby's warmth and the luxuriousness of the executive suite's bed. It didn't take long for me to recall that my father was dead - murdered - and that I bore a substantial portion of the blame. It made the comfort I'd felt moments before hollow, vacuous, and undeserved.

I pulled away and must have sighed, because it woke Tabby.

"Don't go," she said, sleepily.

"I can't sleep," I lied. I could have stayed in bed all day, but not next to Tabby and not in luxury.

"You're pulling away from me again," she said.

I just shook my head.

I heard disappointment in her voice. "I'll give you space."

That worked for me.

I pulled on my old suit-liner and headed toward the door.

"I lied," Tabby said, jumping out of bed and positioned herself between me and the door.

"Don't," I warned.

"Clean liner and a shower," she said. "I let you by last night, but it's not happening today."

"Forget it."

It got worse from there and we ended up having a pretty good fight. In the end, she gave up and stalked out of the room, pissed.

I didn't want to follow her, so I took a shower. At least it was my idea.

When I got out, I heard Mom talking in the other room and wasn't sure how I'd be able to face her. Sure enough, her voice stopped by the door and she knocked. She had to be reading my mind – she did that sometimes.

"Liam? It's me," Mom said through the door.

I wasn't sure what to say, so I just sat there, staring at the floor.

"I'm coming in." She opened the door and slipped into the room, closing it behind her. She'd changed from the Annalise costume to her normal grey vac-suit.

"What happened to your face?" she asked, running her hands along my cheeks and nose. I felt soreness where her fingers touched. "This has not set up correctly. Did they torture you?"

"No, I had a fight and lost," I said.

"Well, Nuage should have provided a surgeon. It's going to be harder to fix this after the fact," she said.

"I suppose," I said.

"I know what you're feeling, Liam," she said, sitting next to me on the bed and running her hand down my back. "You should know something, though. Pete saved me on that station. When we saw that the turrets weren't defending us, he abandoned me in the passage that led up to the back side of the asteroid. If he'd just come with me, he'd still be alive."

"Why'd he do that?"

"He said he could save Dave," she said, pulling my hand into her own. Her hands were always cold and I wrapped them in mine for warmth.

"There couldn't have been time to save him," I said.

"No, but that's the man he was, Liam."

I shook my head and we sat quietly for a while.

"Why'd you tell me that?" I asked, finally.

"He had to know he couldn't get to Dave and he went anyway. I wanted to tell you because frankly, I'm having trouble dealing with it.

"Not that hard to understand," I said. "He thought he had a chance and with you safe, he didn't feel like he had anything to lose."

"But I had something to lose," she said.

I really couldn't tell if she was trying to teach me a lesson or was struggling with what happened.

"He couldn't have lived with himself if he didn't try," I said.

"That's right. Your father, the man I loved, wouldn't have been that man if he'd turned his back on Dave," she said. "But you already know that, don't you?"

"Yes," I said.

"You're a lot like him."

"Not hardly," I said.

"Believe it. When the *Cape's* crew needed you, you went without hesitation. We'll hang Pete's murder on the people who did it. Don't let them succeed, Liam. You've a crew that needs a leader, son. You have to put your mourning aside. People are going to die if you don't pull yourself together."

I blew out a long, shuddering breath as we hugged. I knew she was right, but I was having trouble finding my way through it.

"How?"

"Give you a hint from officer training?"

"Sure."

"Fake it until you make it. You've a crew any officer would be jealous of. Set the direction, then lean on them. They won't let you fail," she said.

"You know, you have to come with us," I said. "No way am I giving Belirand another shot at you."

She smiled. "I figured you'd say that, but you see the irony, right?"

I shook my head.

"I'm pretty sure if I come along with you all, Belirand will get their shot at me sooner rather than later."

"Yeah, but you'll be on more equal footing this time," I said.

"I'm counting on it. Now, get your butt up, apologize to Tabby, and let's get this show on the road."

Clarity of purpose started to replace the fog I'd been feeling. Mom was right about our need to move and I wasn't doing us any good wallowing in self-pity. Dad despised wallowing, self-pity and just about any other emotion that took more than four words to explain.

I spun the ring on my finger and thumbed the quantum crystal, knowing it would pulse on Tabby's finger. It was as close to an apology as I had in me. The response from Tabby was immediate and I knew we were okay.

I stood up from the bed and made my way to the main room. For a moment, I looked at my friends as they talked animatedly. One by one, they recognized my presence and quieted, looking back at me. I felt Mom as she approached from behind.

"Jonathan, two questions," I said. "First, what will it take to put a fold-space drive on *Cape of Good Hope*?"

Jonathan turned to face me directly. How anyone might guess he was anything but human was beyond me.

"Fold-space drives require an extremely rare, manufactured element called aninonium. Anino Enterprise never exposed the formula and had the only manufacturing facility in the known universe. Last night, that facility was destroyed and with it the only known way to create aninonium," Jonathan said.

"Belirand blew up the factory?"

"No. We did."

"So you're saying there's no way to add a fold-space drive to the *Cape*?"

"Not at all. We simply wanted you to be aware of this fact as it changes the balance of our conflict," he said. "Anino Enterprises has a substantial stock-pile of the material. We believe it is critical that the remaining aninonium be loaded onto the *Hotspur* before Belirand discovers its whereabouts and takes it by legal or other means.

"To answer your original question, it will take roughly four days to upgrade *Cape of Good Hope* with a fold-space drive."

"Mom. You've the most knowledge of big ships. Can a heavy cruiser, like the one that attacked the Co-Op, make atmospheric entry on a system with .9g?"

"Yes. They'd be slow and burn an exorbitant amount of fuel, but it could be done," she said.

"Those cruisers that chased us out of Grünholz didn't seem to have much of a problem," Tabby said.

"Those Oberrhein cruisers are babies compared to Belirand's Justice-class," Mom replied.

"Nick, any word back from Jake on missiles?"

"Yes. You're going to hate it. He accepted your deal and has six. They're being loaded right now," he said.

"What's to hate about that?"

"They're the ones we sold him."

"I could have gone the rest of my life not knowing that," I said with a wry grin. "So, something's been bugging me. When *Hammer of Justice* attacked the Co-Op, why didn't the defensive guns fire?" I looked at Mom.

She started to answer when Jonathan cut in, "My apologies, Mrs. Hoffen, but I believe I have an answer for this."

"Please, call me Silver," she said.

"Thank you, Silver. The reason your guns didn't work is because a few members of Belirand's security forces have access to NaGEK's disarming codes. Those weapons were manufactured by the North Americans, who encode what amounts to a virus in the systems allowing them to be disarmed under the right circumstances," he said.

"Can the virus be defeated?" I asked.

"Yes. We could remove the code that performs those functions," Jonathan said.

"Good. Nick, tell Berandor we'll forgive three hundred thousand if he'll move those guns for us."

"What for?" Nick asked.

"Nuage's own Admiral Marsh was ready to hand me to Belirand over a bar fight. It's going to get harder and harder for us to find a place where we can find refuge. We'll need those guns," I said.

He nodded. "I'll negotiate with him. I don't think it'll take all three hundred. Where do you want them moved to?"

"I'll show you. But before that, I was wondering if Jonathan could tell us if he had an estimate on how big their fold-space-capable fleet is?"

"Belirand has eleven ships capable of generating an independent fold-space wave," Jonathan answered.

"Are they all Justice-class cruisers?" I asked.

"No. They have two corvettes, six heavy cruisers, two fast frigates, and a Goliath-class freighter," he said.

Ada whistled at the mention of the freighter.

"Okay, final question. What's the status of the Ophir settlement?"

"It's not good," Jonathan said. "From what we've been able to discern, the settlement has come under a massive attack from the indigenous population. The Yishuv settlement is under siege and trapped in what they're referring to as the Keep."

"Well, that makes things easy then," I said. "We fold-space to Curie, pick up the aninonium, then jump to Ophir. When can we leave?" I asked looking around the room.

"Good to have you back, Cap," Marny said.

"We're ready," Nick said. "You know we can't fold-space directly to Curie, right. We'll have to jump out at least a thousand AUs."

"Sounds like a detail to me," I said.

"Belirand won't like us popping over to Curie that fast. They'll feel like we're giving away their secret," Nick said.

"Yeah, let's not talk about how much I don't care what Belirand thinks. Honestly, the only reason I can come up with for not blowing the lid off their little secret is because it's possible there are big bad scary aliens out there."

"Figured you'd see it that way," Nick said. "We should get moving in that case."

"Armored vac-suits and heavy blasters," Marny said. "And we're going to be exposed so we don't stop for anyone."

Twenty minutes later, we exited the executive suite and entered the elevator. I felt sorry for the older gentleman who happened to be in the car. The seven of us, dressed in black armored vac-suits with heavy blasters within reach, stood in stark contrast to his brightly colored clothes. I didn't blame him when he remembered an appointment and requested an exit at the next level. I was relieved when we exited the elevator directly onto Meerkat's main level where *Hotspur* sat nestled against the bay doors.

"Captain Hoffen. I guess the reports of your incarceration were exaggerated." Bing approached our group, holding out his hand.

"Load up," I said, shaking his hand.

"Cap, she's locked up," Marny said.

I placed my hand on my blaster's grip. "What's going on, Bing?"

"Nuage just called down, they've requested I stall you," he said.

"I believe our arrangement was anonymity," Jonathan said.

"Small city, people talk," Bing said. "Look, you've been good to me, but I can't go against Nuage Security Services."

"Nick. Get us on that ship," I said.

"Working on it," Nick said.

"Marny, shut down that elevator," I said.

"Aye, Cap," she said, jogging over to it.

"Tabby, Mom, defensive positions around the ship. Jonathan, see if you can help Nick," I said.

"Copy," Tabby said as they peeled away.

"Captain, perhaps I can help negotiate," Jonathan said.

"Help Nick first. I'm done with carrot, it's time for stick," I said.

"Bing. I need to explain something to you. Admiral Marsh is about to hand my crew over to Belirand and they intend to do us harm," I said as calmly as I could manage. "I'm telling you this because I've always liked you and don't want to see you hurt. Believe me when I tell you that if you don't give me access to my ship, I'll tear this place down."

"I can't," he said.

"You can and you will. If it'd be helpful, I could shoot you," I said.

"Shoot me? How would that help?" he asked his voice raising an octave.

"Duress. Stop stalling. You have five seconds and then I'm going to start shooting. After that I'll be dropping charges from those bags we're carrying," I said. I hoped Bing wasn't a card player, as I didn't think our clothing would explode as dramatically as I was suggesting.

"It's open," Nick said. "He's still got control."

I fired the blaster into his lower leg and he crumpled to the floor.

"Three seconds, you frak. I'm serious! Your life for my crew's." I held the gun to his head.

"Liam, no!" Mom yelled.

"It's yours," he said raising his arms above his head, shielding himself. I almost felt bad.

"Nick?"

"We've got it."

I pulled the earwig from Bing's ear, leaving a small bloody line along his cheek.

"Open the frakking bay door or the second missile I fire will open it for you," I said.

"What about the... okay! Please, just leave," he said.

I ran across the deck, up the stairs and pulled the exterior hatch closed behind me.

"Charge up the blasters. We might have to shoot our way out of here," I said as I sprinted through the hallway and turned toward the berth deck. Someone had been moving doors around on the ship, but I didn't have time to process it now.

"We're ready," Ada said jumping out of the pilot's seat as I ran through the renovated bridge. Bing did a nice job, I sure was going to miss working with him.

I slid into the seat, pulled back on the flight stick and moved *Hotspur* toward the opening bay door.

"*Incoming hail, Nuage Air Defense,*" the AI announced.

Pushing the throttle, I scraped the doors slightly sliding out of the bay. I turned off the arc-jets that would keep us hovering next to the city and we dropped like a rock, falling freely through the atmosphere toward the clouds below.

Accept hail.

"*Hotspur*, Captain Hoffen here," I said.

"Captain. This is Nuage Air Defense. We're ordering you to return to Nuage Gros immediately for questioning."

"I'm sorry, we're experiencing some technical problems. Our arc-jet controls aren't firing," I said.

The forward holo showed a squadron of brilliant yellow fighters streaking toward us.

"Return immediately or you risk being fired on," the woman's voice said.

"Just a second, almost have it," I said.

Close comm.

I used the arc-jets to spin the nose of *Hotspur* over so we were pointed down. We only had to get a couple of kilometers into the clouds and we'd be out of their airspace.

I pushed the throttle to full. I couldn't outrun them, but they also wouldn't chase us into Oberrhein territory.

"Incoming hail, Nuage Air Defense."

Accept hail.

"Captain Hoffen, this is Lieutenant Crépin. We've been given permission to fire if you don't turn around immediately." A severe looking woman's face showed on the forward vid-screen.

"We can take a few hits, Crépin, and you've no jurisdiction to fire on us," I said. "We're no longer in Nuage Airspace."

I pushed the throttle to the max and we squirted into the heavy cloud bank. It wasn't entirely true that we weren't in their space, but we were in a zone where control was contested by the violent nation of Oberrhein. Crépin would have to make a decision whether or not to escalate tensions with their neighbor by shooting us down. I was hoping they wouldn't. It was ironic that I was using tension we'd helped create between the two nations to our advantage. Admiral Marsh wouldn't be as amused.

It was a tense few minutes, but we finally pulled out of the clouds at six thousand meters elevation into the ever present storms that plagued Grünholz. We were relieved to find that the Nuage ships were no longer in pursuit.

"Sorry, Ada. I hope that doesn't put a wrinkle in your relationship with Luc," I said.

"If it does, then he's on the wrong side of this one," she said. "Besides, I can only take Captain Airforce for so long. Don't get me wrong, I like Luc, but he's a little... I don't know... by the book, sometimes."

"Are we still talking about our escape or are there some juicy details you want to share with the group?" I asked.

Chapter 26

LAW BRINGER

"Captain, you might want to hear this," Jonathan said.

We'd just escaped the gravity of Grünholz and transitioned to fold-space.

"What do you have?" I asked. I was more than glad to look away from the jittering stars outside the cockpit windows.

"Listen," he said.

"Councilwoman Peraf. Acting protectorate director Shem has asked that you and the remaining council members join him in the upper room." A voice emanated from a small device that Jonathan held.

"It's about time," a woman said amidst rustling, as if someone was on the move.

A few minutes later, the rustling stopped and another voice could be heard.

"Acting director Shem, you requested our presence?" The woman who had been identified as Peraf asked.

"I have. Is this the remaining council?"

"Yes. It is just Bedros and myself," she said.

"Understood. Nurit, Amon, would you excuse us?" Shem asked.

No words were exchanged, but a door closed.

"And, engineer apprentice Merrie. Should she not also leave?" Peraf asked.

"No. I have asked Eliora and Merrie to remain behind so that we may discuss eventual outcomes," Shem said.

"You need to be sending out patrols and pushing back the Ophie," Peraf said. "We cannot remain in the Keep for much longer. We're running low on food and water and the smell is horrendous."

"I believe you've already stated that we have two tenday of food and water as long as we are diligent with our rationing," Shem said.

"Do not change the subject," Peraf said. "It is your responsibility to protect this community and you will end this siege now!"

"Peraf. We have fourteen remaining protectors and there are over a thousand Ophie. There is no possible way we will drive them off." A woman I hadn't yet heard said.

"Eliora, is it?" Peraf asked.

"Yes."

"These Ophie are not sophisticated and we have superior technology. They simply took us by surprise. You *will* go out and you *will* drive them off," Peraf said.

"Perhaps I wasn't clear, Councilwoman," Eliora said. "You aren't here to discuss strategy with us. Your comments reinforce the wisdom of that. We are barely holding off the Ophie and you were called up here so you could understand our predicament."

"Councilwoman Peraf is suffering from the same shock we are all feeling," another male voice said calmly. "We have no expectation that you will lead an assault any time soon. Please, tell us what's going on. Eliora?"

"Councilman Bedros. Right now the Ophie are celebrating their victory."

"How do you know that?" Peraf asked.

"Look at the screen," Eliora said.

I could hear what sounded like tapping on an old style keyboard.

"They're animals. They've killed our people and they're having a party?"

"Of course they are. They live for battle. Today was their largest success ever against our people," Shem said.

"Do you have any good news?" Peraf asked. "Or did you just call us up here to gloat."

"That's not fair, Peraf," Bedros said. "If you can't be civil, you should leave. Shem, Eliora, what can we do to help?"

"We're going to be here for a while. Right now, we're hoping to wait them out. The Ophie are not a patient group and, hopefully, they'll start to turn against each other when they have no access to us," Shem said.

"But what? I heard you hesitate. There's something you're not saying," Bedros said.

"We're at risk. If they put enough pressure on the main blaster, they could overrun us," Shem said. "We would not be able to stop them. And there's one more thing."

"Out with it," Bedros said.

"Pele's blaster rifle is at their main camp. Show them, Merrie," Shem said.

"You sure?"

"Yes."

"Is that one of their leaders? What is he doing with that?" Peraf asked. "Move. He's pointing it at us. Damn it, what happened? The screen went black."

"He's learned how to use Pele's blaster rifle. That's a game changer if he uses it to pick off the gunners on our turret," Shem said.

"When will they attack?" Bedros asked.

"We have no idea," Shem said.

I couldn't take listening to them anymore. We had to help.

"Jonathan, have we tried transmitting? We should tell them we're coming," I said.

"We cannot. Their unit is not set up for bidirectional communication," Jonathan said.

"Would you continue to monitor that channel and tell us if anything of significance changes?"

"Yes."

"Nick, how long of a jump is it from Curie to Ophir?"

"You know it's not a jump, right?" Nick asked.

I just looked at him over my shoulder.

"Fine! In fold-space, thirty-six hours. Almost twice as far as it is to *Cape of Good Hope*."

"I don't suppose it's in the same direction," I said.

Nick just shook his head. "It's not linear. There is no direction. Regardless, it's eighteen hours in fold-space between Ophir and where the *Cape of Good Hope* is. And, we're about to drop from fold-space at our half-way point on our way to Curie."

"Joy," Tabby said. "I so love the pastel vomit through the windows."

"Where are we picking up the aninonium?" I asked. I noticed that Jonathan had retired to the back of the bridge and had his eyes closed.

"Anino's platform nine seventy-five," Nick said.

"Oh, right. Belirand would never think to look for us there," I said facetiously.

"He said he has everything all ready. All we have to do is stealth in, pop the ramp, stealth out and be on our way," Nick said.

"How close can you drop us on a jump?" I asked.

"Fold..." Nick caught himself. "Hundred kilometers, give or take."

"That close?"

"Yup."

"Drop us in as close as you can to Anino's platform," I said.

"Are you sure you're not being reckless?" Mom asked from the couch.

"That platform is defended and not within any government's jurisdiction," I said. "By dropping in close, we'll cut off hours."

"Cap, if they have a cruiser patrolling we might not be able to get stealthed before they pick us up," Marny said. "They'd have a good chance of intercepting us before we got to the platform."

"Frak. Right. Good Catch. Nick, I imagine you have a location already identified."

"I do," Nick said.

I glanced back at Mom and she smiled, not even bothering to look smug.

Hotspur dropped from fold space and my stomach lurched uncomfortably.

"Entering fold-space in three... two... one..." Nick said. "Estimated time to Irène is thirty-five minutes."

"Ada, you feel like showing us your new space?" I asked. I needed a change of scenery and some time to think.

"Yes! I haven't even seen it yet," she said.

"I'll take the helm, if you'd like," Mom said.

All of us, excluding Jonathan and Mom, followed Ada down the lift to the berth deck. Instead of turning aft, she turned forward and walked around to Nick and Marny's bunkroom.

"The changes actually started here," Ada said. "Nick and Marny's bunk room was expanded a meter and a half back. It gave us enough room to add a small desk, a little more storage, and a larger bed."

It was surprising how much a meter and a half more did for the amount of usable space. A twinge of guilt hit me as I realized how small their space had been.

"If you'll follow me," Ada said, leading us back around to the hallway that led aft, past the head. "Instead of punching through the aft bulkhead, I just shrunk bunkroom two and moved the armory into the remaining space."

I ducked my head into the new armory where bunkroom two had been. It was about the size we'd had before and had the same neat arrangement.

"You probably saw the big changes when you came in. We added a second, aft bulkhead three meters behind the original and ran it all the way to the top of the hold. This gives us almost sixty meters of usable space, which is equivalent to a new deck. Ultimately, we ended up with a total of two new bunkrooms and a micro-head," Ada continued.

"What'd you do about orientation?" Tabby asked.

"It was a tough call, but I decided to keep things simple and not change orientation. The bottom bunk room is three by four meters and the top two are three meters square with the micro-head joining them. You have to climb up to get to them, but at .6g that's no big deal.

"Pressure barriers?" I asked.

"Yes. The rooms have pressure barriers and hard seals," she said. "Come on up." Ada easily climbed a metal ladder built into the forward bulkhead. The ladder was next to the hatch leading back into the berth deck.

Metal ladders had never been kind to me, but I didn't hesitate to climb up after her.

"That's easy," I said, stepping off the ladder onto a ledge opposite Ada.

The ledges weren't large enough to accommodate more than one person and when Tabby arrived at the top of the ladder she had nowhere to go.

"Which one is yours?" Tabby asked.

"Right here," Ada said, palming open a door that disappeared into the wall.

At nine square meters, the room wasn't huge by land standards. In a ship, it was generous.

"Are they all this big?" Tabby asked, having followed Ada into her room.

I jumped across the hole to the opposite ledge and walked into the room where they were looking around.

"Close," Ada said. "I figured Silver would appreciate a first level room, though."

"This is nice," I said, looking around at the new furniture, paint and carpet.

"It'll be nice to have a place of my own," Ada said.

"It's great," I said. "Thanks for getting this all designed. Was it expensive?"

"No," Nick said looking in from the hallway. "All in about eighty thousand credits and Jonathan insisted on paying for it, since he got a room out of it."

"What's he keep in a room?"

"You'll have to ask them," Nick said.

"It's hard when you do that," I said.

"What, keep surprises?" Nick asked.

"No. Switch back from singular to plural and back when talking about Jonathan."

"It's weird, I agree. They appreciate it though."

I nodded.

"You'll have to bring Mom back to see her new room," I said. "I think she could use some privacy."

"She's holding up pretty well," Marny said. "You both are."

"I'm worried about her. She's putting up a strong front, but she's just holding on. I know she's focused on our mission right now. She said the best way we could honor Dad was to save those people," I said.

"That's right. We can't let Belirand win this one, Cap. We need to make Belirand regret their choices," Marny said.

I knew Marny well enough to hear the unexpressed emotions behind her words.

"Ten minutes," Mom's voice came over my suit's audio.

"Ada, you want to bring us in?"

"You sure?"

"Of course. Tabbs, take second chair? I'd like to show Mom her room," I said.

We trooped back to the bridge where Ada relieved Mom from the helm.

"How'd it look?" Mom asked. I noticed that her eyes were red, but decided against saying anything.

"She added a lot of space. I was thinking we could get you checked into a bunkroom if you'd like," I said. "I think you'll like the finish, it's really nice."

"I could use a break," she said.

I reached out for her hand and we stepped onto the lift down to the berth deck.

"Coffee, first?" I asked.

"I'm fine," she said.

We walked through the aft pressure barrier and I palmed the door to her new room. I smiled. Ada had placed an arrangement of flowers on the small table next to the bed. I wondered how she had managed that given the crazy events leading up to our departure.

On the bulkhead, which was the portside of the ship, I initially thought a porthole had been installed, but soon realized it was a cleverly disguised vid-screen.

"It's wonderful, Liam. And the flowers?" she asked.

"Not sure. I imagine Ada, but we'd have to ask to be sure," I said.

"If you don't mind, I'd like to rest for a bit," she said, sitting on the bed.

"I'll find your bags and bring them in," I said.

"Thank you."

I walked back into the hold and was surprised at how full it was. I knew we had a lot of supplies, but the hold was over sixty percent loaded. The AI directed me to Mom's possessions – all contained in a single, soft duffle - a reminder of the fact that between the Red Houzi and Belirand, she had little left.

"Captain, you should probably come up," Ada informed me over the comm.

I dropped Mom's bag into her room and hurried to the bridge. When I arrived, the lights were low as we were running silent.

I stepped up the stairs into the cockpit and sat between Tabby and Ada. My HUD highlighted two bright white Belirand cruisers steaming toward where we'd just come from.

"That's a quick response," I said in the quiet voice I reserved for silent running. It wasn't as if they'd hear me, but we all did it.

"I cut our engines entirely," Ada said. "I'd like to put some distance between us."

"Good plan," I said. "How long before we reach the platform?"

"At this pace? Too long. I'll kick the engines on once those cruisers clear out and we'll be there in three hours or so," she said.

"Mom appreciated the flowers."

"Good."

For the next twenty minutes we watched as the cruisers grew smaller and smaller as they sailed away from us. Finally, Ada slowly accelerated.

I walked to the back of the bridge where Jonathan still sat on the couch, leaning against the aft bulkhead.

"How much time will we need to load once we get to the platform?"

"Ten minutes. I've arranged to have everything in the loading bay upon our arrival," he said.

"Will we have enough room for all the aninonium?" I asked.

"Yes. The material is compact. We'll be bringing on twenty cubic meters, which is more than *Hotspur* could use in several of your lifetimes," he said. "I've also arranged to load several construction machines and a Class-F industrial replicator."

"That's a huge replicator, it has to be worth several million credits," I said.

"The Ophir settlement will have to be rebuilt if they've been overrun. That replicator has limited value on the platform now that Master Anino is gone," he said

"You miss him, don't you?" I asked.

"It is like that. I believe the most similar emotion you experience is regret. He had much to offer and his passing was a considerable loss for more than humankind," Jonathan said.

"How much help will you need to get everything loaded?" I asked.

"We have stevedore bots standing by. Your help is not required. Would you like to review the load distribution in the hold?"

"That won't be necessary."

"Would you mind if I asked a very personal question?"

I looked at him and tried to read his face, only to remember he didn't likely have the same tells most people did.

"I don't mind, Jonathan. What's up?"

"Do you regret your decision to get involved with us?"

I considered his question. "I regret that I didn't understand the peril I was placing my family in. It is difficult to see beyond that right now."

"Yet, you are not just continuing on, but have assumed responsibility for the Ophir settlement. Are you not similarly concerned you will come to have regrets about that decision?"

"Are you trying to talk me out of this?"

"Not at all. We are trying to understand your motivations. Humans have a creativeness that is unusual among the sentient species we've run into," he said.

"How is that related to what we're doing?" I asked.

"You say you regret not understanding the peril you placed your family in, yet you knew it would place your crew in danger. There was some level of danger you were willing to assume. Your entire crew took less than ten minutes to come to a unanimous decision and you spent most of that time talking about unrelated issues," he said.

"You were listening?"

"We were, but only for the purpose of research. We would not have shared your conversation with Master Anino," he said.

"It was intuition," I said. "We made that decision because we believed we would be successful and the need was great."

"You had very few details on what you were getting into. How were you able to come to that decision?"

"Conflict isn't something you can calculate and know you'll be successful," I said. "It changes too quickly. You simply have to do what is right at the time and make necessary adjustments as things change. It's more about having core principals, one of which is to value life. Perhaps another is to surround yourself with people who can be trusted. Sorry, other sentients who can be trusted."

Jonathan smiled. It wasn't a big warm smile, but it wasn't a bad smile, overall. "You honor us by including us in that list. We want to know why you would do this, having only known us for such a short period of time."

"You do have a lot of questions, don't you?" I asked.

"Yes."

"My dad had a saying – trust a person by their actions, not their words."

"You two are looking pretty cozy over here," Marny said. We must have been out of the thick of things if she was up and walking around. "I'm headed for coffee, would either of you like a cup?"

"I'll have one. Do you need an extra hand?" I asked.

"I think I can manage, Cap," she said.

Jonathan and I continued to talk. He had a lot of basic questions and I didn't think he was even close to the bottom of the list when Ada finally announced that we would be docking in a few minutes.

"Thank you for the talk, Captain," Jonathan said. "We'd enjoy talking again."

"You should join us for poker. We like to talk philosophically when we play. It's even better if we're drinking, although you might get more honesty than you're expecting," I said.

"And now, we have many more questions. We look forward to playing poker with you," he said and got up.

I walked over to where Nick was quietly talking with Marny.

"Any signs of Belirand?"

"Yes. There's a Corvette called *Lawbringer* orbiting the platform," Marny pointed to a long, narrow warship sitting five hundred kilometers off the platform.

"Man, those are gorgeous lines," I said.

"Like a snake, Cap. She has more firepower than *Fist of Justice* and runs as fast as we do. Her only downside is she's short on armor," she said.

"Then they'll be sending her after us," I said.

"Good bet," Nick said.

"Cap, grab Tabby and a blaster rifle, I don't want that ramp open otherwise," Marny said.

"Copy that," I said.

"On it," Tabby acknowledged.

The three of us made our way down to the hold, stopping first in the new armory where we picked up blaster rifles. We found Jonathan standing patiently next to the exit hatch.

"We'll meet you at the cargo ramp once it's open," I said, in passing.

"That won't be necessary. The stevedore bots are fully automated and I need to run up to Master Anino's office before we leave again," he said. "I will be back shortly."

"Would you like an escort?"

"No. Ms. Chen has restored communications and the Belirand agents aboard the platform will not be able to intercept me," he said.

"Wait." I stopped in my tracks. "There are Belirand agents on the platform?"

"Yes. Eight in total. I've provided Master James with a link to the station's security. He should be updating you shortly," he said.

I heard Marny next to me, contacting Nick. A moment later my combat HUD popped up. Two red dots showed in a room adjacent to the platform.

"I'd feel more comfortable if you were accompanied," I said.

"We won't have difficulty bypassing the Belirand agents. They will most likely be focused on you and the loading bay," he said.

"Understood."

I followed Marny and Tabby through the aft pressure barrier into the hold and we jogged through the narrow aisle of food crates.

"We're down," Ada's voice announced over our comms.

"Nick, we're showing the bay is empty. Copy?" Marny asked.

"Copy, Marny," Nick answered.

My HUD marked the spot in the bay where I was to set up and take cover. It designated the space I was to monitor and lock down. I could see two other fire lanes that Marny and Tabby would be covering.

"Ready," I said.

Marny palmed the loading ramp and it lowered slowly, small puffs of atmo escaping as the hold's pressure equalized with the bay.

"Tangos on the move," Marny said.

I wasn't surprised, since the agents had been monitoring the docking bay from inside. My heart started hammering in my chest as the excitement of combat grabbed me. A third and fourth red dot showed in the adjacent hallway and I recognized the four-man stack on the doorway.

"Go, go, go," Marny said as the ramp descended sufficiently for us to disembark.

Adrenaline hit my bloodstream and I raced for my position, sliding to a stop behind a stack of crates.

Identify contents of crate. I requested.

It took longer than I'd expected for my AI to reply, which led me to believe it had to reach out to Jonathan for permission.

"Polymer based plumbing fittings," the AI replied.

So much for deflecting blaster bolts. I took a knee to steady my shooting and present a smaller target.

"They're breaching," Marny said.

The barrel of the lead Belirand agent's blaster scanned the room.

"I'm fragging the door," I said.

"You ready to draw first blood, Cap?"

"Roger that," I said.

"On my mark, three... two..." Marny started counting me down.

I pulled a frag grenade from the side of my blaster rifle. It expanded to fit in my hand and as Marny's count hit zero, I stood and threw it. After playing pod-ball all my life, I was disappointed by my throw. It landed short and skipped into the opening. I'd planned to bounce it off the open door, back into the hallway.

I watched as the red dots scrambled to escape as the frag grenade exploded short of its target.

"Nick, we need to get those stevedores moving," I said.

"On it," Nick said and five bots lifted from the floor and moved crates into the hold.

"Marny, I have turret control," Mom announced. "Add me to tactical."

"Aye, Mrs. H.," Marny replied.

In all, three turrets activated and swung around, pointing at the bulkhead where the invading Belirand agents had holed up.

"Liam, that Corvette is awake and she's steaming around the platform to line up on us," Ada said.

"Jonathan, tell me this platform has defenses," I said.

"It has sufficient structural integrity to withstand a Corvette's attack for a sufficient amount of time," he replied. "I've completed my task and am on my way back. Unfortunately, I've run into a problem. The second Belirand team has done the unexpected and we appear to be trapped."

"Mom, I need you to keep that first team pinned down," I said. "Marny, find a route to Jonathan."

"I've got 'em," Mom said. "I'm in communication with them now. I just need to establish a pecking order, wait one."

A single shot from the aft blaster on the top of *Hotspur* ripped through the atmo of the docking bay. I'd never been on the outside of the ship when one of her guns had been fired, at least not with atmosphere between us. The round tore through the top of the bulkhead above the position of the first team and I suspected it hadn't stopped at that point.

"They're stationary, you're clear," she said.

"Cap, Tabby, on me," Marny said. "Jonathan, I need you to move to location alpha. We'll meet you there. We move now."

Tabby and I formed up on Marny as she took off at a jog. As she did, our HUDs started updating. I knew that the cognitive load of planning an extraction was too much for Marny to also be effective on point, so I accelerated around her. I felt a reassuring pat on my shoulder as she acknowledged my adjustment.

We serpentined our way to an elevator bank and stepped onto the waiting car. Ordinarily, we'd avoid elevators, but Marny must have been confident we had sufficient control of the platform.

The station was rocked by an explosion outside of the bay and I realized that *Lawbringer* had started its attack.

"We're loaded, Liam," Ada's voice cut in.

"Close ramp and move to the aft section of the bay. There's an exit we'll have to enhance," Marny said. "But don't tip our hand yet."

The elevator stopped a floor above where Jonathan was trapped. He was still moving, but the Belirand agents were moving in concert to keep him cut off from an exit.

"Are you going to pull a *Bakunawa*?" I asked.

"Aye, Cap," Marny replied. "Tabby, breaching charge, pattern on floor."

The room we entered showed three outlines on the floor. I pulled my final explosive charge from the stock of my blaster rifle and configured it for breaching, placing it on one of the outlines.

"Jonathan, hold back," Marny instructed. "Strike team take cover."

We retreated and hunkered down, keeping our armored backs to the blast. A moment later, she blew the charges.

"Tabby, in the hole, help Jonathan up," Marny ordered.

Without hesitation, Tabby turned and jumped into the hole. The enemy team had been alerted by the explosion and converged on our location, only a floor below.

"Liam, the bay is taking quite a bit of damage. They've already blown the atmo," Ada said.

"Hang tight, Ada, we're almost clear," I said.

I knelt and aimed down the hallway of the floor below as Jonathan reached Tabby's location. She didn't hesitate, grabbed him and tossed him easily up into Marny's open arms. Even before Jonathan was standing on the floor next to us, Tabby had leapt back up to our level. That was *my* girl.

"Retreat," Marny said. "Package in third location."

I turned and ran down the hallway, Marny close on my tail. Tabby and Jonathan were slow to follow.

"Move, Jonny! We're oscar mike!" Tabby said.

The open elevator greeted us and I raced in, spun around and dropped to my knee, aiming down the hallway. Marny stacked up behind me, standing over my shoulder. We fired past Tabby and Jonathan as the lead Belirand pursuer came into view. None too gently, Tabby pushed Jonathan to the side to clear our firing lane and had to help keep him from falling as he collided with the wall.

"Down," Marny said as Tabby and Jonathan joined us in the elevator car.

Tabby pushed Jonathan to the floor and covered him as Marny also lowered herself. The elevator started dropping as blaster fire ripped into the car through the doors.

"Ada, make an exit," I said. "We're coming in hot."

"Roger that, Liam."

We exited the elevator into the docking bay which barely resembled what we'd left only a few minutes previously. *Lawbringer* hadn't breached the bay completely but the damage it had caused to the platform was immense. We snaked our way through collapsed bulkheads, fallen pipes, and live wires, finally arriving at *Hotspur* which had started firing repeatedly at the too small exit on the opposite side of the bay from where we'd entered and where *Lawbringer* sat broadside to the platform.

I couldn't have been happier when we made it through the pressure barrier that covered the exit hatch.

"Ada, we're in." I pulled the armored hatch closed behind us.

I stopped only momentarily in the armory as I pushed my blaster rifle into its rack on the way to the bridge.

I passed Mom, next to Nick and focused on opening the exit.

"Ada, give me my aft blaster," Mom said.

I wasn't initially sure what she was saying, but it became obvious as Ada spun *Hotspur* around. The thwump of our aft blaster fired, followed by a second, similar thwump. I looked over Mom's shoulder and saw that she'd dumped our entire battery into the two shots, although the battery was refilling. Ada must have one of the engines generating additional energy to refill them.

"It's open," Nick said.

Ada didn't hesitate and backed *Hotspur* out through the hole as Mom continued to fire the top and bottom blasters at the ragged opening.

Tabby had jumped into the second pilot's chair and was bringing up flight status.

"All hands, combat burn in three... two...," Ada announced.

I grinned at the unusual configuration of my bridge. Mom had taken Marny's spot as gunner and Ada was expertly threading us through the wreckage of Anino's once pristine platform. The only spot left for Marny and me was the couch.

I looked at her as I took a seat, just as *Hotspur* jumped to a hundred ten percent of safe operation. Marny winced as she pulled her hand back from her shoulder.

"Are you hit?"

"Just a flesh wound," she said.

"Let me see," I said.

Her glove was bloody, but the armored vac-suit had already knitted the fabric back together.

"Let's get out of here first, Cap," she said.

"Fold-space in one minute," Nick said.

I pulled up a tactical view of *Hotspur, Lawbringer* and the platform. One minute seemed like a lifetime as *Lawbringer* curved beneath the platform in pursuit.

"Missiles en route," Nick announced.

Mom brought *Hotspur's* guns to bear on the flight of missiles tracking us. One spectacularly exploded, but there was no way she'd get them all.

Just then, the universe turned upside down and reality smeared in my vision. I couldn't have been happier.

Chapter 27

SORTIE

"That was a gorgeous bit of sailing, Ada," I said. The adrenaline leaving my body made me feel almost giddy. "And Mom, I thought you were a pilot. You handled those guns like a pro."

"Don't you forget it," Ada said as she slapped Tabby's outstretched hand for a high-five.

"I only hit one of those missiles, and just so you know, the remaining three would have opened this girl up just as easily as four," Mom said although she was smiling.

"Any day you knock down a missile with a blaster is a good day, Mrs. H.," Marny said.

"Just doing my part."

"Would you mind if I asked a question?" Jonathan said. He wasn't riding the post-combat high the rest of us were.

"Certainly, Jonny Boy," Tabby said.

"Make that two. First, what is the meaning of 'pull a *Bakunawa*?'"

"It's an inside pod-ball reference," Marny said. "*Bakunawa* was the name of a Red Houzi dreadnaught we captured. Oddly enough, the particular maneuver Liam referred to ended up being unsuccessful."

"It wasn't unsuccessful," I said. "It just required adaptation."

"Not to mention, one of your old girlfriends to bail your ass out," Tabby said.

"Xie Mie-su was never my girlfriend," I said. "And, I was just as surprised as anyone when she opened the door to the *Bakunawa's* bridge. Jonathan, the maneuver on the dreadnaught was simply where we blew our way through a top deck and dropped down onto our target below."

"Thank you. We'd never confirmed that your crew was indeed the same that captured *Bakunawa*," he said.

"What's your second question?" I asked.

"It is for Ms. Masters. Under heightened emotional moments, you change our name to Jonny. Why do you do this?" he asked.

I gulped and asked, "Does it bother you?"

"No. Our observations have been that nicknames are assigned in human cultures as a sign of acceptance into a social group," he said.

"I love how you bring the awkward, Jonny Boy," Tabby said. "And yeah, I'd say you're part of the team. You looked out for me and mine. How does that make you feel?"

"We don't feel emotions in the same way you do, but I must say that we are very pleased with how recent events transpired," he said.

"Anyone else need a drink?" I asked. "And I think someone needs a med-patch. Right, Marny?"

"Fresh beers are in the reefer," Marny said. "I'll get a med-patch."

"Sit. I can carry beer and med-patches," I said.

"I'll join you, Captain," Jonathan said.

The two of us descended to the berth deck and I was surprised to see Jonathan head aft as I turned forward toward the galley. I mentally shrugged. I could easily carry the beers. I rummaged for a few minutes in the galley and found a bag of salty corn chips and finally stuffed a couple of med-patches into my belt.

Jonathan arrived back at the lift at the same time I did carrying the ancient katana we'd last seen on Curie along with a stack of packages.

"What'cha have there?" I asked.

"We'd like to present this all at once, if you don't mind," he said.

"Not at all," I said as we rose up into the bridge.

Tabby met us at the back and took a few beers from me and the bag of chips.

"Off with your shirt," I said to Marny.

She smiled, shaking her head. "You've a dirty mind, Cap."

"Purely for the sake of crew health," I said.

She gingerly pulled the armored vac-suit down. I had to help peel it away from her shoulder where the suit had injected clotting medicine on her wound. I couldn't help but notice that her suit liner had been burned back, exposing more of her chest than I was expecting.

"Would you like me to ask someone else to help?" I asked, turning away. While I found her muscular physique attractive, I wasn't about to overstep the bounds of our friendship.

"No," she said in a stage whisper. "I'm enjoying the show more than you are. Your face is bright red."

I wiped her shoulder clean and decided she'd have to clean the rest when she had some privacy.

"Frak, how many times have you repaired this shoulder?" I asked, as I uncovered old scars.

"Hard to tell," she replied. "Some of those we got together, though."

I placed the thicker of the two med-patches over the damage.

"That should do it." I handed her one of the beers I'd put on the table.

She pushed her numb arm back into the vac-suit. "Thanks, Cap."

"To life on the edge... with friends," Ada said, holding up her beer.

We all clinked our bottles together and sat back.

"Whatcha got in your hands there, Jonny," Tabby asked.

"One of Thomas Philippe Anino's final requests was that I deliver these to you all. In particular, however, he was so taken by one of you that he asked I make a special presentation," he said.

"You have the floor." I wondered if it was an idiom he was familiar with.

"Thank you, Captain Hoffen. First, I apologize Mrs. Hoffen, when this agreement was made, I was unaware that you would be traveling with us."

"Not necessary," Mom said.

"Thank you. The first presentation is for each of you. The grav-suits - as you, Captain Hoffen, called them - were specifically made for each of you and Master Anino preferred that you have them," he said and handed each of us a package.

"The armor characteristics of these suits are superior to what you are wearing and are considerably more flexible. I was unable to carry the optional helmets and they remain in the hold. While they are not completely necessary, the helmets provide significantly more oxygen as well as increased protection for your heads," he said. "Ms. Bertrand, I've submitted an analysis to your comm queue for review."

"Thank you, Jonathan." Marny stood up and shook his hand.

"I've one more presentation. Even though you were frustrated by Master Anino's initial audition in the Radium Sea, you left a lasting impression on him, Ms. Bertrand. Your instinct to utilize this ancient but deadly katana to defend your crew from the Sephelodon was something he wanted to reward by presenting it to you." He held the blade out to Marny horizontally, bowing his head as he did.

"I can't accept this. It's priceless," Marny said.

"And yet, you didn't hesitate to use it to defend your crew," he said. "It is said a katana will find its true owner. While we do not hold with superstition and legend, it does seem appropriate in this case."

"I... I don't know what to say," she said.

"I believe Master Anino had only one further request."

"Oh?" Marny asked.

"Yes. He preferred that you not use it in salt water," Jonathan said.

We all stared for a moment and then started laughing. While not a very good joke, it was so far from Jonathan's normal repertoire that it was hilarious.

After we'd recovered, I looked at Marny, "What do you think, Master of Arms? Should we be using these suits instead of the armored vacs?"

"They compare quite favorably to our current suits. I'd say it's up to the individual, but I'll make the switch," she said. "The helmets add a significant amount of protection to the head."

"Nick, how long until Ophir?"

"Thirty-five hours and change," he said.

"Okay, let me put some shifts together," I said. "Ada, you have another hour in you?"

"Yes, sir!" she replied a little too sharply. I then noticed she'd already drained her beer.

"Here," I handed her my mostly full bottle. "Let's get you a break. Tabbs, you have first two, I'll take next two and I'll get assignments out after that and I need someone to volunteer to make grub."

"I'll handle that," Mom said. "That is, if I can get Nick to show me around the galley."

"Can do," he said.

"Jonathan, are you monitoring the Yishuv settlement?"

"I am, Captain."

"Please alert me if their situation changes. I'm not sure when their morning will be coming, but it sounded like they were worried about a possible attack at that time," I said.

"Planet Ophir has twenty-six hour days and they are currently well into the evening. We will arrive six hours after daybreak on the second day," Jonathan said. "There will be nothing we can do to help them if the attack comes on the first morning."

"Understood. Thank you. Okay everyone, make sure to get some good rack time. Hard to tell what we're about to step into," I said.

With the exception of the blinking star fields, sailing in fold-space was very much the same as any other trip. We easily fell back into our normal rhythm and time slipped by.

"Captain," Jonathan's voice spoke in my ear and I struggled to wake up. Tabby's warm, not to mention naked body, lay next to me and I didn't want to be pulled from our cozy nest.

"Go ahead," I said, trying to be quiet enough to let Tabby continue to sleep.

"We are seven hours from our arrival at Ophir and the situation has changed," he said.

"Copy. Where are you?"

"On the bridge, Captain," he said.

"I'll be there momentarily," I said and closed the comm. "Tabbs," I shook her shoulder gently.

"No..."

I pulled the covers down, which didn't affect her like it did me, given that her synthetic skin wasn't as sensitive to temperature change. "Tabbs," I turned her onto her back and she rolled back over, covering her head with her hands.

I ran my hands around her back to her stomach and started sending them north.

"Not now," she said and pushed me back.

"Sorry, kid. We're needed on the bridge," I said. I jumped out of bed and started pulling on my prosthetic foot.

"You grope me, then you leave me here?" she asked. "You suck."

"Yup. You're officially a guy now," I said.

I started pulling on my suit and she slithered over to me, wrapping her arms around my waist.

"Don't go. I'll make it worth your while," she said.

"I think there's something going on in the Yishuv settlement," I said.

"Gah. Fine." She rolled to the other side of the bed and pulled on a suit liner.

"Coffee, Cap?" Marny asked as I entered the bridge.

Mom was currently on shift and Marny was seated at the table across from Jonathan on the bridge couch. Marny held a cup out.

"What's going on?" I asked.

"It's about an hour before sunrise, Cap. The enemy has launched an attack on Yishuv. Apparently, one of the Ophie - as the settlers refer to them - gained control of a blaster rifle and has taken out their combat leader, a man named Shem. Their remaining blaster rifle was lost in the struggle and they're having difficulty repelling the attack," Marny explained.

"How is that possible? I was sure they said they had a mounted blaster. That's more than enough to hold the position," I said.

"The mounted gun lacks defenses. Each time they put someone on it, they eventually get picked off. Fortunately, they've kept the Ophie from advancing so far, but their current leader is running out of people who can or are willing to man that blaster turret."

"Frak. Understood. Jonathan, you tried transmitting over that crystal, are you sure it won't work? Can I try it?"

"Certainly," he said and placed the device on the table between us.

"*Yishuv settlement, come in, this is Hotspur,*" I said, holding down the transmit button.

I repeated my call several times.

"What are you doing?" Tabby asked. I gave her the condensed version.

"Try again," she said. "If they don't know it is two-way, it could be in a bag or something."

"Square-wave. Hang on," Nick said.

Generate a square wave at five hundred-twenty hertz, ninety decibels, standard S-O-S pattern, five seconds, Nick said.

In response, a loud, high pitched sound played over the bridge as Nick held the transmitter button down.

"Shite, what in the frak are you doing?" Tabby asked. She'd gone from sleepy to ready to kill in those five seconds.

"Did you hear that?" It was the woman's voice we'd come to recognize as Merrie.

"They heard it," I said. "Do it again, Nick."

Tabby brought her hands up to her ears and glared at me.

Nick repeated the sequence. I chuckled as I noticed that Mom had pulled her suit's helmet up.

"It's coming from Peraf's bag," Merrie said.

"That's ridiculous," Peraf said.

"Empty your bag, Peraf," Bedros said.

"Don't order me around, I'm still the chairperson of our council."

"Do it again," I said. I joined Tabby by placing my hands over my ears.

"Please, Peraf. That's Morse code. It's a request for help signal," she said. "And, we're not generating it."

"Oh fine," she said.

We heard a significant amount of rustling and the muffled voices became much clearer.

"What? Do you hear it now?" Peraf asked, obviously annoyed.

"Yishuv settlement, come in please," I said holding the transmit button down.

"Did you hear that?" Merrie asked. "Who is that? Can you hear us?"

"Yishuv, this is Captain Liam Hoffen, *Hotspur*, we read you. Please acknowledge," I said.

"Who are you?" Bedros asked.

"Descendants of your founder's home world," I said. "We understand you're under siege."

"It's a trick," Peraf said. "The Ophie have figured out how to trick us."

"Don't be stupid," Bedros said. "The Ophie cannot speak our language and they know nothing of our founders."

"Captain Hoffen, do you have offensive capability?" It was the woman, Eliora, who asked the question.

"Yes. We're traveling light, but we should be able to help. We need you to take a defensive posture and hold on," I said.

"We can't get more defensive than we are, Captain," Eliora responded.

"If those Ophie gain control of your blaster turret that would change," Marny said. "I recommend disabling it if you are unable to keep it manned."

"See, it's a trick," Peraf said. "They want us to give up our only means of defense."

"That's asking a lot," Eliora said. "That turret is the only thing holding off twelve hundred angry Ophie."

"If they can fire a blaster rifle, they can certainly use your turret," Marny said.

We heard a muffled exchange. Apparently, they'd thrown something over the crystal transmitter/receiver.

They finally came back a few minutes later.

"Are you able to render assistance?" Eliora asked.

"Yes. We're seven hours out. Hopefully, we'll be able to communicate at that time," I said. "Also, we'll be wearing blue suits that cover our bodies completely. We'll look pretty alien."

"Do you mind, Captain?" Jonathan asked.

"No, go ahead," I said.

"Merrie, this is Jonathan, a fellow engineer. I have a request," he transmitted.

"Uh, what is it, Jonathan?"

"Have you recorded any of the Ophie speech?"

"No," she said. "Wait. Some. Why?"

"I have access to translation software. With a long enough sample, we might be able to communicate at a rudimentary level with the Ophie."

"Just kill them," Peraf said.

"Not if we have any other choice," I said before Jonathan could respond.

"I can replay a small snippet," she said. "I have maybe twenty minutes of a conversation."

"That would be very helpful," he said.

"Anything else?" I asked.

"No, thank you," Jonathan said.

"We'll be monitoring this communication device," I said. "Please hold on. We'll be there as quickly as possible."

"Thank you, Captain Hoffen. One final thing, would you share with us how large of a force you're bringing?"

"We'll drop three," I said.

"Three hundred? You're a Godsend," Bedros said.

"No, Mr. Bedros, three people," I said. "It will be sufficient, we'll have air-support."

"I believe you've underestimated the situation," Bedros said. "The Ophie are quite large and there are over a thousand of them."

"It does sound like a lot," I said. "We'll be trying to minimize Ophie casualties."

"This is insane," Peraf said and the transmitter was covered again.

"Maybe I shouldn't have answered that last question," I said.

Tabby swatted at me and grinned. "We'll have to work on that."

The next few hours seemed to drag on as we heard no updates from Yishuv. Finally, when we were an hour out, we heard the cover being removed from the device.

"Are you still there?" Merrie asked.

"Roger that," I said.

"Our turret has been run over," she said.

"Do the Ophie control it?"

"They do. So far, they haven't mastered the controls and we're trying to mount a sortie to take it back," she said.

"Merrie, listen to me. Can't you cut the power from it, overload the battery or something? You just need to hang on for an hour, we're almost there," I said.

"Holy buckets! Of course, the battery! I'm so stupid," she said.

"Amon, with me, now!"

I heard a door close.

Half an hour out, we finally dropped from fold-space, fifty thousand kilometers from the beautiful planet, Ophir. It looked drier than Earth, the standard by which all interstellar colonization was decided. Only a third of its surface was covered with water, but as far as planets went, it was a jewel.

"Cap, here you go," Marny said handing me a blaster rifle. "I replaced the grenade charges with crowd control. Won't be a lot of help for a thousand, but if you need to stick a handful of lizards together, it'll do the job. Wear this nano-blade. It will cut right through them. We're going to have to put them down quickly if they get on us. Finally, FBDs.

Marny handed me a pile of small flash-bang disks. Our suits would synchronize with the loud sounds and light flashes.

"I don't know what affect they'll have on Ophir natives, but let's hope they're sensitive to either light or sound. Otherwise, we're going to end up having to kill a whole lot of them," she said.

"Jonathan, did you get anywhere in translating their language?"

"No. I'm afraid Yishuv settlement has cut off communication with us," he said.

"First order of business will be taking out that turret," Marny said. "It's the only thing that I have any concern with and we can't afford to fire on its given position.

"Once we're on the ground, we stay in line of sight with each other. I don't want anyone getting trapped," Marny said.

"Drop on the turret first?" I asked.

"Aye, Cap. After that, I'd just be making up stuff," she said.

"At least you admit it," I smiled at her and placed my helmet on.

"Entering atmosphere," Ada's voice came over the comm.

"Better get in position," Marny said.

Tabby and I followed Marny down to the starboard entry hatch and pulled the armored door open. The pressure barrier became the only thing between us and exiting the ship.

"Cap, you've got point. Tabby, you've the number two slot. I'll follow," she said. "I'll mark the turret as quickly as I can."

"Ada, give us a flyover when we get there, would you?" I asked.

"Can do, Liam," she said. "We're close, I can see smoke on the horizon."

As we approached, the scenery beneath us was gorgeous. The trees were lusher than those we'd seen on Mars, although shorter with a thicker canopy. I wondered what type of star fed the vegetation. We were approaching a tall, rocky mountain and I finally got my first glance at the settlement. A small city rose from the forest, totally surrounded by a stone wall.

As we approached the city, the carnage was immediately obvious. At first, it was only thick, reptilian creatures. When we finally neared a fallen gate, the battle became obvious. Dead humans were strewn everywhere, most dismembered with their heads caved in.

"It's horrible," I said and my mind skipped to Big Pete. If we'd lived here, he would have been at the wall defending us. I reached out and steadied myself on the door.

Marny's steady voice cut through my fog. "Cap, get in the moment. Tabby and I need you."

I sighed. She was right and it was our time now. Our goal was to keep from slaughtering the invaders so we'd have a better chance of brokering a peace, but I was having a difficult time working with that.

"I've got the turret," I said. It had swung around and a gaggle of Ophie gesticulated wildly as a shot fired wide of the ship. My AI illuminated the turret on my HUD.

"On my six," I said and leapt from the ship.

For a moment, I simply free fell until I remembered how to activate the grav-suit. It was the same as using arc-jets. I bent my knees and leaned in, speeding toward the ugly bastards on the turret. I pushed my blaster rifle onto my back and pulled the nano-blade. We were going to be in close quarters and I didn't want to spray Tabby or Marny.

When I landed, an Ophie jumped into my path and swung his club. My blade effortlessly cut through him and I kicked his corpse aside. Whatever compassion I'd felt on the ship was long forgotten after seeing the debauchery at the gate.

It was at that point I turned into a machine, slicing, kicking and firing my pistol from my left hand. In a few short minutes, I'd cleared the turret of Ophie.

"CAP!" I finally heard Marny's voice over the comm.

"What?" I asked.

"Don't do that! You have to listen to your comms," she said.

"You were talking?"

"Yes. I'm not sure it was such a good idea bring you down here."

"I'm good, Marny," I said.

"You just slaughtered forty Ophir," she said.

I couldn't focus on that. Not now, at least. "What's the play, Marny?"

"Jonathan, tell Yishuv we've gained control of the turret. If they want to send someone up we'll turn control back over to 'em," Marny said.

Movement caught my eye and I saw a small woman sneaking along the inside wall of the city. I wasn't the only one who saw it, as a lizard-man had caught her movement as well.

"Marny," I said and highlighted the woman in my HUD as I took off in her direction.

"Go, Liam. Tabby, stay with him," Marny said.

I landed in front of the woman, who couldn't be over sixteen or seventeen stans old. She pulled up in surprise and then dropped to the ground, cowering. I clipped the nano-blade to my belt and pulled my blaster rifle from my back, leveling it at the advancing Ophie.

"Kid, get up! We're here to help, but you're too exposed," I said.

Tabby landed next to me and we boxed the woman in behind us against the wall. A group of Ophie approached. I could easily take them all, but I couldn't guarantee one wouldn't slip by before I did.

Tabby fired at an Ophie who leapt toward us with club raised. I clipped a second who followed suit.

"We need to cut the power," the young woman yelled behind me.

I couldn't respond as the Ophie continued to advance. Both Tabby and I were conservatively in triple-shot mode, avoiding full-auto in an attempt to reduce casualties, but they had no fear. Two dozen more Ophie closed in on us coming from nearby buildings.

"Cover me, I've got to get her outta here," I said.

Tabby stepped forward, switching to full auto and lay down a fusillade of blaster fire, the forward rank of Ophie dropping as she did.

While she was laying down fire, I slapped the rifle onto my back, spun around and grabbed the young woman. We sailed upward out of the Ophie's reach.

"I'm clear, Tabbs," I said, turning to make sure she didn't get stuck. I was relieved when she popped up from the group closing on her.

"Cap, drop her off and get back here. We've trouble brewing," Marny said.

"Copy that," I said.

"We're right behind you, Liam," Ada said.

I turned in the air and flew toward *Hotspur*. The sound of the old turret firing caught my attention and I spun around. It was firing into a group of lizard men trying to breach the Keep. I turned back and flew through the pressure barrier.

"Are you Captain Hoffen?" the girl asked, her voice quavering as I set her down.

I pulled my helmet off and smiled. "I am. Welcome aboard. You must be Merrie."

I heard noise behind me as Mom appeared in the small hallway that doubled as an air-lock.

"Go, Liam. I've got her," Mom said.

I pulled my helmet back on and dove from *Hotspur*.

Chapter 28

BAG 'N TAG

I twisted around while falling, and oriented on Marny. A flash from the hillside told me she was taking fire.

"Marny, what's the play?"

The air above me blistered with a blast from *Hotspur's* top turret and the location on the hillside where the flash had initiated, exploded.

"They're amassing. We've got to stop them or we'll have to respond with *Hotspur*," she said.

I was still on the edge of not caring what happened to the Ophir. I knew it was the wrong feeling, but I couldn't help it. Their singled-minded focus on murdering the settlers had struck a chord with me and I wanted to respond in kind.

I pulled up next to Marny and Tabby, who were floating just above the Keep's turret. My AI counted eight hundred Ophie roiling around just past the range where the turret could fire at them.

"Have you made contact with Yishuv settlers?" I asked.

"Just the gunner," Marny said.

"What about them?" I asked, pointing to a trap door that had opened atop a narrow building next to the wall. A lithe woman with a sheathed sword on her back and a thickly muscled man holding a hammer had just emerged onto the roof.

"No, that's new," she said.

"I'll see what's up," I said. "Maybe they have some ideas."

"Aye."

I set down on the roof a couple of meters from the two and held up my hands to show that I meant no harm. Even so, the woman crouched defensively, resting her hand on the hilt of her sword. The man, however, didn't react.

I pulled my helmet off and the woman visibly relaxed. A wave of rancid smells hit my nose that was so overpowering, I choked. I breathed in slowly and stood up straight holding my hand out.

"Liam Hoffen," I said.

"Eliora... and this is Amon," she responded, reaching past my open hand to grasp my wrist.

"Are you in charge?" I asked.

"Yes," she said.

"A woman. She was outside the keep," the man said stepping forward.

"If you're asking about Merrie, she's safe," I said.

He sighed.

"Any way to run these guys off without simply killing them all?" I asked.

"You could do that?"

"We're holding back," I said.

"The Ophie have only four weaknesses, under their jaw, beneath their ribcage, their groin and their Achilles," Eliora explained. "They have a difficult time seeing long distances, which is why they continue to advance. They cannot see your ship, nor can they see your crew floating above the turret."

"But, they were shooting at us," I said.

"The rifle they have has an optical scope," she said.

"Had. Our ship returned fire on the position of that rifle and it is no longer operational," I said.

I followed Eliora's gaze up to where *Hotspur* was gliding past us a hundred meters up.

"They also have particularly acute hearing," Eliora said.

"Oh. That's interesting. Marny toss an FBD into the crowd over the wall. Eliora, don't look over the edge... and it's going to be very loud," I said.

"Aye, Cap. Fire in the hole."

I caught sight of the small disk fluttering in the breeze as it fell into the middle of the largest group of Ophie. I'd forgotten I'd pulled my helmet off, but fortunately, the mass of Ophie blocked most of the blast of light and much of the sound. Even so, I had to blink my eyes rapidly to clear the momentary blindness.

"Frak. Helmet," I said as I pulled it back on.

There were floating dots in my vision, but I didn't think I was permanently impaired.

When I looked back down, the impact on the invaders had been profound. More and more of the trampled field became visible in the area where the disc had fallen as a sea of Ophie clawed and pushed to escape the vicinity.

"What was that?" Eliora yelled, having instinctively placed her hands over her ears.

"Hold on, Eliora," I said. "Nick, did you see that?"

"Yup. We're on it. Give us three minutes and you need to get those civilians inside," he said. "This is going to be extremely annoying. Oh, Merrie said to tell Amon she's okay."

"Marny, you have it out here?" I asked. "I'd like to meet the locals."

"Aye, we're good. I'm having some trouble convincing the gunner to go inside.

"Eliora, we need to get you and your gunner inside," I said.

"What's going on?" she asked.

"Our ship, *Hotspur*, is going to try to drive the Ophie off and my partner requested we get you inside," I said. "Trust me, we need to comply."

"There is a lot of fear, Liam Hoffen. It will be difficult if we go inside," she said.

"Distrust of us?"

"Yes. Understand, we've lost almost half of our settlement to the Ophie this year. Now, you show up with all this technology. People are frightened," she said.

Eliora flinched as I pulled the blaster rifle from my back and handed it to her. I then pulled the pistol from my chest and handed it to the man standing beside her.

"Amon, is it?" I asked.

He looked at me with confusion, accepting the pistol and nodding his head affirmatively.

"You have my weapons and I'm going to take my helmet off," I said, doing so. With my helmet in my left arm, I released and pulled my earwig from my right ear, peeling it off my cheek bone. With a vac-suit, the earwig was redundant and I needed to gain trust as quickly as possible.

"Nick, can you get Merrie a comm setup?" I asked.

"Yup," he said.

"Amon, if you'll allow it, I'll give you a way to both see and talk with Merrie," I said.

"Okay," he said.

He flinched as I reached for his head but allowed me to mount the earwig.

"I know it feels weird at first. All you have to do is talk to Merrie and she'll hear you," I said.

He stumbled a moment and I reached out to steady him, pushing the pistol's muzzle so it wasn't pointing at my leg. "How about you take your hand off that trigger?"

"Merrie? Is that you?" he said. "I can see you, too. Yes. We'll go inside."

Amon turned and lowered himself into the open trap door. I followed him down, although I used the grav-suit to allow me to float. Between my prosthetic foot and holding my helmet, I wasn't about to negotiate the rudimentary ladder.

"What's the meaning of this?" I recognized the voice and turned toward the older woman.

"Captain Liam Hoffen. You must be Councilwoman Peraf." I stuck my hand out to her and smiled.

She pursed her lips and grudgingly accepted my hand. I looked to the man standing next her. "And you must be Councilman Bedros."

He more readily accepted my proffered hand.

"What can you tell us?" he asked.

Before I could say anything, a siren started wailing outside. Even with the stone walls to separate us, the noise was almost debilitating.

Peraf and Bedros started gesticulating wildy and shouting at each other, although I couldn't make out what they were saying.

Finally, *Hotspur* moved off our position and the sound became almost bearable, only to return a moment later and move off again.

"WHAT IS HAPPENING?" Bedros yelled, having positioned himself in front of me.

I'd have preferred to wait for *Hotspur* to get further away, but the man was distraught.

"SCARES OFF OPHIR," I yelled back and waited to see if that mollified him.

"WORKING?"

"I'LL CHECK."

I picked up my helmet from the table where I'd placed it and pointed at the pistol I'd handed Amon. He handed it back to me. Placing the helmet on provided instant relief from the noise and I lifted off the ground and shot up through the still open trap door in the ceiling.

My HUD showed Tabby and Marny spread out, slowly flying over the interior of the city.

"Marny, what's our sit-rep?" I asked.

"They're scattering," she said. "We still need to do a building-to-building search, but the city is mostly clear."

"What do you need from me?"

"We're good out here. Jonathan is manufacturing sirens for the residents and bots to do building inspections," she said.

"Perfect, I need good news."

I flew back to the room where I'd left the Yishuv leaders.

"Well, it's a mess out there, but there aren't any indigenous visible," I said. "We don't know how long that will last, but we're working on defenses."

"What kind of defenses?" Peraf asked.

I pulled my helmet off and once again the smells assaulted me.

"Initially, we're concentrating on clearing the buildings and restoring the fallen gate," I said. "Our ship will provide sufficient defense in the meanwhile."

"We should introduce our hero to the people," Bedros said.

The look Peraf shot Bedros could only be described as venomous, but I really didn't care about their internal politics.

"Of course," she said.

The scene I walked into was appalling, the conditions squalid. Hundreds upon hundreds of people were crammed into a great hall where there was barely enough room. Again, the smells were initially overwhelming and I longed to pull my helmet on. As I scanned the room, I saw wounded, dead and dying. It was horrific.

"People of Yishuv," Peraf called from the stairs where we stood looking out over the great hall.

A hush fell over the hall and all that could be heard was that of groaning and whimpering of the wounded.

"Our prayers have been answered. Our ancestors have sent a rescue mission to bring us home," Peraf said.

I looked over to the old woman, having no idea where she was going with the announcement.

"Standing next to me is Captain Hoffen who has brought a powerful space ship that will destroy the Ophie," she said.

A cheer erupted from the crowd below as many of them rose to their feet.

"What are you doing?" I asked.

"Giving the people what they need," she said. "A hero."

I looked over the crowd who'd quieted down, obviously looking to me to say something.

"Thank you, Yishuv. The indigenous Ophir have been driven off and we are working to secure your city," I said, which caused another cheer to erupt. I held my hands up to help calm them down. "I can see that there is great need as I look out over this crowd and ask that you appoint representatives to help work with my crew."

"When can we go outside?" a man's voice from the crowd asked.

"We haven't cleared all the buildings, but there are no Ophir in the streets," I said. "Going outside would be at your own risk."

"Captain Hoffen has important work to do and must get going," Bedros stepped forward. "We will provide updates as quickly as possible. For now, rest comfortably in the understanding that Yishuv has been saved."

"You just couldn't help yourself, could you," Peraf said.

"Oh stop it," Bedros snapped back.

"We need to talk," I said, interrupting their bickering.

"Of course," Bedros said and walked back toward the small room I'd initially found them in.

"Amon, Eliora, would you excuse us?" Bedros asked.

I raised my eyebrows at the request to remove their lead security person.

"I'd think you'd want to have Eliora stay," I said. "Much of what we're discussing will have a security component to it."

"Won't you provide protection?" Peraf asked.

"For a short time, yes," I said. "You've made a number of assumptions that I'd like to clear up."

"Such as?" Peraf asked.

"Eliora, why don't you stay," Bedros said.

Eliora nodded.

"We're more than happy to have been able to push off the invasion, but we're not here to take you anywhere. I assume you're aware of the fact that your people were abandoned on this planet centuries ago by the corporation Belirand," I said.

"That is one of several legends," Bedros said. "You're saying you know this to be true?"

"I am. I'm not ready to get into all of the philosophical implications, but from my understanding, it's an indisputable fact."

"Go on," he said. He didn't look pleased to have the information.

"In a campaign to expand humanity's reach into the universe," I said. "Belirand, funded by four cooperating nations on Earth sent a colonizing mission to this planet. What the colonists didn't know was that continued contact with Earth was contingent on a number of factors, one of which was no sentient life being discovered."

"You're saying the Ophie are why we were abandoned?" Peraf asked.

"Yes. I can't speak directly to the reasoning behind that, but we believe this is essentially the truth."

"Why did they send you now?" Peraf asked.

"They didn't. Thomas Anino, the inventor of the fold-space technology did. We are fugitives from Belirand, much like you and that's not the end of it."

"This is where he tells us what he wants for having saved us," Peraf interrupted.

"Quiet, old woman," Bedros said.

"While cynical, you're not entirely incorrect," I said. "Belirand has abandoned a ship with forty-five crewmembers under similar circumstances to your own and they need a place to live."

"You're not taking us back to Earth?" Bedros asked.

"No. If we did, Belirand would kill each of you," I said.

"You don't know that!" she snapped. "I'd just as soon take my chances."

"I do know that. They killed my father in cold blood to keep us from rescuing that crew. Finding your settlement was just a happy coincidence," I said. "Currently, you are safer on Ophir than you would be on Earth."

"That's a load of bull crap," Peraf said.

"Be that as it may," I said. "My ship is leaving in thirty-one hours to pick up that crew and bring them back to Ophir. If you don't want to welcome them, that is your decision and we will find an alternative location on the planet for them to live out their lives."

"And you'll take your supplies with you?"

"Many of them, yes. But it's not like that. We'll do the best we can for you in any circumstance. What I need is a decision within the next few hours on whether or not you'll welcome this crew."

"They will be welcomed," Bedros said. "Your news isn't as good as we'd hoped, but we won't forget that without your efforts we would have perished."

Peraf looked angrily at him but didn't otherwise correct him.

"Good. My crew is constructing small flying robots to search building-to-building and make sure they're clear. After that, I believe the priorities will be removing bodies and tending to your wounded. If you'll provide a location, we could get started right away digging graves," I said.

"Those all sound like sensible things to do. Eliora, how many protectors remain?" Bedros asked.

"Six," she said. "Do you have the capability to repair our main defensive guns?"

"You have more than one?"

"Three in total. One broke just recently, the other hasn't worked for fifty stans or longer," she said. "If they were repaired and the south gate rebuilt, we'd be able to defend ourselves."

"I'll ask my partner to look at them. He's pretty handy, so the odds are good. I'd like to get you and one more of your choosing set up with armored suits similar to what I'm wearing. You won't be able to fly, but they'll insulate you from most physical damage."

"In exchange for what?" Peraf asked.

"My ship is leaving in thirty hours, give or take. We can stand around being suspicious of each other or we can get to work," I said, giving her a hard look. "Either way, I'm done being polite. Eliora, do you want a suit or not?"

"Yes. Of course," she said.

"Then hang on," I said. I placed my helmet back on, stepped in close and wrapped my arms around her small body and lifted up, flying through the open trap door. I oriented on *Hotspur*, two kilometers away, and flew in its direction.

"Ada, hold on a moment. I have another passenger," I said.

"Understood."

"What are you doing over here?"

"They had a camp set up. We're dismantling it," she said.

Once through the entry hatch, I set Eliora down.

"Let's see what's going on," I said and led her through to the berth deck, requesting that she put the blaster rifle I'd surrendered to her back into the armory. "I'll give that back when we disembark, but I'm not crazy about visitors having weapons inside the ship."

"It's all so clean," she said in wonder.

"Hold on." I took her arm to steady her as we stepped on the lift. To her credit she only wobbled a little as we popped up to the bridge deck.

"Eliora!" Merrie greeted us as we arrived. "The Ophie are running up the mountain; they're retreating!"

"Nick. What's your timing look like?" I asked. "There are a lot of wounded back at the settlement."

"We were just finishing up here. We can be done for now. Marny may have other ideas, but at least we could offload supplies and get the bots working," he said. "And it's nice to meet you, Eliora. Merrie has been talking about you."

"I'm Ada and she's Silver," Ada said pointing at my mom. "We're headed back. I was thinking of landing on the street in the city near the broken gate. Will that work for you, Eliora?"

"Yes," Eliora answered, overwhelmed by the experience of being on the bridge.

"How are the bots coming for clearing the city?" I asked.

"We made ten of them and should be able to clear the city in an hour," Nick said. "We'll start closest to the Keep and work back to the ship."

"I want to outfit Eliora with an armored-suit and a blaster rifle," I said.

"Agreed," Nick said.

"What do you want me to do?" Mom asked.

"Would you help Eliora get into an armored vac-suit? After that, how about organizing medical supplies with their doctors? There are a lot of wounded," I said. "Ada, could you stay with the ship? Run a defensive perimeter so we can offload supplies?"

"Yup, will do."

The ship settled on the ground.

"Marny, I'm sending the bots out," Nick said.

"Got 'em," Marny replied on our general tactical channel. "Tabby and I will bat cleanup."

"I'll send Eliora out in a suit to help," I said.

"Copy, Cap," Marny replied.

"May I make a request?" Jonathan joined the conversation. I hadn't seen him for a while, but I knew he didn't feel the same needs for physical proximity as the rest of us.

"Go ahead, Jonathan," I said.

"We'd like to talk with one of the indigenous. It would give us a chance to start learning their language," he said.

"Bag 'n tag it is," Marny replied. "We're packing duct-tape grenades. We'll get you a couple of lizard boys to chat with."

Chapter 29

REBORN

Fold-space, middle of deep dark

We'd chosen thirty-four hours as our deadline for leaving Yishuv. We had no idea if Belirand would follow us to Ophir, but I didn't want to be there if they did. We'd deal with Belirand after we finally rescued the crew of *Cape of Good Hope*.

Before leaving, we'd buried most of the corpses, repaired the gate, and brought one more of the defensive guns back online. We also left Eliora and her second in command, Gabe, with armored vac-suits, blaster rifles and plenty of FBDs.

"Captain LeGrande, come in, *Hotspur* calling," I said once I loaded up the comm crystal.

After a few tries, she finally replied. "Liam, thank Jupiter." I was surprised by her lack of formality. "Tell me you have good news."

"We do. There was excitement on Ophir and we had to reroute. What's your status?" I asked.

"What do you want, the bad news or the really bad news?"

"Worst news first," I said.

"Two corvettes just arrived in-system and appear to be searching for us," she said. "We're running lights out, but they'll find us sooner or later."

"What's the other news?"

"I had to shoot my first officer and lock up three other crew."

"What? Why?"

"An attempted mutiny," she said. "The idea of not returning home wasn't very popular."

"But we agreed to take people back if they wanted to risk it," I said.

"We had a meeting and decided it was too much risk to the rest of our families."

"Is he dead?" I asked.

"Yes."

"I'm sorry, Katherine," I said.

"Thank you, Liam. Strange to say, but it's almost a relief that he finally made his move. He had been boiling for weeks. I don't think he would have accepted life on another planet," she said.

"We'll need your crew to be ready to move when we get there," I said. "We can't afford to abort our fold-space flight at this point. I'm not sure where we'd end up, but if those corvettes find you, we'll really be in a spot."

"We'll be ready, Liam," she said.

It was impossible not to think about what awaited us when we dropped out of fold-space near the *Cape*. The hours seemed to drag on. It was a good move on Belirand's part. *Hotspur* could outrun their heavy cruisers easily enough, but corvettes were another thing entirely. Even worse, with two, they'd more likely box us in.

All my worrying turned out to be for nothing when we finally arrived. The corvettes hadn't found *Cape of Good Hope* and we had plenty of time to transfer the *Cape's* crew and much needed medical supplies to *Hotspur*. Unfortunately, our plan to add a fold-space drive to *Cape* wouldn't work. It was too risky to attempt with the corvettes in the area.

I didn't have to announce our arrival to the crew, as we'd all been counting it down on the bridge.

In preparation for the *Cape's* crew, we'd secured the bridge deck and locked down the berth deck as much as possible. There was no way to fit everyone in the hold, nor would it send a very good message to them if we did. That said, we weren't opening up the bridge.

"Captain, we've an incoming hail from *Lawbringer*," Ada said.

Accept comm.

I wasn't sure why I was going to talk to one more Belirand captain. So far, the conversations had been one-sided.

"*Hotspur*," I replied.

"Hoffen?" I recognized Lorraine Tullas' voice.

"Admiral Tullas, you've upgraded," I said.

"What are you doing, Hoffen?" she asked.

"What's it look like. We're rescuing your colleagues from the awful death you sentenced them to," I said.

"You're taking them to Ophir?"

"Yes. It's not such a stretch, is it?" I asked.

"You shouldn't give away our plans," Tabby said, muting the comm.

"They already know. They're tracking our jump destinations," I said. "Why else would we have gone to Ophir?"

"She's a snake and you can't trust her," Tabby said.

Perhaps I shouldn't, but I felt like Tullas had a level of integrity in her zeal.

"Ophir colony failed centuries ago," Tullas said.

"You mean your predecessors left them to die just like you're doing with the *Cape of Good Hope*?" I asked. "We found the settlement - what's left of it anyway. At least this crew will have a chance on Ophir. It's better than what you're offering."

"To die at the hands of beasts? That's better?"

"It would be for me. I'd rather go down fighting than suffocate. Would you take that away from them?" I asked.

"You're not going to try to bring them back to the known universe?" she asked.

"You shouldn't have killed my parents," I hissed at her. "You told me you'd only go after those people we drug into this mess. You lied. Have you already started murdering their families too?"

"MacAsgaill acted without authority. He's being disciplined," she said.

"For murdering three people? Seems like all in a day's work for your team."

"You've got me wrong, Hoffen. I take no joy in this. We do what we do to protect humanity," she said.

"By lying to them about the existence of sentient life outside our systems?"

"Don't be naïve. We're the good guys here."

"Not from where I'm sitting. And why harass us now? By your own logic, *Cape's* crew is going to die on Ophir. Why try to stop us? You and I both know forty plus crew isn't enough to create a viable colony."

"You can have Ophir, Hoffen, for as much good as it will do you. You've sentenced that crew to death, alone on an inhospitable planet, and you'll have to live with that," she said. "For what it's worth, I'm sorry for the death of your parents. It shouldn't have happened, but don't take my sympathy as weakness. You show your face in my corner of the universe and I'll hunt you down."

"Just like you would if you were a hundred thousand kilometers closer right now. I read you just fine Lorraine, no loss of fidelity. You might consider what will happen when you finally get us in a corner," I said.

"Careful," Nick said, muting the comm. He could tell I was starting to get annoyed.

"How's our transfer going?" I asked.

"Just finishing up and those corvettes have been closing on us at high speed for the entire conversation," he said.

"Jump when ready," I said. "There's nothing more for us here."

The last person to board *Hotspur* was Katherine LeGrande. I left Ada at the helm and worked my way through the crowded berth deck, finally finding her in the hold. Davi, the Marine who'd been at her side when we'd first met, stood at her side.

"Welcome aboard, Captain," I said. "Where's Rastof?"

"Over here," Rastof said. I'd forgotten he was about Nick's height and would be hard to find in the crowd.

"Could I get the two of you to join us on the bridge? Davi is welcome, also," I said.

"Certainly, Captain," she said.

The trip back to Ophir was considerably less nerve wracking than the trip out had been. Other than a slightly funky smell in the air, we arrived without any incident only two days after we'd left.

"Taking us in for a low flyover," Tabby said as we came up on the settlement.

The amount of progress they'd made in those two days was astounding. Signs of the battle were still evident, but it was clear that the two construction bots we'd brought with us hadn't rested.

"Eliora, where would you like us to set down?" I asked. "We've a load of new settlers who are anxious to meet their new neighbors."

"We weren't expecting you back so quickly, but go ahead and set down outside the front gate," she said.

"Got it, babe," Tabby said to me. "Get your delegation onto the ramp ready."

We'd agreed that it would be best to have Katherine and Moon Rastof, as representatives of the *Cape's* crew, be the first to meet the Yishuv settlers. And, while it took some effort for Marny, Nick, Katherine, Rastof, Davi and me to work our way through the crowd, we were successful in doing so just about the time Tabby set down.

I palmed open the door and enjoyed the fresh Ophir breeze that met us. A cheer welled up from the crowd behind us and we hastily cleared the loading ramp, lest we be trampled by the crew who not so long ago had been sentenced to death.

When I looked up to the proud gates of Yishuv, people were streaming onto the top wall, all waving brightly colored scarves. A band abruptly started playing as the gates opened and we were greeted by what I could only imagine was the entirety of Yishuv.

Bedros and Peraf hustled through the crowd to take their place at the front of the smiling greeters.

"*Cape of Good Hope*, Yishuv welcomes you," Bedros announced, his voice carrying over some sort of public address system. The crowd cheered and spilled out through the gates.

"Wow, what a greeting," I said, shaking Bedros' hand as he approached.

Even Peraf was smiling and I wondered what had changed for the old girl, although I wasn't about to poke that bear to find out.

"Our settlement needs new blood. Just a tenday ago we were faltering, failing, and on the brink of ruin. Now, look at us," he said. "We're reborn!"

"Councilman Bedros, Councilwoman Peraf, I introduce Captain Katherine LeGrande, formerly of *Cape of Good Hope*," I said.

To say the Yishuv settlement knew how to throw a party would have been an understatement. If I'd expected their recent losses to mute the celebration, I'd have been wrong. It was something I could understand, however. The pain of losing Big Pete was still fresh on my mind and now that both Yishuv and *Cape's* crew were out of harm's way, I was more than happy to join them in drinking heavily.

It was late in the evening when Jonathan found Tabby and me lying on a blanket in front of the roaring bonfire just outside the gates of the city.

"Jonny Boy, sit with us and tell me you all experience the joy of drinking to excess," Tabby said, slurring her words. It was quite a feat for her to get this drunk, given the accelerated metabolism from her replacement parts.

"It's something we've often wondered about," he said, taking Tabby up on her offer to sit on our blanket.

"You need to work on that, because it's a shame to miss out on all the fun," she said.

"Captain, I thought you might be interested to learn we've deciphered the indigenous people's language," he said.

"That's great," I said. "What'd you learn?"

"I just told you, we learned to communicate with them," he said.

"Ooohh. Right... anything else? Like... did they say why they attacked Yishuv?"

"It will take more conversation, but from what we were able to discern, the Ophie very much enjoy battle. To die in battle is their highest honor and calling," he said.

"Sounds like a horrible neighborhood," I said, sending Tabby into a fit of giggles. I smiled at her, loving the fact that she understood drunk Liam.

"That may be exactly correct," he said. "From the basic continent plotting we gathered from *Hotspur's* two landings, we believe it is possible that there could be locations on Ophir that would not be next to this particular species."

"That's a lot of syllables in one sentence. Seriously, Jonathan, I'm not completely tracking. Did you just say there might be a safer place on Ophir?"

"I did," he said.

"Well, frak, let's go check it out."

"Captain Hoffen, perhaps we should have this conversation tomorrow," Jonathan said.

I giggled, which I think might have given away my current state of mind.

Jonathan stood up.

"Don't go away mad," Tabby said. "We just need a night where there aren't any problems to deal with."

"We are not mad," Jonathan said. "We simply believe we might not be achieving our desired objective."

"Oh good. In that, you're right," Tabby said.

It was the last thing I clearly remember about that night. The next morning, I awoke with Tabby lying across me and the blanket pulled tightly around us. My head was pounding and I had to do the needful about as badly as I could ever remember.

"Oooh," Tabby complained as I disentangled our vac-suited limbs.

"I'll be back," I said and ran over to the ship, where I found Jonathan working at assembling a project.

"Good morning, Jonathan," I said on the way past. My mouth tasted like cotton.

"Good morning, Captain," he said.

On the way back out, after placing a sober patch on my temple, I stopped to talk with him.

"Hey, sorry about last night. I wasn't intentionally being disrespectful," I said.

"No apology necessary. Intentional intoxication is one of the more puzzling behaviors of humankind, although Ms. Master's explanation was sensible."

"Did I hear you right? Do you really think there might be a better place for Yishuv?" I asked.

"We theorize that it is possible," he said. "We would like to lead a party to locate a more appropriate location for a human settlement."

"You might receive resistance from the settlers, especially now that we've successfully pushed the Ophie back."

"We will most certainly receive resistance," he said. "That does not reduce the value of the objective."

"You make a lot more sense when I haven't been drinking," I said, smiling.

"Would you believe that over sixty percent of us found that statement humorous?"

"Oh you devils! You do get humor," I said.

Chapter 30

EPILOGUE

The Yishuv council presented a significant number of objections to Jonathan's suggestions, but in the end, they agreed to review whatever findings he came up with. It felt like a significant win on his part, although it might have had something to do my pointing out that the Class-F Industrial Replicator was his property.

It had been six tendays since we'd arrived at Yishuv and the settlement was humming with activity. We'd been taking almost daily trips to drop off surveying bots. Jonathan thought that within fifteen or so tendays we'd have a relatively complete map of the planet, complete with indigenous populations. So far, it had become clear that somehow the Yishuv settlement had been established in the most highly populated region on the globe.

We'd also had time to put Dad to rest. We'd originally thought to send him off into outer space, but Mom reminded me that he'd come from humble beginnings as a farmer. It was a simple service and I felt like he would finally be at rest on Ophir.

Something broke inside me when MacAsgaill murdered Big Pete. I'd felt it trying to get loose when I'd first run into the Ophie and single-handedly slaughtered over forty of them. It was an unresolved anger that I hoped I'd buried with him in the Ophir soil.

As for the crew and passengers of the *Cape*, they were starting to fit. There had only been fifteen actual crew, the remaining thirty had been passengers, bound for service on Tipperary's TransLoc gate. The higher level managers had more difficulty adjusting to a less refined existence, but mostly they all appreciated having a plentiful supply of atmosphere and a safe, warm place to lay their heads.

After all that, our lives became routine, which, if I had any sense, should have concerned me.

"What do you suppose happens to the Co-Op and our claims?" I asked, taking a pull on a light amber beer.

"It's in litigation," Jonathan said. "I've hired legal teams on Earth, Mars and Curie to regain control over these properties. We'll be successful. Not only that, we're putting pressure on Belirand for the wrongful death of your father."

"Let me guess, Nicholas, you already knew this," I said.

"It's difficult to get updates, I didn't want to say anything until we knew more," he said.

"What I've been wondering is what became of *Cape*?" Tabby asked.

We were all playing cards and relaxing in the warm afternoon.

"Captain's last order when she exited was to hand controls over to Loose Nuts Corporation – just in case any representative of your company ever found it," Moon Rastof said.

"She did?" I asked.

"Yup. Surprised she didn't tell you that herself."

I hadn't had much time to talk with Councilwoman Katherine

LeGrande. We were on friendly terms, it was just that I was biding time and she was trying to build a new life for herself and her crew.

"Don't you think Belirand grabbed it?"

"I doubt it," Rastof said. "I set her on a random path... well, random to Belirand at least. I just happen to know someone who can pinpoint her location - that is, if Belirand didn't chase her down while they were still in system. She's almost impossible to track and only wakes up once every forty hours or so to change course.

"Didn't you lose an engine when you fell out of fold-space?" Tabby asked.

"We did," Rastof said. "Nothing we couldn't fix with, say a Class-F Industrial replicator."

"You pirate, you," Ada said slapping down her cards. "And that's a full house."

We all groaned as she pulled the pile of seeds from the center of the table over to her already large pile.

"I've got the new engine plans already put together," he said. "We just need council approval for a thirty-four hour run."

"Don't we know someone on the council?" I asked.

"We do. She said she'd clear the schedule if we wanted to give it a run," Rastof said.

"What's in it for you, Moonie?" Tabby asked.

"I'm not a farmer. I'm hoping you'll recognize you need an engineer," he said.

Tabby held her fist in the air near Ada, who returned the fist-bump.

"What's that about?" Moonie Rastof asked.

"We were wondering when we'd get off this rock. Love the people and all, but frak do we hate listening to grass grow," Ada said. "Oh... and we thought you seemed like crew to us."

"Seriously? You're bored already?" I grinned at my ever-expanding crew. They were not cut out for life on-planet. "What do you think, Nick?" I asked.

"We'd just need a certain sentient to agree to install a fold-space drive for us," he said not even bothering to take off the towel he'd placed over his eyes to block the sun while he pretended to doze.

"We'd be delighted to," Jonathan said.

It was only a tenday later that we found ourselves crammed, crew-heavy in *Hotspur*.

In order to give us enough time to repair the engine, we dropped in seven days from where *Cape* was located. The rationale was if Belirand bothered to drop in after us, they'd be too far away to catch us before we could jump out again.

"There she is," Nick said.

They'd left *Cape* sailing with minimal signs. We'd have had trouble picking her up if we hadn't known how to pinpoint her.

"Try to raise her," Moonie said, looking over Nick shoulder. "Your ident should wake her up."

Hotspur to Cape of Good Hope, Nick said.

"Oh. Right. She's called *Strumpet* now," Rastof said.

Nick gave him a slightly pained look and repeated his call. As he did, the lights of the medium cruiser turned on.

"Mom, take us around to the starboard. I'd like to see how bad that engine is," I said.

"Trust me, I can do it," Moonie said. "I'll just need help getting it lashed on there."

"In the middle of the deep dark, with nothing but us and a renno bot?" I asked.

"Frankly, if it were just you guys, we'd be screwed. Sorry for the language Mrs. H.," he said. "But, with that renno bot I modified, we're in like Flynn."

"Like who?" Ada asked.

"Look it up," Moonie said.

"Silver, I've got positive control of *Strumpet's* catwalk. Bring us in to four meters and zero delta-v," Nick said.

"Copy that," Mom said.

Like Ada, she had a light touch on the controls and easily slid us in next to *Strumpet*. We heard a positive contact from the catwalk as it latched onto our starboard side entry hatch.

"Equalizing pressure," Nick said. "And we're on."

"I'm running a security sweep and reviewing video logs," Marny said. "We're clear for entry."

No matter how good the atmospheric handling is on a ship, if it sits empty for any period of time, the air always tastes a little stale and *Strumpet* was no exception. We'd been onboard several times before, but I'd never made it to the bridge, which is where we were headed.

The ship was gorgeous on the inside. As configured, she had limited cargo room, but was physically twice the size of *Hotspur*. She wasn't as fast as *Hotspur*, but had considerably heavier weaponry and armor. She was built for a crew of fifteen, but was designed to accommodate three times that number in luxurious passenger accommodations. The only difference between *Strumpet* and a Justice-Class cruiser was armor. They had it and she didn't. That said, we'd proven that an angry *Strumpet* could lay down a serious beating on one of her heavier sisters just fine.

When I stepped onto the bridge, it was love at first sight. It was basically the same layout as *Sterra's Gift* and *Mastodon*. Pilot's chairs at the front, gunnery stations to the sides, navigation stations at the back and a nice sized conference table centered behind the Captain's chair. It wasn't quite as spotless as *Mastodon* as there was litter strewn about, but the highly polished wood-grain bulkheads and white synthleather chairs looked, if anything, more sophisticated than that of *Mastodon*.

"Tell me she has a combat bridge," I said, looking at Moonie.

"Nope, but there's an armored visor that slides over the armored-glass while in combat," he said.

"Do it!" Ada said excitedly.

"Actually I can't," he said. "Has to come from one of the principals of *Loose Nuts*."

Add Moon Rastof to crew. Apply standard ship security to Strumpet.

Moonie stepped over to one of the workstations on the side of the bridge and armor plating slid up into place.

"Where is Jonathan with those cool little tea cups that kept the drinks from spilling?" Ada asked.

"We have those," Moonie said. "They're not that hard to come by. There are probably some in the galley."

As we continued to explore the ship, we could see superficial signs of abuse, but nothing the renno bot couldn't easily take care of. There was mostly a lot of trash that had been left behind.

Tabby and I walked in on Marny and Nick who had found the galley. Marny had Nick pinned up against one of the three professional looking stoves.

"Whoa, we'll come back," I said.

"Come on in, Cap. I was just explaining to my little man just what I thought I could do with these ovens," Marny said.

"Cooking really does it for you, doesn't it?" Tabby asked.

"It's all about baking, kids," she said.

"Whoa, what am I interrupting here?" Moonie asked as he rounded the corner.

"I think Marny just volunteered to make dinner. How about we get after that engine?" I said.

"Just need to grab some tools... and I think Jonathan's already on it," he said.

"Let's get after it. Nick, give me a buzz if you need anything."

"Yup," he said. I smiled and shook my head.

It was four days almost to the hour when Jonathan announced he'd completed installation of the fold-space drive.

"So what's all this baking about, Marny?" I asked as we sat down at the beautiful mess table again.

"Grandma. She used to babysit me and we'd bake. I haven't had access to real ovens like this since back then," she said.

"Cool. A fun fact about Marny. What was her name?" I asked.

"Nanna."

"No fair."

"Fine. Rebecca," Marny said.

I felt like it was a win getting Marny to talk about herself.

"We're running low on fuel on *Hotspur* and we're at sixty percent stores on *Strumpet*. We're not going to be welcome at many fuel stops. I think we should hit Belirand," Mom said.

She couldn't have surprised me more if she'd taken off her clothes and run around the room - although I was grateful she'd chosen the fuel thing.

"Silver? Something you want to share with the class?" Tabby asked.

Nick and I laughed at Tabby calling mom out on a phrase she'd used when she was our primary school educator on Colony-40. Mom even smiled at the familiar reference.

"Asymmetric warfare. We strike the behemoth where it's weak. Nobody in their right mind would attack a Belirand outpost, unless they didn't have anything to lose. We need fuel. They have it. So we take it. Eventually, they'll come after us, but that's going to happen anyway. The only reason Tullas didn't come after us on Ophir is because Jonathan took away their aninonium," she said.

"We agree with Mrs. Hoffen's analysis," Jonathan said. "The cost of aninonium will have risen exponentially with Anino Enterprise's sudden departure from the market. No amount of stolen fuel would equal the cost required to send an invasion force to Ophir."

"So, my mom and the pacifist sentients want to become pirates? The world as I knew it has just exploded." I sighed at the insanity of it. "I'll bite. Anyone know where to find a lightly defended Belirand fuel depot?"

"Belirand supply caches are everywhere," Moonie said.

"Undefended?"

"Lightly defended, as long as you have a talented engineer who knows how to hack 'em," Moonie said.

"Hack, as in break their software?" Nick asked.

"Trust me. You get me to a cache and I'll break into it."

"Two ships, how do we split the crews?" Ada asked.

"Easy call," Tabby said. "Moonie, me and Captain Hotpants in

Hotspur. We fly aggressive and like to mix it up. Ada and Silver are better with the big girls and we need a real gunner on Strumpet."

"When do we leave?" I asked.

"How about now?" Nick asked.

But that's another story entirely.

ABOUT THE AUTHOR

Jamie McFarlane is happily married, the father of three and lives in Lincoln, Nebraska. He spends his days engaged in a hi-tech career and his nights and weekends writing works of fiction.

Word-of-mouth is crucial for any author to succeed. If you enjoyed this book, please consider leaving a review at Amazon, even if it's only a line or two; it would make all the difference and would be very much appreciated.

FREE DOWNLOAD

If you want to get an automatic email when Jamie's next book is available, please visit http://fickledragon.com/keep-in-touch. Your email address will never be shared and you can unsubscribe at any time.

For more information
www.fickledragon.com
jamie@fickledragon.com

ACKNOWLEDGMENTS

To Diane Greenwood Muir for excellence in editing and fine word-smithery. My wife, Janet, for carefully and kindly pointing out my poor grammatical habits. I cannot imagine working through these projects without you both.

To my beta readers: Carol Greenwood, Kelli Whyte, Robert Long, Nancy Higgins Quist, Dave Muir, Michael Gray and Matt Strbjak for wonderful and thoughtful suggestions. It is a joy to work with this intelligent and considerate group of people.

ALSO BY JAMIE MCFARLANE

Privateer Tales Series

Privateer Tales Universe

Made in the USA
Monee, IL
17 February 2023

28107328R00216